HIDDEN

Copyright © 2021 Denis O'Brien
All rights reserved
ISBN
ISBN–13:

FOR ANNIE – LOVE ALWAYS

Contents

CHAPTER 1 MARCH 1842	1
CHAPTER 2 JULY 1842	20
CHAPTER 3 AUGUST 1842	29
CHAPTER 4 AUGUST 1842	44
CHAPTER 5 AUGUST 1842	55
CHAPTER 6 AUGUST 1842	63
CHAPTER 7 AUGUST 1842	81
CHAPTER 8 AUGUST 1842	91
CHAPTER 9 AUGUST 1842	99
CHAPTER 10 AUGUST 1842	113
CHAPTER 11 AUGUST 1842	126
CHAPTER 12 AUGUST 1842	133
CHAPTER 13 AUGUST 1842	147
CHAPTER 14 AUGUST 1842	160
CHAPTER 15 AUGUST 1842	170
CHAPTER 16 AUGUST 1842	180
CHAPTER 17 AUGUST 1842	188
CHAPTER 18 AUGUST 1842	198
CHAPTER 19 AUGUST 1842	208
CHAPTER 20 SEPTEMBER 1842	220
CHAPTER 21 SEPTEMBER 1842	226

CHAPTER 1 MARCH 1842

'I promise you, if he does come here I'll have him killed.'
Emma Halley was reluctant to take issue with her husband but his threat to visit murder on her brother struck her as so extravagant that she responded with uncharacteristic assurance.
'Please, Alaric, let us maintain some tenor of proportion. If he is degenerate he is also harmless.'
A confidant of Prime Minister Peel, Alaric Halley was tall, good looking, elegant, well–educated, articulate, cultured and popular. It was this catalogue of admirable attributes that turned the stomach of his brother–in–law Achilles McAra. The contrast between the siblings was pronounced: Emma was pretty, courteous and diffident. McAra had no parallel qualities. It was a stroke of ill luck that had afforded Emma the rare opportunity to invite her brother to her husband's Mayfair residence on the very day that Halley had made preparations to entertain a group of distinguished visitors with whom he shared mysterious financial interests and political objectives. Even by his own spectacularly low standards McAra was not to behave well on the occasion.
Alaric's first guest on that Friday was Sir Hudson Smart who had recently retired from a long career with the East India Company. Towards the end of this service he had been civilian representative in charge of one of the Company's steamers in the brief war with China. On reluctant return to his native Scotland he had procured an estate on the southern outskirts of Edinburgh next to that of his friend Halley, and taken possession of several acres of Perthshire abutting Halley's property in the same county. It had perhaps been his long absence from his native land that had misled him into a recent investment failure that had left him on the verge of hardship. Also attending were two half–pay soldiers – Colonel Culver Roland, now modestly employed as curator of the Crown Jewels of Scotland despite having enjoyed a reputation as a gallant officer at

HIDDEN

Waterloo; and Major Calvin DeWitt, a historian and genealogist of sorts. Awaited but at that hour absent somewhere in the city was Hiram Charles D T Stuart, a native of the United States with a reputation for colossal wealth. This nabob of the Far West had a plan which, he had assured the coterie, would not only rescue them from the brink of the financial precipice but also render their future secure.

There had been obvious reason to query Hiram's declarations of fabulous riches and so from early December the preceding year Alaric had been in the United States prying into these claims. However when Halley had returned from his western odyssey some days prior to the Mayfair assembly he had been able to dispel all doubt. But what had brought him scurrying down from Edinburgh was not solely to report his felicitous findings. It had been reported that Queen Victoria would visit Scotland in the course of the year and this regal excursion would – apparently – afford the opportunity to prosecute Hiram's arcane objective.

Alaric was to be involved in discussions at Downing Street of the arrangements for the visit and it was on the eve of that conference that this get–together at his house was fixed. He had advised his wife that the domestic details should be carefully attended to so that no mishap could intrude on the proceedings. Now that Stuart had been authoritatively identified as the fifth wealthiest man in America Emma should be under no illusion as to the significance of this convocation of privilege.

The spousal diktat injunction against McAra's presence was received by Emma some days after her invitation to her brother and she was in no position to rescind it as her sibling had become temporarily uncontactable. Not having seen him for more than two years but harbouring a clear recollection of his penchant for unpredictable delinquency she could only hope that the interval had effected some improvement in his recalcitrant disposition. By the time Sir Hudson and his companions had established themselves in the drawing room there was no sign of the reprobate relative and Emma, on excruciating edge all morning, allowed herself to relax as time drew on and there was no sign of Achilles.

With the non–appearance of the unwanted caller Halley's outrage had diminished and his humour had improved a little and, as it

HIDDEN

happened, prematurely. The trio of visitors had disposed themselves comfortably around the elegant room and made free with Halley's expensive spirits when an audible and persistent ringing of the doorbell was followed by a loud altercation between the suave butler Samuel Spark and another. This apparent confrontation was brief and superseded by the crash of the hall table and the rare porcelain pieces on it being distributed with shattering force on the flagstone floor. The collective response in the drawing room was one of alarm which a moment later was translated into recoil as the door was thrown open and the newcomer made his appearance having shaken off the futile attention of two uniformed flunkeys.

McAra, a small man who looked as if he had just emerged from a vat of boiling tripe, raised a hand in cheerful greeting but beyond that made no effort to introduce himself or to enquire into the identity of Halley's guests. Instead he concentrated on keeping as upright as possible and staggering to the array of crystal decanters in the far corner. Amid the hostile silence he managed to dispense for himself a colossal measure of gin and, holding the glass triumphantly aloft, reeled across the floor towards a large solid brass and leather packing case decorated with a fading coat of arms. "*Ann an Dia no dhìon dìon mi*," he muttered, running his hand over the raised lettering and, uninterested in obtaining permission to satisfy his intoxicated curiosity, swung open the lid of the receptacle. Unintentionally lurching forward he tried to steady himself by grabbing a metal bracket and releasing a shelf, the effect of which casual insouciance was to expose a second, lower compartment into which he was pitched headlong, bringing the heavy lid crashing down across his back. It was only the plush lining together with the good fortune that attends the blasé befuddled that saved him from more severe injury. With a yell that combined fear and pain he had to be extracted from this near–lethal encounter by Samuel Spark. Having miraculously retained un–spilled every drop of the gin McAra righted himself with a display of unconvincing dignity. Waving a hand at the motto on the lid and making no attempt to guess at the pronunciation he mumbled, 'Arabic, isn't it?' before collapsing onto an armchair.

'Gaelic,' Colonel Roland told him. 'Please keep away from the

HIDDEN

thing. Our friend Hiram Stuart is loaning it to me. It may fall under the eyes of Royalty and it would hardly do for it to bear the impression of greasy assault or for your pungent remains to be found resting in it.'

'Disregard my presence, gentlemen,' McAra invited, pretending that the vicious weals on his neck had left him nonchalant and unscathed. 'I'll contribute to debate as required.'

At which point he swallowed whole the quarter pint of spirit, peered round with an air of bemusement, dropped the empty glass on the carpet and appeared to fall asleep, his mouth wide open and issuing a range of unsweetened airs accompanied by both a dribble of something of a nameless but offensive colour and a series of peculiar burbling sounds that were gradually converted into rasping breathing reminiscent of a terminally ill ox.

'I regret, Sir Hudson, that the house is at present being attended to by an army of decorators,' Halley explained. 'As you know my ownership of the property has had to come to an end. The expense is beyond me now and we must prepare for its disposal. If you would prefer it, though, I shall dismiss them for the day and we can adjourn to a more private venue. Mrs Halley's detestable relation will not be easily removed – he is capable of extreme unpleasantness if propelled against his will. I wouldn't want to inflict any display of his disagreeableness on you.'

Waving away the remark Smart said, 'I doubt your esteemed visitor will intrude on our affairs so long as the snoring becomes no more resounding. Meantime I understand that our American colleague and intending benefactor has gone off to look for a kilt. I take it that he *will* be joining us shortly?'

'Yes – Hiram is aware of the importance of our gathering,' Halley assured him.

'Well, in his absence perhaps you would confirm things across the ocean are indeed as we have been led to believe.'

'His wealth and his California project, you mean? I can vouch for him absolutely. Everything he has claimed I have been able to substantiate.'

'I meant rather whether we are to be satisfied that he's entirely right in the head.'

A long pause.

HIDDEN

'I believe the man is entitled to his... eccentricity.'
'My dear chap, I know our military friends here can be entertained by Hiram's hunting down of his Jacobite ancestors. But this is a perilous thing we're at on his behalf.'
'Nevertheless I believe that it's good fortune that has put this opportunity in our path.'
'But treason, Alaric. Treason. I must be as mad as Hiram.'
'Buck up, man. Since when did the hero of the *Nemesis* at Chuenpi, value his own courage at so little?'
Smart was busily rubbing his forehead with a sweating palm. The reference to his participation in the brief dispute with China did nothing to assuage his unease.
'But the sheer magnitude of the enterprise. And the consequences will reverberate...'
'You may remember the coup against the Mexicans in Northern California a few years ago. Fellow called Isaac Graham was the leader.'
'I did read something about it,' Smart said, 'but what does that have to do with us?'
'That'll become clear with time. For the moment let me say this. It was Hiram who financed the project. But the whole thing was engineered by his man – a chap called Grundy. It was done with great skill and in absolute secrecy. Now listen – Hiram and I have prevailed on Grundy to come home to Scotland Ito act for us.'
Colonel Roland did not conceal his unease with this revelation.
'You have recruited a stranger? He is aware of what is intended?'
'Of course. Mr Grundy's discretion may be relied on. He will, much to our advantage, act as a... a buffer between us and our foot soldiers as Hiram describes them. We ourselves will be anonymous. His experience and proficiency will be invaluable.'
'I don't suppose it's *Walter* Grundy you're talking about?' Major DeWitt asked. 'The fellow who set the record for swimming back and fore across the Forth at Queensferry some while ago?'
'Not the reason for recruiting him.' Halley was becoming exasperated at the direction of the debate. 'The main thing is that he's someone we can control. I've installed him in a modest role in Edinburgh which will allow us keep contact with him in a way that will appear perfectly justified. He will be our instrument – our own

HIDDEN

hands and souls will appear without stain.'
'Talking of Queensferry,' DeWitt said, lowering his voice and glancing at the recumbent and hibernating McAra, 'we need to give some thought to acquiring the boats for there and Leith.'
'And the associated combustive cargo,' Roland added.
'You and I, Alaric, share the misfortune of falling on hard times,' Sir Hudson said, choosing to ignore the soldiers' *obiter dicta*. 'These unlucky investments have ruined me and I know you have fared little better. I doubt our situation can be kept dark much longer. And so I accept the gamble will have to be taken but it weighs heavy on me.'
'Major Dewitt and I have our own reasons for participating,' Colonel Roland said, 'but I see no reason to divulge them.'
'We have no secrets from each other, Culver,' Halley told him 'The Major, if I may say so, is understandably disaffected. A man of his character and standing ought to be situated on a higher rank. And you, my dear chap, – a hero of Waterloo – deserve better than your present humble station.'
Circumspection decreed that no direct reference was made to the group's objective. The oblique exchanges were concluded uninterrupted by anything more irksome than McAra's occasional garbled muttering and the restive creaking of his bony limbs. A minute later Hiram Stuart, roseate with the liberal application of malt whisky imbibed in the course of his retail adventure, was conducted in by Samuel Spark.
Stuart was a large man, short–sighted, florid and emanating the easy charm he had inherited from his multi–millionaire father. There were times when Hiram sowed confusion among his listeners with his pronouncements, though these were generally thought attributable, as Halley had pointed out, to mere oddness sanctioned by untold riches. Convinced that he was a direct descendant of the Stuart Royal Family he had over the previous weeks been led by Major DeWitt through extensive genealogical records in Scotland and now London.
'One crown, one sceptre, one sword,' the American pronounced. *'"Lay the proud usurpers low."'*
'A toast to the king over the water,' Roland said, raising his glass and Hiram, failing in his tartan exuberance to detect the sarcasm,

HIDDEN

performed a delighted if inelegant twirl, his arms extended over his head, his new kilt swirling.

'Hiram's personal passion aside, then,' Sir Hudson said, 'I assume that the risk we run bears the prospect of proportionate benefit for all of us. I take it that Esmeralda still enjoys her trips to Bristol?'

'Certainly. But for now can we concentrate on our more immediate endeavours?'

Smart cast a suspicious glance in McAra's direction and when he was satisfied that the disreputable outsider was comatose he lowered his voice and addressed their host directly.

'Then we may rely on you,' he said, 'to prevail upon our Prime Minister to ensure that the date for the Queen's arrival in Edinburgh is fixed for the 1st of September? And we need to know the time and location of the Royal yacht's berthing.'

'You may depend on me. Anything more?'

'This timetable – the risks. I can think of a dozen safer…'

'The timetable is mine,' Hiram announced. 'It is not for negotiation. The date for my return to America is set in stone.'

'Then you, Alaric, will arrange that little piece of business for us in Bristol?'

'Of course – I'll make the necessary enquiries and Samuel will see it done in a few weeks.'

'And these Chartists or trades unionists or whatever Bradley's people are calling themselves?'

'We ourselves must steer clear of them. It will be for Grundy to come on them any day he deems it necessary. The Red Herring pub in Leith is still where they rendezvous.'

'And these Dreyse things we've spoken about?'

'Grundy will arrange for them. Now, if I can be of…'

As McAra stirred gurgling and delirious from his slumber ululating, 'The maggot's eaten my window,' Sir Hudson seized the opportunity to convey to his host something that seemed to have occurred to him without forewarning.

'Emma is a beautiful and agreeable woman, Alaric,' he announced at a more elevated volume than appeared necessary, 'but I can't discard the conviction that you should never have become embroiled with a family attached to that detestable Roman creed, whether they continue to practise it or not.'

HIDDEN

'I'm of the same mind,' DeWitt said, responding to Smart's brief nod. 'The Colonel agrees with me, and so does Earl Bonaly. Wellington and Peel have much to answer for. They should not have changed position on the standing of the papists.'
Halley aimed a cold stare in his brother–in–law's direction but before he could react to this abrupt irrelevance Samuel Spark reappeared in the room to announce the arrival of Albertine Burgess. This foremost British painter of delicately precise watercolours was carrying a portfolio of work of which Colonel Roland hastily relieved her. Before the purpose of this manoeuvre became clear McAra erupted from his still languorous disposition, a hand clasped across his lips just loosely enough to allow him to utter the pained cry, 'Sick. There is vomit upon my palate. God help me, this may be the end – my guts are streaming out of my mouth.'
Beside himself with rage Halley threw open the door, shoved his brother–in–law out into the hall and called on Emma and any conveniently located domestic to remove the distraught interloper from his presence and from the building.
'But I'm ailing,' McAra bleated as he was manhandled by Samuel Spark out into the fresh air, an environment that disagreed violently with him.
'What in God's name were drinking before you got here?' Emma cried after him.
'Don't know. I found it in a jar somewhere.'
There was a pause while the undesirable was being wrestled onto the pavement, from where he summoned the remains of his failing coherence and called over his shoulder, 'We should do this again. I'll be in touch.'
Halley examined McAra's miasmal wake lingering in the room's still air and contented himself with saying, 'Let us press on now with the matter in hand.'
While the ejected intruder, his costume not entirely free of expelled debris, attempted to dust himself down Albertine Burgess emerged from the building and before she could take her own way McAra detained her with mock meekness.
'You depart in outrage at their treatment of me,' he told her, 'and I'm moved.'
'I should be as happy to avoid your company for the rest of my life,

HIDDEN

as I would that of Mr Halley and his egregious company.'
'Egregious? You speak Norwegian, then? What makes them that?'
'Not that it's any affair of yours, but Colonel Roland has pestered me unmercifully about these paintings that he commissioned until I could cheerfully have cut out his tongue. And today he tears them from my hands without a word of appreciation. I don't despise the fee he paid for them but I hate the very sight of the man.'
McAra steadied himself against a low wall and scratched at his barely concealed pudenda.
'He's a critic of water colours?'
'He's an arrogant boor and I will never compel myself to his employment again. It entertained me to enter an error into every single one of my works to annoy him, and naturally he was too enamoured of the end product to perceive them.'
Having described with some relish these minuscule inaccuracies in her copies of portraits and representations of the Scottish Crown Jewels, the chapel, the great hall and the more dramatic stained glass windows, all at Edinburgh Castle, Albertine wound up: 'And anyway the things were a gift for that awful American so I don't imagine the Colonel was concerned with the fine detail. You men are all the same – strikers of a dilettante pose.'
But a survey of the wobbling McAra suggested that the blanket observation did not stretch quite that far.
A few days later, while Halley himself was conducting business elsewhere, McAra joined his sister in the Quiet Room of Brown's Hotel. Reluctant to lift her veil Emma greeted him with a formal handshake. Her Parisian fashion morning dress hardly concealed her fine figure and McAra, leaning close to her, said, 'I don't suppose the humour is on you for a tumble in Halley's hay while he's away nobhogging in the White Chamber?'
'Please, Mac, don't start that again. And anyway the word is hobnobbing.'
'But I'm rampant at the very sight of you. Be discreet, Em, and have a wee feel of it under the table.'
'Behave yourself. You're my brother, for God's sake. And,' sniffing the air, 'you've been drinking as usual. Ten o'clock in the morning and you've been at the whisky.'
'Just a tot, a tincture, a smidgeon – nothing more. And it's a well–

HIDDEN

kent fact that the occasional dram does nothing to damage the performance. I'm still a stoat beneath the sheets.'
'Keep your voice down, you embarrassing little scoundrel. You could be sent to Newgate for this revolting nonsense. Why can't you behave a bit more like a human being? You're not normal.'
'Normal? Tell me this – why should consanguinity,' McAra stumbled several times over the word, 'be a bar to pleasure? My offer, like my member, stands. What's that shiny thing, by the way?'
Emma touched the gold, silver and diamond–studded brooch in the shape of a thistle.
'A gift from Hiram Stuart. He had his personal jeweller create it.'
'A personal jeweller, by God! Give it to me. I wager I could live for a year on the proceeds of a sale.'
'Alaric would never permit it.'
'And that big box of Roland's I took a bit spill into. I should have got compensated – I could have been killed or maimed. Or worse.'
'Worse than…? Oh, never mind.'
McAra's chin dropped for a moment on his chest as he debated the terms of his next advance. Emma took advantage of the pause to raise her veil and reveal the bruising beneath an eye. He peered at her, lascivious yet concerned.
'An accident?'
'My husband. And you know it's not for the first time.'
'Run away with me. It's madness to stay with him, the animal.'
'I can't, Mac. He's told me plain – if I leave him he'll find me. And then this – 'indicating her injury – 'he says will seem then as the merest trifle.'
'He's a carbuncle on the arse of humanity. What's he want to keep hold of you if this is the way of it?'
'Can you imagine how his reputation would be impaired? For some reason there are those of his acquaintances who look on me as his prize.'
'Look, you've had me come to you for a reason surely?'
McAra spread his hands and emitted so audible a belch that the nearby group of dandies poring over their hand of whist turned as one in his direction. But so malevolent was the responding glower of the ruffianly little man that they hurriedly resumed their game.
'Perhaps. I don't know what I want,' Emma replied. 'Advice of some

HIDDEN

sort, I suppose. But I doubt there *is* anything you can do. Halley is so… He does this to me yet he claims time and again to be besotted by me.'
'You'll not forgive him, though? That would be madness.'
'Forgive? No, but I'm trapped, don't you see?'
Emma let the veil fall back over her face.
'I'm sorry,' she went on, 'I shouldn't have come to you this way. I think all I needed was to tell… someone… The world sees us – Halley and me – as the most fortunate pair. Maybe now that you know, maybe someday… Oh, I can't speak clear.'
'You won't take to the law's remedy?'
'He has warned me against it, and anyway his word would be heard far above mine.'
McAra drew his battered lever watch from the pocket of his stained and greasy waistcoat.
'I have to be somewhere now, but my offer is before you still.'
'Your offer?'
'A coupling with no obligation. Five o'clock, will I say?'
'You're wrong in the head, Mac. Go about your trade and think of me once in a while.'
'And Halley? He'll let you be now, you think?'
Emma shook her head and sighed.
'We'll meet again?'
'I know you, Mac. I doubt wild horses would drag you back to Scotland.'
'I'm your brother, Em. Look to me for succour…'
And McAra hunched forward in an effort to conceal the bulge in the buttoned full-front of his twenty-year old dirty breeches.
'By the way,' he asked, struggling into his hideously misshapen frock coat, 'with what diversion is your beloved spouse occupied over the next day or two? Will you have an hour or so for yourself?'
'It's possible. Alaric is at Westminster for the rest of today. It seems as if the Prime Minister is consulting him on the details of a Royal visit to Scotland. To Edinburgh and Perthshire, I think. There is some working out of the finer points to be done – nothing more.'
'King William's heading north?'
'William died five years ago, Mac. Victoria's on the throne now.'
'Oh, aye – isn't she the one that married a Red Indian or something?'

HIDDEN

'Prince Albert is German.'
'That's right. And my loving brother–in–law has been offering some wisdom to the Prime Minister?'
'Aye. And tomorrow Alaric is due to go to Bristol for some purpose he has chosen not to communicate to me.'
'You'll be with him?'
'Not at all. He's going out of the city by coach and train. He's been at some pains to dissuade me from undertaking the journey and I'm more than pleased to comply....'
'So he'll be leaving early?'
'Very early. He likes to stroll to the corner of Green Park. That's where his brougham always waits for him.'
'Well, you wouldn't want to be setting off in the dark of a chilly morning anyway. Goes straight down Albemarle to Piccadilly, I suppose? Will I see you again before you go back to Edinburgh?'
'Best not. You and Alaric have never been on the best of terms.'
'I'm a coachman nowadays. Got my own phaeton. Man of many talents as you know. Vehicle is outside. Have to be off. I've a longish way to go across the city.'
Emma stood up and, disinclined to embrace her malodorous relative, rested on shaking his grimy hand again.
'I take it I'm correct in assuming you have no plans to return north at any juncture?'
'None, unless you can muster some keenness for, you understand, some warmth of intimacy…'
'Then goodbye, Mac. Maybe we'll meet again in this world.'
Later that day Arthur Bowler, standing in the dock of the Central Criminal Court, set about his cosmetic diatribe couched in a purloined vocabulary.
'I have been treated scandalous,' he railed at the phlegmatic judge. 'Detained without warrant, charged without evidence, subject to the undue rigours of unlawful process, of ill–made authority. Your Honour, recompense is owed. And these louts of the State responsible for my discomfiture must be held to the most draconian account.'
Pausing for breath and to glance at his notes Bowler banged his fist on the oak shelf in front of him, but before he could pursue his rehearsed rant Judge Carswell held up an admonitory hand.

HIDDEN

'Let us agree to accept the reality by which we are beset. You, Mr Bowler, stood accused of the most heinous crimes – no less than three such charges of extreme violence. I am compelled to let you loose upon the populace only in consequence of the disappearance of no fewer than seven witnesses against you and the resolute refusal of others to bring their testimony before me. Be assured, sir, that I have no doubt of your guilt. It is to my abiding regret that I cannot propel you in the direction of the gallows solely on the basis of my certainty of your culpability.'

Bowler emitted a roar which was not to be suppressed by the agitation of his Counsel.

'I protest your indefensible bias, Your Honour. Your assertion cannot be allowed to pass unchallenged. Why, if…'

But the combined stone–faced scrutiny of the judge and assembled lawyers served to terminate Bowler's fulmination.

'I recommend that you go now from this place,' Carswell pronounced, 'and express your gratitude to those mysterious fates which have laboured to set you at unmerited liberty.'

As the March evening drew in Bowler, triumphant and drink–sodden and accompanied by his most loyal underling Horace Trapp, held his own court in the insalubrious taproom of the Eagle and Lamb inn in a fetid side–street of the city's East End. As usual he was surrounded by obsequious minions and unctuous sycophants. Bowler was in the throes of regaling this audience with a colourful account of his escape from the clutches of authority. To intermittent applause, he concluded his energetic narrative with a boast to his listeners.

'I came on posh in court. Impressed that bastard Carswell and here I am – free as a bird.'

There was a general clinking of jugs and glasses.

'But none of you forget this – I put the blade up to the hilt into that snivelling squealer Doland. You could hear it tearing its way in. Got blood on my best jerkin.'

Bowler took a long pull at his mug of port, wiped his mouth and smacked his lips.

'Best was the way you done Jeddler, though,' one of the more inebriated hangers–on remarked with a confirmatory nod of admiration.

HIDDEN

'Aye. Broke his neck,' Bowler acknowledged. 'That's when that crowd saw me. But we kept them quiet, lads, eh?'

'Not a one got near the Bailey. We seen to it like you said,' Horace Trapp confirmed.

'Quiet as the contents of a tomb they'll be. Or...' and Bowler drew his thumb across his throat in an eloquent gesture.

The tide of alcohol and high good–humour carried the occasion well into the night by which time Bowler, perspiring and purple–faced with triumph, was barely capable of standing.

'McAra,' he yelled, spraying spittle into the nearest face, 'get me home, you miserable little Scotchman. I'll bid you goodnight, gentlemen and may the Lord be with the reeking lot of you.'

Steadying the brute's bulk McAra and Trapp guided the lurching Neanderthal out into the sheltering darkness.

'Sing us a song, Mac,' Bowler instructed as he clambered with difficulty into the creaking, noxious coach.

'I'll take you along by the river,' McAra said. 'It's quiet there at this time of the night.'

'Anywhere you like, cabbie,' in mocking imitation of the other's accent. 'Just get me safe to my crib.'

'Rely on it.'

And Bowler relaxed as he inhaled the pleasurably familiar stench of the Thames' sewage and the stink of the urine vats at the tanneries.

Late the following morning Emma Halley, sitting in the foyer of Brown's Hotel, was puzzling over her husband's non–appearance at the regular rendezvous with his brougham. Cautiously irritated, the driver had waited by Green Park for almost two hours then made his way to the hotel to enquire after his absent passenger. At Emma's urgent request a search was made of the route along which Halley would have made his accustomed way in the pre–dawn chill but there had been neither sight nor report of him. By afternoon there was still no word of her missing spouse and a courier had confirmed that Halley's private coach on the Euston train had not been occupied on departure.

At a loss to know what to do next Emma enlisted a lackey to take a note to her brother's lately acquired address in Clerkenwell near Smithfield Market. It was not until night was falling that McAra

HIDDEN

arrived at the hotel. Emma explained that her unease was born not out of Halley's vanishing – any relief from his vituperative company was to be welcomed – but at her dubiety as to the course she should pursue herself.

'If I go home,' she said, 'he'll accuse me of desertion. If I stay and he chooses to be still out of touch I'll be without funds in a few days. I can't help but wonder what's become of him, Mac.'

Her brother appeared only faintly interested.

'It's the damn piles,' he explained. 'I can hardly rest my behind. I've got a cushion on the coach but my suffering goes unrelieved.'

'What do you think I should do?'

'Maybe apply some kind of emollient for me. I tell you, my posterior is on fire.'

'Do about Alaric, I mean. If I don't ever see him again my heart's not likely to miss a beat, never mind break in two. But whatever I do he'll deem it wrong. Help me, Mac – offer a suggestion at the least.'

'I'm perched her on a bunch of distended veins and do I hear a word of sympathy? Napoleon had the piles, you know. And by God it's no surprise that he lost at Waterloo. Right enough, though, it's just as true that we won because I was there if you recall – youngest fellow in the 71st Regiment of Foot.'

'Listen to me, will you – I've told you till I'm tired, Halley's a dangerous man.' Struggling to remain calm Emma fought to hold back tears. 'There's no telling what he'll do, whether I stay here and run up debt or go back to Edinburgh tomorrow.'

'You'll have no trouble from him. I feel it in my water.'

McAra shifted awkwardly in his chair.

'I wager I'm sitting in a pool of blood,' he added.

'Rely on you? You have no idea. These men of his would swat you like a fly.'

'It would be a mercy the way my beam–end is nowadays. Put me out of the misery of the exquisite itch.'

'All I can do is go home, I think. I've not a bawbee or a farthing past the fare to Scotland. And if I chose somewhere else to go he'd find me, make no doubt of it.'

'I'm not exactly in funds, but…' McAra began but Emma waved him away.

HIDDEN

'Please, I understand.'

Emma buried her face in her hands and her brother watched her for a moment, debating whether to reach out to her with his none–too–clean paw. In the end he settled for a wave of the same appendage. 'My dear sister, will you take the advice of your cruelly suffering but loving brother?'

Emma straightened, leaned back in her seat, sighed and nodded.

'Go back to Edinburgh. I promise you "*All shall be well, and all shall be well, and all manner of things shall be well.*" That's Julian of Norwich by the way. Damn queer name for a woman if you ask me.'

'This access of borrowed wisdom doesn't reassure me. Who's to protect me if Alaric opts to accuse me of running home – and away from him?'

'God's teeth – I say it again – you're a fine–looking lady, Em. Look – you're my sister, I concede it. But on the better hand we've never been that close. A dispensation surely from the injunction against – what's it called again? Oh, aye – *incestuous coitus*. You'd find me gentle and accomplished.'

'Please give up this tomfoolery. Can't you see the distress I'm in?'

'Well, I doubt you'll suffer grief from him, so go home. There – that's all I can manage.'

And McAra passed her a few silver coins.

'And be happy. None of this – ' he edged aside her veil and pointed to the bruising – 'should ever happen again.'

His eyes communicated something that no thesaurus could convey.

'Then I must trust you.' An afterthought. 'Will you come with me? For a week maybe?'

'I'm bound to my work, Em. Can't depart the Great Wen. I've payments on the coach to keep up.'

'But there must be prospects elsewhere. You're a clever man, Mac, even if you would conceal the fact.'

'I hide my greatness as best I can. Modesty becomes me. But now I have a passenger to collect. A regular hire that keeps me in exiguous funds.'

McAra clambered to his feet, produced a small flask from his coat pocket and tilted the contents into his mouth with a low moan of satisfaction.

HIDDEN

'I hope you can control the vehicle. You shouldn't be drinking so much.'

'There's no finer coachman in the city.' Then a look of mystification. 'Damn me if I can remember where I left the thing.'

Leaning forward unsteadily he aimed a kiss at Emma's lips and was left to be satisfied with the cheek that was turned to him.

'It shames us that my lechery should remain unrewarded,' he complained and passed wind so protracted and audible that the doorman twenty feet away was moved to draw a precautionary glove across his nose and mouth.

'Exceptional,' McAra muttered, gathering up the insanitary debris he had spread on the table in his search for the money he had handed to his sister... 'Matchless. *Tuebor*.'

Emma watched him reel across the vestibule and out into the street, raising an arm in farewell without turning. Unable to account for the unwarranted confidence with which she suddenly felt endowed she set about arranging for the journey north, less perturbed at the prospect of her husband's inevitable outrage than at the sight of her only sibling translated from the hero of her childhood into the incarnation of a staggering vagrant.

McAra himself stood disorientated on the pavement, alternately scratching his head and groin, trusting that the action would stir some recollection of where he had parked his mud–splattered conveyance and flea–bitten nag. Once that inspiration struck the next challenge was to bring to mind where he had been instructed to collect the monstrous Bowler. Another revelatory swallow of whisky had the desired effect and he emitted an elongated porcine gurk that drew a horrified stare from a passing woman who wrapped a protective arm round her trembling offspring and hurried out of auditory and olfactory range. In an effort at mocking salutation McAra succeeded only in propelling his battered billycock into the street. Lumbering after the defecting item he narrowly avoided being knocked over by a slow–moving horse–drawn cart.

'Mind your hind–end, you cretin,' the driver bawled, dragging his team around the floundering pedestrian.

'Away and shite,' McAra called after him, resorting to his Caledonian demotic and pulling the hat over his long, mangy,

HIDDEN

unkempt hair.

'In your hole with a hot poker, you Scotch bastard,' came the rejoinder from the trundling vehicle.

'Thrawl Street,' McAra reminded himself – the filthy and dangerous location in Whitechapel from which Bowler conducted his brutal and sometimes homicidal business. Lording it over the area and its disreputable inhabitants the arrogant and apparently untouchable thug had come to trust the seedy little man who drove him at any hour around the precincts of his squalid jurisdiction. No matter what resource his activities brought him Bowler had chosen to remain quartered in the neighbourhood in which he had been born and reared, confident of the fearful loyalty and ingratiating attentions of his slum–dwelling congregation.

Nevertheless his operations extended throughout the city and his dominion had for years successfully resisted the efforts of the 4500 officers of the Metropolitan Police and the criminal courts to terminate his savage rule. So terrifying was his domination of the streets and the lethality of his reach that no legal authority had prevailed against him. To offer witness against Bowler or his accomplices had often enough proved a fatal undertaking. It was largely in an attempt to bring justice down on him and his rabble that Commissioner Charles Rowan had established a detective force, an innovation also designed to penetrate the ranks of the seditious Chartist movement. As yet this modest undercover organisation had achieved little in either arena despite the advice of Andrew Laurie, a former officer of the Metropolitan police now responsible for the running of a detective cohort in Edinburgh. In an effort to bring the Bowler branch of the criminal fraternity to heel Laurie had returned briefly to the capital and made his temporary presence well known in that circle but his ostentatious intrusion had not been resoundingly effectual.

It had been some months before his most recent appearance before the Bailey bench that Bowler had required his low–life associates to recruit a personal driver who could be relied on to transport him at any time of the day or night to any of the numberless outposts of his empire. The foul–mouthed, mean–spirited, ill–smelling recent arrival in Whitechapel had seemed ideal. McAra knew his way around the city as well as any native inhabitant and could be relied

HIDDEN

on, Bowler was assured, to keep his own counsel. Sullen, bad–tempered and the owner of a small coach on which he relied for a bare living, McAra was a man whose credentials were impeccable. This yellow–toothed, stench–drenched Scot had made a home for himself in a broken–down outhouse in Spitalfields' Dorset Street – not unfairly described as 'the worst street in London' – which he shared with a pet rat called Balthazar. The verminous, flea–ridden rodent was well past the mid–point of life, by which time he had learned that the best defence against hygiene or ill–disposed humanity was his perennially soused master. Recognising that it was only in this unsteady company that his security lay, Balthazar would be content either to laze around the domestic premises while McAra was eking out their collective living or to curl up on his liege's shoulder when the occasion was mutually suitable. Unfortunately the liverish rat was in the lengthy process of divesting himself of animation and tended to vomit with irregular and projectile vigour while perched on McAra's threadbare tail–coat. All of which commended the glassy–eyed Scot to Bowler when it was drawn to his attention; and so over the winter and now the incipient spring this gangster had cause to invest his faith in his driver's circumspection.

HIDDEN
CHAPTER 2 JULY 1842

Night fell late on the crags and closes of Edinburgh and did nothing to muffle the fumes that rose into the cloying air of the Old Town. Occupants glowered from behind the small, yellowing windows of the tall buildings that bulged out into the High Street and the Grassmarket. They eyed with indifference the coming and going of unsteady shadows, heard incuriously the bawling of drunks, the snapping and snarling of hungry dogs, the rattle of wagon wheels on the cobbles. When it came the darkness was warmer than usual and the suffocating atmosphere did little to improve the accustomed disposition of the regular topers squabbling over a place at the bar of the White Hart, laboriously nudging each other aside between tables or sitting in grim silence, rocking back and forth muttering into half–empty glasses.

John Joseph Haggerty, the bouncer, lounged against the frame of the open door, keen for some outbreak of disgruntlement that would allow him to indulge his enthusiasm for distributing his personal form of discipline, but the sweating mass wedged inside the pub was conducting itself with disappointing decorum. Tamping some fierce tobacco into his long clay pipe he shoved his way out into the relative freshness of the twilight and with a disconsolate air lounged against the wall and with a sigh of boredom examined the process of the universe revealing its mysterious distances in the empurpled sky.

A hundred yards further west Mrs McGinty was perched as usual on her precarious wooden stool just inside the stone lobby of the block of single–end flats. From this position she exerted her unofficial authority as a concierge – though the word would have meant nothing to her. The absentee landlord paid her a pittance to keep watch over the irregular traffic into and out of the place and report to his agent any suspicious characters haunting the environs. By way of entertaining herself in the course of carrying out these duties Mrs McGinty would suck at her moustache with her lower lip and bellow at her daughters in the room next to their mother's

HIDDEN

lookout post.

Repulsed by the plebeian pre–nocturnal brouhaha of the Grassmarket and conscious of the danger of lingering in the area Bertram Hopkin, looking in vain for a cab, walked with increasing but careful haste from the home of his aged mother in the Canongate up through the West Port. A taciturn man perpetually dressed in black he was heading for the estate beyond Falcon Hall in Morningside. This destination on the outskirts of the city he knew only as a sought–after decorator of interiors, well–respected and much in demand by the wealthy denizens of the area.

It was almost midnight before Hopkin reached the city dwelling of Alaric Halley. Well to the south of the bedlam that convulsed the Saturday evening in the centre, the suburban street was silent and deserted but he hesitated in the shadow by the iron gate and glanced cautiously around before pushing his way into the expanse of the densely planted grounds. Willows, alders, poplars, larch and fir loomed over him and the faint breeze started an ominous rustle in the rearing hedgerows bordering the gravel path that wound a tortuous way to the enormous Palladian edifice. A single lamp was glowing through an enormous tripartite window, the panes divided by pilaster–style columns that threw a shimmer of dancing shades on the immaculate lawn.

With a guilty air Hopkin glanced over both shoulders, swallowed deeply, bit his lip and urged by an unaccustomed onset of courage yanked the brass bell–pull by the side of the vast oak door. A long pause was followed by the sound of footsteps in the hall and the grating of a bolt being drawn. A squat, bow–legged figure holding a dim lantern in one hand peered out into the now breathless summer darkness.

'Bertram Hopkin to see Mr Alaric, please.'

'Mr Halley is not here.'

As the door swung open a little further Hopkin was treated to the sight of a drooling *cane corso* restrained in its menacing aggressiveness by a short chain which the surly retainer allowed to slip an inch or two through his fingers. Backing away in haste Hopkin touched his hand to his forehead in a gesture designed to indicate subservience.

'Mr Alaric knows me well. And you may remember me – in my

HIDDEN

profession I compose the internal disposition of great houses such as this,' he managed to say, his mouth dry with fear at the sight of the muscular mastiff. 'I have important information for your master.'

Irritated by the persistence of the visitor the imposing hound began to growl and its eyes acquired an unnerving light, but before the confrontation between newcomer and custodian could develop into outright violence Emma Halley came into view behind the burly sentinel.

'It's all right, Casper – I know this gentleman. I'll see him in the small drawing room.'

With a display of sour reluctance Casper stood aside, hauled the vicious–looking dog to heel and with a jerk of his head gave Hopkin to understand that he would not be torn limb from limb if he entered the hall. Flickering lamplight revealed an array of furniture by Chippendale, Hepplewhite and Sheraton along with rococo mirrors, wing chairs, Bergère chairs, rosewood round tables, an ornate carved oak settle, a Chesterfield sofa, a walnut chaise longue and mahogany bookcases. The facets of crystal glasses and decanters reflected the golden glow of discreetly placed candles and gold and silver oil lamps. Though much of this was his own work Hopkin came to a confused halt in the entrance to the room to which Emma had led him.

'What brings you here at this ungodly hour, Bertram? I'm afraid current circumstances suggest a lack of propriety.'

'I don't understand. A lack of…?'

'It surprises me that you should call at all, and certainly at this hour.'

'Of course,' Hopkin agreed, wiping his brow. 'But a matter has arisen… it is essential, Mrs Halley, that I have an urgent word with your husband. It's of the greatest importance, I assure you – and one that he alone will be in a position to respond properly to.'

'Then you haven't heard? Alaric has not been seen for some months. He has never returned from London where we were engaged on various transactions in the spring.'

Hopkin was dumbfounded.

'I myself have heard not a whisper of it, and none of my employers or associates has referred to any such misfortune.'

'You must not on any account allow these tidings to be brought into

HIDDEN

the light. I reveal them to you simply because of our amicable association in years gone by and your capacity for silence.'

'My God, madam, you must be devastated. How can this have come about?'

'You need to understand that I cannot tell you much. Believe me – I indulge your curiosity only because of our mutual regard. And the Home Secretary has insisted that on no account must news of Alaric's disappearance be more widely broadcast than is already the case.'

'The Home Secretary? But why…?'

'There is anxiety in government circles that either some foreign power or some seditious domestic faction is involved in this mystery. Until the situation has been clarified as far as may ever be we are all under injunction to keep our counsel. Now please explain to me what sudden drama has brought you to my door at midnight.'

Hopkin was momentarily at a loss.

'What I need to divulge,' he said at last, rubbing his damp palms together and staring at the floor, 'is of a sort that knowledge of it would certainly be a hazard.'

'Please, Bertram – you talk in riddles. If you must be so vague I cannot offer to help.'

'I can't put you in the way of danger by sharing what I have discovered. All I will say is that some terrible plot is afoot that will damage the nation. And that it is impossible to establish who is concerned in it. There are, I'm convinced, no lengths to which these folk will not travel to ensure that their undertaking is not threatened with exposure.'

'And you thought Alaric could do what to remedy the situation?'

'He moves in circles that one must hope are immune to treason. I had thought he would be able to identify the safest and surest arena in which to share the intelligence.'

'I'm on good terms with Mr Haining, the head of the police here in the city. Would that…?'

Hopkin leaned forward and spoke so quietly that Emma could barely hear him.

'For the last time, madam, you must understand: I came here in darkness for the very good reason that even my movements may be subject to scrutiny.'

HIDDEN

The ensuing silence dragged itself across the room like a hostile shade. Then, struggling to suppress her impatience, Emma said, 'Listen: in London Alaric and I have often been entertained by Charles Rowan, who is in charge of the Metropolitan Police. Surely he of all people might be entrusted with whatever plot it is that you wish to uncloak. What if I send him a private communication conveying my conviction that you have evidence of the most serious danger to the state? I am prepared to do as much on the condition that I am not setting a mock hare running. You *must* give me your unconditional word that that is the whole truth.'

'Of course. But I suggest that you stress that you yourself have no knowledge of what is claimed to be in the offing.' Hopkin gave himself a few seconds to reflect before going on: 'The thing is this, though. The Commissioner is hardly likely to come to Scotland himself, is he, especially given my reticence on the details?'

'You may rely on my advocacy. All the same, without something material to your case, he may be reluctant to hear what you have to say.'

Again Hopkin made no attempt to conceal his diffidence.

'But you think,' he asked, 'he might take some action, and with the greatest discretion?'

'It will not be the first time that I have had occasion to write to him in confidential of terms. So yes – I might be able to persuade him to respond appropriately.'

'Then please do as you suggest. If I may, perhaps I could call again in some days to learn what is to be done. You might tell Colonel Rowan that I can make myself available to any representative of his at a venue and of an evening to suit him. The sooner the better.'

'I have to say this to you once more, Bertram. Why you cannot tell me the whole tale of what brought you to my house like this strikes me as incredible. If you have deceived me in any way I must warn you that Casper will not be well disposed to you, nor will that fearful creature of his.'

'I swear on all I hold holy that I withhold from you only facts that otherwise might cost you your very life. What I have overheard by accident and acquired by stealth may prove to have direful repercussion.'

'Well, I have reason anyway to be communicating again with

HIDDEN

Colonel Rowan – I need to invite him to report again on the search for Alaric.'

Soon after this conversation had taken place in Edinburgh Arthur Bowler, heading home across London in the relative comfort of McAra's phaeton after holding an evening's muster of his seedy lieutenants, saw in the pale bluish light of a tavern door a victualler with whom he was keen to have more than words. Despite repeated admonition this successful retailer had so far failed to surrender the cost of Bowler's unwelcome aegis. Leaping from the slow–moving vehicle, and without preliminary, Bowler cudgelled the unfortunate trader to the ground and when the man's wife, screaming fear and hate, threw herself at the assailant she was dealt with no less robustly. Achilles McAra was slumped drunkenly on the seat of his coach, but the nag was accustomed to the frequent eruptions of the passenger and came to a halt without instruction. Emerging from the pub the several witnesses to the assault retreated in horror from the sight of the victims lying bleeding and unconscious on the ground.

'Toss a pail of water on him,' Bowler ordered, waving a dismissive hand, 'and remind him that his debts need to be cleared if he wants his skull in one piece.'

It was only when Bowler rapped the side of the coach and required its driver to make off that the drowsing McAra cracked his whip and set his elderly horse cantering into the sweltering night. When the authorities were alerted to the attack a couple of days later the police were satisfied that at last they had been presented with the evidence and opportunity to consign their bitterest enemy to the mercies of the judiciary. In this, though, they were yet again thwarted when the intending witnesses had either been discouraged from coming forward a second time or had confessed to deriving an erroneous impression of the event.

Instead of participating in the subsequent discussion of the affair in the conclave of East End thuggery McAra was content to conduct an amiable debate with Balthazar in the discomfort of his rundown residence. The ailing rodent offered little by way of enlightening exchange beyond a glower of his single operative eye and a lash of his scaly tail when a piece of middle–aged meat was placed at his disposal.

HIDDEN

'He,' McAra explained, referring to Bowler, 'would be to me as I, your master, am to you. But you, my wee friend, have lived a blameless life and dedicated your every waking moment to prosecuting my wellbeing. Is there an over–stepping somewhere? Is there some remedy for the ills of the community called for?'

At which point he staggered to his palliasse, cracked his forehead against a fractured beam and fell either asleep or unconscious until called on the following day. Balthazar had had no insights to offer. It was not long after this fruitless exchange that Emma Halley's allusive communique had landed on the desk of Colonel Charles Rowan. From his office at Whitehall Place he found himself staring down at Great Scotland Yard and puzzling over the contents of the letter. The mystery of Alaric Halley's disappearing from the face of the earth remained unsolved after four months of intensive investigation. What was known was that Halley had set off to stroll in the pre–dawn murk to his pre–arranged rendezvous with his coach at the edge of Green Park. At the time it appeared that there had been no traffic, either horse–drawn or pedestrian and no witnesses to his progress. The man had simply vanished into the sluggish air.

What preoccupied Rowan and his colleagues was that there had been no fewer than four attempts on Queen Victoria's life, the latest only days earlier. While there was no apparent connection with any organisation these incidents had promoted the deployment of plain–clothes officers in the metropolis, much to the annoyance of the more radical politicians who objected to the installation of *'spies'* on the streets of the capital. And no less concerning for the forces of the law was widespread Chartist protest accompanied by a wave of strikes which threatened violent and extensive disorder. It was with all this in mind that Rowan and his fellow Commissioner Richard Mayne felt growing concern over Halley's evaporation into silence and invisibility. And now Halley's wife was hinting at some inchoate intrigue boding ill north of the Scottish border.

'Emma Halley is not a woman whose warning is to be taken lightly,' Rowan said. 'She has been privy to plenty that has passed in front of her husband's eyes. I believe we should at least make some effort to uncover whatever it is that has piqued her concern.'

HIDDEN

'But surely her interest is discovering what has become of her husband,' Mayne said. 'Anything else is probably something of an aside. And anyway,' glancing at Emma's letter, 'the thing is too vague. We have enough to trouble us without diverting resource so far from our own backyard.'

'Nevertheless if Mrs Halley is reluctant or unable to divulge detail I'd say it's for good reason. I'm minded at least to send somebody to interview the source of this warning.'

Mayne changed course and tossed onto his colleague's desk a slim file of hardly legible reports.

'That strange little fellow you put into the East End to keep an eye on that gang of Arthur Bowler's – he's Scottish, isn't he? Nobody but the pair of us know about him, so have a look at this: he's going to be at a bit of a loose end for a while.'

Rowan flicked through the wad of documents and raised an eyebrow at the concluding bulletin.

'Well, well. So the esteemed Mr Bowler has been taken off to heaven in a hurry.'

'Hastened on his way, it seems, by a .31 calibre lump of lead that penetrated his thick skull at some great velocity.'

'A sad loss, no doubt. Judge Carswell in particular will, I suspect, not be desolate at the demise of his most elusive client. Do we know the perpetrator of the deed?'

'Desultory enquires are proceeding. The deed was done at a quiet spot by the river. In the dead of night – appropriately.'

'Then, as you say, Mr McAra is free to undertake this Caledonian commission. You will be aware, of course, that the Halley woman is his sister?'

'Really. My God, is that possible? The man is…'

'Quite.'

'Useful coincidence, though. I mean McAra's being on hand for this.'

'Oh, well. This will get him out of the way for a bit. And the air in London might smell rather better. Have him make himself known to our old colleague William Haining in Edinburgh.'

'Mrs Halley appears to hold to the notion that highly placed people are concerned in this affair – if such an affair there is. What if our Mr Haining is one of these evildoers?'

HIDDEN

'He is a long–time acquaintance and I trust him completely. I shall write to him today with a résumé and an explanation of why I believe it to be as well that it should be looked into by an officer from outwith his jurisdiction.'

HIDDEN
CHAPTER 3 AUGUST 1842

Leaving London on the crowded mail coach from The White Horse Tavern in Fetter Lane McAra soon found he had ample room in the swaying conveyance as his fellow passengers appeared keen to remove themselves from his immediate vicinity and huddle as far out of reach of his distinctive bouquet as possible. The journey north could be addressed by more convoluted means if the traveller was prepared to switch between stagecoach and steam train but McAra was content to be jolted on wooden wheels all the way to Edinburgh. He liked the stopovers at coaching inns which afforded him the opportunity to get fiercely drunk and leave him the next day hardly conscious of the inconvenience of the drawn–out trip. Along with the wheezing and rasping issuing from Balthazar McAra's appalling behaviour in the public bars and uproarious snoring and breaking of virulent wind in the coach did nothing to endear him to his companions but his wild–eyed, snarling reaction to criticism soon dissuaded protest.

En route he re–read the letter his sister had sent Commissioner Rowan in which she had described the approach she had received from Bertram Hopkin – a man unknown to McAra – and her response to his request for an enquiry to be mounted into some vague goings–on. Until the substance of the case had been fathomed there was no question of McAra's staying at the Halley residence – if there was anything to Hopkin's apocalyptic pronouncement it would be necessary for him to maintain a degree of anonymity. But none of this impinged on his anticipation of a restful break in Edinburgh and the opportunity to revisit many watering holes. Emma had arranged with the Commissioner for Bertram Hopkin to meet up with the unknown visiting police officer in the White Hart in the Grassmarket on the evening of Saturday the 13th when the place would be bustling with the sort of activity that would render the assignation more or less invisible. There was an abundance of guest houses in the area of sufficiently dubious aspect to welcome even McAra's odoriferous trade.

While McAra was journeying sedately to Scotland officials at

HIDDEN

Whitehall Place were pondering the security arrangements that would be necessary for the Queen's visit the following month to the same destination. Although Victoria had demonstrated courage in the face of assassination attempts and remained averse to being surrounded by a cordon of visible guards there had been a small but sobering number of prominent fatalities in the past twenty-odd years across the continent. The Commissioners of the Metropolitan Police were therefore obliged to balance the Queen's occasionally irritable dismissal of efforts to shield her from attack with the need to protect her despite herself.

The Royal Yacht was to arrive in Leith on Thursday 1st September and the royal party was to be greeted by the Lord Provost and the Corporation before making its way via Edinburgh to the palace of the Duke of Buccleuch in the village of Dalkeith. In the city itself there was much of historical interest on the agenda, the Scottish crown jewels at the Castle, the famous High Street, the National Monument, the Nelson memorial on Calton Hill and the Robert Burns monument. It was the Monarch's intention that she should be plainly seen by the populace so the opportunities for intending attackers were hardly lacking, so Mayne and Rowan and their advisers had spent many hours poring over maps and charts to identify where the greatest risks were to be run.

The usual litany of potential trouble-makers was recited and added to: the newly formed Young Irelanders in pursuit of Irish self-government; the Chartists with their demands for political reform; striking workers from mills, mines and factories; and the lone-wolf disaffected on whom the authorities had tried to keep tabs with varying degrees of success.

About the time the conference in Whitehall was winding up McAra was, somewhat the worse for drink, lurching down the West Bow in Edinburgh, his dirty holdall in one hand and Balthazar's cage in the other. Confused by the geography of a place he had not seen for years and which appeared to be spinning slowly past him he paused to rest against a window sill and, by an act of extreme concentration, fixed his uncertain gaze on the building on the far side of the cobbled street. In the Grassmarket he was able to make out the sight and sound of Mrs McGinty at the entrance to her hovel, her voice raised in maternal antipathy as she railed at her

HIDDEN

pair of scurrying daughters throwing pebbles at an outraged gentleman whose Bolívar hat was sent tumbling into the gutter by a well–aimed rock. Pleased at this picture of social disharmony McAra chuckled, spat and, reeling a yard or two to his right, was confronted by the open door of a disreputable lodging house.

'The very place for an aristocratic interloper,' he announced to the indifference of the clerk who, not stirring from his position on a basket chair and not so much as glancing at the caged rodent accompanying his client, demanded and received advance payment for a week and directed McAra along the stone–floored corridor to a room less endowed with comfort than Newgate Prison. With a sigh of contentment he sank into the urine–stained mattress and slept the sleep of the just until the hour of his meeting with Bertram Hopkin.

Ignoring Balthazar's furious scrabbling for sustenance he stumbled across the uneven surface of the wide street and found himself drawn to the Black Bull pub where, sifting through the contents of his pockets, he came on enough small change to buy a decent measure of Madeira which he disposed of with commendable dispatch. Over the next hour he worked his way along a shelf of fortified wines until his hangover had been dealt with and he was on the verge of applying himself to the fine array of beers when the purpose of his expedition recurred to him. Closing one eye he managed to determine from the position of the hands behind the cracked glass of his pocket–watch that he was long overdue at the White Hart.

'Ribbon,' he muttered as he dragged himself with the support of the wall of the row of dilapidated houses and closed shops. With no idea of what his contact looked like he had been informed by Emma's letter to his master in London that Hopkin would make himself known by wearing a blue ribbon on his lapel. Ricocheting through the heaving crowd he made a space for himself at the bar of the White Hart. Balancing his head on one shoulder he angled a look along the surface covered in jugs, mugs and glasses of varying size and condition, with the occasional inebriate face–down amid the debris and choking clouds of pipe smoke. But no ribbon was to be seen.

The buxom barmaid, hurrying from order to order, waved a hand

HIDDEN

in front of McAra's vacant stare and demanded to know what he wanted. With difficulty he formulated a request for a tumbler of gin which was banged down an inch from his stuttering hand but held still by the hard–faced dispenser. McAra was incredulous.

'Four pence for a wee thimble? I can't pay that. You'll have to give it to me for nothing. I have powers.'

None too coherently phrased, these statements ran together, and on their being repeated with studied care McAra snatched the noggin and threw the liquor back with speed and precision that were admirable in a man who had already worked his way through enough alcohol to fill a tin bath.

'John Joseph,' the apoplectic drudge bawled over the Saturday night din, 'this wee shite has stole drink.'

A moment later the Goliath Haggerty – apparently just returned from some extracurricular *al fresco* business – had prised apart the throng and had the uncomprehending McAra by the collar of his shabby jacket. As if the offender weighed no more than the threadbare clothes he was wearing Haggerty carted him out onto the pavement, pinned him against the mullion window and, with a display of distaste began to rifle through McAra's pockets, an unrewarding exercise that yielded no more than a pair of copper coins and a crust of bread that for weeks had not been revealed to the light of day.

'Don't you come near here again, you little bastard,' the giant Irishman advised, 'or I'll rip the head off you.'

'Officer of the…,' McAra managed to hiss again, his throat much constrained by the other's monumental fist.

'Fuck off out of it,' Haggerty snarled and tossed the unhappy policeman into the gutter.

Finally and with the greatest difficulty McAra succeeded in raising himself almost erect and shook an admonitory finger in the direction of his nemesis.

'I give you fair warning,' he mumbled, 'you'd do well to keep on my side. Do not make the mistake of turning me into your enemy. You will fear me if I…' but Haggerty responded with nothing more than a back–handed slap that sent the other spinning into the street and turned his attention to dealing with another recalcitrant. Picking himself up McAra made to brush from his clothes the mud that was

HIDDEN

a good deal cleaner than the items it was adhering to. He was setting off unsteadily in the direction of his lodgings when he spotted at the west end of the Grassmarket a group of men and women gathered as an audience to some incident, various lamps and blazing brands throwing the scene into garish relief. Depositing in the receptacle of vengeful memory his wounded dignity and the consequent physical pain he slouched across the wide market space and edged aside the onlookers to the hidden event.

Stretched on the cobbles and covered in blood lay the battered figure of a man and even in his debilitated condition McAra was able to make out that clutched in the right hand of the fallen was a short length of blue ribbon.

'As a doornail,' a crouching passer–by pronounced rising from inspecting the supine casualty.

'I nearly seen it from over there,' someone else claimed. 'A two–wheeler, it was. Driven like the hags of hell was after it.'

'*Nearly* seen it? What's that mean?' somebody else asked.

'Heard it, then.'

'A coach and pair, was it?' McAra offered, breathing something foul in the direction of the witness.

'Nah! What do *you* know? It was just the one dobbin.'

'Aye,' McAra persisted, 'but it was one of them dray things. Yellow, eh?'

'Rubbish. It was black as the hole in the pit of hell.'

'Shite. It was one of them four–wheeler landau buggies. And a four team. You never seen it right.'

'Your mother's arse! It had only the two wheels. And there was a bucket and chain on the back of it. And here's the police. I'm away.'

'Look at that,' another onlooker pointed out. 'A horseshoe that come right off it.'

'Going like a hungry whippet, they tell me,' an old man reported to the newly arrived officers who shoved the little crowd away and knelt to examine the fallen.

McAra caught sight of the horseshoe wedged against the kerb. The metal was burnished and evidently new.

'That's handsome,' he informed a passing reveller looking the worse for alcoholic wear. 'A horseshoe – it's good luck. I'll keep that.'

And stooping shakily he collected the thrown horseshoe and

HIDDEN

stuffed it under his jacket.

'For good luck,' he repeated, as much for his own benefit as for the elderly gentleman who had paused to watch him and recoiled at the callousness of the remark.

'Good luck is it, you sot? Not for this laddie that's lying there in his own gore.'

'There you go, then – it's lucky for me, isn't it? I wasn't even touched.'

The gentleman shook his head in disbelief and strode off while McAra rummaged through the corpse's pockets. He came across nothing of interest and received a terrific blow on the back of his head for his trouble and the appellation, 'Thieving wee twerp.'

'I'm not feeling that well,' McAra confessed as the police went about the business of interrogating the remaining spectators. 'Could somebody maybe give a hand here? I'm just in yon door over there.'

A sly–looking bystander, keen to assist on the off–chance of some modest recompense, wrapped an arm round McAra's shoulders and began to drag him towards his diggings but was instantly repelled by the particularly noxious odour emitted from within the invalid's apparel.

'My alop... plippol... apologies,' McAra managed. 'An incident – an accident – in my nether garments. All night only a solitary tincture of sherry. Must have been corked.'

Late the next day McAra surfaced from a profound sleep that had done little to impact the vicious headache that afflicted him. He studied the runes discarded by fate the night before and was able to read very little into them.

'Like I said to the police nobody saw nothing,' his landlord announced in reply to his query about the fatal felling of Bertram Hopkin the night before. 'The lad might have been at the gin. Must have took a tumble just when the cab was passing. Bad luck anyhow.'

There was still a puddle of blood on the cobbles outside the building despite a casual effort at sluicing it away. Patting down his jacket, coat and trousers McAra confirmed that his funds were exhausted. There was only one resort open to him which he applied to without delay. The long walk in the mid–August heat added a further dimension to the depth and variety of astringent essences

HIDDEN

wafting around him and when he arrived at the Halley estate neither Casper the domestic sentry nor his fiendish hound betrayed any great eagerness to intrude on his aura.

'You remember me – Miss Emma's brother? I need a bit of help,' McAra said, trying unsuccessfully to come within the other's ambit. 'You'd know where I could find a cheap mount? I'm just after an old dobbin – nothing fancy.'

'Aye, well I think I could suggest a place. But you'll not get anything there that's pleasing to the eye. And for sure you wouldn't want to be looking too close at the teeth neither.'

With the address of the equine trader stuffed in a pocket McAra intruded on his sister's therapeutic session of needlework. Emma was for a moment struck dumb by this wholly unanticipated incursion and came close to fainting altogether when McAra explained his presence as that of the metropolis's *'finest detecting officer.'*

'You think you're a policeman? Mac, you poor thing, you've become unhinged. I knew the drink would do for you. But we'll get you well again even if it means the Asylum for the Insane for a while. They tell me Dr MacKinnon is a worker of miracles. And he'll let you be a gardener or a pig farmer or a poultry keeper until you're better and I can look after you.'

And gently she led the dishevelled, shambling waif to a chesterfield almost weeping with sympathy.

'A wee drink, maybe,' the intruder suggested, 'and I'll be as fine a fellow as ever blessed this house.'

'No more drink, Mac, until…'

And it was with staggering incredulity that she cast her eye over the warrant of office her brother waved in front of her. At first too bewildered to make sense of what she was looking at, she calmed herself sufficiently to read the terms of the document over Commissioner Rowan's familiar and confirmatory signature.

'But I don't understand,' she said, collapsing into an armchair. 'Where is your uniform? And why have you never told me?'

'New breed. Best men only. Secret police. Not allowed to say anything. And don't you tell a soul. There was word of a little tumbler of something strong?'

An hour's none–too–coherent exposition later brought proceedings

HIDDEN

up to date.

'Yon fellow Hopkin dodged me. Got himself caved in under the wheels of a cart or something.'

Emma stopped what she was doing, her hand paused in mid–air.

'Bertram's hurt? Where is he? Can he talk?'

'Dead. Squashed. Looked like a pancake with raspberry confiture. I only saw it was him because he had that bit of ribbon about him.'

'My God – how did it happen? Where?'

'Grassmarket. Stepped into the road of some flyer. Nobody could tell me anything more. Nobody saw it, they say.'

'An accident, you think? You had no chance to talk to him?'

'No I waited for him in the pub like it was arranged,' McAra lied. 'But an accident? Aye, I would say so. Poor bastard. Anyway, I've come about one or two other things. I'm after a nag but I'm low on funds so I thought you might want to put your pretty wee hand in yon strongbox of Alaric's. And then maybe you can let me know where this Hopkin fellow used to lay his head before it got mashed on the cobbles.'

'Don't the police give you any money nowadays?'

Having disbursed a mite of his expenses on lodgings and the bulk in pursuit of alcohol McAra had to resort again to untruth and assured his sister that the money due to him would no doubt catch up with him in a few days.

'Mac, you know well enough how Alaric will react if every farthing can't be fairly accounted for.'

'You won't need to worry on that score, though, will you?'

'What do you mean? Have you news of him.'

After a moment's hesitation McAra said, 'No, Em, not at all. It's just that the man's been gone that long he's not coming back, is he? It's been months.'

'And really – there's been no word of him?'

'Maybe he's been a spy all along. Or some other sort of shite. I'd put nothing past him. And, good God, woman, you can hardly be sorry that the bastard's gone. Think on these fists of his and take a wee bit of pleasure that they're nowhere near you now.'

'I can't rest, Mac, until I have sure news one way or another. I'm frightened every time Casper answers to the bell.'

'So about my lucre. If you could see your way…'

HIDDEN

The Halley wealth was cruelly diminished and anyway not a resource which Emma was accustomed to accessing, and her hands trembled as she counted out far more than McAra could need for the duration of even a lengthy stay in the city. With his spending power much increased and not having had a single glass of porter, port or gin all day McAra was anxious to be on his way; and Balthazar would need placating – by this time he would be gnawing angrily on the bars of his cage.

'I think I need new stockings,' he said. 'The reek on a hot day like this is coming right out through the holes. The toes and the heels are gone. See what you think if I take off my boots.'

'Please, Mac, get on your way if there's nothing more I can do for you. And if Bertram's gone I don't see what there is you can do here now.'

'Hopkin's place. Where is it?'

Emma wrote the address in the Canongate on a piece of paper.

'It's his mother's house, near the Tolbooth. You'll pay our respects?'

'Rely on it. I am the soul of compassion.'

The horse dealer whom Casper had recommended was located in the Cowgate, not far from McAra's other destinations. It was afternoon evening before he arrived there and it was under the suspicious eye of the owner that the leisurely inspection of his stock was viewed. Having sought and found relief from sobriety in several hostelries on the way back from the south side of the city McAra occasionally had to stabilise himself by grabbing a mane or muzzle. Feigning knowledge of what he was examining he made ungainly efforts to lift a fetlock or pastern to study the condition of a hoof but had in the end to admit that either none of the horses was prepared to cooperate with his efforts or displayed a hoof which to his untutored gaze was nothing more than a hoof.

'I'll be riding the thing hard and long,' he claimed, giving up his attempts to convey expertise in the field. 'So he'll need to be powerful but biddable and well shod.'

'These are all prime beasts. Finest mounts to be had anywhere in the country.'

Even McAra could see that this was not the most accurate description of the flea–bitten herd. Some were clearly long past that prime and others gave the impression of never having had a prime

HIDDEN

to leave behind. With a show of distrust and overt animus he stumped up a nugatory amount for the least broken–down mare in the place along with a saddle and set of reins both of which betrayed every sign of imminent disintegration.

'I'd like fine to have a farrier take a good look at the way the thing's shod. Probably an awful lot of them in the city.'

'Aye, a lot.'

'Well, there's one of them I hear is an honest man. That's his work, look.'

And McAra produced with a flourish the horseshoe he'd picked up in the Grassmarket the night before.

The dealer held the thing for a while in the palm of his large hand and rubbed the metal.

'That would be Dobbie. He has a place in King's Stables Road market. I have a drink with him every Saturday. Aye, have Dobbie look over your beast.'

'King's Stables, you say. Near enough. Mind my beast, will you, until I'm ready for her.'

Setting off for Bertram's home on the Canongate he stopped at the Tolbooth Tavern to undo the giddying sensation of clear–headedness that had briefly inflicted itself on him and then made for the Hopkin residence whose address he discovered easily enough with a number of concerned neighbours having gathered outside to console the departed's grieving mother. His swaying belligerence cleared a way through. Hooking his arm round Mrs Hopkin's neck he hustled the noisily grieving little woman back into the dingy flat and firmly deposited her on a sofa. He stood inspecting the results of his manoeuvre, waiting for the hysteria to subside and when there was no sign of such a consequence he adopted a more vigorously sympathetic approach.

'For God's sake, missis, calm yourself. You're opening a crack in my head. Look, I'm an old pal of Bert's and the last thing he said was "*I want Achilles McAra to have whatever of my things that he wants.*" His very words.'

'Bertram's gone. He's dead and gone from me, God help me.'

Another bout of weeping was accompanied by a drumming of her tiny fists on her thighs and furious rocking back and forth until her visitor's immense patience was exhausted.

HIDDEN

'It's all right for you,' McAra said, 'I was there. I saw him all battered to bits in the road and his blood all over the place. It would have made slaughterman sick. But there he was – breathing his last and all he does is hold my hand and say I was the very best of his pals and would I rake through his belongings for anything that took my fancy. *Remember him!* That's all he asked of me.'

Irritated that his mendacious account produced nothing beyond a further lachrymose gnashing of teeth he half–fell backwards into a rocking chair and sat sulking until the poor woman was capable of speech.

'What'll become of me now?' she pleaded. 'He was everything to me. My lad, my boy.'

'You'll be fine in a day or two. You don't happen to have a glass of something strong do you? My nerves are in pieces with your howling. I'm too delicate for this world.'

Mrs Hopkin slowly began to subside into a stupor of uncomprehending bereavement.

'I think there's some sherry if Mr Donnelly left any,' she managed to utter, waving at a small sideboard.

'Donnelly?'

'You'll know him. The feu collector for Mr Grundy. Another of Bertram's friends, he said. Just an hour gone. All he took away was that wee bit paper that Mr Grundy was after. A feu, maybe, or something. I never asked. My Bertram…'

Launching himself at the cheap decanter McAra said over his shoulder, 'I'll just have a wee look in Bert's room like he asked. Where…?'

And with a full tumbler to sustain him he barged into the room which his frantic hostess had indicated with a trembling finger. The furniture was sparse – a bed, a wicker chair, a wardrobe with a pathetic array of well–tended garments and a beech cabinet with two drawers. Setting his glass to one side McAra hauled these open and sorted through the unrevealing contents until he came across a neat and clean collection of underwear which he distributed amongst his various pockets, some already occupied by remains of rotten fruit and the corpses of insects unlucky enough to have settled on his lethal person. An extended search produced only the melancholy residue of a lost life. On his way out of the building he

HIDDEN

was waylaid by the lamenting Mrs Hopkin who had recovered just enough as ask McAra as he laid a hand on the door handle, 'Please, Mr Achilles. As his friend can you tell me that he didn't suffer? That would be too much to bear.'

'Suffer? Madam, he was bowled over by a horse galloping at full tilt. He was smashed to the cobbles like a thrown away toy and then run over by the wheel of the careering vehicle. Gore and guts all over the place. Suffer? Of course he suffered. I don't suppose you have a bit of dinner I could have?'

Disappointed in this request but helping himself to some sheeps' trotters and potato parings McAra left the now wholly disordered lady to her deafening wailing. Back at his lodgings in the Grassmarket he shared these luxuries with the ravenous Balthazar to whom he confided the acuity with which he had handled the vagaries of the day. Then, the cage in one hand and scratching at various locations about his person with the other, crossed the street to where Mrs McGinty was stationed as usual and sat down uninvited on the bench next to her. In a gesture conveying the promise of unaccustomed generosity he withdrew a handful of coins from his jacket and, holding them close to his face, nodded and muttered out their value.

'Nasty business that was last night, eh? Pity nobody saw what really happened.'

'Well, folk round here don't always see things clear, 'specially when the police is asking about them. Not that yon coppers did much asking. They was only there a minute before some big chap hauled them off. A copper himself with a moustache that made him look like one of them walrus things I seen a picture of.'

'Aye – the police. Bastards, every one of them. A big chap, was it that got the peelers away out of the way? You'd know him, then?'

'No, no. If I seen him again I would, though. Maybe.'

'Mind you, yon was my chum that got knocked over. I'd like to settle with whoever it was done him in.'

'Settle with them, is it? Well, you'll never find them. The thing was over that quick. And it was all black – horses, cart, the lot. That time of night you couldn't see nothing more. Other thing – I never could see nobody on the coach. Maybe it was just a runaway, but it was awful careful getting up the West Port.'

HIDDEN

'Pity. There'd be a penny or two for anybody that could have told me a wee bit about what went on.'

'I seen that big J J Haggerty and some other that was with your pal when he got hammered with the horse. It was too dark for me to make out the other creature that was with J J.'

'They were *with* him or what?'

'Up to no good, I'd say. Maybe they was shoving him about. But never tell a soul I told you.'

'Never to a soul. Here – ' pointing to a basket of large onions on the doorstep – 'would that be yours?'

'Aye.'

'I've a great likeness for onions. Can eat them from first light till bed. If you can spare a pair of them you can have the whole sixpence.'

McAra picked up the imprisoned Balthazar, strolled back to his base, deposited the sickly rat at the lodging house, and sought relief from the day's activities in a pub on the nearby Lawnmarket. Then giving the impression of an idle visitor he wandered up the esplanade and joined the stream of sightseers making for the Castle itself. Paying his shilling he strolled round the Crown Room to have a glance at the Honours; admired the vast Mons Meg bombard on the ramparts; stared down at the spectacular urban outlook drenched with memories of his childhood; and chatted with a junior officer of the Royal Scots Greys who took the time to complain that a regiment with such an illustrious history was now reduced to garrison duties at home and operating in support of the civil authorities at locations in every part of the country. McAra sympathised.

'I was a hero at Waterloo,' he explained modestly. 'I'm elemental – a force of nature. At fifteen years old I was a great brute of a fellow for my age.'

'What happened to you, then?' the other enquired, casting a doubtful eye over his scanty dimensions.

'I'm awful failed with the work and worry. This must be a canny wee job you have, though,' McAra said, ignoring the implication that he was unlikely to be mistaken for Benandonner. 'Does the Lord Provost call you out now and again to have a go at the tinker lot?'

HIDDEN

'Sir James can be sure of our help if he needs it. These are troubled times right enough. But we're soldiers, not policemen.'
McAra dragged the worn sleeve of his jacket across his face, wiping the green drips from the end of his nose.
'Who would be the Colonel nowadays?'
'Not that it's your business but we've two of them the now – Sir William Grant, him that's the boss of the whole thing; and Culver Roland with his daft wee ceremonial job polishing the Honours and his medals. Why would you want to know that? Are you up for joining us?'
'I'm up for a full shilling of gin and a night with my behind on a soft bed – better than strutting about in a uniform on a hot day. How many of you lads are there in the Castle?'
'Should be six hundred but we're out at Glasgow and Dundee and other places belting the balls of yon Chartist lot. Still enough of us to fend *you* off, eh.'
McAra let fly with a belch that might have rocked the fortress's gatehouse.
'The New Barracks,' he said, 'must give you a good view of the Grassmarket. Would any of your lads have seen any goings–on there the other night? A fellow got crushed under a cart that was in a hurry.'
'The Grassmarket's two or three hundred yards away and the thing was done at night, I hear. Mind you, there's Sergeant Rannoch and his bunch that are after getting back from Glasgow. They've been dead drunk in the pubs on the West Port since. Maybe got a look at the thing. You'll get them there the night.'
'Look at that, would you,' McAra grumbled, nodding at a spindly youth trudging across the courtyard with his eyes fixed on an open book. 'I blame that damn Factory Act and it putting these wee fuckers in school two hours a day. No good's going to come of that. Noses in books and they'll be banging into wee wifies and falling down drains.'
McAra spent the rest of the evening stretched out on his straw–filled mattress half–listening to Balthazar's pathogenic gurgling. And some hours later he learned from the well–lubricated Sergeant Rannoch that a black four–wheeler with a red and white crest on the door had come blazing up the West Port on the night of

HIDDEN

Bertram's demise, nearly inflicting a similar fate on one of the celebrating troopers.

'There's some say it's a thing belongs to one of your local lordships for they know that red and white picture bit on the side of it, is that right, Mungo?' the Sergeant asked.

Mungo, a corporal even less steady on his feet than Rannoch, mumbled an affirmative.

'Bonaly's the man,' he elaborated. 'My dad was his gardener a wee while ago.'

'Queer thing, though,' Rannoch remarked. 'I couldn't see any driver of the thing. It was like nobody was at the reins. A ghost, maybe. Or a wee bit too much drink, eh?'

HIDDEN

CHAPTER 4 AUGUST 1842

It was early the next day that, with much satisfied sighing, McAra relieved himself noisily and copiously in the vile–smelling outhouse. In pursuit of his theory of the adverse effect of wanton cleanliness he scrupulously avoided the shared wash basin in the lobby and tossed his famished rodent the remains of his last onion. Somewhat restored he returned to the dealer to inspect his horse at the livery stable and under the sullen stare of its former owner attempted to whisper mysterious encouragement into the thing's ear and announced that he'd collect the pathetic and unresponsive equine shortly. The rest of the day and evening he spent relaxing in the luxury of the lodging house.

Pursuing his nocturnal expedition he took shelter around midnight in the shadows at the foot of Candlemaker Row until even the notoriously benighted Old Town was deserted and the shutters were being closed over the vulnerable windows of the taverns. There was an oppressive feel to the cloying atmosphere that had retained the heat of the long day under the suffocating integument of heavy cloud that hid the moon and rendered the city streets even darker than usual. At last J J Haggerty appeared, having sampled a substantial amount of the White Hart's fare.

Humming an ancient Irish air as he applied flame to the tobacco in his pipe he was unaware of the slight figure fifty feet behind him dodging from doorway to close–mouth. As he turned into the Vennel at the west end of the Grassmarket something hinting at danger in the brooding silence caused him to halt, turn and peer into the dense murk, but there was no sign of movement. With a snort he carried on up the lane trying to remember how far through the tune he had got. When he reached the steps at Keir Street he caught his foot on a cracked paving stone and landed awkwardly on his knees, sniggering at the condition that had – not for the first time – waylaid him. It was then that he was propelled forward by a blow to the skull behind his right ear.

'What in the name of Christ…'

Spinning round he raised an arm to ward off any further onslaught

HIDDEN

but the gesture did nothing more than carve an arc through the weighty hush. His assailant had moved quickly out of range and Haggerty caught sight of the shadowy outline made instantly recognisable to him by the overwhelming stench that he recalled from his extricating its owner from the bar a few evenings earlier.
'You little weasel,' he hissed, starting to clamber to his feet and bunching his great fists. 'I'll break your back, you wee bastard.'
But one step was enough to bring into view the fact that the other was pointing a strange looking pistol at him.
'I warned you,' McAra reminded him, 'you'd have reason to fear me. Now make a charge at me and I'll blast the pate off your neck.'
'What do you want? I've not got more than a bob or two if that's what you're after.'
'You're a murderous bastard,' McAra pronounced. 'You should be run in to the Calton Jail but I've a better notion.'
'What are you on about? Leave me be or I'll find you and break every bone in your horrible wee body.'
'It was you shoved yon fellow Hopkin in front of that coach the other night. I have a good witness. You'll surely be for the rope round your neck in the Lawnmarket.'
Haggerty blanched.
'It's a lie. I never... It wasn't...'
'But I'm a grand friend to have,' McAra announced. 'And if you have a name for me – the name of whoever it was paid you to do the thing, well, I might forget I ever set eyes on you.'
'The name? What name? Nobody...'
The sound of the pistol shot reverberated between the walls of the lane and Haggerty, clutching at his wounded foot, embarked on a long falsetto squeal.
'Somebody'll hear you, right enough,' McAra remarked, 'but they'll not care a fart to come looking. You're lucky I've had a drink – I was aiming for your bollocks. Still, maybe the next one...'
And he raised the pepper–box revolver until the rotating barrels were focussed on Haggerty's crotch. Clutching himself protectively in this area of his anatomy the big Irishman came to amicable terms with his attacker.
'Walter Grundy. That's all I can tell you. He got Breccan Donnelly and me a pair of sovereigns for doing the thing. I never knew the

HIDDEN

man Hopkin would get done proper. I never knew they was going to kill him, I swear.'

'And where can I come across Mr Grundy and Mr Donnelly?'

'Donnelly was Grundy's man for giving a hand sometimes with getting in the feu money. Gone back to Ireland somewhere. And Grundy I never seen myself. He's a factor or something for some big wigs at Dowe's on Leith Street. You'll get him sometimes in the Red Herring pub.'

'And why would Mr Grundy wish ill on poor Bertram?'

Haggerty, still covering his groin with one hand, was dragging off a boot to ease the pain in his foot and a puddle of blood spread on the cold stone.

'How would I know? Jesus Christ, you fucker, you've lamed me.'

'And I'll see you hung if you're not telling me the truth.'

With which admonition McAra was gone into the undisturbed small hours.

The premises from which Walter Grundy was reported by Haggerty to conduct his business were at the east end of Princes Street and were set up in a thoroughfare by no means devoid of agencies offering refreshment on the following sweltering August afternoon. Tying his stridently breathing mount to a hitching rail McAra was seduced by the nostalgic scent of mingled stale porter and damp sawdust blossoming from the open door of a pub called The Old Caravel. Soon enveloped in its embracing twilight he was left almost alone to enjoy the variety of drinks on offer. He had worked his way half the length of the lower shelf before the effects of this commitment to endeavour had wreaked its inevitable result. Falling asleep at a corner table he eventually awoke in the evening to find that he had slid to the floor and the tavern owner's dog had emptied its bladder at exactly the area of his trousers that would suggest he himself had been responsible for the accident.

The irate McAra chose to remonstrate first with the quadrupedal miscreant but receiving in response only a baring of fangs redirected his outrage at the thing's master. This bleary–eyed bluster was no more successful in producing apology. Instead the unhappy policeman found himself deposited swiftly and painfully on the roadway outside the bar to the delight of half a dozen brats who pelted the fallen officer with handfuls of gravel. Unable to

HIDDEN

recall where he had secured his nag McAra half-crawled, half-staggered for fifty yards in either direction, tried to clamber aboard the first tethered mount he reached and was rewarded with a vicious kicking by the owner whose lack of affection for a potential thief took proportionate physical shape.

Still in possession of a few fragmented faculties he concluded that the solution to his predicament was to take refuge in the next public house from which he was not to be excluded on the grounds of his apparent mental and bodily instability. This was the Red Herring, the least reputable establishment in an area not renowned for its respectability or gentility. That destination he achieved not wholly by chance and his distributing of coins on the counter was a passport to something exceeding further solace. Recognising a source of companionable bonhomie three or four of the hefty occupants of the place surrounded him, clapped him amiably on the back, exchanged some incomprehensible badinage and awarded themselves the benefit of his unwonted generosity. The name Bradley was to lodge somewhere amid the smithereens of his memory of the night's work as did some raucous boasting by his new-found friends of recent and imminent anarchy. Oh, there were plans, all right, McAra thought he recalled a fearsome trade unionist confirming – plans that would coincide with the unwelcome Royal foray across the border. His mumbled enquiry after Mr Grundy had led nowhere.

By the time the day had slipped away into yet another breathless night McAra, wild-eyed, his matted hair standing on end, his pantaloons spreading a nauseating effluvium in the already mephitic air and his jacket and shirt clinging precariously to his figure, went careening back and forth across the now deserted roadway until he spotted a familiar face in the window of the last saloon before the curve that would bring him onto Little King Street. At his unsteady gaze this unprepossessing physiognomy returned a lip-curling snarl that somehow drove him to righteous fury and he launched a right-handed punch that smashed the glass, quickly removed from view his targeted reflection and bequeathed him a set of bleeding knuckles. Distantly conscious that the misunderstanding might have repercussions from within he weaved his hasty way into the protective cover of darkness. Having

HIDDEN

lost his bearings he took refuge from the iniquity of the locality and collapsed into a niche in a low wall, giving himself up to a slumber attested to by tumultuous snoring.

Not in the finest condition in the morning McAra resurfaced, spruced himself up by evacuating bladder and bowels on the muddy patch of ground where he had spent the previous eight hours and, some sense reinstalled, was at last able to identify his horse. By this point the creature was so hungry and thirsty that it could do no more than shuffle with painful sluggishness the three miles or so via the Grassmarket to the Halley property on the outskirts of the city. Struggling under the combined weight of his unsteady rider and Balthazar's residence now tied to the pommel, McAra's mare stumbled resolutely on while her master sorted through the various routes down which he might conduct the next component of his research, munching a fresh onion and trying to inhale as little of the clean and clear air as possible. On arrival at his destination even Cerberus, Casper's monstrous *cane corso,* betrayed no inclination to approach the bedraggled, whey–faced and noxious visitor whom the expressionless gate–keeper seized with some revulsion. Having ripped off the shredded clothing he tossed the unresisting McAra into a cast iron bath in an outhouse and ran tepid water on the whining recumbent until something resembling a human could be identified under the discoloured pellicle of the sluice.

Newly apparelled in a set of garments belonging to Casper, McAra presented himself in front of his sister as if he had recently emerged from an episcopal conference; and neither he nor Casper uttered a descriptive word of the condition in which he had appeared an hour earlier. Combining lying alongside an approximation of the truth with his ordinary facility McAra proceeded to render account of his exploits of the evening before. While Casper secured and tended to the flagging horse McAra joined his sister in the drawing room where he deposited his pet rodent on a chiffonier with a mirror in which Balthazar, unwittingly pursuing his master's example, could snarl at his own reflection.

"I've been seeing an old wife that called me by my given name,' he told Emma as he slumped in a chair whose expensive covering deserved a less aromatic occupant. Casting around for evidence of

HIDDEN

potable relief he wondered, 'Why is it that you never do that for me?'

'You'll remember that when you reached the age of twelve mother and father felt that the name was... not entirely appropriate.'

'I don't remember that. And it has no sense. I'm a master of the Tsakonian for a start.'

'No, you're not. You don't have a single word of it. Anyway maybe they just felt you didn't look enough like a Greek. Please don't press me on the matter. I suggest you reflect on it at your own leisure.'

'They weren't Greek, though?'

'Of course not – papa was from Edinburgh.'

'He was a tragic figure – passed on when he had his whole life in front of him.'

'He was 82. And remember – mama was from Kinsale.'

'Kinsale? So I'm half Portuguese?'

'Oh, please, Mac...'

'Well, we're a small family now and we shouldn't be calling each other by surname. We Jews should stick close by each other.'

'We're not Jews, Mac. We've been Catholics since God woke up.'

'Oh, aye. And wasn't it me that Old Hookey got to write the Bill that emaciated us back in '29?'

'No, it wasn't. And you know well enough that's not the right word. You do that just to annoy me, don't you?'

'Well, I'm a collapsed Catholic anyhow and I could deal very severely with a dram. A single malt would be the very thing for a drouth like the one on me.'

Emma rang a bell for Casper who appeared, bowed to listen to her request, marched out and a minute later came back, set down the whisky and silently departed. McAra went on: 'Now's the time. We're alone. I'm a desperate man, Em – let's make free with each other. An hour in that great bed of yours and you'll never want another man.'

'That's certain, but not the way you mean it. You have to stop that nonsense once and for all time. And listen – since Bertram is dead I have to say it again – there can be little point in your staying on in Scotland.'

'I heard yon Sir Smart Hudson fellow hates Papists. But I venture he'd drop his underlinen fast enough if you so much as smiled at

HIDDEN

his lucky bamboo.'

McAra gulped down a measure of spirits, cracking the glass against his teeth and a second later an upper incisor was plunged into the dregs. He fished the fugitive tooth out with his long–unwashed fingers and tentatively pressed it back in place. When this performance led to no satisfactory outcome he dropped the yellow fang into a pocket and with a smacking of lips downed the last of the whisky.

'I'll need to sort that later on.'

'Well, what will you do now? For all we know there's nothing to investigate. Once the Commissioner hears that the only person who said there was something that needed looking into is dead now he'll want you back in London.'

'My bowels have been awful loose since I came back up here. And the smell! Balthazar can hardly stand it. I'm a martyr to my organs. I'm ravaged by disease.'

Noting that Casper had had the good sense not to leave the bottle of malt in the room, Emma wrested the glass from her brother's hand and with an eloquent gesture began to usher him out.

'There's some other thing I need to have a good think about at the now,' her brother informed her. 'I've been doing some secret work in a pub down on Leith Street. There's folk, I can tell you, all afire to bring their strikes and riot to us.'

'What does that have to do with poor Bertram's story? There's nothing the Government don't know about these people.'

'They were loose in the tongue because of the drink, but lucky I was all sober.'

'You need to be careful. These folk aren't on the best of terms with the law.'

'Well, that's the thing. See, I'm as sharp as a tack when I'm not in the cups and I caught them saying something about how they were going to have the police and the army run about like lost sheep the way some fellow Bradley wanted.'

'And who's Bradley?'

'So I gave them a few more lumps of that money you gave me – I mean, I gave them nearly all of it by the time I was away. So if you don't mind I'd like a few bob more. Because that last lot went on the business of the state.'

HIDDEN

'You're lying to me as usual, Mac. Or bigging yourself up. Were you at the drink again last night?'

'God and Mary, not a drop I had – take a peek at me. Do I have the look of a man that's been on the spree?'

Emma studied her brother with some care but could hardly deny that he appeared in uncharacteristically good vestiary form, ill–fitting as the outfit was.

'All right, as long as Alaric doesn't turn up back on his own doorstep.'

'That's the way of it, Em. You're a grand girl. I don't suppose you've changed your mind about a quick seeing to? Look for yourself – I'm in the very pink of pure spotlessness.'

'Now tell me – who is this Bradley?'

'I couldn't make it out if he was mixed up in the business or if he's a man to be made a monkey out of.'

'I wish I could trust you, Mac. But you've lied from the cradle about everything.'

Casting around for a bottle or decanter McAra was disappointed to see no immediate remedy for the hangover he was concealing and was about to suggest a shared resort to a pre–prandial noggin when he summoned to mind another enquiry he intended to pursue.

'There was some other bugger I was after. Who was…? Oh, aye, you likely know a fellow called Bonaly – that would be his surname, I suppose? Erle Bonaly, anyhow.'

'Bonaly? He'd hardly be one of your street Apaches.'

'His name came up. I'm not sure why. But you do have some news of him?'

'He's our neighbour, Mac. Alaric is in his circle.'

'Where would I go,' he asked, 'to have a wee sit–down with him?'

'Oh, please, Mac – I promise you, nothing in this world would convince a man such as he is to find himself even in the same room as you.'

'I'm fair–minded. If he felt too abashed in my presence I'd be the very body of empathy. But are you not curious to know why I would want a tête-à-tête with him?'

'I must say it again – he's not to be numbered among the recusant.'

'Well, I wonder if you could get me seeing some of his flunkeys?' McAra asked as he was hustled into the hall. 'If you think the man

HIDDEN

himself wouldn't be that keen, that is.'
'If you would tell me what it is that you need to speak about maybe I could arrange it. Casper is on quite good terms with his *chef de la maison*.'
'He's not a Frog, is he? Can't stand them. They tried to bayonet me at Waterloo. And they eat slugs.'
'Snails, and no, he's not. His name is Oliver Skewton and he's as polite an Englishman as you could ever meet.'
'Right, then. I'll be here again in a day or two. See if Casper can get the thing done for me. Make certain, though, he knows nothing of my true calling.'
'If the earl himself is out of the way you'll be able to go to the grange. But don't you dare make a nuisance of yourself. Or involve myself or Casper. We are only too aware of your true calling and it has nothing to do with the maintenance of order.'
'You'll hear of me nothing but affection and praise. It's known that I have about me a wonderful air of stillness that is much admired. Now if you have a handful of Halley's ill–gotten riches I have the nation's bidding to perform.'
'Alaric's wealth is not what it was – far from it. Anyway, when will you be back here?' Emma asked, taking some money from a drawer. 'If you can resist my company for a wee while I should have been able to arrange for you to meet Skewton.'
'"*She looked at me as she did love, And made sweet moan.*" How can you bear to be parted from me for so long? I promise you, we two could knock a fair tune out of my "*silly instrument*."'
'Keats as usual. And now Chaucer? What a cultured boor my brother is.'
'The late Mr Keats? He had that line off of me. And Chaucer? Got the gist of his wee stories from my table talk.'
'Keats would never have heard of you. And Chaucer's been dead since...'
'He's dead too? I hadn't heard. I'll write to Mrs Chaucer in my first free minute.'
And rising to take his leave McAra hesitated, then said, 'Have you had the privilege of your nearest neighbour's company latterly?'
'I assume you mean Sir Hudson Smart. He's had no concern for me since Alaric disappeared and anyway he's been much occupied the

HIDDEN

past days with a clique of guests. His large American friend Hiram has been quite attentive to me, though I would prefer he found cheer elsewhere. But never was a man more proud of his heritage or louder in his approbation of the land of his forefathers.'

McAra's interest was aroused and he resumed his seat.

'Tell me all about your newest suitor and Mr Hudson's acquaintances.'

'Sir Hudson. Oh, they're a tiresome lot. You should remember you came across them once. A couple of military chaps – Colonel Roland who served with the 79th at Waterloo; Major DeWitt who seems to have rather fallen on hard times. Hiram is said to be the one of the wealthiest men in America – or the world. I can't remember. You know, Mac, I can't dispose of the conviction that the clothes you're wearing are not only on the generous side. They look very like…'

'No time for sartorial jousting, my dear sister. Must be on my way. My regards to Casper and his fearsome cur.'

Back in the city centre McAra, having deposited his rat at their common residence, had no difficulty in finding the farrier Dobbie, an imposing figure, the short sleeves of his shirt rolled up over blotchy red arms with muscles that would have flattered the thighs of a heavyweight wrestler. He wore a leather apron and when McAra arrived at his shop he was bent over a raging brazier emitting a heat that extended far beyond the shimmer and dance of the air above it. At the end of a pair of tongs was a lump of metal which was being beaten into shape by the blows of a 40–pound hammer. Gnawing with relish on yet another of Mrs McGinty's onions McAra watched this operation with a combination of admiration and revulsion. Physical labour did not figure in his lexicon of worthwhile pursuits and he possessed an innate aversion to the sight of any sort of prowess in that field. Despite the competing sulphurous aromas filling the place the assorted emissions which accompanied McAra's presence were sufficiently declaratory to give the leviathan pause in his activity and turn his perspiring attention to his audience.

'Aye?'

McAra produced the horseshoe he had collected from the cobbles of the Grassmarket and held it out for inspection.

HIDDEN

'Great work,' he announced. 'My master's had a good look at it and he'd like five or six of his mounts shod the same.'
'Easy done if you'll bring the animals in.'
'And he'll pay well over the odds. There's one wee thing he'll want first. This one has come loose of a hoof somewhere in the Old Town. There's no danger, is there, of that being a sign of a fault in the size or shape of it?'
With a careful display of annoyance the tradesman hefted the shoe in his mighty hand and bestowed a scowl on this prospective client. 'The things is made to measure,' he said. 'I've never had no complaints.'
'Good enough. I don't suppose you can tell me who I should be sending this back to. My master's a good man like that.'
'And what good would that do? Leave it with me and his Lordship's folk'll be sure to come looking for a new one so I can put this back for him.'
'His Lordship, is it? My master's that thick with Buccleuch and Tweeddale. If it's one of them…'
'No' as grand as that. It was some fellow of Earl Bonaly's brought it in. Well, the coach was a bit broke up and after the horse was sorted it was to be fixed up somewhere. Anyhow it was just the one mount as needed it. I can tell my own work as soon as I see it.'
'The Earl, is it? Fine. I'll be back in a day or two with half a dozen dapple greys for you.'
'Who's your master, did you say?'
But, unleashing a wailing fart of alarming duration, the secret policeman was gone, possessing confirmation of the identity of the vehicle's owner.

HIDDEN

CHAPTER 5 AUGUST 1842

By the time McAra had returned to his lodgings Balthazar was in a frenzy of hunger and at his master's arrival hurled himself about his confinement with all the violence his aged and ailing body could muster. Having placated the creature with such scraps as he could conjure from his clothing and the floor of his room he turned his attention to his next project. It was much later that McAra found Mrs McGinty at her accustomed post in the Grassmarket and for a few coins was prevailed upon to provide some unidentifiable sustenance for the impassioned rodent.

'Yon beast Haggerty,' the crone said, 'is hirpling like he's been stood on by a Clydesdale. Foot's all bandaged. A wee bird tells me he's in a good mind to find you out and have words.'

'There's nothing gets past you. You said there was another with him the night when that fellow was run over in the road. I hear Donnelly was his name and he's away home to some place in Ireland. You wouldn't know if that's the right of it?'

'A careful wee shite of a creature and bad with it. He's the runner for Dowe's.'

'The runner. What's that?'

'He collects the rent and feus and stuff like that for the quality. Dowe's would be their agent, like. They take a wee share and pass on the money to the likes of them fancy folk at Trinity or The Grange or out at Morningside He's not been in the Grassmarket since but he'll still be hereabouts in the Old Town. His missis is gone back to Ireland but you heard wrong about him. He's aye here yet but I do hear he might be away himself soon enough.'

'You wouldn't know where I could put a hand on him?'

'A place in St Mary Wynd. You wouldn't miss him – he's a right head of ginger hair and somebody took a lump off his ear a while ago. Watch out for him, though – he carries a blade in his sleeve.'

'Here – have another shilling for your wisdom. You'd not be sharing that with anybody else now, would you?'

'Not the shilling nor the wisdom.'

McAra again quartered his decrepit mare at the livery stable and as

HIDDEN

night began to drape the seedy closes and the 14-storey-high tenements he made his surreptitious way back to the boarding house, taking some trouble to avoid passing the White Hart in case Mr Haggerty was on duty despite the mutilation of his extremity. Balthazar was comatose, a trickle of waste matter dribbling from the orifice at both ends of his balding body. Picking up the cage and throwing a rag over it to cover its somnolent inhabitant, McAra sauntered off to St Mary Wynd prepared to wait for his prey as long as it took.

'A breath of air will do you good,' he told Balthazar as they lurked on the shadowy street corner. It was almost midnight before the distinctive figure of the little Irishman came into view. Waiting for a moment or two to allow Donnelly to force open the door to his lodging, McAra lit his pipe and contemplated his approach to the coming encounter. In ten minutes a flickering light appeared through the filthy rag of curtain behind the almost opaque window and McAra, glancing around to ensure there was nobody in sight, gathered up Balthazar's cage, crossed the street and rapped on the rotting wood panelling of the rickety door.

'Open up, Donnelly,' he said loudly enough to be heard, 'I've a message from Haggerty and it's damn urgent.'

The door was swung open a crack and the suspicious Donnelly peered through the narrow gap, a long-bladed knife grasped in his hand.

'Let's see the look of you, then.'

McAra produced a collection of coins that caught the poorly reflected light from inside and the occupant of the dingy apartment nodded him in with a display of reluctance mingled with rapacity. The atmosphere in the near-derelict room would have poisoned a normal human being, but McAra was unaffected by the purgatorial pungency. Throwing himself into a dilapidated armchair he placed Balthazar's shrouded transportation on the floor and allowed his uneasy host to tote up the modest fee on offer.

'And what is it your man Haggerty's after this time?' Donnelly asked briskly secreting the handout about his person. 'And how's he not here himself?'

'Haggerty told me all about the wee job you and him did the other night in the Grassmarket. Now there's big trouble brewing for you;

HIDDEN

and it's already got your pal in a bad way.'
'Well, Jesus, will you come out with it or not?'
'Haggerty's been shot, and I'd say you'll be the next for a taste of a lead ball.'
Donnelly shrank back in his seat, a wave of disbelief washing over his amorphous features.
'Shot? Is he dead or what? Who in the name of Christ would shoot him?'
"He's only hurt bad. He'll likely get over it unless he gets caught up with again. It was some fellow called Grundy that had it done.'
'Grundy? This is malarkey you're telling me – him and me and Haggerty are chums.'
'It's Haggerty himself has said the thing to me. It's him thinks Grundy's trying to bolt the door on anybody that knows the full story about the Grassmarket business. He says you'll need to look out for yourself.'
Donnelly sat open–mouthed with incomprehension and apprehension.
'Haggerty's done right by you. He's given out that you'd taken to the Bog of Allen or some such. But Grundy's in a fair way to get you murdered – in your bed or out of it."
'Jesus Christ, I was only doing what Grundy paid us for. I don't know nothing else. All I done was get your man Hopkin out of the White Hart. It was Haggerty flung him under yon horse.'
McAra could see suspicion rise in the other.
'What's all this to you anyhow?' Donnelly asked, his eyes narrowing and his lips tightening.
'I'm here to help you, man. You're at Dowe's, aren't you – the feuing place. So you'll be able at the least to put a few names in my way for it's plain enough that there's been somebody behind making poor use of Haggerty and you.'
'What are you telling me? I can't make head nor tail…?'
'Never mind. I'll think for the both of us. Get me a list of the big nobs Dowe's collects the loot for. That's where I'll find out who it is would be after you and Haggerty – and what for. Let me have it and I'll find out who's paying a bit of money to put you in the ground.'
'What would you do that for? Why would you be looking out for

HIDDEN

me?'
'Only because Haggerty wants me to. But if you think you can deal with this yourself I'll be away the now.'
Donnelly's anxiety about his perceived precarious position discomposed his irregular features and out of habit he ran his finger over the wound that Mrs McGinty had mentioned.
'Listen, there's that Alaric Halley himself and that the Earl of Bonaly could be one of them. Maybe he's the one you're after. And there's yon Sir Hudson Smart. And a soldier fellow called Roland.'
'Aye, it's them I thought,' and then without warning McAra leapt from his seat clutching the side of his head.
'Holy God, will you look at that – I'm a dead man. My brain's coming out of my lug.'
And in his extended palm was a gobbet of a brown semi–liquid. Even the repugnant Donnelly was repelled and McAra's near-hysteria evinced not a shred of sympathy. Shaking the viscous substance onto the floor the policeman collapsed back into the chair with a long moan of agonised volume and endurance.
'Now,' McAra went on, having composed himself somewhat, 'you'll need to tell me what it was you got away from Bertram Hopkin's place for that's something I'll need as well.'
'What? Who told you about that? You're up to something. You're lying about Haggerty and Grundy and Dowe's.'
Admiration for this bout of perspicacity overtook McAra's frenzy over the fragility of his physical wellbeing.
'If that's the way of it,' he said in a tone of patient calm that impressed himself more than the properly wary Irishman on whom McAra's duplicity was dawning, 'I've a wee friend here that'll explain the thing to you.'
As if on cue there came a scrabbling sound form beneath the cover of the mysterious burden McAra had placed on the floor.
'What in the name of God is…?'
With a gesture conveying calculated drama McAra whipped the soiled cloth from Balthazar's cage and the sudden exposure to the dim lamplight instantly prodded the verminous occupant of the cage into a fractious hissing filling the gap between bouts of extrusive belching. Lighting on the nauseated Donnelly the rodent's one good eye glistened with visceral loathing and its squamous rear

HIDDEN

appendage thrashed against the bars of his confinement.

'He's been awful sick for a long time,' McAra pointed out. 'Miracle he's survived. Anyhow I'd not be too keen on them teeth getting into me. Be a horrible death likely. Slow but sure.'

'Fuck off. I'd stick the thing stone dead with this – ' Donnelly brandished his knife – 'before it got near to me.'

'Aye – well, you wouldn't be the first to think he'd manage that. But it's Balthazar that's with us yet, and many as aren't. Ill he might be but you never saw anything move as fast.'

On instinct Donnelly lifted his feet clear of the floor and cowered back into the chair.

'This Hopkin thing Grundy wanted the hold of. What is it? Where is it? I hear it was stole out of some big house.'

'Keep that trap thing shut then and I'll tell you. It was Hopkin got it out of that big place of your man Hudson Smart. It was some kind of drawing – a map–like thing. I couldn't make head or tail of it, but I never really took a good look at it.'

'Grundy's got it then?'

No. I had to leave it at Dowe's for some soldier lad to collect.'

'A map, you say. Where of?'

'I don't know. Maybe Scotland or something. Not a right map. I couldn't make nothing of it.'

As he left McAra leaned his head to one side, tipping yet more of the glutinous matter onto the frayed shoulder of his tattered jacket. 'One last wee thing,' he said. 'Haggerty doesn't want you near him until this is all sorted. Steer clear or he'll throw you from here into the Forth.'

The city was cloaked in an oppressive darkness as McAra made his way back to the Grassmarket, the clothed cage dangling from one hand. Distressingly sober, he sought out a dingy pub a couple of hundred yards from the lodging house, rapped on the bar and ordered a pint of port. From his pocket he squeezed a middle–aged chunk of mould into Balthazar's cage and reflected on the progress of his investigation. As an aid to concentration he signalled half an hour later for another pint of the fortified wine – brought to him by a supercilious midget – and made his slightly unsteady way out to the back of the building to the *al fresco* jakes, resigning himself to an interview with the local Chief Constable before too many more

HIDDEN

days had elapsed.

By the time he returned, having in the pitch dark misdirected a significant flow of foul-smelling urine down his trousers and over his boots, he had lost interest in his meditation and was compelled to turn his urgent attention to the havoc being wrought by his pet whose cage door had swung open to allow the enormous rat access to the flagstone floor of the tavern. A group of ladies of the night were gathered shrieking in the corner, holding their skirts high and stamping their feet in a vain attempt to discourage the furtively vicious looking Polyphemus. One of the more heroic topers was advancing with a great lack of conviction on the furry monster and waving an empty bottle in an effort to convey threat to the intruder. Before circumstances became extreme McAra grabbed his four-legged associate by the neck and with a growl of disapproval at its escape bundled it back into incarceration. The outraged proprietor, rendered valiant by the securing of the gate of the cage, roared instruction to McAra to depart his premises.

'Pish all over my breeks,' the policeman complained, ignoring the order and collapsing wearily onto his stool. 'Could you not have a lamp out there?'

And with one hand and a disconsolate air he tugged his soaking pants away from his scrawny limbs while with the other raised his jug and threw back an enormous swallow of the port.

'Right,' the owner shouted, 'you'll not sit there and make folk sick. On your way, you wee runt before I break your head for you.'

With that he started round the end of the bar bearing a wooden truncheon but his lumbering approach was brought to a halt when McAra's patting at his trousers unintentionally cocked the hammer of the concealed pepperbox pistol – one of a pair – and let the weapon off with a muffled roar. The ball tore through his coat, struck the floor and went whining across the room, missing one of the petrified prostitutes by a hairsbreadth and smashing the solitary window. For half a minute McAra stared in disbelief at the charred and smoking hole in his grubby, muck-spattered coat.

'Buggered arseholes,' he complained finally. 'That's my best ulster.' And turning in the direction of the appalled inn-keeper chose to vent his spleen more forcibly.

'My best damn coat. A pretty penny that was. And you... you

HIDDEN

chuntering half-wit,' his voice rising as the enormity of the self-inflicted damage grew on him, 'you brought this on me. You'll make this good or by Christ I'll see you thrown in quod, you bawling cretin.'

A stunned hush fell on the place as this unexpected reaction to the potentially lethal incident took noisy shape.

'You'll be hearing more of this,' McAra carried on, rising from his stool, downing the last of his second pint of port, scooping up Balthazar's residence and swaying dangerously on his way out into the night. Across the street he caught sight of the last few customers of the White Hart being urged from the pub by J J Haggerty who was leaning on a crutch and holding his bandaged foot clear of the ground. The injustice of Bertram Hopkin's unavenged death, confirmed by Donnelly, drove through the fog that was gathering on McAra's brain. He concealed himself in the shadows and watched the exodus until all went quiet, the door of the tavern was locked and bolted and the bouncer, swigging from a flask, set off with painful determination towards the west end of the Grassmarket.

The steps of the Vennel were proving a difficult hurdle for Haggerty to negotiate when his discombobulated adversary made his presence known.

'You louse,' J J hissed, turning to confront his enemy. 'When this – ' he waved a hand at his injury – 'is cleared, by God, I'll crush you like a cockroach. I'll rip the face off you. I'll stuff your bollocks up your hole. I'll squeeze the guts out of you. I'll hack the tadger off you. I'll…'

Tiring of this diatribe and unimpressed by its vehemence McAra wasted no time on exchanging crepuscular pleasantries. Still furious at the disfigurement of his attire and still the worse for having too speedily dispatched the port, he produced the weapon that had caused his public humiliation and without preamble, shot Haggerty in his hitherto intact pedal appendage. The Irishman collapsed on the stone stairway with a roar of pain and incredulity that brought some candlelight tentatively to the smudged windows on the far side of the road but interest proved short-lived despite the prolonged ventilation of his agony.

'Third time lucky,' McAra said, returning the revolver to his pocket.

HIDDEN

'That'll be between your eyes. Unless the gangrene gets to you first. Make sure I don't see you again.'

With that he left his bawling victim to crawl homeward and seek assistance. Back in lodgings Balthazar, freed from his cell, slouched around the room looking for something to eat before emptying himself and settling down with a sigh of contentment at the night's proceedings. Watching this performance with approval McAra turned his attention to the ancient cheese and relatively fresh onion he extracted from the depths of his damaged coat. Furiously clawing the more intimate regions of his body, he set about marshalling what he thought he perhaps already knew. But far from promoting insight the Madeira did nothing more than encourage the pleasant recollection of the retribution inflicted on Haggerty and the anticipation of a long night's sleep in the embrace of a good conscience. Slumped on the stone floor McAra patted his shoulder and the obliging Balthazar clambered up his sleeve and settled down drowsily to the thunderous sound of his master's dossing. The man dreamt of sororal intimacy. What the rat dreamt of was more elevated.

HIDDEN

CHAPTER 6 AUGUST 1842

Too delicate next day for demanding work McAra collected his horse from the livery stable and, leaving the tetchy Balthazar to his own devices, he rode out to Morningside and skulked around his sister's home while Casper went looking for Bonaly's steward. Instructed by Emma, Casper had revealed nothing of her brother's profession.
'I don't suppose,' McAra asked Emma as he lounged in the comfort of her drawing room with a curative bumper of Dutch ale on top of a half bottle of malt, 'that you can tell me anything new about those chums of your neighbour's you said something about the other day?'
'Only that Sir Hudson Smart drones on about all his yesterdays in India; or how interested he is in the trip that Alaric made to Alta California. And he claims to have won the little war with China last year all on his own. Like you Colonel Roland boasts about how he slaughtered the French at Waterloo and Major DeWitt sulks and likes to look handsome and dangerous. The lot of them are said to harbour some animosity towards Romans like ourselves but they've never put such a thing to me.'
'Alta California? Near Falkirk, isn't it?'
'It's on the Pacific coast. You might have heard about the Graham Affair?'
McAra affected a blank response.
'No, I didn't really think so,' Emma went on. 'Anyway, it hardly matters. Sir Hudson and his coterie think they can help the Americans wrestle the place from Mexico and one day turn it into a state. Or something like that. He's vague about it all.'
Before McAra could quiz her further, Casper arrived, his slavering canine bodyguard at his heel.
'Skewton has an hour to himself if you can get over there to the grange now. I'll take you if you like.'
'Aye, fine if you'll ferry me on the barouche. I've always wanted to be on one of them.'

HIDDEN

With a sigh Emma nodded to Casper and in five minutes the two men were on their way to the Bonaly estate, McAra perched petrified on the seat beside the driver and holding on with one hand while the other was occupied with intermittent raising of a port bottle. By the time the carriage arrived the policeman was conspicuously the worse for the brief journey, a condition not wholly induced by the precarious juddering of the vehicle. Oliver Skewton was waiting for his guest at the gate to the walled garden and was moved to catch McAra by the arm as he descended from his roost and narrowly avoided crashing to the ground as he struggled to ensure the safety of his misappropriated supply of wine.

'You may call me Oliver,' the major–domo intoned and accompanied the pale–faced policeman into the immaculately cultivated gardens.

'And you,' the obliging visitor responded, 'may call me...'

But confusion had momentarily overtaken him and he couldn't quite recollect his own name.

'The thing is,' he continued after an unembarrassed pause, 'you'll likely be aware of my reputation as the finest driver of a coach in the whole of London and I'm here on vital business.'

'Which is?'

Once again McAra was at a temporary loss and filled the gap with a long drawn out moan as he clutched his stomach.

'You are indisposed, sir?'

'I'd love,' he muttered, 'to castrate a camel.'

'I'm afraid the opportunities for that sort of work in Edinburgh are limited. Is that the occasion of your clandestine mission? Look here, sir – I'm given to understand that you've been sent here on an obscure errand of commerce but I'm much put upon – the Earl's factor has made off somewhere and left me to assess the estate's financial standing and prepare a detailed report. So I have precious little time to spare.'

'Not a fellow called Grundy?'

'The same. You know him? He's taken it into his head just today to take up some sort of position in Argentina and not a word of notice.'

'A pity. I meant to pay him a visit but another pressing engagement cropped up.'

HIDDEN

'May we proceed?'

With an effort that distorted his addled features McAra concentrated on the task in hand by closing one eye and pointing at the array of shiny black coaches in the shade of a fifty yard long awning. 'Very nice. Not unlike my own.'

Reaching the splendid line–up of hansoms and clarences, McAra shoved the wine bottle into the waist–band of his trousers and, imitating what he took to be the posture of an expert, proceeded to examine the vehicles, murmuring grunts of satisfaction and exhalations of passing concern.

'This is the lot of the Viscount's fleet?'

'All the Earl's vehicles with two exceptions – one of the phaetons was stolen a few days ago. And his landau has just been taken to be serviced.'

'And the police haven't recovered the phaeton?'

'I cannot conceive of your concern but no, there has been no sign. I'm informed that the search continues.'

'It bore the Baron's coat of arms?'

'A red and white crest. The only one to carry it. The Earl inherited the vehicle and it was his pride and joy.'

'Stolen from here, was it? These walls and gates look quite… secure.'

'Stolen while it was being repaired. At the coach–works in Low Calton.'

'What was wrong with the thing?'

'One of the Earl's friends borrowed it. An old colonel of the 79th, I believe. Broke a hub and some spokes. Nothing serious. But look here – if your interest is in the acquisition of a vehicle please be so kind as to say so. I have no wish to be interrogated this in this manner.'

'Would there be somewhere I might relieve an overtaxed bladder?'

'Your own, I imagine?'

Conducted to a lavatory at the rear of the house McAra chose to accompany urination and an astonishingly extended flatus with a roaring rendition of "*Go gentle breeze that fans the grove.*" In a simultaneous attempt to remove the wine bottle from his belt he lost his balance, fell backwards and lay supine while liberally spraying walls, floor and his lower limbs, subsequently to be

HIDDEN

rescued by the concerned Skewton and the nauseated Casper. Awakening the next afternoon in the civilised surroundings of his sister's home he lay whimpering beneath the ferocious onslaught of post–event debilitation. By the time evening was falling and the realisation had dawned on him that no attention was going to be paid to his increasingly noisy indisposition he donned the putrid accoutrements in which he had been clad the day before and presented himself in better fettle and humour than his hostess felt he deserved.

'You're the most dreadful creature I've ever had the misfortune to encounter,' Emma informed him as he sat down and addressed dinner with undisguised relish. 'It's no wonder mother and father sent you away.'

'Remind me,' he said, dropping shreds of half–chewed boiled beef from his mouth, 'what you were telling me about something called the Graham Affair.'

'Have you no shame? Can't you exercise even a modicum of control over your behaviour? You smell like an abattoir. Really, Mac, this is the end. I can't have you destroying what's left of the family's reputation.'

'Isaac Graham, wasn't it? But there's damn all else I can put my finger on.'

Emma threw up her hands in despair and tossed a napkin at him.

'Please wipe your chin and cover up the mess you've made of the table cover.'

'Would there be a concoction... a beverage, maybe? A little something to take the edge of a certain dryness I've conceived in my...'

'Isaac Graham. He led a gang of Europeans against the Mexican authorities in North California. For his pains he wound up in prison in Mexico but I think he's free now. Why on earth is that any of your concern?'

'That can mean only one thing.'

'Which is?'

'I haven't a clue. There was still a drop of Madeira in my bottle. That would be enough to set me up again.'

Feeling deserted for far longer than was good for his relationship with his master, Balthazar was in the worst of humours by the time

HIDDEN

McAra arrived back at the lodging house in the Grassmarket. His cage was shuddering as its occupant lurched savagely around his precinct, making plain his profound dissatisfaction with his abandoned lot. Placating the beast with some brackish water and a lump of something from which a rancid fungus had to be scraped the policeman divested himself of the most offensive of his garments and contemplated his next move. With some disappointment he discovered that he had worked his way through the last of Bertram Hopkin's previously immaculate underwear. In the end he decided belatedly to have words the following day with the boss of the Edinburgh City Police to whom he was to have reported on his arrival.

Negotiating entry to the constabulary headquarters office on the High Street proved a difficult task. The surly doorkeeper treated McAra with deep suspicion when he presented himself on the sweltering summer morning clad in a heavy coat designed to cover the less appealing aspects of his costume. The heat of the day had created an effluent vapour rising mystically from the unimposing character who demanded access to the head of the force and the aroma of onions and bodily malfunction further deterred any favourable reception. Even the production of the copy of a letter of introduction from Commissioner Rowan and a stained card bearing the crest of the Metropolitan Police were hardly enough to accommodate the newcomer.

Finally conducted to the inner sanctum by the resolutely hostile constable, McAra peered round with mild approval at the well-appointed office and dropped his credentials on Haining's desk. Not invited to sit down he chose to embark on a voluble censure of the subordinate who had barred his way for so long.

'A senior man,' he insisted, 'a Joint Commissioner of the Metropolitan Police such as myself deserves better. I don't doubt you will register your disapproval with the minion concerned.'

'Have you been drinking, Mr McAra?'

'I won't, thank you. I've had one or two today already.'

'Then let us shed all pretence. You are no Commissioner of Police – I know you to be of the humblest rank. And Colonel Rowan tells me that the sole reason for your being a man in plain clothes is that your appearance in uniform occasioned severe harm to the

HIDDEN

reputation of his force. I have his letter here and I see that you were to report to me as soon as you got to the city, and not at this late stage. So what can I do for the Colonel's emissary?'

McAra pulled up a wooden chair and did his best to outline the chain of events that had brought him north. Whatever lay beneath the opaque surface of the purported machination was, he explained not entirely truthfully, so hard to discern that conjecture had so far been the only recourse.

'You have no idea, then, of what this nebulous intrigue consists of? Or, if it even exists, of who is implicated in it?'

The limb of the Metropolitan law shifted his buttocks on the hard seat trying to bring some relief to the prickling irritation of his anal affliction. Unsuccessful in this he got to his feet and, with a barely suppressed gasp at the assuagement, applied his gnarled hand to the affected area. Completing the performance of this delicate operation he returned to his place and asked the Chief Constable whether there had been any investigation by his men of the circumstances of the death of Bertram Hopkin or the theft of the Earl of Bonaly's coach. Not impressed by McAra's imperious style and lack of etiquette, or his lack of any justification for combining the two events, Haining briskly informed him that the force were aware of the Hopkin incident but, from the evidence available and the absence of witnesses, his deputy Andrew Laurie had come to the conclusion that what had happened in the Grassmarket was an unfortunate accident. Some desultory exertion had been put into finding the driver of the vehicle but there was much more to preoccupy his men at present. And the Earl's phaeton had indeed been reported stolen. It appeared that all that remained of it was lying in charred ruins somewhere on the outskirts of the city.

McAra had been examining something he had harvested from his nostril and though he had been paying some attention to the other's exposition a look of horror froze on his face.

'There's blood in that,' he almost wept, holding up for scrutiny the object he had detached from the innards of his nose. 'A haemorrhage for certain. God in heaven, I'm at death's door.'

Haining offered no word of sympathy and quickly averted his eyes from the proboscidean excavation.

'Do I seem pale to you?' McAra persisted. 'I think I feel faint. Blood

HIDDEN

loss would be the cause. Who will be guarding our beloved young Monarch and Prime Minister Peel when they get here?'

'My own deputy Mr Laurie will be in immediate charge. I'll thank you to join him on his inspection of the location of the Royal Yacht's mooring and the Royal route here. Here –' handing over a note – 'is where and when you need to meet him. I give you this instruction only because I'm driven to assume whatever was the danger being hinted at that brought you here in the first place, it must bear on her Majesty's wellbeing – and that of Sir Robert Peel – while they're on this side of the border.'

'What in... oh, I'd forgotten about this,' McAra announced, withdrawing from his pocket the tooth he'd jettisoned during his call on Emma. 'Would that fix back in, do you think if I got somebody to find the hole and give it a good shove? So the Queen comes by boat?'

'The *Royal George* will be docking at Granton. Mr Laurie will be at there tomorrow afternoon. Now kindly find yourself some fresh air.'

'Fresh air!' Repulsive as the prospect was McAra managed to stand up with some difficulty.

Haining rang the bell on his desk to summon the uniformed officer who, at a nod from his principal, grabbed McAra by the scruff of the neck, yanked him from his seat and hustled him out of the building, taking a moment to greet and tall, rangy uniformed officer sporting a moustache that drooped well beyond his chin. This new arrival was hailed as 'Mr Laurie, sir.'

A little the wiser for the interlude McAra sauntered down the High Street, collected his doddering mare and rode her the short distance to Low Calton where the coach–works were located.

'You'll want the nag put down, is that it? For we don't usually do that but if you let me have a half sovereign I'll take the poor thing off your hands.'

'I'm going to call her Hebe,' McAra said. 'Goddess of everlasting beauty and youth.'

'She's just bone with a wee bit skin on them.'

'I'm told the Bonaly phaeton was nabbed out of here. I hear that's big trouble for you. In fact the coppers might run you in right now.'

The ruddy humour drained from the foreman's puffy cheeks.

HIDDEN

'How's it your business, then?'
'And the team was away with it?' McAra persisted.
'Aye, two fine black geldings they were. The whole thing got took. But the fault was never mine. The lad that came for them was a right rangy fellow I never saw before. And a scrape across his face that somebody had had a good hack at. Said he was from the Colonel and he needed it for one more day.'
'Colonel Roland that would be?'
'Aye, that's the man.'
'Good chums are they – Cardinal Bonaly and Marshal Roland? And it was the Marshal himself brought it in?'
'Aye, they are – and aye, himself.'
'I hear the wagon was broke up – wheels and that.'
'Aye, but it would run a few miles more no bother.'
'The police have been here already, is that so?'
The foreman shrugged.
'Lot of good that's done. But, aye, they've found the thing – or what's left of it. Out at Portobello. Officer came across it last night and was here a wee while ago to boast that he was the one discovered it. Was after a reward but he got nothing off me but a black look.'
'Is the thing still there at Porty?
'Aye, so far as I know.'
'Where can I find a reliable gunsmith nowadays?'
The foreman frowned and thrust his face close to McAra's, but the effort to convey well–merited dislike and civic disapproval was quickly redirected by the outflow of halitotic effluvium.
'There's John Dickson & Son. You'll get them on Princes Street.'
McAra nodded and at the third attempt succeeded in boarding Hebe and secured his place in the saddle by grasping the reins with one hand and her shaggy mane with the other.
'You'll be away riding to hounds, then?' the sardonic onlooker suggested.
Small but imperfectly formed the rider peered down at the man, closed one eye and aimed a green gob at the ground between the foreman's feet. There was little need to use the apathetic mount to make the short journey to the gunsmith's shop and the trip was completed without injury to either horseman or mare. The interior

HIDDEN

of the gunsmith's premises smelt pleasingly of metal lubricant and flaxseed and the police officer paused in the doorway to inhale and appreciate the dense atmosphere. A cough from a dingy corner revealed the presence of a large, stout, cheery storekeeper rubbing his hands with a rag and beaming a welcome. McAra wasted no time in prosecuting his enterprise.
'I wonder if you've come across a breech–loader. A German needle–gun. Very recent on the market.'
For a man whose appearance had suggested imperturbable good humour the arms dealer did little to conceal an air of careful antagonism.
'A dangerous weapon in the wrong hands,' he announced. 'Not that it's any of my concern beyond being a chap in that sort of market, but might I ask what your interest in it is. I mean, the Dreyse's not an easy thing to get hold of, especially here.'
'My interest? Wouldn't you be the fellow I'd come to if I wanted to get a hand on one? But if you're a cautious sort that's to your credit. At the least you might tell me a thing or two about the gun.'
'Right you are – if that's all you're after. It's a rare weapon – not more than a dozen in this country, I'd say. Has a fancy bolt–action and they say it's accurate to a couple of hundred yards with a decent marksman.'
'But there's nothing secret about it, is there? So I wondered why you're that busy giving me those fine black looks of yours.'
'I'm not over–fond of being tested on my own business.'
'Anyway tell me this – can you get me one of these Zündnadelgewehr rifles or not?'
'*Zündnadelgewehr*? My, my, you're real well informed. But no, I couldn't. You'll need to join the Prussian army for that. The thing's not been on the go for more than a year or so.'
'If you can't get one,' McAra pressed on, 'who in Edinburgh can?'
'If you have to know – aye, I did manage to get a pair from a dealer in Birmingham. But they were for a privileged customer. He'd not have me give out his name, though.'
McAra's stomach began one of its convulsive and insistent rumblings which both men paused to listen to, the one with admiring satisfaction, the other with superior disdain. When the intestinal performance was exhausted it was pursued by a passage

HIDDEN

of escaping gas which threatened the integrity of the officer's already sorely tested britches. The ensuing stunned silence was broken finally by McAra.
'I might have a few florins about me…'
The shop–keeper threw up his hands.
'You'll have to swear that you heard the name from somebody else.'
'You can rest easy on that score – I swear. Often.'
'It was Earl of Bonaly's factor lad – Grundy from the Dowe's company. But he said they were for Bonaly himself and I had to keep quiet about it.'
'Is that so? And did Mr Grundy explain why the Baron was that keen to be master of these exotic items?'
'The Earl. Aye. Bonaly is said to be one of the finest rifle–shots in the land. He has medals galore for the practice. And Grundy didn't mind paying well over the odds if I could get them at short notice.'
Happy with the outcome of his day's labours McAra quartered Hebe at the stables and wandered back in the direction of the lodging house. Mrs McGinty was ensconced in her habitual position at the tenement entry and McAra decided that his interests might be best served by a brief encounter with this principal source of intelligence.
'J J's in a bad way,' she informed her benefactor on receipt of the required deposit. He had been confined to the men's ward in the East Division of the Charity Poorhouse, maybe to survive but certainly at the cost of losing a foot. Even if Haggerty did not know where McAra was staying it would not be difficult for the big Irishman to find out and to engage a vigilante to wreak reprisal. This possibility represented the minor inconvenience of diverting some of the policeman's vigilance and McAra, feeling a twinge of conscience rather than apprehension, counselled himself that he ought to have shot the man in the head instead of at the opposite end of his prodigious body.
As he set foot in the musty passageway of his living quarters he slipped the pepper box revolver into the sleeve of his coat and tiptoed along by the wall to his room. Waiting for a moment with his ear pressed to the door and hearing nothing untoward he burst into the mildewed apartment to find it occupied only by Balthazar, skulking in his cage and, long without the solace of company,

HIDDEN

emitting a squeaking, hissing welcome. Trawling his pockets he came across some scraps which he tossed at the forlorn creature. Then as a precaution he placed Balthazar's cage against the door and fell asleep safe in the knowledge that the beast would emit tumultuous protest at any nocturnal intrusion. He dreamt of rectal ligation.

Early next day McAra dabbled his fingers in a bowl of muculent water and, having completed these assiduous ablutions, examined his reflection in the cracked yellow mirror dangling from a rusty hook.

'Nice. Very nice,' he offered as compliment to his image. 'More than presentable. Ruggedly handsome, would you say? Or handsomely rugged. You takes your pick. So, who'll be the lucky lady tonight?'

Then an afterthought: 'Though maybe sometime I should pick out some of that queer stuff living in the side–whiskers.'

He breakfasted on a large onion, picked up the rat's cage and, with a wave in Mrs McGinty's direction, strolled to the stables to retrieve Hebe who recoiled sharply from his belching exhalation and surrendered reluctantly to his inept saddling under the ostler's disapproving gaze. After a serene ride the length of the coach route of Leith Walk, past the Anchor Soapworks on Water Street – at the sight of which he shuddered in the warm sunshine – he directed his exhausted and cantankerous mare along the bank of the Forth while his pet, sharing something of his master's disposition, cowered under the dirty rag that enveloped his cage, so averse was he to the clean air coming in from the river.

Beyond Newhaven Harbour McAra found a pub from which a couple of hours later he was ejected by a furious proprietor. Having dropped off to sleep by the water's edge he didn't reach his destination until well into the afternoon. Not wholly recovered from his encounter with the best part of a bottle of gin and a couple of pints of porter he turned up at the Duke of Buccleuch's private harbour at Granton where, attempting an elegant dismount, he pitched head–first into a dunghill. Rescued by a washerwoman of mighty proportions and strength of arm as well as the good fortune to suffer from dysomia, he spent half an hour picking at and beating his clothes until almost all that remained as evidence of his

HIDDEN

excremental encounter was the lingering effluvium and some fragments of ill–digested hay and grain.

Leaving in Balthazar's charge the trembling Hebe gnawing on the sparse vegetation at the river's edge McAra wandered along the pier. There was little to see by way of preparation for the Royal visit. A handful of indolent workmen were standing around admiring the lengths of timber and bunches of bunting that were presumably to be assembled and erected at some juncture.

'We've nearly met once before,' announced the raw–boned tall figure sporting a huge moustache and sounding oddly hushed for a man of his dimension. 'Andrew Laurie, deputy to Mr Haining.'

McAra shook hands with the loping giant who was no longer in uniform, the informality of his dress attributable to his being on a confidential assignment.

'I'm sorry about the smell around here today,' Laurie said sniffing the air. 'The tide is out but it doesn't usually whiff quite as bad as this.'

Seeing no reason to enlighten the other on the provenance of the rank rancidity that permeated the atmosphere McAra dismissed the apology with a cheerful shake of the head that did nothing to improve the steadiness of his gait. Laurie leaned forward smartly and caught him by the arm in time to prevent his precipitation into the harbour. Suspecting that the agent of the metropolis's constabulary was suffering from the aftermath of some form of apoplectic stroke Haining's lieutenant led McAra to a pile of wooden pallets and carefully placed him in a more or less sedentary position on it.

'I hear that you've not been entirely in accord with us on the matter of that affair in the Grassmarket a few nights ago. Mr Haining's not best pleased, I can tell you, but I'll be happy to have your version. I gather it's different to the one given me by my lads.'

'If you're going to go on about it I'll say this – if I soiled my drawers it was because some bastard must have slipped something in my tea.'

'I meant that chap Hopkin being killed.'

Still befuddled but gradually summoning his wits McAra sorted through the skelfs of his memory. Slowly he recounted to the best of his selective recollection the course of the events that had

HIDDEN

brought him from London but making no reference to his relationship with Emma. It was fortunate that he had so recently rehearsed these for the Chief Constable and the hesitancy and slurring impaired his rendition only marginally.

'You came across a witness to the Hopkin affair? But you've no idea who that is?' Laurie asked, perching next to the inebriated but coherent McAra.

'Just some fellow that buggered off into the dark,' McAra lied. 'I never saw him again. But here's the thing – I'm gathering up other witnesses like flies to a turd. All I need now is that one arrest and the whole thing will be plain enough even for that wifey Polly Femus to see.'

'Polyphemus, maybe? Well, anyhow, I'll have the lugs off my men for not bothering with a right search for somebody that saw what happened.'

McAra nodded, reminding himself that Mrs McGinty's description of the official intervention she had seen at the time coincided with Laurie's bearing and feeling his eyes closing, he struggled to resist a great desire to drowse in the heat of the summer day.

'If there's a threat to Her Majesty or the Prime Minister,' Laurie went on, 'this is a likely site of it with them being in the open and hard to protect. It's what Mr Haining thinks as well, so you and me are here to have a good search about the place. Get a feel for the way somebody might get close enough to do some damage.'

He gave McAra a moment and when he detected no comprehension on the other's part he mistook the lack of reaction for profound rumination.

'So if you're with me,' he said, squinting as his eyes caught the brilliant scatter of light on the water, 'we can put our heads in the one place and do our damnedest to make the Queen and Peel safe here in the city.'

With an effort that almost burst his brain McAra pulled himself together and picked his way through what Laurie had been saying. 'Is it the true thing that the Provost and the Town Council aren't in on the details of Her Majesty's wee trip?'

'Aye, well, there's bugger all love lost between them and the London lot,' Laurie remarked, 'so it wouldn't surprise me if nobody up here's in the full know of it. All I can tell you is that I'm the

HIDDEN

fellow supposed to look out for Victoria and her entourage when they land here.'

As if aiming an invisible pistol Laurie extended his arm towards the clock tower and lighthouse at the end of the pier.

'We'll have a wee gape at that thing over yonder. Somebody's broken into it a few nights ago. The caretaker found the door open and had one of my lads call me.'

With difficulty McAra staggered to his feet and, clutching the other's arm, swayed his way to the end of the dock.

'Clear off, the pair of youse or I'll have the law on youse.'

The two officers had to shield their eyes against the brilliant sunlight to make out the shape of a stocky little figure coming at them on hastening bow legs with the carriage of a man negotiating the deck of a ship in a storm. He appeared to be dressed partly in a uniform and partly in the garb of a trawlerman.

'We *are* the law,' Laurie assured the new arrival.

'And what about the wee drunk fellow?'

'Be careful of your language,' McAra warned as he produced his own token of authority, 'or you'll get the jail for your trouble.'

'Aye – you scare the innards out of me. Anyhow it's about bloody time youse turned up. There's a thing that youse need to see.'

'It was you gave out somebody's been at that tower thing, was it?' Laurie asked. 'Well, we're here the now, aren't we, to see what's what.'

'Name's Gordon. There's a gang of wee blighters out of Leith never done with a bit of fishing off the end over there. Same time every damn day. That's them you can put your eye on the now. Every time I chase them away they're here as soon as my back's at them. It's easier to leave them be so long as Buccleuch himself's not here to see it. And it was them that seen the boat away yesterday.'

'I can't make out a word of what you're on about.'

'Jesus, give me a minute and I'll show it you.'

Gordon shoved at the door of the little tower and it gave way where the rotten frame beside the lock had been easily splintered. At the head of the short, narrow stone stair was a tiny chamber in which a man could just crouch down, and a slit window, devoid of glass, gave a clear view of the entire length of the dock. Across the sill lay a sand–filled sack in the middle of which was a deep crease as

HIDDEN

if something narrow but of some length and weight had been laid over it. Laurie cast around in the half–dark of the tiny chamber and lifted a pile of sacking off the floor to reveal a rifle, a weapon in obviously pristine condition that smelled of lubricating oil and linseed.
'God Almighty, would you look at that,' he said to McAra who was propped up against the rounded wall staring vacantly through the glassless window.
'What?'
'It's a gun, for Christ's sake. A gun and it's fifty yards from where the *Royal George* will be putting in.'
'Is George still the king, is that it?'
'No, you idiot. That's the name of Victoria's yacht.'
And Laurie raised the rifle to inspect it properly in the poor light.
'What was that you were on about – a boat?' Laurie asked Gordon who was squeezed between the two police officers and making no secret of his revulsion at McAra's less than fragrant proximity.
Their informant shrugged uneasily.
'I seen an older bit lad once or twice but I left him be for he looked a bad lot, and he's away now.'
'What's a bad lot look like?' Laurie asked.
'Dirty, like. Not as bad as this wee fellow that's with you, but nasty enough. But I took him for no harm. Queer voice – not from hereabouts, I can tell you that. Bit of his lug missing so you'd easy know him if you saw him.'
'He came in off a boat, you say?'
'No, but he was away on one. That's what that gang over there told to me.'
Wrapping the gun in the sack and tucking it under his arm Laurie led the way back down the spiral stone stairway and out into the open air.
'We'll away and have a word with the fishing hooligans,' he told Gordon. 'You be sure to keep all this to yourself.'
At the sight of the two men approaching the three youngsters dropped their homemade fishing poles and made to run past them along the pier but, for all his size, Laurie was a fast mover and collared the biggest before he could make his getaway.
'What's this about some man breaking into the tower?' he

HIDDEN

demanded, holding the delinquent by the hair. 'You saw him at it, eh?'

'I never saw nothing except he run out of the place and got down yon ladder there.'

He pointed at the top rung that was visible at the end of the harbour wall.

'And there was a boat there for him, was there?'

'Aye – one that just came in up the river. One of them wee things with a chimney and that.'

'What's this fellow look like?'

'A dirty onion – bit like your pal there. Ginger hair and a lump of his lug bit off.'

'What about the boat? What was it like? Was there a name on it or anything?'

'It never stopped long. Once he was on it it was away like shite. There was a name on the back of it – *Belly* or something like that, I think it was. And it was brown, like. And it had a red and white picture on the back of it.'

'Is that a few coppers in your pocket?' McAra asked and shook the scowling truant till the money rattled. 'You're an awful rich Palaemon.'

'I'm no pal of yours. And the siller's my business.'

'Give it to me and I'll see you don't hang.'

Laurie shook his captive loose and turned to McAra.

'For God's sake, man, behave yourself. What we need to do is find this boat. I'll have the lads get round the harbour here and over in Leith. I don't have to tell you this is a damn serious business.'

'A damn serious one right enough,' McAra managed. 'But they're not that canny are they, these folk? This whole thing going on when these tinkers are at the fishing right in front of them. They're not that clever, would you think?'

McAra's doubting attitude was beginning to irritate Haining's deputy.

'It's fine for you coming up here for a week or so and then pissing off back to London. But this is my city and I'll not be the one blamed for having a Royal murder happen here.'

'I wouldn't mind a dog of the hair,' McAra remarked as he went off to check on his horse which quailed at his advance and cheerfully

HIDDEN

resumed grazing when he restricted his attention to the wellbeing of the somnolent Balthazar by poking the remnants of an onion into the cage. When he returned Laurie grudgingly said, 'Let's get a drink over by – a hair of the dog, if that's the way of it – and have a think about this.'

McAra was aware, though, that he was still confronting the world through a gauze–like film induced by his over–indulgence and the blow to his head incurred in the course of his being expelled from the pub to which Laurie had nodded. An early re–visitation to the place was unlikely to be welcomed by the host so, feigning an eagerness to enjoy the air, he prevailed on his companion to join him on a stroll by the river until another venue was to be found nearer to Leith and along the route by which the Royal visitors would be approaching the city. McAra's tongue felt like sandpaper and it was scouring the roof of his mouth. Conversation was not going to be relished but he was resigned to conveying the impression of an authority on matters of security. Laurie himself seemed to be pursuing his duties seriously. At every fifty yards or so he paused and noted a position from which a potential assassin could launch an attack on the regal procession. Windows, closes and rooftops were pointed out and duly recorded in the big, moustachioed policeman's journal.

'It's a good thing that the timing of the affair isn't decided yet,' he told McAra as they took their seat in a darkened corner of an ale house. 'It gives us a chance to have a good look at anybody getting too set up in all these places.'

'You'd need an awful lot of folk to do that surely?'

'There's no option. This is all down to me and nothing's to go wrong, believe me. I'll have every damn copper and trooper in the city standing guard the whole length of the way. I'll put a whole lot of them in ordinary garms – like yourself.' A pause to sniff the pungent air. 'Well, not exactly like you maybe.'

'I have veins,' McAra confided, smacking his lips at the arrival of a foaming tankard. 'Veins.'

'I'll draw up a plan – every man will know to the inch where he's to be and what he's to be watching out for.'

'I fear I might not be long for this dene of distress,' McAra continued. 'There are bits of me protrude that shouldn't.'

HIDDEN

'I'll see there's not a man in or out of uniform that's not minding the crowds on the first of the month. Tonight I'll be seeing Colonel Grant at the Castle and we'll set up the Greys to join my own lads. The bloody Chartists are on the streets in Glasgow and Dundee so the troopers are right thin on the ground here.'

'So there's not six hundred of them at the Castle now?'

'No. They're hard pressed supporting the civil power. Mind you, Colonel Grant's doing the thing right. He's set up Popham telegraph chains between here and the other two cities. If they need reinforcement or any other thing the signal can be got through quick.'

'I've abandoned God. Do you think maybe that's why my life's been so cursed?'

'Have you heard one word I've been telling you? Isn't this what you're supposed to be here for?'

'A soldier and a bobby in every nook and cranny along the way. It'd be a fine day to be a bit of a burglar wouldn't it?'

'You think there's more important work than looking to the safety of the Monarch or her Prime Minister?'

'I'm only here to help. There's not been a round fired at her that I've not thrown myself in the way of.'

'What? When?'

'And there's been the kings of Spain and Portugal and Hawaii. All after me for my skills, of course. But how can I be everywhere at once?'

'Are you drunk, McAra?'

'Given my calling it's lucky I'm a man who can handle his liquor. Never been drunk in my life. *Semper vigilo.*'

And McAra rounded off this self-directed accolade by bawling, 'I have thoughts. Thoughts!' Then, 'Bats! Everywhere. Bats!' and on the instant lapsing into profound unconsciousness with his tankard still gripped in both hands.

HIDDEN
CHAPTER 7 AUGUST 1842

Regaining his senses the next morning McAra found himself face down in a pile of strong smelling hay in the livery stable in the Cowgate, home to Hebe and the irascible horse trader who now loomed over the prostrate policeman. A few curt and expletive–heavy sentences described how the sedate nag had arrived back at base with her rider slung over the saddle. It appeared that Laurie had draped his colleague across the horse's back and patted her on the haunch in the subsequently justified expectation that she would, given time, wander home.

'My life,' McAra muttered as he climbed stiffly to his feet, 'is one of unrelenting misery and suffering. I stay cheerful only for the benefit of others.'

Contrite, he offered the starving Balthazar his *mea culpa* and, rodent cage in hand, repaired on foot to the Grassmarket and his residence while the ostler did what he could to restore Hebe to some condition of mobility. A few hours' overnight rest and recuperation brought McAra back to the stable in much improved shape and humour. It was another day of high sunshine and a gentle breeze and the unhurried ride to the coastal suburb of Portobello further revived the spirits that had been flagging under the assault of his recent surrender to excess. Balthazar had, by his confrontational demeanour, indicated his desire to be left undisturbed at the lodging house.

The remains of Bonaly's phaeton lay conspicuous on the sand and as soon as McAra had dismounted to inspect the wreck he was assailed by an incensed resident brandishing a hefty walking stick and bristling with indignation.

'Get this mess off my land,' he snarled, puffing out his wheezy chest, 'or by God I'll put a dozen dents in your skull.'

'Your land, is it? The beach belongs to you?'

'Aye – this bit does. Now get some cart and haul this shite out of my sight.'

'And who was it left it here? Did you see?'

'Don't try to tell me you don't have the truth of it. I saw it myself.

HIDDEN

That lanky scar–face was going to take his whip to me. And now see what's happened – these bloody wastrels have been tearing the last of the thing apart. Two wheels was took off that was covered in paint or blood or some other damn thing, and tossed inside. And the seats torn out, the hood ripped apart. Now get rid of the rattletrap that's left or I'll have the law on you.'
'I'll have you know I'm the chief of police and I'll have you tossed in the Calton for waving yon bit wood at me. And setting yourself in the way of an investigation. Now tell me more about this midden.'
Doubtful of McAra's undisclosed credentials but loath to take the risk of confinement in the notorious jail the rubicund protestor reeled in his ire and, still cautiously distrustful, explained he had been walking his dog late at night when the coach had been driven at speed onto his land. When he had taken exception to the intrusion he had been discouraged from further expression of disapproval by the threat of violence issued by the driver who had with some difficulty set the carcase on fire.
'Well, he got the horses free, did he? And what then?'
'Rode one of the mounts and had the reins of the other. Up past the Figgate House. To yon horse–flesh dealer Clapper that sends mounts to the army down in England somewhere.'
And he aimed his stick at the imposing if somewhat rundown three storey building overlooking the beach.
'You knew this fellow. Seen him before?'
'Aye, by God – Josiah Dicken's his name.'
'You told my officer about him?'
'He never gave me a minute of his time, he was that desperate to be somewhere else.'
'I'll see to all this. Rely on me. Where could I get hold of Dicken? How would I know him?'
'You'll get him the now – in the Porty Dug pub up there –' waving a hand at the near–derelict building at the far end of a patch of waste ground – 'and you'll know him easy enough. A great tall bastard he is with a scar right across his face that would make a leper sick.'
McAra dismissed the still incandescent land owner with as imperious a gesture as he could muster. Hitching Hebe to the

HIDDEN

remains of the ruined phaeton he wandered off in the direction of the tavern that had been indicated to him. Inside there were only a couple of topers at the bar, both visibly the worse for their endeavours, but in the darkest corner he was able to make out the unmistakable figure that had been described to him. Sauntering across the sawdust floor he sat down next to the skeletal giant and without preamble addressed him in a low tone.

'Ernie Norris,' McAra pronounced, lying with his usual facility. 'You'll not have heard of me, but we have acquaintances in common.'

The other shook his head with slow deliberation.

'I doubt it, you wee weevil. Pish off out of it.'

'Weasel, surely?'

'What is it you're after? I've better things to do.'

'You're handy at the taking off of things, I hear. And there'd be twice as much for something the same again. If you're interested in a few sovereigns, that is.'

'You'll hear me admit to nothing. Except maybe a big jar of rum and a bottle of porter.'

'Right you are.'

Not ordinarily given to acts of even the most microscopic generosity McAra bought a round of black porter and tumblers of rum. The latter held no appeal for him if only because it was the only alcohol that made him almost immediately physically sick if taken internally. However it turned out to be the sole spirit on offer on the sparse gantry and the prospect of watching someone else drink spirits, especially at his expense, while he abstained would have induced an even more virulent malady. Returning to his seat he edged near enough to Dicken to whisper, 'That was good work you did with the Bonaly coach. Don't worry – I know all about the business. So what about it – will you go again? The same trick, but a lot more money in your sea–bag. And a team of four for the army this time. What do you say?'

'And what's this about the Bonaly thing?'

'I've just been reading about that Baron Frankenstein. What a bastard. Oh, clever – aye. But…'

'What in the name of Christ…?'

'I tell you – if he'd put a brain like mine in the monster he'd have

HIDDEN

had perfection. But what I need to be sure about is if you're up to laying hands on a landau with a four–in–hand. A folding top front and rear. The thing needs to be done exactly the way of Bonaly's phaeton.'

Accepting that McAra was well aware of his role in uplifting the Earl's transport, the sailor relaxed into frankness.

'Aye, I could manage that. And the money would be... better?'

'Have no doubt of it. But it has to be handled the very same.'

'Dropped off at the same place?'

'You'll need to tell me about that. Most like it'll be exactly the same but my customer wants to be right sure that'll suit him. He'll let you have half in front and the rest when you're done. But are you clear – you can find what it is he's after?'

'Have no worry about that.'

'Anyhow, what's the place the vehicle will be left?' McAra asked.

'You said the same as before? Out of the way at St John's Hill. And I can collect it again down there at Porty beach?'

'That was the way of it? You didn't run the thing at the Grassmarket?'

'What? Where? No, Mr Grundy wanted a top driver and I'm no more nor a top bit thief.'

'That's who it was took the Bonaly one out of St John's Hill? A pal of yours?'

'What's that to you?' Dicken asked, with a frown of suspicion.

'To me – nothing. To my master plenty. He needs to be sure of every man with a finger in his purse.'

'His name's Newsome. I was supposed to leave it at St John's Hill hang on to have a word with the fellow taking the rig but he was the sourest little bastard you ever put an eye on. Is there more rum in yon bottle would you think?'

'Aye, no bother.'

And, feeling a tightening in his chest and a creeping paralysis in the hand reaching for his wallet, McAra reluctantly signed for another round, and ten minutes later was placed in the unpleasant position of having to order yet another. Having downed both rum and porter in the blink of an eye, 'I'll be away the now,' Dicken pronounced as he climbed unsteadily to his feet, implicitly acknowledging that he had had enough. 'When will you come for

HIDDEN

me with the job and the money?'
'Oh, soon enough. You'll be here, sure you will? But this Newsome – so you got nothing out of him?
'Always here. And nothing out of Newsome.'
'What was he like? Can you describe him at all?'
'How's that your affair?'
Again hint of doubt was entering Dicken's voice.
'I need to tell my boss how we can lay hold on him if we need him.'
'You'll need to have that out with Grundy, but you'd easy find him. One of these dwarf things, works sometime in a pub in the Grassmarket; but, Christ, he was up on that coach and turning the team fast as you like. Oh, aye – a driver all right.'
McAra went swaying out of the pub at the man's heels. The blast of fresh summer air combined ill with the quantity of hastily consumed rum and as Dicken went striding across the deserted lot the contents of the policeman's stomach were rapidly dispatched down his front.
'Aw, for fuck's sake,' came the muffled complaint from the unfortunate lawman, 'that's my best waistcoat. And there's beans in that.'
Pawing at the affected garment he was immediately resentful of his companion's indifference to his plight and to the fact that he alone had had to shell out for the man's drink. Casting a quick look around and confirming that no–one else was in sight he overtook Dicken and slipping the short truncheon from his sleeve brought the club down with exemplary precision and force behind his victim's ear. Rifling the unconscious thief's pockets he extracted exactly the sum he had spent in the Porty Dug and discovered a metal disk that had imprinted on one side the word CHUENPI and the date 7 January 1841 and on the other, in ornate letters, HEIC NEMESIS.
'A nice wee memento of the occasion,' McAra congratulated himself, already oblivious to his literally nauseating appearance. Back at the beach he found a gang of guttersnipes busy dismantling the remains of the Bonaly coach and prodding Hebe with a sharp stick. His modest frame would not of itself have had any intimidating effect, but his malevolent deportment combined with the generous sartorial spraying of vomit and the blood–stained

HIDDEN

cudgel was adequate to scatter the hooligan posse and bring relief to the much–put–upon horse.

'Time to let Prince Bonaly learn what became of his conveyance,' he informed his nag as, with all the elegance of a quadriplegic gibbon, he swung into the saddle, just resisting the impetus to topple over the other side. 'Morningside, Hebe, at the gallop.' And the aged mare, head drooping and legs shaking ominously, took the first tentative step on the long journey from the eastern suburb while her master concentrated on averting his attention from the mephitis rising from the steaming regurgitation on his jerkin. The trip would probably have taken less time had it been undertaken by foot, but its duration at least had the effect of banishing the worst of the after–effects of the drink that Dicken had unwittingly paid for. Riding slowly past the neighbouring estates of Sir Hudson Smart and Alaric Halley McAra dismounted at the towering gate of the Bonaly property and yanked the bell–pull with wearying repetition until the conspicuously irritated Skewton appeared, examined him critically through the bars and opened up with the worst possible grace.

'I'm here on the same business as before. Is the Count at home?'

'Oh, it's you again. The Earl is here, yes. May I ask…?'

'It's imperative I have words with His Highness. I have news of his missing carriage.'

Continuing to appraise him through narrowed eyes Skewton, repelled by what he was looking at and smelling, asked, 'Have you had an accident?'

'Many, over the years and I thank you for asking. But concern for my health will have to wait, though if you'd care to brush me down a little I'd offer no objection.'

Recoiling further into a sanctuary of distaste the steward led the visitor along the gravel path to the front door of the mansion. A butler took Skewton's hurried announcement and several minutes later reappeared with a long–handled yard brush which he aimed at McAra's chest in an effort to dislodge the abundant spattering of puke that defaced his attire.

'That'll do. I've no time for these trifles,' McAra announced briskly when the operation proved to be vain. 'Take me to his Lordship. And make sure my mount is tended to. He's a thoroughbred stallion

HIDDEN

and needs careful attention.'

'The stallion is a mare, you oaf. Your credentials as a coach driver seem to leave much to be desired.'

Hebe was quivering from ear to hoof and giving off every sign of being on the verge of expiration. Her breathing consisted of a long, low moan, her ribs appeared to be about to burst through her mangy coat and her innards were emitting sounds that heralded imminent defecation. While McAra was conducted into the cool depths of the majestic edifice Skewton summoned a stable lad to expend some restorative energy on the poor creature.

The Earl of Bonaly was tall and rotund, his puffy cheeks thickly populated by an immense curling moustache. He wore a capacious velveteen outfit that combined a variety of greens with a spangle of miniature yellow shapes embroidered into jacket and trews. About to offer his hand in greeting he withdrew the appendage on greater familiarity with the cut of McAra's jib.

'I gather you have news of my misappropriated carriage, sir. It was my father's and so I have a great love for the vehicle and I'm most grateful to you for recovering it.'

McAra meanwhile was busy bowing before this aristocratic dilettante and also noting that some of the detritus that had been clinging to his waistcoat was dropping bit by revolting bit onto the antique Isfahan rug. A surreptitious rubbing of the ill–digested offal with his boot served only to ensure its adherence to the priceless carpet.

'Aye, your coach thing,' the policeman said, finally drawing himself upright. 'Well, my friend in the local police tells me it's nothing more than a pile of shite now. Mangled. Kids dropping their breeks in it. Everything ripped off it. Not a wheel–spoke whole. Totally ruined. Fucked altogether. You wouldn't have a glass of something to cheer me up, would you? I've had a wee internal complaint that loosens every inch of gizzard in me.'

Appalled, he said, at the fate of his much–loved phaeton Bonaly could only gesture to his underling to fetch some brandy and led McAra into the opulent withdrawing room where the visitor crumpled into a vast wing chair and began belatedly to button up the flies of his fustian trousers.

'The thing got stole out of that place on Low Calton. Some fellow

HIDDEN

that said he had to get it back to a Colonel Roland. But your man was just a thief with a clever tongue on him.'

'Yes, that's as I understand it. Colonel Roland's a friend of mine and he's often had the vehicle in the past. I'm grateful for your conveying this sad intelligence but may I enquire…'

'And apart from the Colonel who would have known that the thing would be at Low Calton?'

'I'm afraid I have no idea. What on earth encourages you in the belief that it's for me to proffer answers to ill–mannered questions? If you wish to purchase what is left of the carriage do simply say so and make me an offer.'

Still tussling with his mutinous garment McAra was also making the most of his newly–arrived therapeutic intoxicant.

'Well,' he sighed, having listened to all this while concentrating more on how to manoeuvre another tincture into his glass, 'let me have a wee think about this. I wouldn't want to be mixed up with some queer gang that you might be part of. There's something fishy here and I'm an honest contractor.'

Bonaly almost choked with incredulous appreciation of the improbability of the stricture.

'I hear you're a grand shot with a rifle,' McAra persisted. 'Are you a man for shooting deer up yonder in Perth? I'd like fine a quick sight of this Dreyse thing you've got hold of.'

'Dreyse? I'm a patient sort of fellow so I choose to exercise restraint, but you really do go too far now, sir. If you have in mind to buy the wreckage of the phaeton or a coach from my collection I shall be content to accommodate you and in the most charitable fashion. You may at some point present yourself here in the future when you are properly in your wits.'

And the Earl rang the bell on the table beside him to summon the formidable butler.

'Please conduct this gentleman from the premises with all possible deference and despatch. And be sure to register his person as a guest to be welcomed only when his gait is steady.'

And all circumstances of gentility evaporated as soon as McAra, his four limbs now flailing impotently in mid–air and en route for the exit, was out of the Earl's sight and hearing.

'If you reappear here I'll have Ares and Charon tear you to shreds,'

HIDDEN

the butler announced portentously.

Hurled from the portico and landing at speed on the drive McAra took his time about reassembling his faculties and his appendages and scraping the fine pebbles from his face and hands. Satisfied that he had conducted the interview with discretion and sensitivity he limped to the rail where Hebe was secured and still under the eye of the unctuous Skewton.

'Very informative,' he claimed, still dusting himself down. 'I believe Mr Bonaly and me have had a productive debate about whatever it was I came here for. Would you have any inkling what that was?'

'You'd found *the Earl's* phaeton. You were to report on that.'

'Oh, aye – it's coming back to me. The Duke suggested I get in touch with that fellow Grundy. How would I do that?'

'Grundy? Well, he's nothing more than an overseer of the collecting of feus and tittle–tattle. And anyway I've told you – he's gone away. So if you want words with him you'll find him in South America – God knows how far away that is.'

'You'll know a fellow called Hopkin, eh?'

'I met him once or twice. A fellow with a wonderful eye for the embellishment of superior dwellings. But if it's him you're after now you're too late – he's dead. Had an accident in the city, so I hear.'

McAra prodded himself in the stomach and issued an agonised groan.

'There's a great hard lump coming up in there. I'll be lucky to have a month or two left in this vale of tears. I suppose you and Hopkin would have been pals, sort of?'

'Not the same at all. Harmless chap. My responsibilities…'

'Aye, aye. But you'd have spoken a word or two maybe once in a while.'

Skewton glanced around and though there was no–one else even in sight he lowered his voice to a confidential *sotto voce*.

'Bertram wasn't the most discreet of men. An accomplished eavesdropper, a sometime explorer of others' possessions. Used to regale me with gossip from Sir Hudson's soirees.'

Grasping the pommel of his saddle McAra was about to mount Hebe who was chomping at some long grass and simultaneously

HIDDEN

giving vent to noisy and pungent unconditioned reflexes.
'Hopkin never mentioned some pals of mine by the name of Dicken or Newsome?'
'Not to me that I remember. Why?'
'And when's your chum Grundy due back?'
'He never said. And never said what the business that was taking him away was.'
'I'll need to…'
And turning away from the grazing mare McAra leaned his back against a wooden post and began to wriggle violently against it and loosed off a long suspire of relief.
'Fleas,' he explained. 'Or some other thing. You should see my behind – suppurating sores the size of an elephant's balls.'
'I believe it's time you were on your way, sir. Be sure to keep all this to yourself for it's none of your affair. Now I have better things to do than bandy words with an oaf who wouldn't recognise the truth if it struck you with the bible and called you Beelzebub.'
'Aye – I'll away now. I've forgot, though: the Grand Duke threatened to feed me to Arse and Sharon. Would that be a biblical reference and all?'
'Ares and Charon. Salivating hounds as they are I doubt even they would find you to their taste.'
McAra twisted round to grope at his back.
'Sweet Jesus, no – a hump. I'm growing a hump.'

HIDDEN
CHAPTER 8 AUGUST 1842

McAra wasn't unduly concerned for the wellbeing of his pet rat. Precarious as its health was it had been left free of its cage to wander the lodging house room, eating and drinking whatever had been discarded. In return for this dispensation Balthazar was expected to ensure that there was no illicit intrusion on the seedy property and his master had no doubt that, in his absence, the irascible creature would deter ingress. Given that conviction of security McAra was in no great hurry to return to the Grassmarket and rode no further than the neighbouring Halley estate. Casper and his accompanying *cane corso* (which at least had the merit of being neither Ares nor Charon) made no secret for their shared distaste for their visitor and it was with a marked lack of enthusiasm that the policeman was permitted access to his sister's salon. Emma was sitting at a walnut kidney desk poring over a wad of documents and shaking her head in mystification.

'I've had nothing to drink all day,' McAra lied as usual. 'I just dropped by to see if there was anything decent on offer.'

His wish had been anticipated by Casper who, taking Emma's casually tetchy gesture of approval, placed a crystal tumbler of brandy at the disposal of the dissolute officer. Turning away from her examination of the papers Emma was more repulsed than usual by her brother's condition.

'I had to rescue a drowning infant,' McAra claimed, 'that in fear for its life disgorged its contents on me. It's thought that I'll probably be required to attend on the Lord Provost for some kind of reward. And what's detaining the scrutiny of my beloved sister today?'

Edging away from the unwelcome scent Emma threw up her hands in frustration.

'I have to accept,' she said, 'that something dire has happened to Alaric. Neither Colonel Rowan's police nor the Home Secretary's informers have succeeded in discovering what became of him after he left Brown's Hotel back in March. I thought perhaps it was time for me to make some sense of my own situation. Financially and socially.'

HIDDEN

McAra brightened.

'There'd be money, right enough,' he said, laying down his glass and rubbing his hands together. 'We'll need to have a good close look at what's to be had, eh?'

'It's hardly a matter for you, Mac. But there *is* something that's very strange set out in this correspondence from Coutts. Alaric told me several months ago that large investments of his had come to grief, and yet…'

'I know a bit about it. My eyes were closed but my ears were open.'

'You're as duplicitous now as you've always been.'

'Are you thinking what I'm thinking?'

'I don't know. What are you thinking?'

'I've no idea.'

Exasperated Emma picked up a bundle of the papers she had been going through and waved them in front of her brother.

'Alaric's resources had become terribly depleted and yet these statements show large funds being deposited in our accounts. I say "*ours*" but of course I mean my husband's.'

'So we're better off than you thought. This is excellent news.'

McAra gloated.

'None of this has anything to do with you – keep that in mind. As yet it may not be my affair either. But look at this anyhow – these deposits are from one of Hiram's banks in the United States. Alaric had thoughts of undertaking a business venture in California so it just seems that the money is travelling in the wrong direction.'

'It is if it's not coming my way. More of that later on. I might as well let you know that there's some doubt about whether Stuart is altogether right in the head. I'm a great student of the way men's brains work and it's my diagnosis that he's bound for Bedlam. I should go round there now and tie him to a post until we can get him a place beside my friend Haggerty.'

'Who's Haggerty?'

'Let me see these statements from Coutts. I have a fine head for figures. I'll be able to clear this up in a minute.'

Assuming a professorial demeanour McAra donned a pair of spectacles from which one lens was missing while the other was smeared with some greenish adhesive emetic. For a while he scanned the columns devoted to deposit, withdrawal and technical

HIDDEN

notes on exchange rates, varying interest rates and references to extraneous matters with which the account holder would be familiar.

'Some bastard,' he reported, 'has done this in the Vigenère cipher. No living man could make it out.'

'It's easy enough,' Emma pointed out and explained at speed what the tables showed: Hiram Stuart had been ploughing huge sums into Alaric's accounts.

'It's an inverted arrangement, isn't it?' she reflected. 'I supposed that Alaric would be sending money across the Atlantic to support his acquisition of land. And probably to bribe agents or buy up property. Instead he seems to be being paid for doing it.'

'A gift horse,' McAra announced, toasting the family's unanticipated good fortune with the brandy. 'You should let me find a good home for it. I'm regarded as one of the country's leading brokers.'

'Do you think I should take this up with Mr Stuart? I really ought to be properly informed about what's going on.'

Alarmed at the prospect of enormous fiscal advantage slipping away McAra hastened to assure her that there was much that could be done by way of clarifying the situation without direct reference to the source of the potentially excess income.

'You think this might have to do with whatever Bertram Hopkin was going to tell you?' Emma wondered.

'Who's Esmeralda?'

Emma frowned, annoyed at her brother's penchant for non sequitur response. It took her several moments to dredge up a recollection of the name.

'It's not a "who," it's a "what." That's the name of Alaric's ship.'

'Sailing where?'

'Between Glasgow and Bristol, I think. What do you want to know that for?'

'Who collects the feus and rents for Alaric?'

'Oh, I don't know. It'll be here somewhere.'

And Emma shuffled through yet more of the forms on the desk until she came across a contract with the name of Dowe in the heading.

'There you are, but what's that got to do with the business that brought you up here from London? I thought you were supposed to

HIDDEN

be investigating some conspiracy that poor Bertram was so exercised about.'

'I am. Could you see somebody taking pot–shots at Her Majesty or the Prime Minister when they get here?'

'You think that's what Bertram had uncovered? A plan to assassinate the Queen. Or Sir Robert Peel?'

'And yon's a right posh shite, that Skewton over at Bonaly's place. I had to teach the two of them some manners just now. Anyhow I'll be away and see this Dowe lot. Don't go saying a word about all this money – it'll not go wrong.'

It took the exhausted Hebe the rest of the afternoon to reach the office of Dowe & Son on Leith Street.

'You should be carrying that thing, not the other way round,' a passing drunk jeered as McAra tied the horse to a brass ring at the door of the establishment.

'On your way, or I'll punt your fundament from here to the Forth,' the policeman replied and for his pains received a punch on the chest that sent him reeling while his assailant looked in horror at the still–sticky spew that clung to his fist after its vigorous contact with McAra's waistcoat. Recovered slightly, the officer hurried into the building before the brief altercation became more heated.

'I'm after a good pal of mine,' he informed the elderly occupant of the office, massaging the area where the blow had landed. 'Walter Grundy's the name of him. He said he was with you in some trade – if you're the fellow in charge.'

'I'm Hector Dowe, aye. But you've no right to come in here covered in sick.'

'Don't try to show off your wit. I'm not a man to be trifled with. I led the charge of the Scots Greys at Waterloo.'

'I'm not trying to entertain you – I'm trying to inform you. Grundy is away in Ardentinny for a few days. He's been commissioned to find a boat for a client and he's been told of a nice wee smack that's moored down there. And likely doing a bit swimming in the loch for the man's a rare gift and love for it. Ardentinny's where his cousin lives.'

'What's a feu and rent collector doing looking out for boats?'

'He's his own man on his time out of this place. He can do as he pleases.'

HIDDEN

'When's he back? Before the first of the month?'
'He's a sound man so I don't force him to anything. Anyway he's away over there for some days yet. So Major DeWitt tells me. That was him collected some papers for Walter the other day.'
'Well then Breccan Donnelly?'
'Works for us at times. An acquaintance of Mr Grundy's. Hard worker, I hear, but I don't know him personally. Or where he is the now.'
'Where would a man find Mr Grundy in Ardentinny?'
'I told you – at his cousin's. A fellow called Donn.'
'And what about a wee fellow called Newsome?'
'Never heard of him.'
'Dicken? Bradley?'
'Them neither. And what's all this got to do with you anyhow?'
Leaving his faithful rocinante to be stabled for the night and having conducted a debriefing session with the yawning Balthazar, McAra excavated from his fragile recall the location of the tavern from which he had been briskly discharged a couple of nights earlier. He courted the possibility that his behaviour on that occasion would be forgiven and forgotten. Wiping down the front of his waistcoat, pausing to admire his reflection in the cracked mirror in his room and, disconsolately toting up the funds available to him, he strolled the length of the Grassmarket and inserted himself into the anonymous crowd in the dilapidated howff.
He decided it was advisable to restrict his intake to reasonable measures of spirits rather than pints of porter. The experience of coping with the tenebrous latrine after distending his bladder with an overabundance of liquid was not one to be too readily repeated. The important thing about the venue, of course, was that it numbered among its staff the insouciant pygmy who had dispensed the pints of Madeira or sherry – McAra couldn't quite remember – that had prompted his urinary adventure. He couldn't be sure that this was the Newsome that the mariner Dicken had nominated but he calculated that the probability of two such Lilliputians haunting the same proximate habitat was low.
Trusting that the disgrace that had attended his last visit to the pub was hardly a matter of outrage he nevertheless restricted himself to the shadows and to half a dozen large whiskies while keeping an

HIDDEN

eye open for the bustling manikin. It was not until near to closing time that the opportunity for an exchange arose.

'Josiah Dicken has some good news for you,' McAra whispered as the creature he took for Newsome set about clearing his table. 'Meet me on the corner of Candlemaker Row when you're done here.'

A little light–headed but more sure–footed than usual he took his leave of the place along with the last of the inebriates and positioned himself in the shade nearby to wait for the assignation. Propelled by a combination of avarice and caution the little man sidled into view but stayed some ten feet out of McAra's reach in the deserted street. When the policeman made to take a step in his direction he retreated further and whipped a long–bladed razor from his belt.

'Keep off and tell me what Josiah has for me,' Newsome hissed.

'My cousin Nathanial is a professional molester,' McAra advised him in a voice so low that the other was obliged to move nearer to catch what he was saying. 'Farm animals, flightless birds, tailless simians. A calf rhinoceros once.'

'What? Speak up.'

For once less handicapped by over–indulgence McAra moved with rare swiftness and his short truncheon sent the blade spinning through the night air.

'Come here, lofty,' he commanded and, bending down, grabbed the other by the throat. Newsome was fast and agile and the ensuing struggle ensured that all dignity on both sides was thoroughly abandoned. The dwarf aimed a kick at McAra's groin which produced a very satisfactory yelp of pain but also elicited a stabbing blow of the club which left Newsome doubled over in breathless agony while the officer clapped a pair of rusty handcuffs on him.

'If you've done harm to my gonads,' McAra muttered, rubbing the affected area with his free hand, 'I'll twist the lungs out of you, you wee wart. Now,' yanking the midget's locked arms up his back and shoving him into a cul–de–sac weighted with a medley of aromas of visceral and vegetal origin, 'you better clench your buttocks when you hear what I've got to say to you.'

'You're not going to despoil me, are you?'

'I'm the chief of all the detectives of the Metropolitan Police, their

HIDDEN

most decorated officer and the one you'd do well to treat with respect.'

'A peeler, is it? Jesus, you're not much bigger than me. Did they shrink you for work up here?'

'You're a murderous little bastard and you're bound for the hemp round your neck for what you've done.'

Newsome stopped struggling and became dangerously watchful.

'What is it you want off of me?'

'For now I just want you to meet a pal of mine – not far, but for luck I'll keep a hold of that hair of yours. Make a run for it and I'll have the scalp off you. And we'll keep the shackles on for the good of us both.'

And not resisting the impulse to beat the minuscule miscreant every twenty steps or so McAra dragged him up the steep length of Candlemaker Row and into the close where the East Division of the Poor House sheltered the men's hospital ward. Despite the ungodly hour the porter at the gate watched with indifference the odd couple make their squabbling entrance. The ward was dimly lit by pale, flickering oil lamps and the atmosphere was heavy with curses, moans, shouts, wheezing and the scent of imminent demise. Covered by a dirty grey sheet, J J Haggerty lay pale and unmoving in the bed nearest the door. Protruding from the bedlinen was a distended and swollen foot, covered in bleeding sores from which rose a foul–smelling discharge. Haggerty's eyes followed his visitors as they inspected him from either side of the bed. Whether he recognised McAra or not was unclear. He remained unmoving, the sweat streaming down his face, his vast body pulsing with fever. Rising from a candle–lit station at the end of the corridor a burly nurse came rolling towards the two incomers and in a hoarse, angry whisper ordered them to leave instantly.

Back on the cobbles McAra halted his prisoner and looked down at him with a gleam of satisfaction.

'That,' he said, 'is where you're bound, and in the same condition, if you don't do exactly what I tell you. And remember this – I have an army of agents that will find you in five minutes if you try to tiptoe out of my reach.'

'What the fuck was that? The man's as near as dead.'

'That's what he got for crossing me. If I feel in a better way about

HIDDEN

him I'll go back in when it suits me and cure him.'
'Cure him? How can you cure him?'
'I'll cut his throat. Are we chums now, then? And think about this before you tell me – you're a murdering little swine and you'll get damn all help from anybody if I have you pulped, burned, opened up from throat to cock and eaten by dogs.'
'You're off your head, man.'
'Aye, I am that, and don't you forget it. Now this is what you need to do to make sure you don't end up in the bed next to yon giant fucker.'

HIDDEN
CHAPTER 9 AUGUST 1842

Two days later McAra and his sister were closeted in the Halley estate.
'You really should move out here and stay with me,' Emma said. 'That poor horse of yours looks as if she's about to expire. And so do you.'
'It suits me to be in the city,' her brother assured her as he probed his long, tangled, unkempt hair. 'I need to be on hand to keep order in the streets. And I have very satisfactory accommodation – well located and luxuriously appointed.'
'Well, tell me now, how is your investigation proceeding? Have you discovered what happened to Bertram that night in the Grassmarket?'
'Oh, no – please no!'
A look of unbridled horror froze on McAra's face as he withdrew his hand from his thatch, peered open–mouthed at his palm and emitted a prolonged gasp of calamitous incredulity.
'There's something moving in there; something living, in the name of God.'
'Nits? Lice? Oh, Mac, you can be the most revolting beast.'
'No, no, it's something far bigger. I could feel the legs. And there's a drove of them. You'll have to get them out for me. Come over here and see if you can get hold of them.'
Emma stayed exactly where she was and waited until the outburst subsided.
'You were going to tell me if you have come any nearer to solving the case – do you have suspects? Was there even a crime?'
'You know – it's good to be back home again in Glasgow. I might move back permanently.'
'Edinburgh, Mac. We're in Edinburgh, always have been.'
'Edinburgh, aye. Now you need to remember that I'm the custodian of state secrets so anything I say must remain between us alone.'
'Don't say a word if you don't think it's the right thing to do.'
'I've got a wee fellow in the cells at police headquarters in the High Street. Maybe he'll be moved to the Calton but I've a strong feeling

HIDDEN

that'll not happen.'
'And this wee fellow had something to do with Bertram's death?'
'In a manner of speaking, aye. He killed him.'
'And you can say nothing more then?'
'He was driving that coach of Bonaly's that ran Hopkin down. I can easy lay hands on witnesses that'll testify to it. There was some that thought the coach was on the loose with nobody on the box seat but that was because the top of this customer's napper wouldn't be much more than a couple of feet off the floor.'
'And the witnesses saw this little fellow drive the thing?'
'I'll maybe need to tell them that they did. Anyhow I know where to find them and they'll not be too keen to disappoint me.'
'Please don't say that you'll compel them to false witness. You're an officer of the law, Mac. You can't force folk to tell lies.'
'I never heard that before. But I've plenty of work to get done before I'm away back to London. I've been thinking about all this loot that's found its way into Alaric's purse. From your man Hiram whatever his name is.'
'Stuart. What about it?'
'You shouldn't be in any doubt by now – your devoted husband won't be coming back, will he? If my men down south can't find him and neither can them Home Office sneaks you can be sure he's gone for good. Maybe he fell in the Thames or maybe a Spaniard stole him away.'
'Don't make mock. I'm not pretending that all was well between us – certainly not. But how can I fail to wonder whatever could have become of him? And it makes me concerned for my own safety. What if Alaric has been assassinated by enemies of this country? He's been an adviser to the Prime Minister and the government for a long time. What if these cutthroats believe that I too am privy to secrets they don't want known any more widely?'
'You can rely on me for your protection, but that won't be necessary, I swear to you. And another thing – I'm struggling with trapped wind; and when it does escape the consequence is hideous.'
From the corner of the room came Balthazar's exasperated gouging at the bars of his portable residence which produced a shudder of abhorrence in Emma who had already tried without success to have the monster deposited as far outside the building as Casper could

HIDDEN

manage. McAra offered some placatory tutting, crossed the floor and shoved a piece of onion through the bars and proceeded with relish to finish the rest of the vegetable himself.
'But if it was some pygmy riding the coach how can we be sure he simply couldn't control it and killed Bertram by accident?'
'I'm a master of detection. I know things. *Things*.'
'And these witnesses? What is it that they know?'
'Other things.'
'Oh, Mac, don't be so Pythian.'
'I know. I can be too pithy for my own good. It means folk don't take me serious enough.'
'That's not... Well, let's forget it. What will you do now?'
McAra casually took hold of the brandy bottle as he was returning to his seat and, dispensing with an intermediary tumbler, glugged down a quarter gill.
'It's what *you* might do. This Hiram Stuart laddie – since he's been ploughing money into the Halley accounts I think you're entitled to find out why, don't you?'
'Sorry, Mac, but I've no intention of becoming mixed up in whatever shady dealings are going on in America or anywhere else.'
'Hold, it's coming, it's coming.'
And McAra rocked over to one side, raised a buttock and unbridled a benchwarmer of such ferocity and impetus that Casper threw open the door to ascertain that no firearms had been discharged, and retreated at speed from his brief encounter with the fetor.
'Thar' she blows,' McAra pronounced with some gratification. 'Mind you, that's going to force the veins down to my knees. The itch will be terrible.'
Emma sat expressionless while her brother contemplated the anal distress in prospect. Finally he reverted to the topic he had raised before this intrusion of faecal fume.
'My dear Em, you're a responsible citizen so think about this: something very shady is going on with that Yankee fellow and who knows who else. The Halley funds are yours now and if they were meant to recognise Alaric's efforts at something disreputable there'll be searching questions asked of you if you've not bothered to enquire into the wellspring of this mysterious generosity.'

HIDDEN

'Don't inflict one of your moralising speeches on me. I'd rather hear chalk scrape on a slate.'

'So you'll do it? Good. Likely the best approach is the direct one. You get your pretty little behind over to Sir Hudson's place and tell your beloved neighbour that you're stepping into your husband's finely crafted footwear.'

'I'll do no such thing. I know Sir Hudson only faintly and that only because of his association with Alaric. He'd smell a rat right away.'

'Don't cast aspirations on Balthazar. You can be sure that there will be no risk entailed in the expedition. For all we know it's a completely innocent fiscal affair or an act of astounding generosity. Maybe none of this has any damn thing to do with the Hopkin killing.'

'No, I'd be too nervous to do it, Mac. I'd be shaking like a leaf and they'd see right through me.'

'Nonsense. You're a beautiful woman and they'll fall at your dainty wee feet.' A pause. 'I don't suppose you've changed your mind about a little fling with your comely brother. Believe me, my dear Emma, that you can't deduce from my modest stature the dimensions of my privy parts. They're there for your delectation at any time.'

'And what would it be, anyway, that I would say to Sir Hudson that would explain my sudden interest in Alaric's affairs?'

'What could be more natural, woman, than that a widow would desire to be apprised of such matters as family bank accounts?'

'Please don't place me in that category. Despite what you tell me, Alaric might turn up tomorrow.'

McAra shook his head in wonderment and applied himself once more to the brandy bottle, allowing the silence to lurch uncomfortably into a full minute of incipient acrimony. It was Emma who finally capitulated.

'All right – if I consent to do this you'll have to give me the words. And you'll have to tell me what you're going to be doing while I hazard life and limb in Sir Hudson's lair.'

'I'm away on my holidays to Argentina. But first I need some funds out of you for a wee plan of mine that I can't say anything about just yet. And would you put up a few shillings more to rent a little place in the Old Town. Just for a week or two? And don't say a

HIDDEN

word about it to anybody.'
'You want me to find the place, is that it?'
'No. I've got it already – but you'll need to grease the landlady's palm. Here's the place.'
And he passed her a filthy piece of paper with an address scrawled on it.
'One other thing,' Emma said, 'before you present yourself for inspection in foreign parts. Maybe you remember you spoke about a fellow called Bradley? Mr Skewton told that he used to be seen sometimes with Grundy. Well, it seems that he's a vigorous proponent of revolution of some sort – not quite in the mode of the French, you'll no doubt be pleased to learn. But taken by some to be a danger to public order. I've been unable to find out more about him though.'
'There's one big favour…'
'Oh, God, Mac…'
'A fellow called Latimer. Give him a wee job, would you?'
'Who? What is it you're up to?'
'Just going about doing good works like always. I've put his details on this bit paper.'
'Wait,' she said, glancing at his note, 'I've heard of this lad. Isn't he the winner of the Lowland Carriage Driving contest? We hardly need a charioteer, Mac. Just a plain, ordinary driver will do us.'
'You know how much I like to help out the lower classes, Em. Take him on for a bit, eh?'
'You don't like to help anyone out. And there is no class lower than your own. But all right…'
'There's one other minuscule good turn that'll be hard for you, for I know you love me to distraction. Every chance you get let Squire Bonnylicks and Sir Smarty Hudson hear you say I'm not in my right mind. Tell them I'm off my head with drink.'
'Unlike you I have an ability to tell the truth so what you ask is no difficulty. I'll spread hourly the word you ask of me.'
'They still know nothing of my juristic calling?'
'If you mean do they know you're a police officer then, no they don't.'
With Casper driving him in one of Alaric Halley's curricles drawn by a matched pair of palominos McAra set off early the next day

HIDDEN

for the Edinburgh and Glasgow Railway terminus at the new Haymarket Railway Station. This elegant part of his lengthy journey was swiftly succeeded by severe deterioration in circumstance. Having to wait for the best part of two hours the policeman found a nearby pub where, in funds thanks to Emma, he devoted his earnest attention to the contents of several tumblers of port and brandy as a cure for the flatulence, the effects of which were afflicting others more than him. By the time he reeled onto the train he was bawling the words of "May Day":

"O May, thou art a merry time,
Sing hi! the hawthorn pink and pale,
When hedge–pipes they begin to chime,
And summer flowers to sow the dale."

While the rendition was audible the full length of the third class carriage it was not entirely appreciated by all and a beefy traveller, whose wife and unprepossessing offspring were upset at the performance, waxed critical by belting McAra twice on the side of the head, making his point and simultaneously relieving the officer of his self–imposed obligation to entertain the company.

When the train arrived in Glasgow he had to be roused by a porter concerned at the deplorable passenger's profound unconsciousness. Gathering his scanty luggage and even scantier senses McAra emerged into the brilliant sunshine in George Square and was rescued from the indignity of having to relieve himself in public by being arrested and conducted to the police station in the Trongate. Able to extricate his credentials from the depths of his carpet bag after some hours in detention he was brought before the senior officer on duty and with difficulty explained the purpose of his expedition, an exposition that was only clarified after the mumbled term "feeling fleon" was interpreted as "fleeing felon."

'A detective, are you? Aye, well, it would seem you detected a fair few pubs between Edinburgh and here.'

'We detectives need to mix with the raffriff if we're going to hear what's going on.'

'That would be riffraff. And Ardentinny, is it?' the unsympathetic sergeant said, scowling at the increasingly dog–eared letter the Commissioner of the Metropolitan force had provided McAra with.

HIDDEN

'You've a damn long way to go yet, wee man. And how is it that you're going to bring your fugitive to justice? On your back, is it?'
Transporting the truant Grundy from the wilder shores of Argyll to Edinburgh was an undertaking to which McAra had given no thought. Unperturbed, though, at his own oversight he assumed his wonted air of mandated competence.
'I'll have you know that my assistant is Willie Haining, the chief of the Edinburgh force. So you'll be well advised to give me your full cooperation.'
'You'll find your tail cooperating with the end of my boot if you're not careful. Listen, you'd have more than forty miles to go to Ardentinny, and that only if you get the ferry out of Coulport. Else you can go all the way the side of Loch Lomond and that'll be a good seventy miles. How'll that suit you, hiking along with a prisoner in tow?'
McAra's knowledge of the geography of his native land was proving to be less than complete, as was his capacity for forward planning. After a moment's reflection he hauled himself up to his full diminutive height and said, 'You'd need to know that I'm here at the specific request of the Queen herself. There have been threats made against her and I'm the man to find out the truth about them. So you'll have to let me have one of your wagons and maybe a driver too.'
'Threats, eh? And that would be from the Ardentinny Revolution, I suppose? Have they set up the guillotine for Her Majesty on the Banks of Loch Long? Aye – these are dangerous times, right enough.'
Before McAra could formulate a sufficiently acid response a hirsute figure in uniform emerged from the office behind the desk, nudged the derisive sergeant out of the way and beckoned to the Metropolitan officer into the smoke–filled room, closing the door behind them.
'I'm in charge of this station and you'll make sure to treat my men with the respect they deserve. Which, right enough, might not be that much. But this thing about Queen Victoria – I've it on good authority that she's due in Scotland at the start of next month. That's not something that's to be spread around, so I'm told, but if you have the word on it I'll be believing that you're here on Royal duty.

HIDDEN

Tell me this first, though – the names of the commissioners at the London force.'

When McAra, having coaxed his mind out of the alcoholic twilight in which it had spent the greater part of the day, pronounced the names of Rowan and Mayne the Inspector announced that he was satisfied with his visitor's *bona fides*.

'I'll assume you're not here on some gallivant and I'll do this for you – I heard what you were saying about Ardentinny. That's a long way out of that door so I'll let you have a van with a good man to drive the thing. He's a bright enough lad and you'll find him handy enough if your fugitive isn't too keen on coming away quiet. I'll want to hear nothing more about the business for I don't want the blame if you make a salmagundi of it. Just get my man and his wagon back here sometime without a dirty mark on either one of them.'

McAra's self–indulgence meant that it was too late to set off on the long road trip that day and the canny Inspector was running no risk of his misspending the evening in the multitudinous Glasgow taverns, so he was kept under lock and key at the station until early the following morning. Having gone briefly out of the way to the Broomielaw Quay where he made some perfunctory enquiries McAra was well on his expedition before the city was properly awake, the wagon, drawn by a pair of sturdy draft crossbreds and manned by Hughie Cassels, a surly officer in mufti. The route took them along the north side of the Clyde through the west end, past Clydebank and Dumbarton and on to Cardross and Helensburgh. Having exhausted his repertoire of tasteless witticisms and meticulously curated tales of his own grandeur McAra was at last compelled to unwonted silence in the face of his companion's stony indifference. Aside from a half–hour pause for lunch and a couple of halts to rest the team when around six words were exchanged, the journey to Coulport was made in a silent cocoon of mutual animosity.

The weather was stiflingly hot but the expedition had begun before five and the well–tended horses completed the route in less than six hours without a solitary application of the whip or yell of encouragement. The small ferry from Coulport carried the vehicle and its laconic occupants across the shimmering and untroubled

HIDDEN

surface of Loch Long to the Ardentinny shore on a waft of idyllic calm. There were only two vessels in the tiny harbour of the village – a handsome single–masted cutter called *Ceasg* and a dilapidated twelve foot row boat. McAra had no idea what Grundy looked like, where he was staying or which boat the truant had been delegated to acquire. But since there were so few houses to be seen he estimated that he would have no difficulty in identifying and laying hands on his prey. Leaving the Glasgow officer to look after the horses and lounge by the waterside he strolled along the pebbly beach until he encountered a disconsolate figure perched on a rock and vigorously shaking the dregs from a bottle into his mouth.

'Bloody finished,' this disgruntled loner complained by way of introduction. His movements were slow and mechanical and McAra, with great experience in the field, gauged that the lethargic gesticulation was more accountable to the contents of the bottle than to the soporific afternoon.

'Is there a Major chappy around maybe?' McAra asked, sitting down on a neighbouring outcrop. 'Or Mr Grundy?'

'What's it to you?'

'I need to catch up to the one or the other. Business, see? And I've a few bob here that might get you through the rest of the day if you can point me in the right direction.'

His new–found friend's face lit up, consonant with the glow in the western sky.

'Grundy's been staying at Archie Donn's. They've been bickering about how much he'll pay for the rent of yon nice big yacht over there. And if you're in the market yourself that's my handsome wee rowing boat that would be going for a song. You'll not get a better at the price I'm asking. Call me Jamesie.'

And he waved a thumb at the stone cottage a hundred yards back from the shore, looking out over the loch and surrounded by a neat garden enclosed by a low fence consisting of white–painted wooden uprights linked by heavy chains.

'I think maybe the Major's just come down as well in some great bloody hurry. He'll most like be at his own place. That's it over your shoulder. Awful busy keeping to himself as usual. He shot my dog last year. Bastard.'

'Right, Jamesie; now where can I find Mr Donn? It's best I get hold

HIDDEN

of Grundy first.'

'First wooden cottage along the shore – no distance at all; just past the inn.'

'Here's the price of a beer or two,' McAra said, handing over a few coins which were quickly secreted in the folds of the man's ragged jacket. 'I'll away and see if I can have a word with him. It might be a good idea if you never saw me here the day.'

'I never set eyes on you.'

And McAra set off swaying gently in the direction Jamesie had indicated.

'We'll need to find a kip for the night,' Cassels opined, grabbing McAra before he could terminate his mission. 'And there's about three bloody houses in the whole village. I'll see if we can get rooms at the inn over there. But what about your runaway? Do you want a hand to bring him in the now?'

Having barely issued a single word between Glasgow and their destination Cassels was suddenly more animated at the prospect of a roughhouse. As if readying for some much–delayed excitement he was repeatedly punching his hairy fists together and his eyes had widened with anticipation.

'No, best leave it till tomorrow so we don't have to shackle him in the wagon overnight. I'll have a quick scout around to see what's what and then meet you in the boozer.'

Cassels watched him limp off towards the selvage of trees along the edge of the sand and noted with faint amusement the other's lop–sided gait and repeated tugging at the seat of his baggy trousers. Keeping to the shelter of the firs McAra plodded on over the rough terrain until, despite the shortness of the walk, the sweat was pouring from his urban brow and down his moth–eaten shirt. With the late afternoon sun behind him he melted – almost literally – into the shadows and, reaching Donn's timber residence, he scanned the place from the shade of a half–uprooted tree. There was no sign of activity or of any form of transport. Satisfied with the outcome of his clandestine excursion he headed back to the Major's more substantial cottage where, too, there appeared to be no movement or any team of horses. A brightly painted post chaise stood at the rear of the building but was missing a wheel which he could see propped against a wall and apparently waiting some form

HIDDEN

of attention. With no evident means of escape for his quarry McAra decided to leave any action until the next morning. Back at the inn Cassels informed him that two rooms were available but would have to be paid for in advance.

'I've not got so much as a bawbee about me,' the Glasgow man said. 'You'll have to cough up for them.'

Open–mouthed with incredulity McAra staggered against the door of the tavern.

'Me? You're bound for the Parliamentary Road Asylum. Me? You need to get a right hold of yourself. I'm in charge here and I'm telling you to get your hand in that bloody pocket of yours.'

Cassels regarded him for a moment with cool dispassion, reflected on the exchange and retorted with a shrug, 'Up to you, you little toad. I'll kip in the wagon and you can find yourself a comfortable bunk on that beach out there. I hear there's rain coming up tonight, so good luck to you.'

'Rain?'

McAra gritted his teeth and with a look of unalloyed hatred sorted through the contents of the purse he kept on a string under his arm. Emma had provided him with more than enough money to conduct his affairs for at least a week but he had had plans for its deployment which did not include accommodation or extending hospitality to a colleague. Shielding the extent of his resources he announced that he could probably fork out just enough to lodge himself alone. Cassels nodded slowly and told him, 'Well, well, that's grand for you. And you'll be able to pay your own way back to Edinburgh – if you can find somebody to take you. For I'll be away on my own first thing in the morning, and no place for you or your prisoner.'

Exasperated beyond words McAra pretended to continue his pecuniary researches and, feigning gladness, reported that he did, after all, have the capital to house them both.

'And there'll be some for a bit dinner – and a wee drink, eh?'

Almost swooning McAra reluctantly consented to this unforeseen imposition, ponderously bestowed on the dishevelled inn–keeper the amount required to assure the pair of sanctuary for the night and led the way to a rickety wooden table where he took sole charge of ordering the most frugal meal on the sparse menu. Overruled on

HIDDEN

the issue of drinks he accepted the urgent necessity of an initial two pints of port which, with the swapping of law–enforcement badinage, shortly became four. Darkness had fallen and candles and lamps lit by the time the officers made for their respective rooms, and it was only half an hour later that McAra tiptoed into the bar to buy a bottle of brandy which he clutched to his chest and crept upstairs fearful of betraying this surreptitious activity to his undeserving colleague.

Around two o'clock, long after the lights had been dimmed and the occupants of the hostelry retired the entire establishment was thrown into confused and fearful wakefulness by the shrieks emanating from McAra's room. Assuming nocturnal invasion or assault Cassels and the inn–keeper himself raced to the point of origin of this frenzy. When the door was sent crashing open the two were confronted by a sight neither of them – understandably– could have been prepared for. McAra lay recumbent on the bed, naked from the waist down, his knees drawn up near to his head. Beneath his exposed rump lay the empty brandy bottle in a small puddle of the spilled contents. Despite the irruption into his boudoir the little policeman's high–pitched wailing continued unabated, and was sustained even after his lower limbs had been wrestled free.

'Douse me," he yelped between screams. 'Drench them!'

'What in the name of God's the matter?' the proprietor demanded as he and Cassels, having rescued the sufferer from his yogic posture, stood irresolute and helpless by the bedside.

'Water, for the love of Christ,' McAra managed between gasps.

Cassels grabbed the stone pitcher and held it over his tortured colleague's mouth as the rest of the staff and guests of the inn crowded into the room.

'Not there!'

And tilting himself backwards McAra, his face empurpled by agony, indicated with a shaking hand his bared behind. The intending carers glanced uncomprehending at each other until Cassels seized the initiative and dashed half the jugful at the quivering buttocks.

'Holy God, more – more before I go up in flames. More, you lazy brutes.'

A stout maid rushed out to return in short order with another flagon

HIDDEN

and, doubled over with laughter, flung the full draught at McAra's scrawny rear. Having unleashed this palliative stream she paused to cast a critical eye over his no less uncovered genitals before, clutching both hands to her mouth, hurrying out past the throng of onlookers to guffaw in relative peace in the darkened corridor. After the application of another round of cold water to the affected area McAra calmed down somewhat, let loose a prolonged sigh and stretched out his full length on the soaking mattress, unconcerned at the concentrated interest of the assembled company on his unveiled crotch and the gradual subsiding of the frenetic thrash of his legs.

'Out, the whole lot of youse,' the inn–keeper bawled at last and, with disappointed unwillingness, the audience removed itself from the scene.

'What the fuck happened here?' Cassels demanded when he alone remained to witness the last of McAra's convulsions.

'It's your fault. Hardly a minute to myself on that bloody ride up here on your buckboard thing. A few stops and I'd have been as right as rain.'

'My fault? Have you gone off your head?'

'It was that wooden box seat of yours. And did we have more than a minute or two off it the whole way here?'

'You were the one that was in a hurry to get to this damn place.'

McAra issued a low, whining groan and tried to find a more comfortable pose.

'This arse–ache is killing me. It was the same for the great Bonaparte. That's why I let him go at Waterloo. A fellow sufferer. I had him by the throat. I could have put him in the clutches of the Duke, you know. But…'

'What are you havering about?'

Not enthusiastic about explaining his predicament McAra set about the task with as much delicacy as he could muster.

'The piles were slaughtering me and I'd had a drink or two. I thought I might doctor the things myself. There was half the brandy still in the bottle so I poured it…'

Cassels leaned back and laughed his jeering laugh until the tears streamed down his cheeks.

'And they'll be putting this remedy in Dunglison's, will they?'

HIDDEN

'Aye, Cassels, you're very funny. Leave me alone to breathe my last.'

HIDDEN
CHAPTER 10 AUGUST 1842

Not in the best of health the next day McAra lingered long abed nursing a splitting headache and persistent discomfort elsewhere in his overtaxed anatomy. When he did make an appearance he found Cassels had been running back and forth along the sand for an hour and was now throwing punches at an imaginary opponent in the yard in front of the inn. Breakfasting on a couple of sizeable onions McAra announced that he was setting off for Donn's cottage to lay claim to the presumed offender Grundy. Cassels brightened and recommended that he accompany his colleague in case violent resistance was offered, but McAra dismissed the proposal, confident that his imposing physique and magisterial bearing would suffice to quell any defiance on the runagate's part.

By the time McAra was thundering on the door of the Donn cabin it was mid–morning and after the rain storm of the previous night what had started as a day of stifling heat was clouding over ominously again. The air was heavy with the threat of another downpour which was already gathering against the lowering western sky. His temper not improved by the tenacity of his hangover and the dilatory reaction to his insistent knocking, McAra was on the verge of booting the door open when the resident put in a cautious appearance.

'I'm buying nothing off youse tinkers,' this person warned, scratching his chest through a dirty shirt whose discolouration was further enhanced by a variety of stains representative of mishandled sustenance. 'I'll not tell you again.' And he displayed a short, heavy club that he had been holding behind his back.

'I'm here on the Crown's business, so I'll have none of your shite. Now, let me have words with Grundy before I knock your teeth down your throat.'

Amused at this exhibition of belligerence on the part of a man not much more than half his size Donn was in the process of leaning forward to covey reprimand when he caught a whiff of the other's breath and recoiled in haste.

'Grundy's away a good while ago, you wee fart. And anyway what's

HIDDEN

Her Majesty after him for?'
'That's no affair of yours. You'll have to let me in and make sure he's not lying low in your hovel.'
'Come on in if you have to – it's no trouble to me, but he went away first thing the day on the boat I hired him – over to Coulport.'
Still doubting the other's honesty McAra performed a swift tour of the two-roomed shack and was obliged to acknowledge that his quarry had gone.
'How was it your man got himself off that early? Did he hear somebody was at his heels?'
McAra had no intention of admitting to himself that his own sluggard start was the cause of his losing the opportunity to apprehend the elusive Grundy.
'He got a right scare last night. There must have been a murder at the inn – we could hear the screaming in the small hours. He didn't want to be here when the police turned up. Don't ask me why. So far as I know he never done nothing wrong, but there you are. At least he leased the cutter off of me.'
'A murder…? Oh, aye, well, that got sorted that all right. Where's he away to?'
'How would I have that? Likely Edinburgh but he said nothing to me. I'm not his keeper.'
McAra silently cursed his anal affliction and the misjudged attempt at self-medication that had provoked his target to make himself scarce so hastily.
'I suppose his soldier pal went away with him?'
'No – the Major's here for a day or two yet. He's waiting for the wheel of his buggy to be sorted.'
'And what's the use Mr Grundy's going to be making use of that *Ceasg* he's had off you?'
'No idea. If you put a glass to your eye you'd see the thing moored on the other side. What's it to you?'
McAra stumped off into the drizzle. Shivering in the unexpected chill he stopped off at the inn to don his grubby jacket and to lay the blame for Grundy's premature departure on Cassels.
'He saw you trotting up and down that beach looking just like what you are – a copper. You scared him out of my hands. I'm warning you, your Inspector'll be hearing about this.'

HIDDEN

Leaving that lying assertion and pointless admonition hanging over the grouchy Glaswegian he made his way through the now teeming rain to the nearby home of Major DeWitt determined to find out what the expedition to Ardentinny had been designed to achieve. He was about to raise his fist to the front door when the occupant presented himself for inspection. Convinced that the Major was a wretched conspirator given to compulsive degeneracy McAra was disappointed that he showed neither surprise nor concern at this discomposed visitant's intrusion on his rural solitariness.

'I can give you a shilling if you get all the weeds out of the front garden there,' the Major said, 'but I'll tell you this – I'm a man who demands perfection. And those chains round the plot could do with some hard burnishing.'

'You are the Major Dimwit?'

Unruffled the ex–soldier inclined his head.

'I am Major DeWitt. What is it you want, you rancid little twerp?'

'My name is McAra. There's a copper down here with me that has me by the balls for some wife called Hopkin says me or you got somebody to pinch some of her son's important papers. I know it wasn't me, so…'

A measure of recognition spread over DeWitt's face and he afforded himself a smirk.

'Ah, I know you. You're that failed coachman. The lovely Mrs Halley's loathsome brother. We met briefly, didn't we? In London, was it?'

'Never mind that. I'm not getting the jail for the likes of you and your fancy pals.'

And not waiting for an invitation, McAra bustled into the lobby. He cast around to gauge his bearings and made himself at home in a chair set to one side of the grate in which a welcome log fire was blazing. A sudden gust of wind shook the window and the rain began to rattle against the glass.

'Where's your pal Grundy away to?' McAra asked, belching poisonous fumes with abandon and hauling at the crotch of his breeches in an attempt to render himself more comfortable. 'What was it the pair of you were up to here? Mind me, now, for I've that murderous copper waiting for me out there.'

'Mr Grundy is hardly accountable to me or to you for his

HIDDEN

whereabouts. And why I'm here in my own home is not a question I feel the slightest need to respond to.'
'You'll need to understand things a bit better. You can answer me here or yon brute of a bobby will be dragging you to the High Street in Edinburgh and beat your skull or your organs of procreation until you tell him what he wants to know.'
The Major opted for his favoured patronising smile.
'You're paddling beyond your depth, little man. I have things to do – go and play in the sand or find somewhere safe to discard that pungent apparel.'
'You'd do well, ensign, not to make an enemy of me. I have powers. *Powers.*'
'Certainly you have the appearance of a Hellenic hero.'
'And martial elegance, it's generally agreed. Dicken and Newsome would be your cankerous cullies, would they? Oh, I've got the word on the whole pack of youse.'
'Our Hercules has been toiling at his vocabulary, eh? I've no idea what or whom you're talking about. May I recommend you lead your posse off into the sunset and find your mucous way back to the Great Wen if only for the sake of Mrs Halley's continued good health.'
'Mrs Halley's…?'
'I believe you catch my meaning, McAra. She's a fine–looking woman. We would all wish her to remain so. For her sake, be careful what you say and do.'
'My bladder's near exploding,' McAra said finally. 'I'm telling you, there's disease in there.'
'What are you mumbling about?'
'Often the passage of wind is an aid to loosening the stricture on the liquid excretion. But today… I tell you there's something immovable lodged there in the hind–quarters. There must be some sort of implement… You think some accident might befall my lovely sibling?'
'Unlikely if you were very soon to absent yourself from Edinburgh. From Scotland, indeed. One can, of course, do little more than conjecture.'
The rain was now drumming so heavily on the roof that even conversation was difficult. McAra plunged his hand into the depths

HIDDEN

of his ill–fitting trousers, withdrew it, held the tips of his fingers to his nose and appeared to approve of the aroma transported by the gesture.

'I see,' McAra said and nodded thoughtfully. 'I see. Well, I don't suppose you have a coat or umbrella you could lend me? I need to get back to the inn or yon police fellow will have his baton at me. And likely you next.'

'Aye, I'm fair shaking at the prospect. Now you mind what I've told you.'

Huddled under a military cloak McAra stumbled through the filthy afternoon to seek and find comfort in the bar in the company of the silent Cassels whose impression of his companion became more favourable with every round of porter and Madeira. What accounted for McAra's unexpected open–handedness was not to be determined in the course of fragmentary conversation that, as the hours wore on became ever less coherent. Cassels' brief enquiry as to the provenance of this unwonted generosity went without response and he was content to make the most of the situation without further interrogation of his gloomy benefactor. The weather ensured that there could be no question of leaving the village that day and by evening the host lit the fire, leaving the two men slumped in its flickering aurora. After a dinner of mutton pie and potatoes and yet more fortified wine the officers went swaying up to their rooms, McAra singing

"When I was young, I said to Sorrow,
'Come and I will play with thee:' –
He is near me now all day;
And at night returns to say,
'I will come again tomorrow,
I will come and stay with thee.'"

An hour later the inn was deserted and plunged in total darkness as he made his unsteady way back down the stairs where his heart leapt at the sight of the untended gantry which, uncharacteristically, he passed by with only a drooling glance and tiptoed out into the wild night.

Next morning the weather remained unseasonably cool and wet and, not averse to another spell away from the rigours of inner city

HIDDEN

policing, Cassels offered no objection to McAra's suggestion that they spend it winding up his investigation in the village. With Grundy gone from sight the only other source of information relevant to the obscure case he was pursuing elsewhere, he said, was the retired soldier to whom he'd already spoken briefly.

'He's a right fancy bit of a fellow and if he's a poor witness I might find it in my heart to give him a prod with these toe–caps,' McAra informed the Glasgow man. Cassels was not the type to stand in the way of robust interviewing and as the pair proceeded through the depressing mist down which a persistent mizzle was falling they were waylaid by a deeply irritated Jamesie.

'One of youse is the law, eh? Well, some shite has been at my wee boat. It's rammed into the glaur, there's water in the thing up to your ankles and the paint's been scored right off the gunwale. Somebody's took it out last night, I'll bet, and left it looking like a dunghill. Youse'll need to find out the scum that done it.'

'We'll have the best men on it this very day,' Cassels sniggered. 'You can rest easy on that.'

'Aye, youse are very funny. Youse haven't hear the last of this if you don't get it sorted.'

Leaving the fulminating fisherman to contemplate the injury done to his vessel the policemen approached DeWitt's cottage just as the light rain turned to a deluge.

'Come on, General,' McAra shouted as he thumped repeatedly on the door. 'It's Her Majesty's bodyguard. Open up, you lazy redcoat, or I'll set fire to the place.'

When no response was forthcoming Cassels circled the building peering in through the mullion windows but seeing no sign of life. 'He's been hauling something out here,' he said, indicating drag marks in the mud outside the gate. 'A pair of the fence posts have been pulled loose and the chain's been torn off them.'

'Maybe it was him that had a go at Jamesie's mighty galley,' McAra said and pushed at the door which swung open. A quick survey of the interior showed that the house was unoccupied.

'Take a peek here,' and Cassels pointed to a large damp patch on the stone floor of the lobby. 'He's been scrubbing at that. Might have been blood by the look of it.'

'Aye, maybe. Anyhow, for my money the bastard's taken himself

HIDDEN

off before I could get anything out of him.'
'Well, you might be right, but the wagon's still at the side of the house and there was no horse near the place.'
'I'll just have a trawl about and see if we can work out what he's been up to.'
And McAra set about scanning the furniture, pulling open drawers and lifting table coverings, cursing every few minutes at the lack of windfall until he found, tucked away against the underside of a drawer in a rosewood bureau, a folded piece of vellum which, when opened up, proved to be a sketchy map in coloured inks.
'Never got that by candle–light,' McAra muttered.
'By candle–light? You were only ever here in the day.'
McAra shrugged.
A continued search bore no further fruit, nor any sign of the Major himself.
'Ah, let him find his own way to hell,' McAra concluded. 'I think this is what I was after anyhow.' And he brandished his acquisition.
Back at the inn his munificence continued on display to accompany his abrupt high good humour. Poring over the map in the privacy of the snug with pints of port to hand the two men were able, after animated discussion, to translate the chart into some recognisable pattern.
'What's this got to do with the man Grundy, though?' Cassels asked as they settled down to another dinner, McAra more relaxed than on the previous evening.
'I've been brought into this affair by the Palace,' McAra claimed, 'because of my great capacity for insight. If I tell you what it's all about I'll have to swear you to silence on it until the whole business is finished with.'
'No bother. I'm the very man to have at your side.'
'It's not widely known, but the Queen is due in Edinburgh shortly. We – that is me and Prime Minister Peel – got word that there was some kind of plot connected with the visit. There are some traitorous fuckers crawling around in Leith or Edinburgh.'
Cassels raised an eyelid but otherwise remained glacially restrained.
'And your Major DeWitt or the fellow Grundy would be mixed up in it?'

HIDDEN

'There's nothing much to go on yet but I'm the man to get to the bottom of it.'

'Jesus, what the name of Christ is that awful smell?'

McAra waved a nonchalant hand.

'Nothing. A wee complaint of mine. Now this'll be beyond your powers of comprehension but I read this map as being a right important clue to what's going on.'

'And how do you get to that? There's nothing on it that says anything about your Leith or Edinburgh.'

'I told you – you don't have the nous for this kind of work. You need to be the sharpest of the sharp. Like me. For now I can't say for certain what this bit chart has to do with what's afoot, but it's something.'

'It's something? That's what the sharpest mind can make of it?'

'Don't get sarcastic with me. You're an ordinary peeler. I'm the country's top secret agent. Do you want to get in on this or not? For if you make a decent fist of it I'll let Prince Albert know, and that would do you no harm, eh?'

Cassels rubbed his nose and with an effort suppressed the inclination to punch McAra's face through to the back of his skull.

'So tomorrow will you take me in that wagon of yours along the way of this map and see if we can make out what's what? Or are you bound back to Glasgow and a life of perjury?'

'Perjury? I never said a lie in court. Except when I needed to.'

'It's the port playing a trick on me. Maybe the word's penury. Like when you've not got a halfpenny in your pocket.'

'I can't stand the sight or smell of you, but I'm in no hurry to get back to the Trongate.'

The air of antagonism was a little less coagulating the following morning when the pair summoned the ferry to re–cross the shimmering calm of Loch Long to Coulport. Affecting nonchalance McAra asked the skipper how deep he thought the loch was. Told that it was around a hundred feet he nodded and was offered for confirmation the view that nothing heavy resting on the bottom was ever likely to break the surface. He then spent the rest of the crossing heroically throwing up over the side of the vessel and loosing off a barrage of assorted but equally nauseating effluvia. Cassels took refuge from this odiferant onslaught in his

HIDDEN

wagon, emerging only when the boat had arrived on the far side of the loch.
'There's the *Ceasg* tied up,' McAra managed through pale lips. 'Who's that for?'
The ferryman shrugged.
'Some fellow that came over yesterday. There's a few bob in it for me if I keep the thing in trim.'
'He'll be back soon then?'
'Somebody will be was all he said.'
The well–rested team hitched to the wagon carried the officers the few miles to the hamlet of Portincaple which was circled in red ink on DeWitt's map which McAra read as significant. On that drowsy August day the only establishment that looked to be of interest was the blacksmith's shop. Relieved to be at some distance from his passenger Cassels dismounted and asked the smith if he knew of the Major or had had any dealings with him. The officer's description of the former soldier brought a hint of enlightenment to the big man's face.
'He came down here a day or two ago asking after horses but I usually just shoe the things. Then away he was on the ferry to Coulport. Just back the way youse came.'
'He was on his own, was he?'
'Aye, but he was after asking if a friend of his had come by. That was a fellow came up here maybe a week or so earlier. Then he was back yesterday in the opposite direction. And off he went on a good wee mount up the side of the loch like the devil was chasing at his rear.'
'He never said what he was doing down here?'
'Aye – he gave me his life story from the time in his ma's womb until the very hour he came up that road there. And I heard all about every bowl of oatmeal he'd had from the age of five.'
'No need for that – you'll get my boot in your sporran for your trouble,' McAra warned from the relative safety of his elevated place on the wagon.
'Away and shite in the woods, you wee bugger or I'll pull the arms off you.'
'You've a rare, canny gift for the questioning, true enough,' Cassels remarked once they were back on the dusty track heading towards

HIDDEN

the village of Arrochar at the end of the loch. 'I'll bet your prisoners just break down and confess as soon as you open your mouth.'
'You watch me careful, and you'll learn a few things, boy.'
'Mostly how to let my insides get a good airing, eh?'
And the ten miles on to Tarbet were conducted amid a welter of mutual antipathy that the dawn armistice had called to a short–lived halt. By the time they arrived at the village on the western shore of Loch Lomond McAra's ill–feeling was to be assuaged only by the liberal application of porter and the afternoon was well advanced before the wagon was again in motion, both men in much better humour and singing
"I sat beside the streamlet,
I watched the water flow,
As we together watched it
One little year ago."

The next location which DeWitt's map had highlighted was Luss which was reached by early evening, but McAra had slyly acquired a bottle of brandy in Tarbet and long before arrival at the next stop on their itinerary he was confined to the back of the wagon, repeatedly caterwauling the first two lines of Eliza Cook's "The Old Arm Chair"
"I love it, I love it; and who shall dare
To chide me for loving that old arm chair?"

until Cassels reached in through the swinging door, seized the bottle and hurled into the roadside grass. With no idea what McAra wanted to do in the village the irritated Glaswegian tethered the crossbreds a little beyond the last house and strolled the length of the single clearly defined street, not feeling entirely sober but certainly in much better condition than his travelling companion whose muted tones continued to issue from his captivity in the now–locked van. The only activity in the warmth of the approaching twilight was to be located by the rhythmic sound of metal being beaten and, following the trail set down by McAra's enquiry at Portincaple, Cassels traced it to a small livery stable at the rear of a low stone cottage at the north end of the hamlet.
Identifying himself in terms less grandiose than those his colleague

HIDDEN

would have used he repeated the description of Major DeWitt and, neither knowing nor caring why, if the soldier had come by within the past few days.

'Big, upright fellow with great whiskers,' the stable–hand confirmed, pausing from his work at the anvil. 'Aye, we've an arrangement for a change of mounts coming up. Fine customer – I've had the money off him already. He's not a robber or anything is he? I got the siller in good faith. A bit over the odds if the team he brings in is up to the mark.'

'When's the business set for?'

'Not fixed, but soon enough. All I've to do is make sure the team's here and ready any day next week.'

None the wiser for the exchange Cassels asked for his own team to be fed and minded for the night and sauntered back to where his wagon was furiously rocking to and fro and from which a hysterical voice was bawling 'Help! An elephant! There's an elephant in here! Herds of anchovies! Get me out!'

With a grunt the policeman unlocked the vehicle and set McAra at staggering liberty. Wild–eyed and waving his arms the disorientated officer gradually sank into mumbled reticence, sat down by the roadside and, straight–backed and immobile, fell asleep for an hour while Cassels found a tiny shop where he bought some bread and cheese to sustain himself throughout the operatic snoring and muttering of his unfettered confederate. Some time later he was chatting idly with the proprietor of the livery stable when the latter pointed back in the direction of the wagon. McAra had come to and was bounding about on all–fours making strange, throaty, barking noises at a passing butterfly.

'I best away and get a collar and chain on that,' Cassels sighed, 'before it gets into a field and starts worrying the sheep.'

'A passing fever of the brain, nothing more,' McAra claimed as the sun went down, but after a night lying under the wagon with a sack pulled up to his chin he was not in the most ebullient of humours when the pair set off the next morning. In Drymen they paused for breakfast, McAra once again compelled to extract a handful of coppers from his rapidly diminishing capital. Another glance at the map he had expropriated together with Cassels' account of the stopover in Luss had persuaded him that he had already learned

HIDDEN

from the journey all that he was likely to derive from the expedition.

'I've had enough of this traipsing around the countryside,' he announced as they set off eastwards again. 'I need some decent buildings about me, and streets and real pubs and women. If you're still ready to go with me let's get back to Aberdeen.'

'I'm still with you if somebody's going to go on paying me. So how do we get to Aberdeen from here? And what do we want there?'

'Aberdeen? Nothing would drag me up there. What do you want to go there for?'

'But you said... Never mind. It'll be Edinburgh, right? What about my money?'

'Never mind your bloody money. I'm in charge of the police through there so you'll get your pay, and more. If you do right by me you'll likely end up with a peerage and an estate in Caithness.'

'Aye, no doubt. Just make sure my pay's coming in.'

'God almighty, man. Have you no pride? No dignity? Look at me – sent all the way up from London at Her Majesty's request, putting my life in danger in every back alley in Edinburgh, trying to put some discipline in the Glasgow force, uncovering these fucking shenanigans in the arsehole of Argyll and keeping you out of trouble in every damn village we've been through. And do I go on about money? Do I complain about my lot?'

'Aye, you're a right wee hero and that's a fact. Now tell me which way you want this wagon pointed and get in the back out of my sight. You'd make a pile of shite look like a decent dinner.'

'Don't try that tone on me, you fucker. I'm a sinister chap.'

And having issued approximate course–plotting directions McAra retreated to the cool interior of the vehicle to sulk and nurse his virulent hangover. The onward journey to Edinburgh was conducted sedately and the sole lapse in decorum came on the dusty main street of the village of Gargunnock – where yet another team of horses was apparently to be kept on standby – when Cassels called a halt to progress at the chortling yell of "*Gardyloo, gardyloo, you bastards,*" from the rear of the wagon. Hurrying to discover the occasion of the joyous clamour he found his passenger, having made the most of the contents of yet another bottle which he had secreted about his person, hanging over the

HIDDEN

tailgate triumphantly spraying an artistic zigzag of ochreous urine through the unmoving air.

HIDDEN

CHAPTER 11 AUGUST 1842

In her brother's absence Emma Halley had given some thought to his proposal that she somehow inveigle herself into the circle of notables apparently gathered around Hiram Charles D T Stuart. Although she was on distantly friendly terms with Earl Bonaly it had been her husband Alaric who had conducted relations with this group of distinguished dignitaries and was privy to their clandestine business. That she should abruptly manifest some concern with their *sub rosa* schemes was quite likely, she thought, to incur the suspicion of the clique's members.

Emma doubted her capacity for duplicity and, having neither her husband's overbearing assurance nor her brother's tactless assertiveness, she had been at a loss to work out a plan of action. However this difficulty was overcome by the Earl's unexpected incursion into her affairs the day after McAra's departure for the west of Scotland. Bonaly, only an occasional and peripheral member of the group, had always struck her as the most easy–going and on his visits to consult Alaric he had been at pains to exchange pleasantries with her and invite her views on the state of the world. There was something about his portly, cheerful, twinkling personality that put her at ease.

'My friends thought,' he said, 'that in Alaric's long absence you might be persuaded to take his place among them. For myself I have no conception of what course they are planning.'

Surprised at her own suspicious intuition, Emma calculated that the affable emissary's approach was designed to open a channel to the substantial resource that had found its way into her husband's account. Resorting to her brother's propensity for unprincipled guile she took this unanticipated opportunity to insert herself into the confederacy which McAra had tried to encourage.

'Such is our marriage,' she lied with the unwonted proficiency as her devious sibling, 'that we communicate with each other the particulars of our affairs and so I am quite prepared to take my husband's place, but only if my incursion were to be unanimously welcomed. I have no wish to appear an intruder.'

HIDDEN

'I come with the group's specific request and invitation. I am no more than their humble delegate. Their affairs, I'm afraid, remain a book closed to me.'

Having arrived at the outcome she had designed Emma was in a quandary. Her brother had pressed her to take the chance to obtain some insight into the mechanism of this cryptic coterie; but now that she had so easily and unexpectedly accomplished that occasion she quailed at the prospect.

'You must understand that Alaric and I have been the most cherished and devoted of companions. I will do nothing that I consider would run against the grain of his judgement. If I consent to meet Sir Hudson and the others it must be on that basis alone.'

'It would be out of the question for it not to be so. I shall make the arrangements.'

Silently cursing the imp that had goaded her into this coming encounter she summoned Casper to see the Earl out into the stifling summer heat. But before he had reached the door he emitted a cry of alarm and seized Casper by the arm, pointing at the cage in the corner.

'What in Heaven's name…?'

It was left to Emma to explain.

'That's my brother's friend and bodyguard.'

'A rat!'

'Yes – and so is Balthazar,' she said and settled into an armchair to turn over in her mind the extent of her regret at her own unanticipated audacity.

Much later the same day in the back room of the Red Herring pub Sebastian Bradley was holding confidential consultation with his most dependable accomplices including the former seaman Josiah Dicken. The latter had just emerged from the offices of the Dowe company on the other side of Leith Street and was not in the best of humours. He had been in search of Walter Grundy, only to be informed that this mysterious agent had taken himself off on private business to the west of Scotland. In the course of his conversation with Hector Dowe he had learned that someone else had been anxious to have words with Grundy.

Bradley was becoming impatient at this diversion from his agenda. 'Who cares a damn where Grundy is the now? We've our own work

HIDDEN

to get sorted out.'
'I give a damn,' Dicken answered, unwisely raising his voice and drawing the other's long, choleric look. 'And I'll tell you why. This fellow that was after Grundy – the way Dowe described him I tell you it was that was the fellow that near burst my head and had the price of a couple of drinks out of my jacket.'
Bradley sucked in his lips and thought for a few moments before inviting Dicken to run through in more detail Dowe's account of the officer's appearance.
'That little fucker, eh? Aye, might be the same as the one that some of my lads ran into here a while ago.'
'And did he have the tin out of their pockct? He's a sly wee bugger, I tell you. And did they mind what they were saying to him? He's a cunning rat and that's for sure.'
Bradley hesitated and turned over in his mind the vague reports he had had of the encounter between his too garrulous underlings and McAra several days earlier, and these were just enough to set his mind at rest.
'They said the wee snake was well out of it that time. He'd have no mind of anything from that night, he was that pissed it was all he could do to crawl into a hole somewhere.'
'Still and all it would be a sound enough idea to get shot of him the first chance we get – dump him in the harbour at Leith or spade him into a hole up in the Pentlands. Would you be up for that?'
'Don't you go pulling that down on yourself. The last thing we need is for the police to be taking an interest in us the now, and that would likely be the way of it if you done the wee fellow in. He's just a drunken nuisance. I wager the man's mind has gone the same way as the rest of him so never pay him heed even if you can find him, that is.'
'Aye, I wonder, though…'
But Bradley ignored Dicken's homicidal contemplation and sat pensive for a while as the rest of his muttering company exchanged glances that carried in them a hint of disquiet that a misstep now might expose their endeavours to the eye of the law.
'Another thing,' Dicken went on. 'There's been no sight nor sign of that dwarf Newsome.'
'He'll be lying low then, but we need him. He's the best driver in

HIDDEN

the city and our folk have made it plain enough – it's Newsome they want and they'll take nobody other. The main thing is that all he knows is when they want him. They've said nothing to him about the where. So if he's taken there's no great harm to us. But anyhow you get out there and find that grumpy goblin.'

With this item duly disposed of and Dicken dispatched on his mission Bradley set about outlining the operation he had been charged with mounting to coincide with the forthcoming Royal visit. Walter Grundy had pointed to the great advantage of the Royal visit as a platform for broadcast of the cause, and that the actions of the agitators would be supported by generous funding if they came off as he had designed. Over three hours he rehearsed the components of the complex campaign he had assembled. Dissenting voices were heard, if only briefly. Most of those present were senior members of the Chartist movement but belonged on different points of a broad spectrum.

It was to the more radical of them that Bradley's undertaking appealed, and especially to Harold Pendle from the Glasgow branch. Only three months earlier the movement had presented to the House of Commons its petition demanding voting rights and dramatic changes in the electoral system and in the organisation of parliamentary constituencies. Despite the document having over three million signatures its terms had been rejected and frustration was rapidly being translated into widespread unrest. Although this had been dealt with robustly by the authorities the demand for reform remained undiminished. Reaction to the dismissal of the petition's provisions was mixed – moderate activists favoured maintaining their case by continued lobbying and peaceful demonstration but the majority of those gathered in the Red Herring were in favour of more violent means of achieving their objective.

While Bradley had continued to espouse the most extreme measures to compel recognition of the campaign he had, too, been careful to conceal the consequent future Grundy had promised him and Dicken by the shores of the Pacific. And he was especially careful to divulge nothing of what Grundy asserted his unrevealed paymasters might be intent on. Even the more bellicose of his followers could baulk at the suspicion that the assassination of a

HIDDEN

Monarch might be in the offing, though the life of the Prime Minister was unlikely to be held so sacrosanct.

'We need to stretch the coppers and soldier boys to breaking point,' he said once the doubters' protestations had been silenced. 'We get things going at Leith, Portobello and Queensferry. And in Glasgow and Dundee on top of that. Youse will know best yourselves how many you can call on and who the best men are for the job. Broken widows – that's one thing, but there has to be plenty of noise with it. Sticks and stones, lads – and torches as well. I'll want to hear in a day or two how many you've all managed to call up. We need nothing short of proper riot, you hear? There's some of you have been at this game already so you need to use that when the time comes.'

The demonstrations he planned had to be coordinated so that the resources of the civil and military authorities would have the greatest difficulty in offering adequate response. Locally an assault on the Royal Exchange where the City Council held its meetings was to take place as early in the day as possible. As a finale to his oration he produced what he considered to be the *pièce de résistance* – several small boats had been expropriated and were already strategically stationed in the harbours of Leith and South Queensferry. Just before the Queen's arrival these, loaded with whatever combustible materials had been stockpiled would be loosed on whichever ferries, steamships, clippers, barques, yachts or schooners could be set alight. It was probably too much to hope that the RY *Royal George* could be got at but at least an attempt would be made.

'This is our chance, lads: we'll be heard or be damned.'

'And what about this Newsome?' Harold Pendle asked. 'Say he's gone over the side? Then what?'

'There's folk want Newsome in on this,' Bradley said. 'The wee titch is a genius with the horses and somebody needs that bit talent – they never told me what for, exactly, but that's the way of it. That's all I want to say the now.'

'One weak link and we're all bound for the jail. What's this Newsome to us?'

'To *us*, nothing. Leave it at that.'

'One more thing,' Pendle put in. 'My boys are up for this and no

HIDDEN

mistake. But some of them aren't that happy with the idea that there's others behind the plan that we don't know, nor nothing about them. And they're the ones that won't be beat with police clubs or shot at or thrown in the Calton. Are you going to tell us who they are and what it is they're after?'

'They're after the same as the rest of us. These are people with money and clout but want to see our folk get a fair deal from these bastards in Westminster. They'll be no good to nobody if word gets out about them. Their money'll be lost to us and so will some of the best of them that are behind the tactics. But you don't have to worry – I'm the man to keep them in their right place when the time comes.'

Bradley's extempore assertion expressed conviction but was without substance. He had been locating refuge in the reflection that even if the plot went utterly wrong there would be little or nothing to connect either him or Dicken to it. The workers' protests were part of a long–established movement and even if Walter Grundy – the sole intermediary between them and the covert intriguers – were taken he could hardly incriminate the pair beyond their role in organising their dissidents. Bradley was no naïf – he understood perfectly that whatever was motivating the mysterious community prepared to finance the coming agitation it was not a desire to promote the interests of his own constituency. If assassination for obscure political or dissenting ends was their objective it had nothing to do with him.

By the time the meeting was adjourned and the participants gone their separate ways night was falling on the city and Bradley emerged from the back room of the pub to escape the suffocating reek of sweat and tobacco smoke. Wrapped in an unnecessary great coat and with a broad brimmed hat pulled low on his forehead the figure at the otherwise deserted bar beckoned him into his company. Waiting until the barman had filled their glasses and gone to clear the debris from the snug the anonymous newcomer spoke quietly and without looking at the other.

'She'll be arriving at that private harbour at Granton on the first of the month – that's a Thursday. That's all the City Council have heard. They don't have the exact time."

'What I can't make out,' Bradley complained 'is why you put a

HIDDEN

marksman's nest on the pier just to be found out? Where's the sense in that?'

'Look, there's a copper up from London supposed to be spying out the lay of the land. He's useless but there'll be more of them by the time the Queen gets here. So if I have him pointed in the wrong direction it'll be all to the good for us. The rest will follow him.'

'Well, I suppose you know what you're at. What I can't see is what's in all this for you.'

'That's my affair but I'll say this to you and no other – I'll not be short of a florin when the time comes. And I'll make sure there's not a soul knows how I've come by it.'

'Fair enough. I've no bone to pick with you or with these folk that Grundy's fronting. Whoever they are.'

'You're right to leave it lie. I have it that they're up against Peel for going the way of the Papists back in '29, so maybe…'

'Don't worry. I couldn't care less if they're Presbyterians or Parsees so long as they're handing out the money for what my folk are about.'

Bradley paused for a moment, then decided to voice his concern at the news Dicken had brought.

'Yon midget Newsome's gone right out of sight and these bankers of ours aren't going to be pleased if they don't have him when the time comes.'

'I can put your mind to rest on that. He got himself thrown in the cells up on the High Street but I'll have him out tomorrow. He'll be ready when the time comes.'

'This is a damn serious thing we're at.'

'Aye,' Andrew Laurie said, 'none more serious.'

HIDDEN
CHAPTER 12 AUGUST 1842

Horace Trapp, once the enforcer and good friend of the now deceased London gangster Arthur Bowler, was a vengeful man, and a resourceful one. Hardly surprised at the lack of enthusiasm or diligence on the part of the police in pursuing the perpetrator of his boss's murder he had elected himself the chief investigator. His first inclination was to suspect that some villainous rival had been responsible but his extensive contacts across the metropolis had uncovered not the slightest indication that any of Bowler's felonious competitors had pulled the trigger.

A more alarming possibility had been that one of his own gang had mustered the resolution to do the deed. If that had been the case his own position would have been in jeopardy. But no–one had emerged as a potential successor and no attempt had been made to purloin the funds Bowler had laid up in various locations that had been secured not by secrecy but by fear. A liberal scattering of bribes among the denizens of the underworld and the less principled members of the capital's police force had generated only a single, not particularly helpful, revelation: that Bowler had been dispatched by the high–speed application of a .31 round. But, as the informant advised Trapp, that titbit was unlikely to lead anywhere – a weapon of that sort could be found in the pantry of every murderous hooligan in the city.

It remained to consider that the assassination had been committed by someone in Bowler's palace guard. Their numbers were few and their fidelity had been unquestioned for years and again Trapp had unearthed nothing to suggest that any were implicated. The sole resort left to him, it seemed, was to discover what had become of Bowler's faithful driver – he knew that Bowler had been accustomed to sharing confidences with the obnoxious Scot and at least there could be no question of his bearing any responsibility for Bowler's fatal mishap. McAra had been not only like an obedient whelp but was always too drunk or too lazy to take such unspeakable action. In fact there had to be a real possibility that the diminutive creature had shared Bowler's fate and maybe have been

HIDDEN

dunked in the Thames amid the sewage and cholera. Still, Trapp thought, if he could be found he might shed some light on the event. The most likely thing was that he was lying low somewhere in fear for his life, tarred, as he would be, by association with Arthur Bowler.

But despite all his resources and diligence Horace had failed to identify McAra's whereabouts or doom until he remembered how Bowler used to tease McAra with his mocking imitation of his accent and references to his belonging on the scaffold in the Lawnmarket in Edinburgh. Heading north on a mission to track down Bowler's former subordinate without more definite information to guide him struck his ruffian troops as futile and this view was communicated to him in decisive terms. With Bowler's dispatch it was for Horace to lead the gang, keep order in its ranks and direct its larcenous and often gory endeavours. His absence would leave the ship rudderless. And anyway even if McAra had departed for Edinburgh, which was by no means certain, there was little chance of tracking him down in a city whose population was far in excess of a hundred thousand.

But Trapp was determined to establish who was behind the killing of Bowler and to mete out revenge, and McAra, having taken fright and fled from a slayer likely to associate him with the same Bowler, might well be able to point to the culprit. And the size of the city notwithstanding Trapp had two reasons for believing he could find McAra – there would hardly be a city centre pub that he was not recognised in; and if his lodgings in London had been anything to go by he would be quartered in some squalid residence in either the Old Town or Leith. That, at any rate, was the view offered by Magnus Wallace, a bleak, ill–tempered Highlander and the brutal disciplinarian now keeping the rank and file in line. He was vaguely familiar with the city and not unaware of its less salubrious neighbourhoods. Having issued a warning that only routine business was to be conducted in his absence Trapp, recruiting Wallace as his travelling companion, headed for the mail coach to Edinburgh for which Trapp had arranged tickets.

'We're off on a fool's errand,' Wallace advised him as he reluctantly joined his new boss on the way across the city. 'There's hardly a cat's chance that we'll find the wee drone. And even if we do, what

HIDDEN

then? The man's too far gone in drink to tell you anything. And mind this – Bowler's dead and gone and all this running about after whoever done him in is a waste of time. It'll not bring him back and we've better things to be doing.'

'Better than getting hold of who murdered my best friend, is it? You'll do well to hold your tongue and do what you're told. If it got out that Arthur could have a bullet put in his head and I never done a thing about it where would that all come to a stop? Some bastard would have the lot of us in the river.'

'If the coppers nor nobody else couldn't find who done it you should be in the Hanwell if you think McAra can do it for you.'

The pair were loudly disputing the wisdom of the expedition as they had arrived at the White Horse in Fetter Lane where, amid the racket of the stabling of some seventy horses, the northbound coach was minutes away from leaving. Their two travelling companions inside the vehicle were unwise enough to express their amusement at the altercation which drew an intimidating reaction from Trapp who invited them to keep their levity under tight control.

With some forty hours of intimacy ahead of them the four passengers in the coach kept themselves occupied by remaining in surly silence through the changes of teams at Ware, Buntingford and Royston and not until the stop at The George at Huntington – almost sixty miles from London – did the quartet resign to some degree of association. The stilted conversation wandered around such pressing issues as the weather, the discomfort of long-distance travel, the quality of the food that had been on offer at The Hardwicke Arms and the probability that, with the rapid expansion of the railways, the days of the stagecoach were numbered.

By the time they reached the change at The Bell and Angel at Stilton enough familiarity had settled over the travellers – now weary and less guarded – for more casually amicable exchanges to lighten the claustrophobic atmosphere in the lurching carriage. The man and woman sitting opposite the thugs introduced themselves as Mr and Mrs Landry and, talking for Wallace as well as himself, Trapp, in reply to an idle enquiry, announced that they were businessmen heading for a meeting in Edinburgh. Stumbling over the detail of their "*business*" he decided that they were involved in the alcohol trade. This proved to be an unfortunate choice as the

HIDDEN

elderly couple across from them explained that they were landlord and landlady of The White Hart and other establishments in the city. Hastily switching tack Trapp claimed that he and his friend were novices in the field, were on their way to hear the advice of a distant relative but would be happy to absorb any of the finer points of the trade that the opportunity of the journey might afford.

With no interest in the subject aside from a long–term inclination to sample large amounts of its products Trapp and Wallace paid little heed to Landry's tireless expounding of the vagaries of the of the life of a publican. By Newark Wallace had fallen asleep and Trapp was pretending attention to the monologue while inwardly cursing himself for not attending to Wallace's enjoining against the journey. All the same, the encounter, he thought, might prove fortuitous when he began to recognise from Wallace's earlier remarks the references made by the couple to the parts of Edinburgh where they plied their trade.

As the coach was approaching Barnby Moor early the following morning the sky seemed to lower about it and in an instant the torrential summer rain turned the dusty road into a quagmire that at first merely slowed progress but within half an hour sent the vehicle slewing on a bend to embed the rear wheels in a gurgling ditch. The guard and driver, prepared for the unpredictability of the weather, donned waterproof capes, instructed the passengers to clamber out and, watched by their miserable clients, tried to assist the horses heave the coach free. Despite much shouting at the team, cracking of a whip and shoving at the back of the diligence the coach stayed stubbornly stuck in the cloying mud. Drenched and despairing of these efforts Trapp and Wallace took charge of the operation. The pair shoved the exhausted guard aside and with a single heave had the vehicle back on the road.

'By God, gentlemen,' Landry pronounced with admiration when they were under way with no damage done, 'you almost leave me speechless. I've never seen strength like that. I can tell you there would be no shortage of work for you fellows at the front end of a pub if you *are* minded to try your hand at the profession…'

'Not our line of work. We're more… managers than…'

'Of course, I beg your pardon. Well, we'd be more than happy to advise you on that side of the trade. We own pubs but we don't

HIDDEN

ourselves often venture into them.'

Another protracted but more cordial silence enveloped the drowsy travellers until their journey was again broken by a planned half hour halt at The Swan in York while the horses were again changed and a table for dining had been reserved for the passengers. The ensuing strange interlude was to become fixed in the memory of both Landrys. The inn was busy with a clearly wealthy clientele and conversation was general but muted. As bowls of mutton stew were being distributed by bustling drudges in décolleté dresses and colourful aprons the main door was quietly opened and three men entered, glanced round at the assembled customers, closed the door behind them and announced their intention by producing double barrelled percussion cap pistols and advising quiet and a cooperative attitude.

'Purses, watches, jewels and money on the tables, ladies and gentlemen,' the tallest of the intruders instructed. 'No need for anyone to be damaged. Give us a minute and we'll be gone from you forever.'

The invading trio betrayed little sign of confidence in successfully prosecuting their engagement – so nervous were they that their weapons visibly shook in their hands. Not that this rendered them more amenable to debate. The slip of a sweaty finger on a trigger was a more predictable outcome than it would have been had the thieves conveyed an air of calm professionalism. Shock, disbelief and fear accompanied by one or two fainting fits served to delay accommodation but as one of the raiders passed among the tables holding a sack the solicited valuables were produced with varying degrees of reluctance. As this collector approached the table occupied by the Landrys, Trapp and Wallace the latter pair made no attempt to offer up belongings for exaction. Instead they sat stock–still, expressionless and the epitome of self–possession.

'Let's be having it,' the intruder ordered and, coming within inches of the huge Scotsman, waved the gun in his face. Probably the man had made many mistakes in his short career but this was to prove the last one. Moving faster than an eye could have followed Wallace seized the pistol, tore it from its owner's grasp, brought the butt crashing down with fatal force on his skull, shifted his grip and, with the speed and dexterity born of years of experience,

HIDDEN

aimed the weapon and, in one movement, thumbed back the hammers and casually shot both the other intending robbers through the face.

Rolling his eyes, Trapp turned to Landry and said almost apologetically, 'Amateurs.'

The ensuing uproar – screams, shouts, aimless dashing about, hysterics – left Trapp and Wallace undisturbed in their place sipping wine until the brouhaha died down and the landlord, quivering from head to foot, ran from the building to summon whatever help was to be had. In a short time the place was invaded by constables, a doctor and a posse of inquisitive passers–by. A cursory interrogation of the many witnesses was adequate to exculpate the unruffled Wallace and with the arrival of a local magistrate statements were heard and written and relative quiet was restored. It was, however, several hours before the Edinburgh–bound coach and its passengers were permitted to take the road again and the atmosphere in the vehicle was, not surprisingly, dense with unspoken intensity. Through several further changes of teams and halts over the next two hundred miles hardly a word or look passed between the badly shaken Landrys on one side and the unperturbed gangsters on the other.

Arriving in the Scottish capital half a day late Mr and Mrs Landry, still in a condition of incredulity, insisted on entertaining their companions to a late dinner at their rooms above The White Hart in the Grassmarket. Knowing nothing of the city the two men accepted this hospitality without demur and behaved impeccably throughout the evening, amusing their hosts with fictitious tales of their labours and ambitions for the future in the wine trade. Only after Mr Landry had had many more drinks than he was accustomed to did he revert to the appalling incident in York.

'Gentlemen,' he said, 'I have to commend you on your courage and ability to look out for yourselves. And for others, of course. May I ...'

He hesitated, not sure how to put or pursue his point. Trapp anticipated the issue.

'Ah, my friend – London is no place for the timorous. Over the years we've had to learn to fend for ourselves – not an easy thing for the law–abiding, but there you have it.'

HIDDEN

'Well, you know, Edinburgh has more than its fair share of problems in that regard. Our pubs most certainly can be places of hazard as well as recreation. If you were inclined to learn a little more about how to run them I'd be delighted to have you installed as supervisors in any of our establishments. You might find the experience useful.'

'Ah, we'd not be up to, I'm afraid. What we'll be after is the more refined market down south – Hampstead, say, or somewhere of the like. We'll not be looking to deal with the rabble, if you take my meaning. We're a little too… genteel for the rough trade.'

Mr Landry could barely suppress a smile but was disinclined to let the matter rest. He had a very specific appointment in mind.

'I quite understand,' he said. 'But knowing how to deal tactfully and even sympathetically with a clientele perhaps a bit too given to over–indulgence will always be a useful competence.'

This was not quite the experience he was proposing. Of the half dozen pubs he was master of none was free of the criminally troublesome and the casualty rate amongst his doorkeepers – including J J Haggerty – was high. If Trapp and Wallace could be recruited as landlords in name but bouncers in reality Landry was confident that good order would be maintained wherever they were stationed.

'For an instance,' he went on, 'the very pub below us attracts both the quality and the common herd. The nicety of judicious management is there for the absorbing. And for the moment the post of… *overseer* is unfilled. The previous incumbent is… indisposed.'

'Ah, we're here on our own concern.'

But a surreptitious thought had crept across Trapp's mind. If the object of his expedition was to track down McAra there was no reason why in addition some profit might not be turned at the same time. Wallace had made no effort to disguise his belief that the whole purpose of the jaunt north was not worth the modest expense – it would be little short of a miracle if McAra could be tracked down, and even more surprising if, in the unlikely event of his being found, he would be of the least help in solving the mystery of Bowler's murder. But Landry's suggestion was dropping into the lap of the pursuers the opportunity to offset outlay and their

HIDDEN

reckless absence from London.

'But if it would be of some small assistance to you...'

Tapping Wallace on the knee Horace leaned forward and with the air of a man keen to offer assistance left the implied concession dangling. Generating income through taverns and taprooms was well-known to the two visitors. Actual participation in the business was, in Trapp's view, optional. Conferring the benefit of guaranteed protection from the depredations of the unwashed was an alternative not entirely unknown to him and his colleagues. In fact, a flurry of shouted expletives from the street below accompanied by the sound of breaking glass drew the attention of Landry and his guests who gathered at the mullion window to peer down at the altercation.

'A too regular event,' Landry sighed as he retreated to his place at the table. 'You'll forgive me if I have given the impression that I think your... well, those abilities you have demonstrated between Barnby Moor and here... you know,' a shrug of the shoulders, an opening of hands in mid-air, 'I'm not suggesting, of course, that your talents don't extend beyond... the physical. No, no. I'm sure you would be more than capable of... you know, running the business. If you wanted to...'

Trapp and Wallace listened to this hesitant encomium with well-concealed amusement and, allowing a gap of propitious silence to open up, Trapp himself, quickly following up his deviously tentative proposal, said, 'You've been a generous host, sir. Certainly it would hardly inconvenience us to have some regard to your proposition.'

'Why, gentlemen, I'd be delighted if you would at least bestow some consideration on it. As I say, I own half a dozen public houses. You might want to visit them to see... if they might... suit... in any way...'

Landry tailed off, unable to formulate clearly what he hoped these prospective employees might bring to his business. There was, though, no need for him to be more precise. The interlude on the pavement outside the apartment could afford no plainer requirement of them.

'May we offer you accommodation for the night?' Mrs Landry asked. 'And perhaps tomorrow you could sample the atmosphere

HIDDEN

of The White Hart down below us and then tell us what you think.'
'Too kind, madam.' Trapp raised his glass to indicate that some sort of alliance of their fortunes might well be in the offing.

After a pleasant and genteel evening and a night of comfortable sleep in the relative luxury of the Landrys' residence Wallace and Trapp spent the day touring the area in the faint hope of setting eyes on McAra or at least of hearing something of him. After all, as Trapp had repeatedly remarked, the little fellow's behaviour, appearance and general comportment combined to make him a distinctive figure. But the hours of daylight and their slightly less disreputable citizenry brought no early enlightenment. That evening, after being again regally entertained by the Landrys, the pair presented themselves quite late at the bar of The White Hart to observe, as they told their hosts, the conduct of the business.

The forbidding presence of the giant Wallace and the stone–faced thuggishness of Trapp produced a mixed reaction. The bar staff viewed them with trepidation and served with ingratiating politeness and obliging haste. As closing time approached the clientele became noisier and prone to internecine jostling, raised voices and mutual hostility – all the pleasures of a night's cheerful imbibing with acquaintances and unfortunate strangers. However any commotion was reserved for the cobbled Grassmarket outside, the topers filing uneasily past the two strangers.

'Which one of youse is the new fellow taking J J's place?' the recently recruited blousy, self–confident barmaid asked when only Trapp and Wallace remained.

'J J? And who would that be?'

'I never knew him then but he was our doorman that got his foot shot off. No use to us now, is he.'

'A foot shot off? Still, if he's the size of Mr Wallace here there'd still be yards of him left. How did that happen to the poor lad?' Trapp asked, savouring the tall glass of malt that rewarded his very presence.

'Some row with a visitor. J J could be short of temper.'

'And now he's short of feet? It sounds like the work has a bit danger stuck on it.'

'You'd be the first I ever saw that was bigger than yon Irishman. There'll be no trouble for the likes of you. Or for this pal of yours

HIDDEN

here – man that's as wide as he is tall.'
'Well, maybe we're in a good way to make sure you don't need to worry about folk that go around shooting the bits off your bouncer or anybody else. Listen, we're friends of Mr Landry and it's looking after places the likes of this that we make a living. Who's the boss in here?'
'That would be me. Tessie Doyle. I'm the manager and I'll not have nobody forget it.'
'A lady at the helm, then? You wouldn't see that everywhere. So it would be you would be in charge of making sure the place is proper looked after.'
'Me and none other. Mr Landry leaves the whole lot up to me. I can promise you a fair wage and decent bed and board.'
'Aye, well, it would need to be a fair wage to keep this wee place in good order. There must be plenty spent in here of a night.'
'That wouldn't be nothing for you to worry about. And you'd get the pay if there's a rammy or not.'
'And Mr Landry has more pubs in the city, I hear?'
'It's no business of yours, but Mr Landry is wealthy enough not even to visit them so long as he gets the money his missis reckons is about right. Anyhow, never mind that. Are youse here for the job or what?'
'We'll be having a wee look round the whole lot of them and let you know. And we'll be telling you the cost of our services when the time comes.'
'No, no, laddie. I'm the one who'll be telling you.'
Trapp and Wallace together issued a short, derisive laugh.
'Aye,' Tessie put in while the muted sniggering continued, 'well, it's me and Mr Landry make up the rules in here. So if you think it's otherwise you can bugger off and pish in the Forth.'
'Just tell us the other pubs we've got to go and see. Mr Landry wants us to have a peek at the whole lot of them.'
For the whole of the next day Trapp and Wallace trawled round the city examining the Landry estate and by evening had made up their minds that it offered sufficient promise of reward to make the journey to Edinburgh worthwhile whether they tracked down McAra or not. They debated the wisdom of billeting themselves on the Landrys for the duration of their probably extended stay and

HIDDEN

decided to take lodgings in an anonymous back street in Leith from which they could operate without detection. When they returned to The White Hart, banging on the door before the pub was open, they pushed past the puzzled barman who let them into the shadowy interior still smelling of the previous night's spilled beer and choking tobacco fug. Tessie was already in her cubby–hole at the rear surrounded by small pillars of coins which she was sorting into cloth bags.

'Right,' she said, hardly glancing up, 'are you for the job or not?'

'We are, dearie,' Trapp told her, reaching down for one of the bags and weighing it in his hand with a nod of approval. 'And this should see you all right for a day or two. Now you just let me or my pal here know if there's any trouble to be sorted out and we'll be here as quick as you like.'

Tessie made no protest. She understood exactly what the pair were up to. This wasn't the first time such protective measures had been extended, and in the past J J Haggerty had resolved the issue to Tessie's satisfaction. But now there was no J J and the only resort would have to be to Mr Landry's horde of hard men who could be summoned from his various establishments when extreme circumstances demanded. No doubt the rest of the taverns in his bailiwick were being subjected to the same dispensation and these incomers would have quite a shock in store for them within the next day or two.

But Trapp and Wallace were not opportunistic part–timers at the game and when Tessie reported to Landry she found him and his wife in a condition of unconcealed agitation.

'It's different this time,' Mrs Landry explained while her husband sat unmoving with a look of despair frozen on his face. 'You're right enough, Tessie, about what these beasts are after – but it's not just the pubs, it's us as well. They know where we stay, and they've found out about the girls.'

The Landrys' two daughters and their families lived in different parts of the city.

'They're not on their own, this pair. They're out of London and they can call on God knows how many of their tribe any time it suits them. It's what they do for a living – it's no wee hobby for them. We'll just have to work out what we can stand and give it to them.

HIDDEN

Can we speak about this when Mr Landry feels a bit better?'
'But what about the usual bunch of lads? Surely they…'
'Please, lassie, it's not the same as before. This gang are too much for us. It's bad enough about the pubs, but us and the girls! Just let it go, Tess.'
'But…'
'We've seen for ourselves what these animals can do. There's one thing, though, that might make it all not quite as bad. They're up here after some friend that was working in London. They think he's probably hereabouts in the Old Town or down in Leith. If we can find him they say they'll cut the money back a bit.'
'How would we find somebody that we don't know nothing about?'
'They've a description and a name for him so listen – J J had an eye on all our places from here to the port. He's their best chance to find out where they might catch up with the fellow. We're still giving him a wee sum while he's in that hospital thing. I know he's in a bad way, but maybe they can get some useful word out of him.'
'J J's not in his right mind half the time. They'll likely get nothing from him but noise.'
'Anyhow, tell these creatures where he's at and leave it to them. And you mind yourself, Tess. Don't go taking on these people with that tongue of yours.'
'And you'll just let them get away with this? I'd take a great big knife to the pair of them.'
'No such thing. We need to look out for you as well as for ourselves. There's no man here to stand up to this lot, and you'll not try it yourself.'
'I seen J J myself a day or two ago with that money you let him have. I never knew him when he was clear enough in his brains but, Jesus, he's in a fair way now to be off his head altogether.'
'Aye, but he's about the only chance we have of cutting our losses over this business. We'll have nobody else hurt over this – you mind that. You tell Trapp and Wallace we'll do our best by them and leave it at that.'
Seething with resentment as much as at the Landrys' surrendering to the demands of the vicious marauders Tessie passed on this information to the London duo when they next materialised in the pub. It was clear enough, though, from their demeanour and the

HIDDEN

way they chose to go about their business that these were not men to be trifled with and that there lurked in the distant background of the English capital a crowd of ruffians they could call upon. So she directed Trapp and Wallace to the place on Forest Road where Haggerty lay perspiring, incoherent and helpless on a grimy bed. His great bulk was much diminished but it was evident to his visitors that this had once been a colossus on the scale of Magnus Wallace himself. But despite their efforts at communication, at first unctuous and subsequently cajoling, they could extract nothing of value from the patient whose response failed to extend beyond moaning and unintelligible shouting.

About to leave the malodorous ward on the instruction of a foul–tempered attendant the two men were waylaid by an obsequious, hand–rubbing, nondescript man with red hair and a chunk of his ear missing. Cowering before the hefty pair Donnelly made to stand aside to let them take their departure but hearing the nurse's acid valediction realised that they had been calling on his one–time friend.

'He's no better, lads,' he confirmed unnecessarily. "Never will be now. On his way out, I hear. My good pal, he was.'

Trapp was inclined to ignore this trespasser on his time and presence, but on reflection decided to test whether there was anything to be learned from it.

'We're looking out for a chum of ours that Mr Haggerty might have come across. I don't suppose you can help us? It's an important thing and there'd be a sovereign or maybe two in it for anybody that can point us to him.'

Shamelessly mercenary Donnelly abandoned his usual caginess. It was of no concern to him if these terrifying bruisers were in pursuit of someone for their own nefarious reasons. If being responsible for the visiting of injury on some metropolitan fugitive was the return for modest gain it was unlikely to weigh much on his conscience.

'Thick as thieves, we was, J J and me,' Donnelly assured him. 'If J J knew the fellow like enough I would as well.'

'A little Scotchman. Plenty of them to be had in Edinburgh right enough. But this one's easy seen. We thought Mr Haggerty might have come across him in one of these pubs in the Grassmarket. Has

HIDDEN

a mate that's a rat he keeps in a cage.'

Donnelly, keeping his own counsel while seeing some easy money accruing, decided that he was after all curious to know what Trapp and Wallace had in mind for the object of their hunt. Reacting to the hint of recognition that flitted across the Irishman's face Trapp elected to enhance the description with unnecessary further detail. 'Smells like a dead whale, would drink the pish off a sick ferret. I can tell – you've something for us, but don't worry that we wish him ill. He's a pal of ours and we want his advice, that's all.'

As if having had a revelation divulged to him, Donnelly said, 'Jesus and Mary, I met the fellow. He was going to set the beast at me. Now I wouldn't know where he is right at this minute but sure I could find him out for you.'

'You'll not be the poorer for it.'

And Donnelly saw himself avenged on his erstwhile assailant and a little wealthier for his trouble.

'You leave it to me. And where is it I can get you when I've set eyes on him?'

Nursing that information Breccan Donnelly, forgetting the original compassionate purpose of his visit, headed for his usual haunts confident that within a day or two he would be in possession of the intelligence that would bring risk–free reward.

HIDDEN
CHAPTER 13 AUGUST 1842

Not desolate at her brother's protracted disappearance from their Edinburgh locale Emma Halley was sitting late and alone in the parlour reflecting on the unanticipated course her life had followed since the spring. If she felt vaguely guilty at her lack of regret at her husband's unexplained vanishing, the sensation was mitigated by an impious relief. What the mystery had served to evoke was a clear–sighted recollection of the man's unpredictable and intemperate ill–humour accompanied by its regular but private resort to aggression, together with the oppressing realisation that any attempt to free herself of his dominion would be met with vindictive vigour. Halley himself had never made any secret of the extent of his reach or the monumental esteem in which he held himself. As Emma had assured her brother, Alaric would have wasted no time in ensuring that if she had fled his attentions she would have been tracked down and severely chastised for her desertion. The security that his now much diminished wealth had previously brought them both had long since proved to be illusory: she had spent fifteen years of her life in a state of recurring fearfulness while, finally, his resources had been no bulwark against his own eclipse.

Still turning over in her mind that perplexing reality she carefully placed between the bars of Balthazar's cage the sort of succulent collation that the creature was never provided with by his master. As a mark of appreciation the rodent bared his yellow teeth and squinted suspiciously at his benefactor. The summer evening was slipping into night and a vast silence had fallen on the house and the whole of the sprawling estate. The room was on the upper floor of the building and Emma, reaching for the decanter, divided her attention between pouring a schooner of sherry and watching the amber stars open out in the obsidian sky. Lost for a moment in the contemplation of this celestial display she realised with a cry of disbelief that, despite the twenty foot elevation, a grinning face was pressed against the widow.

Dropping her glass she reeled backwards with her hands thrown up

HIDDEN

in horror. For some seconds she was unable to comprehend what was confronting her, and then she emitted a long, piercing scream. Casper, about to retire to his rooms, was passing her door on the landing and without pausing to consider the propriety of his action he burst in, a short club at the ready. Immediately catching sight of the apparently aerial intruder and reassured that the window itself was intact he spun on his heel and charged down the stair calling on his salivating mastiff for support. The monster hurled itself snarling into the grounds as soon as his master had unbolted the entrance to the mansion. Armed with his elderly blunderbuss Casper followed hot on the heels of the fearsome canine to find the unaccountably cheerful trespasser perched on the branch of a copper beech that abutted the front of the house.

'Tree–ed,' the miscreant shouted down and gave himself up to laughter and to hesitant surrender. 'Like one of them King Charles fellows. Arboreal refuge must be a family resort. We'll get back to earth once we're rid of these Hanoverians.'

'You have thirty seconds to climb out of that,' Casper called, 'and get down here or I'll blow you to small pieces with this thing.'

'Happy to oblige. But maybe the dog could find his way back inside.'

'The dog stays. He'll attack only if I give him the sign.'

Still hugging the trunk of the tree and astride the creaking branch the man remained ebullient but cautious.

'An accommodation,' he suggested. 'The hound retires in good order and I present myself for proper inspection.'

'Fifteen seconds,' Casper said, thumbing back the hammer of the gun.

'I lower my colours in the face of superior force, sir.'

And the interloper scrambled from his perch, occasionally letting out a jovial curse as he and his too long kilt caught on an unforgiving limb of the beech. Grounded, he stood stock–still against the bole, raised his hands in mock capitulation and eyed Cerberus with nervous friendliness.

'Hiram Charles D T Stuart at your service. Your temporary neighbour and all round good fellow.'

By this time Emma had gathered her wits and appeared on the porch to witness the confrontation.

148

HIDDEN

'Why, Mr Stuart,' she said, her composure regained and her safety attested to by the presence of her retainer and his menacing hound, 'there is a bell–pull. I'm sure you had no intention of catching me in a state of *dishabille*.'

'My dear madam, nothing could have been further from my intent. I have a weakness for the dramatic entrance – nothing more pernicious, I swear.'

The watchful Casper eased the gun into a less threatening position and signed to Cerberus to squat at his heel.

'Should I expel this fellow from the grounds, Mrs Halley? It would be for the best, I think.'

Emma thought for a long while, then beckoned Stuart to follow her into the hall.

'You may go to bed, Casper, but I should be very happy to have Cerberus join us in the drawing room. And there will be no need for tea or any other refreshment. Mr Stuart will explain himself briefly and then take himself off into the night.'

When Casper had, with a show of unease, gone away grumbling under his breath Emma led her uninvited guest to a chesterfield and herself settled down in a rocking chair with the distrustful *cane corso* spread–eagled on the carpet between them.

'And now you may wish to explain yourself, sir.'

'I am delighted that you have been brought to my notice, madam, by Lord Bonaly, our mutual friend. It has been painful to me to be bereft of the company of your husband. Always had the highest regard for him. I have no doubt that you will assume his mantle and be an invaluable contributor to our small enterprise.'

'Brought to your attention, sir? Am I some item to be examined? And through glass, at that?'

'Your pardon – Emma, if I may? My frontier manners leave much to be desired in such a sophisticated presence. Now – my scaling of the tree, eh? There are spies everywhere, you see. We can't be too prudent. I needed to survey the lie of the land.'

'And you're satisfied that I am not in the thrall of an army of secret agents?'

And not for the first time over recent days Emma discovered an unfamiliar persona in herself that had the capacity to transmit self–possession combined with a dry scepticism. It was impossible so

HIDDEN

far to estimate whether Stuart was merely off-centre, was utterly mad or was so instinctively cautious that his behaviour could be construed as reasonable; Emma was prepared to withhold judgement until the man had provided some justification for his unconventional arrival.

'I have some doubts about Earl,' he said. 'There's something that's not right about the man.'

'*The* Earl, you mean. It's a title, not a name.'

'Oh, he's useful, of course, him being a Lord. Has the ear of folks in your parliament. And he's keen, too. He could be of a hell of a lot of use to me as a… Well, it's hard to explain. But I tell you, there's a mighty odd softness to him. Can't see him on the frontier even if he can shoot the eye out of a fly at fifty yards. No, sir; he's not – well, I guess you can read the lines he's written on. Same ones as…'

Stuart shrugged and offered a gesture that invited a response from Emma who, understanding not a word of his disquisition, maintained her inscrutable reserve. Having waited in vain for a contribution the American ploughed on with his impenetrable monologue.

'Let's forget Earl for the minute. As fine a rifleman as you'd find in the Sierra Nevada, I'm told, but eccentric. Not like the rest of us. Now, about your Alaric – he will have explained to you that he was with me on this mission of ours. I need to hear that you run along the same road.'

What struck Emma was that the man spoke clearly and calmly, that he had a significant point to pursue, but that his ability to convey it was circumscribed by either a concealed agitation or some imbalance in his mind. As if reading her thoughts he grinned and said, 'When the game is as dangerous as this one, any sane man's first resort is madness.'

More baffled than ever Emma opted for concurrence in the incomprehensible.

'You must understand my caution,' she told him, not understanding it herself. 'Alaric was – is – the soul of discretion. I share that disposition. And so when I wade into these waters I need to be persuaded that I will not be taken by sharks.'

Stuart appeared to endorse her sentiment.

HIDDEN

'Very wise, ma'am. Exactly as Alaric. So you'll join us at Sir Hudson's tomorrow afternoon. Let's say three o'clock? But say nothing of tonight's visit. Now – is it safe to use the door, do you think? Should I go out a window, maybe at the back? Are the guards to be trusted?'
'There are no guards, Mr Stuart, nor anyone else. You may leave in perfect safety.'
'It's no secret – the Mexicans have their agents everywhere. But don't concern yourself, I know them. My hat – where's my hat?'
'You had no hat.'
'*Uneasy lies the head that wears a crown.*'
Having uttered the quote Stuart looked distraught for a moment, casting around for the non–existent headgear, and then, edging past the somnolent Cerberus, seized Emma's hand, kissed it, informed her that the mermaid would await them and tiptoed out through the hall and into the velvet night. Not an iota the wiser for the encounter his hostess rang for Casper's assistant, the newly employed Felix Athol Latimer, to remove the hound and ensure that all the doors were properly locked and the windows closed. Now annoyed rather than relieved that her brother had so far failed to return from his expedition she pondered whether the invitation from Hiram Stuart was to be taken seriously and if so how she was to present herself the next day at Sir Hudson Smart's; and if Stuart really was as unhinged as his call had suggested or if he was in some convoluted manner judging her soundness as a prospective colleague. For once Emma felt that the advice of her devious, untrustworthy and suspicious brother would have been welcome.
After a sleepless night she chose to await developments rather than take the initiative and engaged Latimer to drive her into the city, leaving Casper to prowl the grounds and ensure that any weaknesses in the estate's defences were repaired. With McAra's various tactical admonitions echoing in her mind she had Latimer deposit her on Princes Street and strolled in the crowded gardens for half an hour. Sauntering up The Mound switching a large basket from one arm to the other she occasionally angled a parasol to keep the blazing sun from her face and to give her the chance to observe any possible unwanted interest in her. Satisfied that she was not being followed she turned into the narrow opening of Anchor Close

HIDDEN

connecting the High Street to Cockburn Street.

A tap on the featureless third door set deep in the wall evinced the sound of wooden furniture scraping on the stone floor and a moment later a tiny hatch was drawn back. The lane was too dark and the opening in the door too recessed to permit a clear view of the occupant, but Emma wasted no time on prying.

'I'll leave the basket here. Pick it up when I'm gone. You're not to open the door for anyone except a man called Latimer. Always ask for his first two names before you let him in. Now, quickly – what do you have to tell me?'

'Yon McAra turned out to have the right of it. I was let out and told to go to my own crib and wait there. I wasn't to leave on no account. That's what Mr Laurie said to me. But I done as Mr McAra let on and come straight here. Don't you worry, dearie, I'll not budge from here.'

'That's all?'

'They was coming for me on the first of the month.'

'Oh, another thing. There's a pair of very rough–looking gentlemen at either end of the Close. Are they friends of yours? I found them quite intimidating.'

'No friends of mine. It was McAra that put them there. He says he has a dozen or more of them that can be here night and day to make sure I'm safe here. And I've not to leave this place myself or they'll not be too gentle on me.'

These non–existent ruffians were a figment of McAra's imagination which he had instructed Emma to confirm as threatening reality for reasons which she was disinclined to enquire into. Setting off down the steps to Cockburn Street she tried as far as possible to avoid the puddles of urine and the less appealing deposits. Another careful glance in either direction persuaded her that her detour had gone unobserved and she returned to Princes Street where the patient Latimer was smoking a pipe and whispering in the ear of the chestnut trotter drawing the Halley chaise. On the way back to Morningside Emma advised her driver to carry a cudgel if he was called on to visit the Close in the next few days. Latimer was a recent recruit to the household and knew nothing of Alaric Halley or his activities. He was easy–going, obliging and, importantly, unquestioning and the prospect of

HIDDEN

adventure appealed to him, even when he was told to keep some aspects of his new occupation strictly to himself.

By the time the chaise had reached the south side of the city the hour of the assignation designated by Hiram Stuart had come and Emma presented herself at the gate of Sir Hudson Smart's mansion where she was welcomed by a houseboy dressed in a kurta decorated in traditional chikan embroidery. Although her husband had regularly attended secretive conferences there he had never invited his wife to join in and she was acquainted only distantly with her neighbour.

Sir Hudson was physically significant, a dried out man but still of some girth and height, whose skin had the appearance of crumpled parchment. He had spent the greater part of his life in post with the East India Company and, having risen to near the top of that organisation, had been, against his will, retired to Edinburgh still restless and questing, determined to fill his remaining years with stimulation and challenge. Smart was one of the few officers of the Company to survive the cholera pandemic that had swept the sub–continent and on his return home had created with unnerving accuracy and nebulous sentiment a sweeping Jodhpur residence in the heart of Scotland. The room to which Emma was led was furnished in the Mughal style with rosewood, teak and acacia tables, chairs and cabinets inlaid with bone and ivory. Around the walls and placed at random on the furniture was a bewildering array of huge ferns, bamboo, cascading grape ivy, areca palms and gigantic rubber plants.

'But the cost, Mrs Halley,' he sighed, 'is becoming unbearable. I am living beyond my means in a past that is beyond my reach. But, please, make yourself comfortable in the embrace of better days in a better place.'

'You would prefer to back in India?'

'I have tried to bring it with me, and not only in my memory, as you see. But it's not only the country I miss. Some of us feel so deeply a vocation to bring good order and prosperity wherever possible under the aegis of the Empire. I am of the ilk, you see. On the subcontinent I could by a gesture bring about improving change, wealth, happiness even. And now that I'm offered the opportunity to engage myself with similar endeavours on quite the other side of

HIDDEN

the world...'
'Improving change? But not for all, I imagine?'
'That would be a noble aspiration but one can do only what one can do. If I describe the product of my labours for the Company as the fruit of Aphrodite you will understand. And I miss a certain excitement – especially that of the days I spent afloat for the Company putting the Chinese in their rightful place.'
Smart paused, reflecting on something he wanted to say but was uncertain of the terms in which to couch it.
'I may be mistaken,' he said, casting around for a tone of affable delicacy, 'but I thought I'd caught a glimpse of your brother the other day. May I ask if he continues to be... afflicted?'
'By excess? Unhappily, yes. His living as a coachman is precarious. I believe he has in mind to plunder Alaric's purse though he claims his motive for calling on me is purely fraternal.'
'Perhaps I could offer him a little gainful employment. In the garden or as an assistant to Kapil?'
'I'm afraid his riposte to your generosity would embarrass us both, but I thank you for your kindness. Besides I intend to keep him at arm's length for the duration of his stay. He has found quarters in the city and if I may be frank with you I would prefer if you made no reference to his very existence either to your colleagues or to our neighbours.'
'I quite understand, my dear Emma. You need have no fear of my incaution. Now let us return to the matter in hand. I believe that our friend Hiram suggested you attend this get–together today. I'm afraid our little gathering is going to be even smaller than I had intended. Hiram himself has been called away to... Well, I'd best explain his absence when our colleagues join us.'
As he spoke Smart occupied himself dispensing tiny glass of a gold–coloured liquor which was unfamiliar to Emma. Replacing the crystal decanter he gave the impression of being about to launch into some confidence which he wanted to share when his Rajputanan servant announced the arrival of a quartet of newcomers. Of these one was a soberly dressed figure who appraised her with narrowed eyes; the others looked to Emma as improbable acquaintances of a man of Sir Hudson's ranking and reputation. Still dumbfounded at her own newly acquired artifice

HIDDEN

she confined to a vague smile her reaction to introduction.
'Gentlemen,' Smart said as they seated themselves and accepted the proffered alcohol, 'as you are aware Mr Halley has been lost to us. May I, then, introduce Mrs Halley who will assume her husband's role with us. And this…'
But before he could trot out the names of the four visitors he was silenced by their patently unfavourable collective reaction.
'No offence, missis,' Josiah Dicken said, 'but I never seen you before. And I don't know nothing about you.' And turning to Smart went on, 'You're right out of order here. This isn't no time for some wife coming in on us without our say–so, her called Halley or any other damn name – begging your pardon, missis.'
Sir Hudson remained standing, the decanter in his hand.
'Whom we recruit is for Hiram to decide. Hiram is meeting Lord Bonaly today but if you object then I suggest that you raise the matter with him when the opportunity occurs. For the moment you may take it that Mrs Halley is one of us.'
And Smart, with a grimace of irritation, carried on with the introduction of Dicken, Sebastian Bradley and a couple of members of a Chartist Committee whose names she failed to catch.
'These gentlemen have been strangers to me – to all of us, in fact, except to our intermediary Mr Grundy. But I think the time has come for us to become a little acquainted on condition that our meetings with them remain absolutely clandestine and as few in number as possible. And it will continue to be the case that Grundy will be the channel of communication with them. For their benefit as much as ours there must be as few direct dealings between us as our plans permit.'
Bradley led his host to the outer room and in a low voice said, 'I never wanted to be on terms with you folk, but at least you can tell us what it is that Mrs Halley has to do with us. This is hardly work for women.'
'As Alaric's wife and confidante she has every right and responsibility to be here. Besides, Mr Bradley, her being with us is very much to your advantage so I recommend that you bear with us.'
Bradley was unconvinced but gave some thought to this.
'I say you're risking an awful lot for not very much. The Halley

HIDDEN

wife is not Halley so…'

'Be still, my friend. I know what I'm at, and besides, without Mrs Halley we have no access to two vital elements of our commission falling within her husband's ambit: the funds deposited in Alaric's accounts; and entrée to the powers at Westminster. Bear with me – all will be fine.'

With which Sir Hudson conducted his doubting colleague back to his faux Indian retreat and beamed his apologies on Emma.

'Mr Bradley is concerned that your own interests may not wholly coincide with those of ourselves – and of Alaric,' he told her.

Emma studied the two men for a long moment and said, 'Perhaps he mistakes my prudence for disapprobation. Then say nothing in my hearing that might perturb him. I can only assure you all of my constant approval of any of my husband's undertakings.'

Bradley indicated with a shrug that he accepted her role as Alaric's surrogate and once the issue of her husband's whereabouts had again been aired and the tetchy, arid debate had subsided Smart set the agenda running. From his brief rehearsal of the affair in which Halley had become involved Emma was able to extract little more than the barest outline, but it was soon clear that the main item to be disposed of was the reason for her own attendance and that of Bradley and Dicken.

'There are confidences I have to maintain,' Smart said. 'But at least I can repeat this – Hiram Stuart has made these enormous resources available for those very specific purposes known to us all. But as we are all aware it is absolutely essential that on no account is his interest in these affairs to be revealed. Hence Mr Halley's volunteering to act as intermediary.'

'If we all know the thing let's get on with it,' Bradley interrupted. 'The time is on us – I need that money urgent or the business isn't going to go the way you want.'

'I understand, but the delay has not been the fault of anyone here. It must be attributed to Alaric's disappearance, and to nothing other. But now that we can welcome Mrs Halley to our enterprise I believe we can move on swiftly. Emma, my dear, you have the floor.'

On the basis of what Sir Hudson had been saying Emma had hardly the vaguest notion of what was being discussed. Assuming that

HIDDEN

what was being referred to was the enormous deposits placed in one of her husband's bank accounts she was nevertheless cautious about revealing her ignorance. Not for the first time she inwardly cursed her brother's implicating her in this hazardous mission.

'Please, Sir Hudson,' she said, conscious of her colouring rising, 'being such a new recruit I hardly feel able to lead off on the matter at this stage. I am here merely to take direction. Consider me the most willing collaborator. I will place no obstruction in the way of progressing our plans.'

'My dear, I know this is foreign territory to you. We others, for one reason or another, are not unfamiliar with the risk involved in such activity. However you may be assured that there will be no untimely intercession by the authorities. We have made certain of that at the highest level within the police.'

Dicken got to his feet and began to pace the floor impatiently.

'For Christ's sake, will youse all get on with it. I don't want to be listening to all this polite shite.'

Bradley seemed to be of the same mind but expressed the view less vehemently.

'The thing is that the Queen gets here in a few days so there's a whole lot I need done right now. It all costs money: materials to be paid for, and transport and boats and provisions and bribes and more besides. If you want the business going off proper I need to have the funds before the end of the week. And mind this well – me and my lads don't want to know one damn thing about your side of the affair and that includes whatever you're up to elsewhere. You do as you will, and so will we.'

'None of us is standing in your way, Sebastian,' Sir Hudson assured him. 'Emma – may we expect the monies to be available in the time our friend Mr Bradley is so keen on?'

'I see no problem with that. Of course I shall have my lawyers consult Alaric's bank manager about the position this very day. Obviously they are aware of my circumstances and will ensure that the business can be transacted promptly. The day after tomorrow should be possible.'

'Cash. It has to be cash,' Bradley insisted. 'And in bills and coin I can easy pass around. Any trouble with the bank and the whole thing's got to be called off. There has to be nothing that associates

HIDDEN

me and Josiah with your business or your partners. And you'll say not a word more about any of this in my hearing – I don't want to know.'

'The whole amount, then?' Emma asked, her mind turning to the vast capital sitting in her husband's account. 'Alaric has always been responsible for conducting our financial affairs but I don't doubt that the sum can be made available to me at short notice.'

'Mr Dicken.' Smart concentrated his attention on the seaman. 'You have some experience in these matters. No doubt you can ensure the safe delivery of the funds?'

'Easy enough.'

'Then, my thanks to Mrs Halley for her stepping so helpfully into Alaric's shoes. May we agree to assemble again the day after tomorrow to take stock of Sebastian's progress and any other matters arising? Including, certainly, the distribution of the budget.'

Bradley shook an extended finger at Sir Hudson.

'Remember that through Grundy your Hiram fellow has made promises to me and Dicken. Without he keeps his word to us I can call the whole thing off.'

'As for the side of things that concerns parliament,' Smart said to Emma, 'no doubt we can leave it to you to ensure that that channel will be open to Mr Stuart.'

At a loss to understand this and hardly sustaining her air of cooperative composure Emma returned with a demure smile Sir Hudson's declaration of appreciation. She agreed a rendezvous at the bank with Dicken and made good her escape. Almost fainting with the stress of controlling her trepidation by the time she arrived home after a brief consultation with the family's solicitors she sank into a chair and had Casper bring her a large tumbler of gin. A few minutes later her nervous disposition was hardly steadied by the abrupt sound of doors crashing and raised voices, to be followed almost immediately by the entrance of her brother and a thickset companion, the pair still engaged in exchanging ill-tempered and personal remarks.

'Where in the name of God have you been, Mac?' she asked, setting her drink aside and standing up in the hope of conveying some semblance of authority.

'An incident. A misunderstanding. An outrage on my person.'

HIDDEN

Cassels grabbed the protestor by the shoulder and threw him onto a chaise longue. Introducing himself by name and profession the Glasgow officer, bestowing a furious glower on the dishevelled McAra, explained that it had been their intention to be back in Edinburgh a full day earlier.
'But this wee creeping thing,' he went on, 'managed to get himself thrown in the cells at Constitution Street yesterday afternoon.'
'Oh, Mac, what now?'
'Not my fault, my lovely Emma. My actions were... misconstrued. Just a little song...'
'You were locked up for singing?'
'You'll know the one, Em – a nice wee thing:
"I've been roaming! I've been roaming!
Where the meadow dew is sweet,
And like a queen I'm coming
With pearls upon my feet."

And the next minute I was being rushed into the clink in Leith.'
'There must have been something more to it than that?'
Cassels took a seat and with a scowl said, 'More to it than that? I'll say there was, the poisonous reptile that he is. Believe me, madam, I'm a Glasgow man, born and bred, as hard as you'll find, but what he was at would make a cannibal sick. I couldn't begin to tell you.'
With a shrug McAra asked after Balthazar's wellbeing and concluded the episode of his home–coming by asking, 'Would there be a drop of brandy...?'

HIDDEN

CHAPTER 14 AUGUST 1842

Late in the evening, after McAra and, mainly, Cassels had rendered their account of the excursion to Argyll it was Emma's turn to describe the events that had filled her time in the course of her brother's absence. McAra pronounced himself well pleased with what he heard even though much of it appeared opaque to Emma herself and irrelevant to Cassels.

'I suppose I need to be getting my breech and the wagon back to Glasgow,' he said. 'My money's run out and now that there's this nice lady to keep you out of the clutches of respectable people I can't see there's anything much to hold me here.'

'You'll miss a bit of the fun if you bugger off now,' McAra told him. 'And yon Inspector of yours just said to get you back *sometime*. Emma here can fix you a bob or two for a drink and I'll let you give me a hand with the job entrusted to me by the Palace.'

'I can fix…?' Emma, with a sigh, left the sentence hanging. Her retelling of her encounters with the Earl of Bonaly, Hiram Stuart and Sir Hudson and the others had been detailed and precise and as he watched and listened to her talk Cassels put in, 'It's a complete bloody mystery to me.'

'You're right, Mr Cassels, It's so hard to make one's way through this maze. Why are people like these involved in some dangerous conspiracy? And what if we get caught up in a scheme to murder the Queen or the Prime Minister? My God…'

'No, no, Mrs Halley. I mean how can it be that a lovely, clever lady like yourself is related to this ill–formed imbecile?'

'You flatter my brother, Mr Cassels, but regrettably there is no doubt as to our close blood relationship. But may we think a little more about the matter in hand? Can you or my benighted sibling cast some light on my darkness?'

'It's not darkness, your brother's pure deranged. God almighty, he's been claiming he went to that University in Paris.'

'You didn't believe him?'

'Not a single bloody word.'

From the very depths of his being McAra issued a broadside of

HIDDEN

flatulence of such amplification that it stirred the drowsing Balthazar to a sibilate turmoil.

'This Hiram,' he said, oblivious to the revulsion in the company – both human and verminous – his abdominal distension had caused, 'when he was peering in the widow – did he catch sight of your boobies? Can I snatch a wee peek?'

'Let me run through what you've told us,' Cassels said to Emma, tweaking his nostrils, 'and what damn wee bit I managed to get out of this twerp over the past few days and see if we can sort it out. What started the whole thing off was the man Hopkin whispering about some plot to do with... with what?'

'With some danger to the state, he said. And it seems clear enough now what that is.'

'And that was what got him killed, was it?'

'So my brother thinks. And, yes, it seems likely.'

'Run over by a coach belonging to that Lord Bonaly. The thing got stolen for the job.'

'Allegedly.'

'Aye, right. And your brother managed to get hold of the wee fellow that did the killing. And somebody called Grundy was behind it.'

'Grundy seems to be in the middle of it all, that's true. But from what I've been hearing it seems that there are others that Bertram Hopkin suspected of being real conspirators.'

'I can't see why somebody like a Lord and all these rich folk would be lined up for a terrible thing like this.'

McAra's ear–splitting snoring represented the extent of his contribution.

'What I might as well tell you is that precious little will remain in my husband's accounts,' Emma went on, 'after I withdraw the money that Hiram Stuart put in my husband's account.'

'I don't know about this rich Yankee but what is it that these others are really out for? Why would folk like them want to see Victoria murdered? Or Peel, come to that.'

'Maybe I can find out more when I see them tomorrow.'

'Jesus, madam, you'd be mad to try that. Me and your brother will put the City Police up to what we think is going on and everything'll be fine.'

'Mr Cassels, you know that's not certain enough. Bertram believed

HIDDEN

even the police were not to be put above suspicion. I don't understand these things, but think about these Dreyse guns like the one the police found at Leith. Mac said that the Earl of Bonaly had got hold of two of them; and if they're as dangerous as my brother says surely something needs to be done about the missing one. And, you know, I think the target might be the Prime Minister rather than the Queen but… oh, I can't make out what's going on.'

While McAra slept the sleep of one whose conscience was permanently unblemished Emma and Cassels continued to mull over the fragmented tale they had pieced together and dined on an elaborate six course meal. By the time the lamps were lit and post–prandial brandies served they had come to the conclusion that they had no alternative but to share their concern with Chief Constable Haining himself and probably the commander of the Castle garrison. Emma would arrange the withdrawal of the money the next day but when attending the rendezvous with Sir Hudson would do nothing more than play the role of a true believer in the cause – whatever it was – and say nothing to place herself in jeopardy. If all went well the conspiracy would be exposed and terminated well before the Royal Yacht berthed at Leith. They were deflected from their closing deliberations by the strangled cry emitted by the somnolent McAra as he struggled back to consciousness.

'They've ate all the toads! There's grudges everywhere! Stop spitting on the stones, you lazy shite!'

Hearing what recourse his sister and Cassels had alighted on he waved a dismissive hand and without delay embarked on a stomach–turning assault on the remains of the dinner, fending off the efforts of the maids to clear the table. With a dribble of cold gravy dripping from the corner of his mouth and an array of gobbets of roast lamb, chicken and assorted vegetables decorating his tattered brocade waistcoat he settled himself in a chair and with a series of satisfied belches dismissed their entire project.

'Just remember I'm the master here,' he instructed. 'I come with the full authority of the Palace, the government and Pope Gregory himself.'

Tugging at the fork of his holed and scruffy breeches with one hand and gesturing with a brimming glass in the other he carried on, 'The whole thing is as clear to me as… as a clear thing. It's imperative

HIDDEN

that no premature move is made. Leave this to the professional among us – me. Would there be any pickles or cream rolls? Onions?'

'The sense has gone out of the man altogether,' Cassels said. 'He was bad enough before but now he wants us to sit around doing bugger all while the Queen or Robert Peel gets a bullet in the eye.'

'Have a good look at these thighs,' McAra invited, further adjusting his garment to admire his lower limbs. 'Superb. I should have trained for the ballet.'

Emma threw up her hands in despair and Cassels turned his attention to the rattled cage in the corner.

'What in the name of God is that bloody thing?'

'You've been overfeeding him, Em,' McAra complained. 'He was sleek and fit when I left and look at him now – fat, lazy and nothing on his mind but grub.'

'If this is Edinburgh,' Cassels said, 'I'm damn glad I belong somewhere else.'

'And in the morning,' McAra told him, 'you get seeing our Castle. And maybe some of our pubs.'

With young Latimer skilfully driving one of Halley's barouches – McAra and Cassels on the front–facing bench and Balthazar's cage opposite them – the police officers were deposited the next morning on the High Street and crossed the cobbles to the headquarters of the local force. Once Latimer had been instructed to drop off Balthazar at the address in the Grassmarket and keep himself in readiness for further orders McAra as usual announced to the gatekeeper his unique jurisdiction and powers of entry at the top of his voice while waving his increasingly grubby letter from the Metropolitan Police Commissioner. With evident distaste and maintaining as great a distance as possible from the rank presence the constable showed the pair into the Chief's office.

Succeeding with difficulty in keeping his air of *sang froid* Haining contented himself with applying a cold stare in McAra's direction and issuing no invitation to sit. Scratching himself energetically in the assorted areas of his asymmetrical construction McAra peered round at the panelled walls, the pictures and the luxurious furniture.

'At the request of Prince Albert himself,' he began, 'me and my man are here to ensure that all precautions have been taken to protect

HIDDEN

not only the Royal party and the Prime Minister. But listen – it's obvious that what's really going on is…'
'What's really going on is the heroism you display in the face of your of your astounding array of ailments. You have no need, you baboon, to assume these false airs. Colonel Rowan in London has made plain to me the extent of your delegation. God knows it's far beyond anything that I can see you're entitled to, but… very well.'
Haining unlocked a drawer and laid in front of his visitors a stack of papers on which were an illustration of the direction through the city to be taken by the Royal entourage together with appended notes on the allocation of security resources along the way. McAra gazed without comprehension at the documents like a man struck by an apoplectic seizure.
'I'll have my staff consider this,' he said and passed the sheaf to Cassels whose responding but wordless glance might have ignited an alabaster statue. 'But let me tell you the right way of what's going to be…'
'I'll remind you,' Haining interrupted, 'that you were supposed to accompany Mr Laurie the full length of that route several days ago. I understand from him that you were on that occasion afflicted by some incapacity. Please make certain that sort of dereliction does not recur.'
"Dereliction? I have a delicate constitution. You're aware that my assistant Laurie came across a rifleman's nest on the pier at Granton? I need to point out that…'
'Mr Laurie is *my* assistant, not yours. And, yes, I am fully aware of his discovery. I can tell you that the timing of the Queen's arrival has been kept even from the City Council; she will have her own bodyguards in addition to the protection we will be providing. And Mr Laurie has learned that there are those opposed to the Emancipation Act who might well have the PM in their sights. As for the party's exact route – which you have there – it must remain a secret.'
'If I need you for anything else, Haining, I'll call on you.'
Before the Chief could discard the patina that he had with difficulty laid over his seething enmity McAra was scurrying from the building with the inscrutable Cassels at his shoulder. In a pub on the other side of the street the two pored over the wad of papers,

HIDDEN

Cassels noting the locating of police and military units along the planned route; and the diminishing reserve of forces to be stationed at the Castle and at various points within and on the periphery of the city.

'I see they're having that many coppers or soldier lads keeping an eye on the crowds between Granton and the Old Town. It looks clear enough they're expecting another Edward Oxford or John Francis waiting for Her Majesty?'

'Who's Oxford? And Francis?'

McAra was concentrating on guzzling as much porter and brandy as his meagre means would permit and his interest in the question came a poor second to that exertion.

'Them assassins in London. Good God, man, Francis had his try just a few months back.'

'Francis? Oh, aye. Would you have a shilling or so for a wee drink? I think I'm out of funds for a while.'

Emma had been generous with Halley's money and Cassels had, with no more than mild embarrassment, accepted an amount that represented some weeks' salary.

'There'll be nothing like the Francis affair here,' McAra told him when another round had been placed on the table.

'But what your sister was saying last night! For a start there's a bastard going to be out there with some bloody gun.'

'That brandy – you got me the cheap stuff.'

'Christ, man, either the Queen or the Prime Minister's going to be in mortal danger and you never said a word to that Haining about it. I'm for telling him the whole of what we've heard and...'

'Now, now, my friend. Calm yourself. Get one of these cheap noggins for yourself and then we'll have a wee stroll up to the Castle like I promised you. You're a Glasgow man and you need to get a bit culture in you.'

None too steady on his feet by the time they left the tavern McAra led the way up the gentle slope to the esplanade and through the portcullis. Challenged by an armed sentry McAra ostentatiously brandished his credentials and affecting an air of command disproportionate to his appearance demanded access to the garrison Colonel.

'Nobody gets in the now,' the soldier insisted. 'They're getting ready

HIDDEN

for the Queen.'
'Have you lost your mind? I'm Her Majesty's personal body guard. If you don't let me through you'll get the jail.'
'Clear off, you cow's dropping or you'll get this bayonet up your arse.'
Before this warm exchange could run its course Sergeant Rannoch appeared from the guard house to find out what was the occasion of the contretemps and recognised not the incensed McAra but his thickset companion.
'Officer Cassels of the Tron Division, isn't it? You'll remember us lot from that rampage in your streets a couple of weeks ago. Are you here to join up? We'll get you a flintlock instead of yon heavy stick of yours. And a dandy kilt and all.'
'Never mind the clever banter,' McAra said. 'You know me fine, you impudent lump. I'm here on the Queen's business. I've to see your Colonel and sharp about it.'
The Sergeant stared at the hobgoblin and slow recognition dawned on him.
'Aye, now I mind you from the West Port. And what makes you think the Colonel wants to see the likes of you?'
He sniffed the air and, retreating in alarm, said, 'What is *that* you've put your foot in? Have you been at the stables? Fall in a slurry pit?'
'None of your cheek. Get me to Colonel Grant or you're up for a court martial.'
With an accomplished scowl the trooper conducted the unsavoury representation of the law to the Colonel's administrative quarters in the New Barracks and left them to their unwelcome conference. Like Haining the garrison commander was confident that all manner of safeguard was being put in place for the Royal visit. The delegation was to call at the Castle to view the Honours of Scotland and afterwards they would be shown the National Monument on Calton Hill, and the Nelson and Burns Monuments. The visit to the city would conclude with a reception at Holyroodhouse.
'The Prime Minister himself has concocted the whole route,' Grant told the delegation. 'First it's the rounds in Edinburgh, a few days at Dalkeith Palace and then on to Killiecrankie and castles in Perthshire – Taymouth, Dupplin, Drummond. You police laddies can call on my men at any time if it looks like there'll be trouble

HIDDEN

though God knows we'll be small enough in number by then. Oh, I know all about these Chartist folk and the trade unions and the kirk. Everybody's carrying around a grievance the now. But you'll know that there's little enough been put about on the fine details of the visit so I wouldn't think there's much to worry about.'

'That's an awful big comfort right enough,' McAra said. 'So you'll have been well advised about the goings–on at Leith and Queensferry?'

The Colonel frowned and shook his head.

'There's a strong smell of onions in here,' he said. 'Have you...?'

'A favourite of mine. Could you go one? I've got a handful in my pocket.'

'What's that about Leith and The Ferry?'

'If I was you I'd have some of your right fine troopers have a good look at any wee boats in the harbours early in the day Her Majesty gets here... See if they're stacked with something like pine and rosin and ready for the river.'

'You're being awful coy. What's this about?'

'You wouldn't want the *Royal George* set alight, would you? Or any of them frigates that the navy has sitting out there on the Forth.'

'If you know what that's all about you need to tell me. And it's a thing for the police, surely, and not the army.'

'It's just that I'd like a fine fellow like yourself to be getting the medals, and not a certain officer of the local force. But do what you like. I've got nothing more to say about it and on the subject of burning my arse is alight with the piles. So you'll not have an onion?'

'My lads are going to be hard put to it to keep the streets clear right across the city. If you can't tell me more I'll need to forego the award.'

'What in the name of Christ was that all about?' Cassels asked when the pair were on their way back to the High Street.

'Piles. They're veins that poke out of your behind and itch like buggery.'

'Not that. The thing about boats?'

'Just keeping folks on their toes. Here – give this wee note to my sister, would you? I'm for an early night at the Grassmarket. How about a wee noggin in Deacon Brodie's?'

HIDDEN

As they left the esplanade McAra called Sergeant Rannoch across and asked him if he remembered the famous artist Albertine Burgess.

'About as bonny as a heifer's udder if I mind her right,' the soldier recalled before he was stricken by a serious bout of indifference at McAra's brief description of the female artist's covert, trivial marring of Hiram Stuart's commissioned paintings of the various nominated artefacts at the Castle.

'Away and paint your arse blue,' he advised the policeman.

In the pub Cassels spent over an hour on a further examination of the papers Haining had passed to them while McAra, having attended as best and as audibly he could to subdue the irritation in his nether regions, proceeded to ingest three large yellow onions and down two and a half bottles of port. By the time his appetite had been sated he was, defiant and not a little inebriated, bawling as far as the fourth verse of 'Dream Pedlary':

"If there are ghosts to raise,
What shall I call,
Out of hell's murky haze,
Heaven's blue pall?
Raise my loved long–lost boy
To lead me to his joy. –
There are no ghosts to raise;
Out of death lead no ways,
Vain is the call"

before Cassels, exasperated beyond all measure, was at last driven to seize the drunk by his matted hair and haul him without ceremony from the sheltering twilight of the inn out into the beautiful summer evening. Summoning the imperturbable Latimer, who was caressing the mane and murmuring into the ear of the chestnut mare, he had the ostler dump McAra into the company of his irascible and lethal rodent at the lodging house in the Grassmarket. At something of a loss to know what to do next he had the young driver convey him back to the Halley estate where he discussed with Emma over dinner the arrangements for her risky encounter the next day with Dicken.'I'll say the truth to you,' Cassels said, 'this affair is not one you should be treading into

HIDDEN

without some assurance of safety.'

'I can't dissimulate my anxiety, but I'm now so far engaged on this scheme I can hardly retreat from it. It seems to concern the most vital matters.'

'Then rely on me. None of these folk will have the name or face of me. I'll be watching when you and Dicken are at the bank and on the way back out here. You'll not see me and I'll not interfere unless you're set in some danger.'

'I'm sure there'll be no problem. The money's going to these people anyway, so why would they want to risk robbing me of it?'

'Aye, they'd all be honest men, right enough and wouldn't ever make off with as much as that you'll be carrying. But just in case there's a wee bit of a lapse... Oh, aye, and your brother said to give you this bit paper.'

And glancing at the dog-eared document Emma drew some comfort from the knowledge that the muscular Cassels, looking far more like a denizen of the underworld than an upholder of the law, would be keeping a benign eye on the next morning's proceedings. As night drew on this Galahad excused himself and set off to run several times round the periphery of the state, his fists thrashing the air, presumably alive with invisible assailants. Cassels' approach to life and to their shared profession, Emma thought, was not identical to that of her brother. Amused by the contrast she retired to her salon and opened the note she had received.

'Laud our Mister Latimer's skills and achievements to Smart or yon Yankee fellow,' it said. 'Just let the thing come up natural. Don't play on it too hard.'

Emma sat in the shadows, shook her head in bemusement, sighed and tossed the document in a bin. In the case of her brother, she reflected, gnomic just meant he was a gnome.

HIDDEN
CHAPTER 15 AUGUST 1842

The following morning Latimer collected Emma, drove her into the Old Town and watched her climb the steps of the Royal Bank's headquarters at Dundas House in the improbable company of the rangy, scar–faced, ill–dressed character who had been waiting for her. Neither he nor Emma nor Dicken noticed the heavy–set horseman across the square apparently examining his mount's fetlock. Inside, the bank the manager Charles Wharton approached the mismatched couple with an obsequious rubbing of sympathetic hands.

'A letter, my dear Mrs Halley. A most upsetting communication from your family lawyers. A tragedy. And not so much as a whisper of your husband's...er, fate. I understand that you now have full authority to deal with his affairs. Whatever we can do for you will be our pleasure, mixed of course with our deepest sympathy.'

Wharton's private office was a haven of calm appropriate to the seriousness of the business before him. The air smelled of beeswax, the vast oak pedestal desk with its panelled red leather inlay was bare of decoration or object except for a voluminous buff folder on which Alaric Halley's name was prominently displayed, the heavy curtains were drawn halfway across the great widows to create a pleasant pale amethyst twilight.

'Naturally,' Wharton began, bowing his head over the thick file but leaving it unopened, 'my only wish is to comply with yours, and I gather that you want to withdraw from your husband's account a very substantial amount. In light of your lawyers'... shall we say, benediction I am happy to have made the necessary arrangements. In fact the funds in question are available this very instant. However, may I offer you counsel on the matter. What you intend to do with them is none of my affair, but to be in possession of such a huge amount is quite likely to put you in some imperilment. It might be prudent to proceed to a sequence of instalments and the disposal of these assets over a period of time during which any temptation to deprive you of them would be mitigated by the relative modesty of the amount at any given time.'

HIDDEN

'Never you mind that. This is for the woman to deal with, not you.' Dicken leaned forward and rapped on the desk.

Taken aback by the abrasive intervention Wharton recoiled open-mouthed and fixed a puzzled stare on Emma.

'I do apologise for Mr Dicken's discourtesy,' Emma said. 'As the guardian of our household's security he has less aptness for civility than for the safeguarding of our wherewithal. But I'm afraid these funds are to be disbursed exactly in accordance with my husband's pre-established compact. You need have no concern for my safety, though – as you have witnessed Mr Dicken can be suitably protective.'

Still shaken by the ruffian's intercession Wharton could only clasp his trembling fingers and acquiesce in Mrs Halley's instruction. Extracting a small brass bell from a drawer he summoned a teller and behind a cupped hand issued the required order. Some five minutes elapsed before the three heavy portmanteau bags were brought in by a trio of clerks, set out on the desk and opened.

'I'm afraid,' Wharton muttered, 'that it will be a time-consuming operation, but obviously you will wish to be assured that the amount is precisely as sought and as referenced in this receipt.'

'There'll be no need for that,' Dicken butted in. 'You can be sure I'll come knocking on your door if there's any shortfall.'

'But...'

And hefting two of the bags, leaving Emma to struggle with the third Dicken barged out past the bowing staff, across the main concourse and into the brilliant August sunshine to deposit the money on the front bench of Latimer's vehicle.

'Don't worry, missis,' he told Emma as he snatched her load from her and placed it with the other holdalls and climbed into the carriage without waiting for her, 'nobody's going to have that lot off us.'

And from the pocket of his pea-jacket he pulled an old double-barrelled flintlock pistol which he left to rest on his knee. Not concealing her distaste for the actor or his performance Emma pushed the weapon aside and told Latimer to take them back to Morningside.

Welcoming her and her repellent bodyguard, Sir Hudson conducted them into his sanctuary where Sebastian Bradley and his

HIDDEN

Chartist lieutenants were already ensconced. Even the most perfunctory preliminaries were dispensed with as Bradley and Dicken made haste to pile the bank notes on a table beneath the bow window and begin the lengthy task of counting under the eye of their associates. While this occupation was being prosecuted Smart, apparently amused at the avaricious enthusiasm it was stimulating, led Emma to an inner sanctum where he asked whether the visit to the bank had gone as planned and whether the cashing out had aroused any unwanted concern or attracted any adverse comment. Satisfied by her account he settled to an exchange of casual gossip of which Emma took advantage. She reported the peculiar aerial invasion of her privacy by Hiram D T Stuart.

'Aye, Hiram is a little eccentric at times,' Sir Hudson said. 'For quite a long while we were averse to his behaviour and we had to doubt just about everything he told us. But we've long gotten over that. Thanks in the main to Alaric's transatlantic researches.'

'Everything he told you about what?'

Smart narrowed his eyes and hesitated over responding but decided that his visitor had become a fully–fledged co–conspirator.

'I'm sure Alaric must have explained the thing to you, but maybe he wanted to exercise a degree of circumspection, what with your brother's less than reliable disposition.'

'I have no desire to interrogate you, Sir Hudson. Please feel free to dismiss me at any time.'

'That would be quite inappropriate, Mrs Halley.' Smart emitted a short laugh. 'When Hiram came to us it was on the recommendation of our old friend Major Calvin DeWitt who had come across him in the Americas. He – Hiram, that is – is enormously rich and owns vast tracts of the Far West. It's his intention to acquire even more and to see the whole of California free of Mexican dominion. Because your husband and Lord Bonaly and those of their circle are so influential politically he was keen to enlist their support – and mine on a more modest scale – in encouraging Washington and London to take a sympathetic interest in the project. But we are experienced and careful businessmen and none of us was prepared simply to take his word for all this.'

'Which accounts for Alaric's mysterious sojourn across the ocean?'

'Quite. We needed to be absolutely satisfied that what had been told

HIDDEN

to us was to be believed. After all, as we've just agreed, Hiram can be more than a little… strange.'

'And Alaric's researches bore the desired fruit?'

'Indeed they did. Hiram had financed an incursion into Northern California by an Isaac Graham with the intention of creating a serious diplomatic incident that would in the longer term enlist the sympathies of both Britain and the United States and open the way to annex the area.'

'But to what purpose? Why would you and Alaric and the others have the least concern for such an undertaking?'

'Ah, so your husband has not been entirely frank with you. Well, it can do no harm to inform you now. There is, after all, nothing illegitimate about the project. The position is this – Hiram, as I've said, has been acquiring swathes of the region but in present circumstances there is a severe limit to what he can do with them. In due course, though, there will be no difficulty with his exploiting his tenure.'

'And how will he exploit it?'

'Gold, my dear. Huge deposits of the stuff are thought to exist there. It's a long-term prospect apparently, but the geology favours it. Preparatory work has already been conducted on the lands Hiram has put his name to.'

'And Mr Stuart will reward you with the freedom to extract gold from it?'

'Precisely. The agreement will be formalised, of course, before we make the essential initial approach to our own government here at Westminster.'

'And has Mr Stuart obtained financial benefaction from you – from us?'

'Ah, my compliments, Mrs Halley. Naturally I see what you're driving at. And the answer is a resounding *no*. The contract is a simple one – we provide the jurisdictional impetus and Hiram consents to our mining his lands.'

'Then what's in it for Hiram?'

'His wealth is largely inherited and is so colossal that money is not a factor. But the office of governor of a new State has huge appeal to him. It may,' he added with a small smile, 'even represent the first rung on the ladder to the Presidency.'

HIDDEN

Concealing her amusement at the prospect of a lunatic at the Washington helm Emma considered all this for a few minutes before coming to the crux of her enquiry.

'What do Mr Bradley and Mr Dicken and all these people have to do with your grand scheme?'

'The Great Democracy, my dear Emma. Isn't that how the Americans now designate themselves? Hiram has been so impressed by the civilised manner in which the demand for voting rights has been pursued – through petitions and, yes, strikes and demonstrations, but not through revolutionary violence. Hence his support for the movement.'

Emma was unconvinced and Sir Hudson, reading her ill–concealed reaction, saw an exit from their brief alliance that would be welcome to them both.

'I can see that without your husband's guiding hand our exertions have become a burden to you. But there is something else – we have not taken Mr Bradley or Mr Dicken entirely into our confidence but now that the funds have been released and placed in the hands of these gentlemen perhaps it would be for the best if we – you and I – now went our separate ways, my dear. Your security is as important to me as my own.'

Emma seized the opportunity to quit the imbroglio her brother had propelled her into – she had read and understood the spaces between the lines of Sir Hudson's various perorations.

'If it will not discommode you, Sir Hudson, I shall withdraw and leave you gentlemen to your labours. They are much too complex to find lodging in a mere woman's wits.'

Mutually pleased with this outcome the pair were about to say their goodbyes when they were interrupted by a shout from Bradley who had looked up from counting Hiram's heaps of cash and was staring out of the window.

'Good Christ,' he called, 'that's Felix Latimer.'

He turned to Dicken and signed to him to join him in peering out at the yard.

'I seen him win the East Coast contest,' Bradley went on. 'And the Lowland last year. I never seen a man could handle a team the way he can.'

Giving way to an onset of juvenile adulation the two men

HIDDEN

temporarily lost interest in the hoard and hurried outside to shake the hand of the star driver. This stroke of good fortune relieved Emma of the chore of introducing Latimer's name into unrelated discussion as McAra had asked her to do. A surreptitious glance at Smart was enough to tell her that he too was aware of the young man's fame. Why her brother had wanted Latimer's presence to be broadcast to Sir Hudson's coterie was a mystery to her but she was now absolved of yet another of the duties McAra had taken to imposing on her.

'Felix Latimer is in your employ?' Smart asked, pretending to nothing more than mild interest. 'I shouldn't have thought your limited travel arrangements would have merited what must be a substantial outlay – or offer the young fellow enough to keep him engrossed. I gather he has led an exciting life at the reins.'

'He's very talented but racing four–in–hands hardly suffices to pay bills and keep a decent roof over one's head. We merely wanted to help him a little.'

'You know, my dear, I believe I could be of some assistance in that respect if it would make life a bit easier for you and for Felix. Once in a while I require a fine, fast driver to deliver documents and goods at the highest speed. Of course the new railways are invaluable for the purpose but you will be aware that as yet their extent is extremely limited.'

Assuming that this proposal was what McAra had designed to elicit Emma offered a polite gesture of acquiescence.

'I don't doubt that Mr Latimer would be happy to take advantage of your kindness if the occasion arose at a time when I had no need of his services.'

Distracted by keeping an eye on Bradley's two companions who had been edging nearer to the money stacked up on the table in the next room, Sir Hudson indicated confirmation of the arrangement Emma had suggested. Correctly surmising that her presence was no longer either required or welcome she excused herself with unbounded relief. Flattered by the sycophantic praise being lavished on him Latimer nevertheless hurried to offer his arm to Emma as she climbed into the carriage and, leaping easily onto the driver's seat, he flicked the trotter into action.

A couple of hours later McAra was wakened by the sound of his

HIDDEN

own moaning foreboding of the severity of the hangover that was about to afflict him. In that he was not to be disappointed – the after–effects of his carousing in the Deacon Brodie would have brought to a halt the charge of a foul–tempered hippopotamus. It hardly helped that Balthazar had been spoiled by Emma's generous hospitality the deprivation of which and its replacement by whatever his master could prise from the depths of his regalia sent him scurrying back and forth across the bare stone floor and hurling himself in fury at the unforgiving walls.

'I'll rip the tail off you, you bastard,' McAra croaked as he struggled into his mangy attire. 'I'm undone by that alcoholic swine Cassels. Slipped something in my coffee and me deep in the Crown's business. You can sink your teeth into his privy parts the first chance you get.'

Not won over by this unwarranted carping Balthazar spent a few minutes spitting and hissing before retreating to sulk in his cage, every once in a while issuing what sounded like an extended eructation. McAra's ablutions consisted of dunking his head in the rain barrel in the yard and, refreshed if not recovered, he stumbled across the cobbled Grassmarket, squatted down beside the hawk–eyed Mrs McGinty and paid her for four of the large onions that dangled from the door–frame.

'Yon wee Breccan Donnelly's back,' she told her ravaged customer. 'Asking if anybody knows you or where you're hanging your breeks.'

'And did somebody have that to give him?'

'Aye – some tosspot out of the White Hart that give you a hand home the night of the coach knocking over that laddie across the way.'

McAra was tempted to head for Donnelly's place to find out what the Irishman was after, but still under the weather he opted for the Beehive Inn where comfort and solace were to be found. In better humour by the time he was escorted from the pub and flung into the gutter leaving a trail of assorted matter in his wake he was able to convince a cabby that he was sufficiently continent to merit transport to the Halley estate on the edge of the city. The journey was conducted at an uncomfortably high speed, the driver on tenterhooks for the duration, his anxiety for the condition of his

HIDDEN

vehicle increasing with every hundred yards. Sprawled face–down on the gravel drive, his pockets having been turned inside out by the cabby in search of the fare, McAra was hoisted to a more or less upright position by Cassels and dumped on the floor of an outhouse where he lay lamenting the cruelty of the world until Casper, not for the first time removing the policeman's clothes with his now customary distaste and a pair of large gloves, doused him with several buckets of water, and finally introduced him to a clean outfit in which he appeared for dinner looking as if he had just attended a ceremony at the Palace of Holyroodhouse.

Complimented on his suave and admirable attire he beamed on his sister and fellow officer, held knife and fork at vertical readiness, nodded appreciation at the platter of roasted turkey with potatoes and its side dishes of vegetables placed in front of him, announced, 'I can levitate. Self–taught,' and, profoundly unconscious, promptly plunged face down into the red current gravy. The next day somewhat chastened, but in companionable humour, he listened with interest to Emma's account of her engagements with Sir Hudson Smart and his guests.

'There's something I want to do in town today,' McAra said. 'If Latimer's about he can give me a lift. Anyhow, I need a word with him.'

Dropped off in the West Bow McAra made his way to the Beehive Inn from which he could keep an eye on the door to his lodgings across the street. Exercising an unfamiliar discipline he restricted his intake of intoxicant and waited for sight of Breccan Donnelly. When the little Irishman, constantly casting around from the depths of a begrimed greatcoat, pushed open the door of the building and disappeared inside McAra hurried across the cobbles and, keeping his hand on the six–barrelled pistol in his pocket, descended on his unwelcome visitor by barging him from the stone corridor into the feculent room. Balthazar's reaction to the sudden intrusion was to shake his cage with such sibilate ferocity that Donnelly was persuaded that the creature would be at his throat in a second.

'Let me be, you bastard,' he protested. 'I've a bit of news for you.'

But before he could disclose the shape of that revelation two hulking figures came thrusting into the nidorous accommodation and without preliminary tossed the quivering Donnelly into a

HIDDEN

corner.

'Now then, Mac, you still have an eye for your old pals surely,' Horace Trapp bellowed, grabbing the policeman by the shoulders in a gesture so obstreperously ambiguous that it registered either high good humour or homicidal rage. For a moment McAra felt inclined to distrust the acuity of vision that sobriety had induced. It seemed improbable beyond measure that Horace Trapp and Magnus Wallace could have appeared at his very door. These former colleagues had plied their disreputable trade exclusively in the back streets of their province in London and there remained a significant incident in the past and in that location the details of which McAra, had no desire to share with them.

'Horace! About time! So you got my letter?'

McAra's indomitable sly duplicity hadn't deserted him even in his hour of relative abstinence.

'Your letter? What… no I never got no letter off of you. But forget that. I near had you down for a dead–and–goner like Arthur but we thought it the best to do was follow this thing –' indicating Donnelly. 'That's what we're here about. There's killing needs to be done on account of him.'

McAra quailed inwardly but displayed nothing other than counterfeit pleasure and relief at the duo's unanticipated arrival.

'And it's here that it needs to be done, Horace. Like I said in my letter…'

'I said – never mind your letter. I got no letter. We done come here for vengeance, Mac – vengeance. You know the word, eh?'

Now alarmed that the life of the world's most accomplished investigative agent (and liar) was about to reach a sudden and painful conclusion McAra held up a hand and said, 'First we have to get that thieving wee bog hopper out of this place. He couldn't keep his trap shut if the Queen herself was going to fill it with smouldering turf.'

At a sign from Trapp, Magnus Wallace seized Donnelly by the neck, shoved a handful of coins into his coat and dispatched him from the premises with the violent application of his boot to the other's rear.

'You're the best and wisest of men, Horace,' McAra went on. 'It's a miracle you knew what was what without my letter. And here you

HIDDEN

are…'

'Will you, for fuck's sake shut your mouth about some fucking letter. Say to me what you think brings us to this bloody town full of Scotchmen and pish pouring out the windows.'

'I found him, 'McAra announced with no idea as yet where his declaration was going to take him; or whether the assertion was to bear the content that Trapp's reference to the late Mr Bowler was intended to adduce.

'What?'

Both Trapp and Wallace gazed at him with their accustomed combination of suspicion and distrust.

'I worked it out. I found the fellow that did for poor Arthur. It's why I'm up here – to do him in, the way he did in my friend Arthur.'

Trap and Wallace exchanged a long, quizzical glance before the former's face lit up.

'See, Magnus! What did I tell you? Our man here's as sharp as a snickersnee.'

And Horace Trapp clutched the pathological deceiver to his huge chest.

'Let's have it, then, Mac. Who is it? And how did you get the trail of him?'

'It's all in my letter… Oh, shite, you said you never… Well it was the work of a clear brain and a clear eye, and I'm the very man for it.'

'Never mind the boast. Get to the pith, will you.'

'Aye, but look – it's not short, this story. Come on over the road there to the pub and I'll give it you with a wet throat.'

HIDDEN
CHAPTER 16 AUGUST 1842

When, once again bearing Balthazar's transportable residence, McAra arrived at the Halley estate the next morning he was still in a condition of nervous extremity and, to the surprise of his sister, Casper and Cassels he betrayed no signs of a crepuscular encounter with excess. He had been convinced at the first sight of Trapp and Wallace that they had pursued him to Scotland with the sole intention of exterminating him. But while his sister and Casper were consulting the skeleton staff in the kitchen he invented for Cassels the reason for that belief with the same instinctive facility as he had turned to when confronted by the thugs.

'Why? Because I destroyed their gang. Single–handed. Great beasts, they are, the pair of them – a good seven foot each and muscle from hair to heel. I had to handle them pretty rough – beat them till they could hardly walk.'

'So where are they now? In the Calton? In the Royal Infirmary?'

'And clever enough with it – they found me out, didn't they? All the way from London, the bastards. But they'll be in no hurry to take me on again. The only hurry they'll be in is to get their huge arses back to the Great Wen.'

'You had them arrested right enough?'

'Trapp and Wallace. That's their names. But it's McAra they'll not forget, by Christ. The blood that came out of them! Balthazar could hardly believe his luck.'

'You'll need to guard your back these nights then.'

McAra shifted uncomfortably on the bench seat.

'Did you ever get crotch rot?' he asked. 'There's something wrong in my drawers. I never had any shortage of women obviously, but when I'm on this kind of duty it's not so easy – I just wondered if a man can…' he waved a hand in the direction of his loins…'spoil himself. You know – interfering with your own…tampering with…? You're a man of the world, Cassels. What do you think?'

'So you were feared that Trapp and Wallace had come up here to cut that dirty wee throat of yours? And what were you up to anyway that you were mixed in with a gang like that?'

HIDDEN

'Proper policing. Not for the likes of you. A secret mission. They thought I was one of them. The Commissioners needed somebody with nous. Nous and brawn.'

'Aye, I can see that, right enough. And how will you be dealing with these gents now?'

'There's a fellow called Laurie that's a copper here that I might pass them on to. He's like his boss Haining – both of them did their time in the Metropolitan force before they came up here. Not that I ever met either one of them down in London.'

'But you're a pal of Laurie's?'

'And now – Jesus, I can't believe it – there's some damn thing growing between my toes. Whatever it is, it was starting to turn purple last night. I'm not well, Cassels, not well at all.'

An enormous late lunch left McAra supine with a trickle of fine wine meandering through the stubble on his chin and onto the velvet cover of the couch on which he was reclining. He had removed his boots and was gazing sadly at the exposed and discoloured extremities the sight of which the rest of the company – maids, Casper, Emma and Cassels – put strenuous effort into avoiding. Having dozed off for an hour McAra came to with a spasm accompanied by a yell for his long–departed great aunt Bertha. While Cassels was again jogging round the periphery of the estate, Casper walking his dog and Emma preoccupied with her embroidery in the upper salon he summoned a maid, ordered bottle of Bordeaux and proceeded to drink himself into a state of expansive good humour which was shortly overtaken by a repeat bout of blissful somnolence. An hour later it was the sound of a rifle firing that jerked him out of that coma of requited repletion.

'I've been shot,' he wailed, clutching his chest. 'High treason! The horse is on the roof!'

Brought hurrying back by the clamour to this scene of abated contentment Cassels came to a precipitate halt at the sight of the uninjured McAra and glowered down at the horizontal martyr.

'It's nothing but your neighbour loosing off a few rounds, you wee toad. You've been soaking yourself into a stupor and, right enough, you make more sense when you're past speaking but I've had enough. If you don't get on doing whatever it is brought us here I'm away back to Glasgow and good luck to your rotten insides.'

HIDDEN

'I need a holiday. I'm not a whole man.'

'Then I'll be away in the morning, you lazy ape.'

'Now, now, Officer Cassels,' McAra declared, rising from the couch as if resurrected, 'you're duty bound to support this investigation until its conclusion, so hold your water for a day or two.'

'Investigation? All you've done since I set eyes on you is pour drink down into these insides of yours that must be like a blocked sewer.'

In reply McAra fired off a fusillade of burps, plaintive groans and gaseous emissions, raised himself just enough to permit an intake of the residual red wine and, collecting the splinters of his jurisdictional influence, said, 'Prince Albert would not take kindly to your desertion, my man. The safety of the Crown is at stake. Now pay attention to my carefully chosen words – the future of the *Crown* is at stake. We have no more than four days to complete our work. So I insist on…'

But before he could elucidate on what he intended insistence McAra erupted from his repose and rushed towards the nearest water closet, one hand across his mouth the other clutching the seat of his breeches. Appalled at the noise, both retching and thunderous, Cassels retreated to the terrace and, relaxing in the cool evening air, smoked a cigar and sipped a decently small measure of brandy until the lavatorial bedlam subsided. It was some long time afterwards that an unchastened McAra reappeared, his face pale and drawn and a substantial array of regurgitated pork and potatoes and a splatter of wine displayed down his front. From some distance off the intermittent sound of gunfire continued, carried on the evening's still, clear, otherwise undisturbed air.

'Right,' he began, wiping some unsavoury residue from his cheeks and addressing himself to his disgruntled colleague, 'there's work to be done over there before it gets too dark. Off your behind, then, Cassels, and bring your gun just in case.'

'Gun? I don't have a gun, you daft wee nyaff. And who is it you're for shooting the brains out of anyway?'

'Casper,' McAra waxed imperious, 'bring me a firearm of some description. I'll not be taking risks with Mr Cassels' life. These could be dangerous folk we're up against.'

'Earl Bonaly dangerous? Have you taken leave of your senses, sir?

HIDDEN

He's a gentle man. And a gentleman. '
'Be so kind as to leave these judgements to the professionals,' McAra warned him. 'Pray do my bidding and provide me with arms. My own gun is in the armoury at my lodgings.'
'This is not an arsenal, sir. If you insist I can let you have the blunderbuss. But I must advise you – it hasn't been fired since Mr Alaric was here many months ago.'
'Don't attempt to teach me my business, Casper. There is no aspect of the art of the discharge of such weapons that is not an open book to me.'
Duly armed, the gun tucked under his arm, McAra conducted his companion the half mile or so to the copse of downy and silver birch bordering the land belonging to the Earl. From the edge of the wood the sound of a rifle being let off became ever more audible. Sprawled in the long grass beyond the spinney McAra and Cassels could see Bonaly reload his rifle with well–practised skill. A small paper target had been pinned to the trunk of a wych elm more than two hundred feet away and it had clearly been torn apart by the Earl's repeated endeavours.
'Keep watch on this,' McAra instructed. 'My bowels haven't yet settled to composure. I have to do a shite.'
With which he crept off into a thicket clutching the flare–muzzled firearm. With little notion of why he should continue to witness the display of detonative proficiency Cassels did his best to close his ears to the more immediate and prolonged reports of scatological relief. Detached, he watched Bonaly casually raise the rifle to his shoulder and loose off the lead bullet which blasted yet another piece off the mark. The Earl then turned his attention to reloading but before the action could be completed his awareness was diverted in the direction of the screech of horror from the bushes off to Cassels' right.
'God on the cross,' the squeals projected into the limpid air, 'thistles, nettles – my arse, my bollocks; mother of God, ants and all! I'm near destroyed.'
And McAra erupted from the verdant shelter clutching the blunderbuss in one hand and a dozen dock leaves in the other, his undergarments and breeches caught around his ankles. A few hapless steps later he stumbled into the open, wildly applying the

HIDDEN

rumex obtusifolius to the frontal and posterior areas of his lower anatomy. The very epitome of *sang froid* the Earl of Bonaly examined this theatrical entrance without so much as raising an eyebrow while identifying the source of the oral commotion.

Before the situation had been clarified McAra pitched headlong into the long grass and the ancient weapon went off with a deafening roar. Unlike their involuntary and serene host, Cassels was appalled at the probable effect of the accidental gunfire and breaking cover sped to his felled companion. By a miracle of unfathomable chance the charge had gone off and ripped McAra's pants and long–johns to shreds leaving his spindly white lower limbs intact but savagely exposed. Bonaly and Cassels gathered round the stricken officer to bestow on him their separate and differing expressions of concern.

'You fucking moron,' Cassels supplied.

'My dear chap,' Bonaly offered, 'how kind of you to drop in after our previous distinctly unpropitious meeting. I'm afraid my butler did rather exceed his instructions on the occasion.'

McAra tugged his long–unwashed shirt down far enough to cover his genitals and shucked off the tattered remnant of his nether garments. With the subsiding of his enteric paroxysm and having contemplated these disconnected disclosures he announced, 'I am in some distress here. Please be so good as to furnish me with suitable replacements of these damaged articles.'

Bonaly inspected him as he struggled to his feet still grasping the now empty shotgun.

'I regret, sir, that my own girth is three times your own, and I am somewhat taller. I may be hard pressed to accommodate you.'

Bonaly escorted the policemen to the mansion where a servant was commanded to find a pair of pantaloons that might almost fit the uninvited caller. Ten minutes later McAra, was clad in an enormous pair of the Earl's moleskin trousers, the waist pinned to his chest by a length of twine and the vast, bulging legs turned up several times at the ankle to give the wholly misleading impression of elephantine calves. Cassels appraised this vision with dry amusement and said, 'Right – yon Victor Frankenstein did an awful poor job on this one.'

McAra ignored the remark and concentrated on communicating in

HIDDEN

an official tone with the Earl while looking like an exotic breed of giant turtle.

'This creature,' he said, waving a hand in Cassels' direction, 'is my cousin Habakkuk. Unhappily he suffers from a derangement of the senses. He escaped our custody, seized Casper's weapon and set off in pursuit of antelope. He took these to be populating the plains of your estate. As you see I have disarmed him and rendered him harmless.'

Cassels took an ominous step towards the mendacious McAra who dodged swiftly out of reach and placed a placatory finger to his lips.

'We must be careful,' he went on. 'He has moments of clarity. Anyhow, now that we're here may I compliment you on the excellence of your marksmanship. Isn't that one of these Dreyse rifle things?'

'Indeed it is, sir. A gift from my new factor. We are on excellent terms.'

'One of my neighbours tells me you have two of the things. Would you be inclined to sell one?'

'Alas, the other was in my phaeton which was stolen.'

'Ah, a pity. I wouldn't mind a wee shot with the rifle myself. Would you load the thing for me?'

With a puzzled shake of the head Bonaly charged the weapon. With its simplified and highly efficient design, it took the Earl only moments to complete the operation.

'Time to take cover,' Cassels said as his colleague took the gun, and stood well behind the intending marksman attracting a disdainful scowl from his companion. Slowly and carefully raising the Dreyse to his shoulder McAra gave the impression of an accomplished rifleman. Breathing in, he squeezed the trigger and sent the acorn–shaped bullet on an unidentifiable course through the still air, invisible but probably in the direction of the distant Scottish Borders.

'Very inferior weapon,' he pronounced, handing back the weapon. 'Now may I apologise on behalf of my disordered kinsman. I undertake to detain him more securely in future. We will impose on your hospitality no further.'

Then, as if as an afterthought he asked, 'I don't suppose you're a bit

HIDDEN

of a seafaring man? The only circumstance that has a calming effect on the dafty here is an hour or two on the water.'

At a loss to know how to deal courteously with the cranky intruders and concerned for his own physical wellbeing Bonaly shook his head and made much of pulling out and examining his fob watch.

'I do have a rather handsome 21 foot steamboat called *Bellerophon*,' the Earl said. 'I keep her at Leith but I personally seldom venture out in her. Must be a year since I even set eyes on her. Grand on the river but I would hesitate to take her too far out of the estuary. But if you have a mind to…'

'Brown hull?'

'Indeed. Would that injure your cousin's aesthetic sensibility?'

'*Bellerophon*? A coincidence, no doubt. I thought I spotted her out at Granton a few days ago?'

'It's possible. The chap Sir Hudson recruited for me gives her a little exercise now and then – an old sea–faring acquaintance of his from his days in the Company. You'd be safe in his hands.'

Anxious to be rid of his unwanted guests but reluctant to give offence to the silent but patently apoplectic maniac he added, 'Perhaps you gentlemen would care for a glass of something before you take yourselves off?'

While McAra brightened up Cassels chose to intervene.

'It's time we was away,' he said grasping McAra by the arm. 'I need my opium dose. That's what we fought the Chinks for.'

'I'll have my servants return your breeks,' McAra announced as he was led away with a great show of reluctance, then turning to Bonaly, 'I'll leave a small deposit in them. By the way, that wouldn't be Josiah Dicken that looks out for your boat would it?'

'You know him? A fine fellow, but I gather he'll shortly be off again across the sea.'

'A religious man, for sure. Just like yourself.'

'Like me? I regret, sir, I have long since divested myself of all the trappings of the church. Let men pray to whatever eternal silence they wish.'

McAra wrestled a discomfiting wrinkle in his appropriated apparel and in doing so gave vent to so boisterous a gastric gurgling that it shocked Bonaly into silence and drew vehement revulsion from Cassels.

HIDDEN

'I'm a lunatic am I? So nobody'll be surprised if I knock your teeth down your throat in a fit of madness. Just what in the name of Christ were we doing there?' the Glaswegian demanded when the pair had departed the scene of the encounter. 'And what was all that blether about?'

'I had to recover the situation after you near ruined it. Anyhow, the business is too complicated for you. You'll hurt your brain if you try to follow.'

Back at his sister's home McAra inspected his borrowed attire and was satisfied that it did nothing to detract from his elegant allure or from the obvious prerogative invested in him. This estimate was not shared by Cassels who had wearied of his colleague's apparently abysmal interrogative technique and was of the opinion that McAra was now transformed in appearance and fragrance to something not unlike the assembled excreta of a herd of elephants. Preoccupied with picking a range of miscellaneous material from under his fingernails McAra asked Casper whether Bonaly had been entertaining any guests lately.

'Not very recently. Some time back there was a Major DeWitt over there. I was aware of that only because he and Mr Stuart seemed to be having a loud and excited confabulation about some shared interest in Stuart's Scottish provenance. They asked me if they could avail themselves of the library at the Earl's. You may have heard that he has one of the great reference collections in the country.'

'Could you look me up? I believe I have the right to a title in Peru.'

HIDDEN
CHAPTER 17 AUGUST 1842

Closeted in the Red Herring pub the two men were careful, despite the growing exasperation of their exchanges, to keep their voices low.
'All us two have to do is jump on the bloody railway train – we'll be away in Glasgow in two and a half hours. That's it, isn't it?' Josiah Dicken was becoming increasingly edgy as the date for the great venture loomed large on the horizon. Sebastian Bradley was tired of his companion's now incessant bleating about the arrangements that had been so carefully worked out and the tone of his response conveyed his irritation.
'Aye – that's right. Now just keep at my elbow when the time comes, and think about this – after it's over we're set for life. If you think for a single second that you can fuck this up and go your own way I tell you – you'll be in the Forth with a rock roped to you.'
And with an air of frustration and displeasure Bradley tapped the other with a warning finger, swept up his wallet and gazette and stumped out of the place. Sir Hudson Smart had – reluctantly bypassing the elusive Grundy – summoned him to a meeting that afternoon out in Morningside and he collared a cab still smouldering with a combination of disgust at Dicken's sudden expression of misgiving and concern that the seaman's qualms might translate into something that could imperil the whole escapade. More than that he was unhappy at the possibility of his being seen yet again in Smart's company. Scowling out at the city as the vehicle turned from Leith Wynd into the Netherbow he caught sight of a small, louche figure, none too steady on its legs and dressed in the manner of a leper in the final stages of the affliction. The little man was sandwiched between two gigantic and much better attired men and all three were engrossed in conversation.
While Bradley's cab rattled up the High Street Achilles McAra was busy aiming Horace Trapp and Magnus Wallace at the target he had designated for them.
'Aye,' Wallace pronounced, having heard McAra's tale, 'I

HIDDEN

remember Laurie. Tried to scare us into good citizenship. Throwing his weight around, showing off. He was going to clean up the East End – wasn't that it? Silly bastard. He came round with a half dozen hard cases out of the force and thought he'd tidied up the whole place. Then he was away up here and we never seen him after. So he's here for good now?'

'I found him out,' McAra said. 'You can take my word for it. He's been boasting about the thing ever since he came here. And he's been braying that yon Colonel Rowan at the police in London wants him back to sort out the rest of us – give us the same as he gave Mr Bowler.'

'How did you track down that by–blow?'

'I had my suspicions about him from the start. That's what took me up here. If you had the price of a drink I'd give you more.'

Trapp rolled his eyes. McAra was no more and no less McAra than he'd been as Bowler's driver in the capital.

'Never mind the drink. You've done good enough. Where can we get hands on the man?'

'You'll make a proper job of it without me? You know Arthur Bowler and me was very thick together. Maybe it would be best if I done the thing, me being that close with Mr Bowler.'

'Rely on us, Mac. And we'll see you right for a pound or two.'

'Fine, if that's the way of it. I'll give him to you. When's a good time to get it done?'

'We've a bit of business at the White Hart tonight. You can get us there.'

'No, wait – this is the night that Laurie spends in the Beehive boozer. Leave off your trade at the White Hart for another night and you can catch him at closing time. He'll be away home up the Castle Wynd off of the Grassmarket. Mind him, though – for he's a dangerous man and he has friends.'

Trapp prised a few coins from his jacket and thrust them into McAra's outstretched hand which was enough to send the little man scuttling into the World's End bar which he departed reluctantly some time later to the accompaniment of a hefty boot applied with vigour to his backside.

'And learn to sing a damn sight better before you come back,' he was counselled at the top of the barkeeper's voice. In a state of some

HIDDEN

confusion McAra lingered seated on the cobbles until he was almost run over by a two-wheeled dray carrying a load of beer barrels and some crates of vegetables.

'I'll have you murdered,' he yelled after the driver who ignored what appeared to be an incensed vagrant, except to hurl a rotting cabbage at his head. Still sporting the clinging remains of this delicacy and clutching a miraculously intact and unopened bottle of brandy McAra succeeded in taking stock of his situation and brought to mind the purpose he had previously allocated to the afternoon. Disorientated by the brilliant sunlight he wobbled up the High Street and into police headquarters, nodding at the officer guarding the door who by now was accustomed to seeing the caller whom he took to be suffering from a chronic brain condition that affected his motor skills.

'I need to see Andrew Laurie,' McAra announced at the third attempt. 'I have a couple of gifts for him and a bit news.'

Assuming the bottle was included in the intended offering the sentry waved him through, retreating from the fumes that rose invisibly but nasally discernible from the visitor.

While McAra was being conducted into Laurie's private office Sebastian Bradley was pacing the floor of Sir Hudson Smart's drawing room. He was still furious that his co-conspirator Josiah Dicken was, with rather less than forty eight hours to go, voicing unease at the tactics already worked out so comprehensively.

'Please restrain yourself,' Smart said, waving his visitor into an armchair. 'Bear this in mind – we have lost Alaric Halley; now Major DeWitt has disappeared. We can't afford to suffer any more casualties, so you must make certain of Dicken's loyalty. This is no time for anyone to be pulling out.'

'I can handle Dicken all right. But we have to have all our people in the right place at the right time on the 1st and that means he has to make sure things will be going proper at Leith and Queensferry. Them boats need to be fired on the hour and it's only Dicken can get these sailor boys at the job.'

'He won't let us down, my friend. He has as much at stake as any of us. So mind your own.'

'Don't you worry about my folk. They know their business. Or they think they do, and that's the main thing.'

HIDDEN

Sir Hudson uttered a short, false laugh.

'Aspirations to democracy, eh? *Vive la revolution*!'

'I'll not be patronised. I'm not without education and neither are these people. There are rights that they're entitled to and if it takes commotion in the streets and burning boats and buildings, by God, they'll win what should be theirs already.'

'Come, come, Sebastian. Be honest with me. What will it profit the nation if your unwashed hordes can vote a government into or out of power? Do you really believe they'll understand one single issue of import to the wellbeing of the state? All they'll want will be more money for less effort and for their trade unions to dictate the conduct of parliamentary affairs until the rest of us are bled dry.'

'I'll not hear that said. The few have run the world for too long, and they're the ones that have sucked up the wealth that belongs to the many. And what are you and your kind at anyway? We're nothing to you – and you're bugger all to do with us.'

Smart tossed a cigar to his guest and watched him strike a light.

'Your hypocrisy knows no bounds, does it, Bradley? How much more do your trade unionists pay you than they could ever hope for themselves? But more than that – in a few weeks' time you'll be wealthy beyond your dreams and you'll not be looking back with one iota of regret.'

Bradley looked long at the cloud of smoke he had sent drifting towards the ceiling before answering with a shrug.

'I've done what I can. I may not look it but I'm supping from the bottom of the bowl. I'm tired, Sir Hudson, and my spirit's gone. I've fought the cause for thirty years and more and…'

'And now you can go with a clear conscience, eh? Let's not fall out over our motives. We've become Hiram Stuart's creatures, not because he's made us that but because that's been our choice.'

'Hiram Stuart should be tied to a wall in Bedlam and your Major DeWitt has him worse than ever.'

'It's called genealogy, Sebastian. We're all entitled to a past at least as much as to a vote.'

Bradley curled his lip and sat in silence for a long while.

'Then tell me about your Earl fellow,' he said at last. 'What's he to do with the rest of us for it's his coach that'll be for the Castle on the 1st, is it?'

HIDDEN

'Don't you make a puzzle out of that. I can assure you that the Earl has his role – whether he knows it or not is hardly your concern. I trust you are not having second thoughts as late in the day as this? A word to the wise – it would be a very great mistake for you to think of pulling out now.'

'Don't threaten me. Without me and my people you've got nothing.'

'I'm not threatening you, dear boy. I'm trying to help you realise that the less you know about this whole scheme the better it is for you. The nation will not soon forgive us for what we're about to do.'

Bradley was looking round for something to break. He and Josiah Dicken had been spreading around vast amounts of Stuart's money to ensure that the authorities would be hard pressed to perform their duties across the city. There was nothing new about demonstrations of disaffection being mounted to coincide with great public events, and the visit of the Queen would be the perfect platform. And there was no love lost for Prime Minister Peel in Scotland. But both Bradley and Dicken had been enlisted for a purpose of which they knew nothing other than that it was to their personal advantage. In return for deploying their organisational skills they had been promised a future of wealth and comfort in the New World. It was obvious that their years to come were to be mortgaged beyond redemption by what Smart's acquaintances were about. Having been at the beck and call of Grundy from the beginning Bradley had until now been dissuaded from demanding of Sir Hudson what was the project Smart himself and his colleagues were undertaking that so heavily relied on his support. While he had no desire to put his own impending benefit at risk he chose this moment to raise the issue.

'From the first nobody's said to me nothing about what you're after,' he said, watching Smart with a studied intensity. 'And from the start I've not asked. Grundy's made it plain enough there's nothing to know but what he tells me. But I'd be an idiot if I couldn't make it out for myself. Yon Bonaly fellow is a fine marksman – I know about the prizes he's won. And I know about them Prussian guns you got. The lot of us is going to be hunted forever if youse manage this thing.'

Sir Hudson returned Bradley's piercing gaze in stony kind.

HIDDEN

'You'd do well to mind your own affairs,' he said after a long pause. 'My time in this world *is* my affair. A life on the other side of the ocean is a price I'm prepared to pay, even with the law at my heels for the rest of it. But you – you and your fancy friends – why in the name of God would youse...?'

Some faint dawning spread over Bradley's face.

'Wait a minute. It's Peel you're after, isn't it? Grundy's told me about you and your mates that think he's been consorting with the Pope's parishioners. God, man, this is the 19th century. Won't youse ever grow out of it? Do youse really...?'

Bradley had run out of catechistic inspiration. Though he had resisted his wife's urgent and unrelenting enquiry as to the hidden risk, now that the denouement was imminent he found himself plunged into violent inward debate. He knew from Dicken that murder had already been done to protect whatever secrets Smart's group were harbouring. To be a party – even indirectly – to assassination hardly pricked his republican conscience, especially as he could be confident of being out of reach of constitutional retribution, but he was unable to discard the notion that he and Dicken were little more than useful implements in the hands of Sir Hudson's faction.

Finally he contented himself with, 'You'd do well not to cross us. If you try to cheat us out of...'

'Us?'

'Dicken and me. We're not to be trifled with.'

'My good Sebastian, we have no intention of doing any such thing. You're both essential members of the team. And anyway Hiram has the highest regard for you. He has great hopes for you once you're settled on the other side of the Atlantic.'

'And my wife and kids?'

'Of course, they'll be with you. Arrangements are being made. Obviously precautions will have to be taken. The police may be watching them.'

'Jesus – this is dangerous ground we're on.'

'The greatest danger is not to you chaps,' Smart insisted. 'All your business with us has till now been conducted through Mr Grundy. That arrangement has been to our mutual benefit surely. I recommend that it should continue so until the final stages. In the

HIDDEN

event of catastrophe – which I certainly do not foresee – your collusion will remain forever occluded.'

Emerging from his brief conference with Andrew Laurie, McAra stood swaying on the High Street until he was able to flag down a hackney carriage that carried him out to the Halley home on the city's south side. Emma and Cassels had been talking in low tones but fell silent on his arrival except to express irritation at his demand for the fare to be found and delivered to the driver who stood waiting at the door holding a handkerchief to his nose. Balthazar betrayed no sign of enthusiasm at his master's return having dined for some days on very superior sustenance and now expecting reversion to harder times.

'I've business in town tonight,' McAra managed to say a moment before he dispatched a cloud of evil-smelling vapours from the majority of his bodily outlets and tumbled to the floor with a muffled cry for help. Neither Emma nor Cassels nor Balthazar offered consolation or assistance until McAra awoke an hour later shouting that an alligator had sold his shoes. After dinner, and after Balthazar had, with bad grace, devoured the scrap of unidentifiable fruit his master had scooped out of the innards of his jacket Cassels suggested he transport his host back into the centre of the city, but McAra was in no hurry.

'I don't need to be there until about tossing out time at the boozers,' he said.

'I've never known you to favour that dread hour,' Emma commented. 'What are you up to now?'

'Police business. Instructions from the Palace. But first I want a word with young Latimer.'

'He's tending to something at the stable.'

Coherent but still far from sober McAra found the coach driver and obtained from him the details of the offer made to him by Sir Hudson Smart and congratulated himself on the accuracy of his anticipation of these.

'You'll be free, I hope,' he said, 'to take up the engagement?'

'So long as her ladyship is content. There seems to be a fair amount of money in it for such a canny wee job. Sir Hudson has a bet that I can do the thing faster than his American friend says is possible.'

'And it's all set up the way I said?'

HIDDEN

'Near enough, but there's to be two coaches – I'll be with the second one on Barley Street behind Leith Walk. When the first one turns up these folk switch to mine and the timing's to start from there.'
'The passengers?'
'Just the two – Sir Hudson himself and Mr Stuart.'
'You wouldn't have a sixpence about you I don't suppose? My money must have fallen out of my pocket when I was putting my coat on.'
'Your coat? On a day like this?'
But Latimer, showing no sign of resentment, handed over the silver coin and leaned forward to pull McAra's coat properly onto his shoulders.
'That's a good weight you're carrying,' he said and tapped the heavy bulge that protruded from the pocket of the garment. 'So you're still a man for the flintlocks?'
'Better than that, but you look to your own affairs. I hope you've kept a good eye on Hebe for I'll need her the now.'
'She's over there in the last stall. You never *paid* for that thing, did you?'
'She's like me – very deceptive. I'll away and get Balthazar home and get some kip before my appointment. What time are you lined up for on Thursday?'
'Seven in the morning but it might be a good bit earlier or a wee bit later. I'm supposed to get the whole lot of the thing done in daylight so it'll be touch and go. Mr Stuart says it's impossible and he's feared that it's too much for the one driver. He doesn't know me, though, eh?'
'Everything's to be in place the whole distance, then?'
'Couldn't be done else. Aye, it'll be test enough but I can do it, man.'
'Good luck to you, lad.'
'It's not luck I'll need – it's the fresh teams on the spot and sound wheels.'
'And that midget is still convinced we have him under guard day and night?'
'Aye. And he still thinks if he puts his nose out the door he'll be found and broken in tiny bits.'
Back in the house McAra begged another sixpence from Casper before returning to the drawing room and pressing his sister for a

HIDDEN

pair of sovereigns and settling, with a display of disappointment, for a handful of more modest coinage. Turning to Cassels he said, 'Give me a couple of bob, Habakkuk, and I'll see you right in a day or two.'

'Away and shite, you dirty little cadger. If you call me that name once more I'll plant a hoof in your cullions.'

'I need embrocations, ointments. I fear my time in this vale of tears may be brief – the curse of the piles, you see. And who's to tend to me? And you, my dear sister, think I'm a scutch on the family eblotcheon. Even if it's my uncle Tobias Lunge that eats bark.'

Some hours later, aware that Andrew Laurie would be at his usual post that night in the Beehive pub, McAra set up in his tumbledown lodgings to watch proceedings on the far side of the Grassmarket. Balthazar had to accustom himself to a return to less appetising rations than he had swiftly become used to at the Halley household and munched forlornly on some indescribable scraps that his master had found in the gutter where Bertram Hopkin's dried bloodstains were still on display.

It was not until darkness had properly descended that McAra left his lookout post and stationed himself in dense shadow at the entrance to a close and waited. His plan depended on events over which he had little control but he was content to leave the night's happening to spool out as it would. The time had come, he felt, to take precautions against his official role being exposed. Only chance, it seemed, had prevented its disclosure already and now the opportunity to kill three birds with one stone had fallen into his grasp.

As always it was well after closing time that Andrew Laurie, exercising his heavy-handed sanction, left the Beehive pub detectably under the influence of an excess of his favourite brandy. By this late hour even the Grassmarket was deserted and Laurie, humming tunelessly, turned east and made for Castle Wynd which would take him in the direction of his home on the New West Approach. With a nod of satisfaction McAra saw the two towering figures emerge from their hiding place a few yards up the steep lane and he crept to the corner where he could witness the savagery he had choreographed. Laurie was a big man and a hardened street fighter but in his condition and taken by surprise he could be no

HIDDEN

match for Trapp and Wallace. In an instant he had been brought crashing to the ground and lay helpless against the onslaught of two flailing pairs of hefty boots.

'Timing is all,' McAra reminded himself as he took up his position only several feet from the brutal affray; and he watched until he was satisfied that the critical stage in the affair had been reached. Laurie was barely moving and clearly no longer capable of offering resistance. Even in the enclosed arena of the pitch black wynd McAra could see that the victim was rapidly losing consciousness and that there was no sign that the thugs had any intention of giving up their attack until the outcome was fatal to the fallen policeman. The first shot took Wallace in the back of the skull and spread blood and shattered bone in a strange aura around his head as he sank to the cobbles; the second missed Trapp who dodged from sight with speed remarkable in so large a man, and disappeared into the enveloping night.

'Help, murder! Murder in the Wynd!' McAra yelled half a dozen times before scurrying off to his lair on the far side of the Grassmarket where Balthazar welcomed him with some indifference when he was loosed from his cage and nuzzled up to his boss who, exhausted by the events of the day but not entirely dissatisfied with their outcome, promptly fell asleep on his straw mattress. When he was awakened the next morning by the thunderous banging on his door it took him some minutes to recall where he was.

'Suleiman the Magnificent ate my clock!' he was squalling as he came on the remains of his senses to the racket outside and the impatient chattering of his ill–favoured rat.

'Mr Haining needs to see you urgent,' the uniformed officer announced when McAra had prised the door open and was staring wild–eyed at the mid–morning bustle in the Grassmarket. 'The head of the force,' the policeman felt obliged to add when he'd taken in the vision of the rumpled tramp answering his summons.

'I need the bog,' McAra told him. 'I'll be with what's–his–name in a wee while.'

HIDDEN
CHAPTER 18 AUGUST 1842

Having conducted his toilet duties and related ablutions with no more care than usual McAra groomed himself conscientiously by shaving with a rusty open razor that tore lumps of greying skin from his cheeks and chin. With wads of filthy paper clinging to the self–inflicted wounds and the stench of an accidentally spilled chamber pot rising with the warmth of the late August morning he strode forth in the best of humours to his appointment on the High Street. He had, he felt, reason to be well satisfied with his endeavours over the past few days and was confident that these were about to be applauded and probably rewarded.

Conducted with conspicuous distaste to Chief Constable Haining's office by a uniformed officer McAra attempted to beam on this distinguished figure but soon discovered that the effort merely had the effect of showering the floor around him with what looked like blood–stained confetti drifting down from his face. To Haining's quizzical puzzlement he announced, *'Virescit vulnere virtus,'* and slouching onto a wooden chair, disposed his unsavoury anatomy in as elegant a pose as its dimensions and shape permitted. Bearing the signs of a man under great duress Haining stared blankly at his visitor for a long moment before proceeding in a voice cracking with emotion, 'You will not yet have learned that my assistant Mr Laurie was ambushed and savagely thrashed last night. He is in a parlous condition in the Infirmary.'

'My God, sir, what devil was responsible for this outrage?'

'We have identified the perpetrators. We have yet to put names to them but we expect to do so shortly. Tessie Doyle, the bar manager at the White Hart, was able to tell us that they've been here demanding money with menaces from the pubs in the area. She thinks her employer a Mr Landry will have come across them.'

McAra allowed his jaw to drop in horror at this intelligence.

'Mr Laurie has been of great assistance to me,' he said, his brow furrowed with concern. 'I hope he'll soon be fully recovered. And I trust these animals have already been caged.'

Haining thumped his desk with both fists.

HIDDEN

'Mr Laurie was *not* your assistant – he was your senior officer. And, no – these animals as you call them have not been detained. In fact one of them is dead and the other has disappeared. Mr Laurie seems to have managed to shoot at them even as they were coming close to ending his life.'

McAra assumed the air of one struck with wonder.

'Mr Laurie was carrying a weapon? Was it the one I...'

'It came as a surprise to me, I can tell you. He's never done so in the past, but perhaps those threats arising from Victoria's imminent arrival…'

'Victoria?'

'The Queen, you simpleton. Have you forgotten already the purpose of your being here in the first place? And your being at Mr Laurie's side while he was preparing the arrangements to secure the Royal procession?'

'Oh, aye; I mean no, it's just that… well, the shock of him getting done over like that, you know.'

Haining peered at him with more than a modicum of suspicion and reached into the drawer of his desk to produce a six–barrelled pepperbox pistol.

'This,' he said, 'was found in Mr Laurie's hand. Two shots have been discharged, and that must have been with some accuracy given his dire circumstance.'

'A hero certainly. You've had the opportunity to compliment him on his actions?'

'Of course not. The man is still unconscious. He may never be brought round.'

'It's a queer–looking thing,' McAra remarked, reaching for the weapon, but allowing his hand only to quiver over it. 'I came across it in my duties in London. I thought it might be of interest to my friend Mr Laurie. A wee gift, sort of. I'm not a man for pistols myself. Never handled one of the things. Should I go and see him?'

'Good God, no. He hates the sight of you. We all do. You're a repulsive termite who's done nothing but get in the way of our work.'

'With me it's our work comes before all things. Maybe I'll have the wee gun back, though.'

'Your work? You've been nothing but an obstruction to our

HIDDEN

investigations. You've embarrassed the forces of the law with your drunken antics and achieved not one single advance in the enquiries you were dispatched here to conduct. Our Queen or the Prime Minister is at the highest risk and your efforts at protecting them have only impeded implementation of proper measures. There can be no doubt that their lives are in present danger.'

Haining's face was pale, tinted by anger and anxiety. In a voice rasping with frustration he wasted few words on his audience. With Laurie's debilitating injuries ensuring that he could no longer assume responsibility for safeguarding the visiting dignitaries that duty would fall to the Chief Constable himself. Laurie's discovery of the Dreyse rifle at the Granton pier appeared to confirm the assessment of jeopardy. There were reports of widespread street unrest timed to coincide with Victoria's visit and already the forces available to Haining were severely stretched.

'You need have no fear, Haining my lad,' McAra replied to this litany of woe. 'All is already clear to me. Their plan is to…'

'Don't you dare address me in those terms. What is revealed to *me* is of more importance. Your execrable presence here is an outrage. Your behaviour is a public disgrace. I want you gone by tomorrow morning. Take your loathsome self back to London by the first available means. Do not on any account linger within my jurisdiction or I'll have you thrown in jail pending trial for… for treason. Or something like it.'

McAra confronted this ultimatum with equanimity.

'I advise you to take heed of what I say,' he replied. 'Their Majesties appointed me directly and I have ascertained by observation and intellect the details of the plot part–revealed by the murdered Bernard Hopkin. If you will afford me the courtesy…'

'Your powers of observation are confined to identifying the contents of a pub gantry. What may be said of your intellect had best be left unsaid.'

'Maybe we could share a glass of something strong as a farewell gesture? At the White Hart or the Beehive. If your resources would stretch to it.'

'Get out of my office. Now. And one other thing: send that Glaswegian thug – Cassels or whatever his name is – back to the Tron station immediately or I'll have him thrown out of his post.

HIDDEN

By God, I've heard all about the pair of you.'

McAra shifted to one buttock the more effectively to discharge an apparently interminable blast of vile effluvium.

'In the circumstances,' he said, 'I hope you'll be able to let me have a letter commending the high quality of my service that I can present to Commissioner Rowan.'

The Chief Constable half rose from his seat, an expression of absolute detestation written large on his rubescent features.

'Morton,' he shouted, 'drag this creature out of the building and out of my life.'

The broad-shouldered constable appeared in haste evidently in the hope of contretemps but McAra, anticipating a certain disharmony, was already dodging out of reach and scuttling to the exit.

'A little gratitude would have…' he called from the relative safety of the corridor, but concluded from the menacing approach of Haining's subordinate that completion of the suggestion would not be in their shared interest. Instead of opting for extended debate he strolled up the High Street, across the Esplanade and, on showing his ever more crumpled letter from Commissioner Rowan, was permitted entry to the garrison commander's quarters.

'The Queen herself,' he announced, 'has required me to ensure that adequate measures are in place to ensure all is secure at the Castle.'

Colonel Grant gave the impression of being less than complacent. He had spent a large part of the morning in consultation with his Company officers, police liaison and some sinister and unsympathetic officials from London. Government agents were in no doubt that widespread public disorder was planned to take place over the course of the Royal visit and especially on the day of Victoria's arrival in the city. These were viewed as an intended distraction from what was an evident plot to murder Her Majesty or the Prime Minister. Grant was sure that his own manpower resources would be sorely tested, as would these at Haining's disposal.

'If there's one thing you can be confident of, though,' he told McAra, 'it's that within the confines of the Castle that Her Majesty will be at her safest.'

'Aye, well, you better keep in mind what I said before – there's things will be going on at Leith harbour and out at Queensferry that

HIDDEN

will need looking at. If boatloads of gunpowder or some kind of combustible stuff are let loose anywhere near the Royal yacht or the Forth ferries you'll be up to your bollocks in shite if you've not got plans to deal with them.'

Grant shook his head in frustration.

'You say that, but you don't let on how you've come by that intelligence. How am I supposed to take it seriously else you give me the right story of it?'

'I'm not here to bandy words. My spies are everywhere – take it from me that you need to have your men in the right place to put a stop to the business.'

'Good God, man, as it is I've got to support the civil power from Portobello to Corstorphine and Granton to Morton Hall. Not to mention Dundee and Glasgow. You should know that I've instituted a Popham system of signalling between the cities but that does nothing to increase the speed of the men themselves. And the police are in no better condition.'

'I'm called back to London for a conference at the palace. I'll register your concerns, but even my great powers have their limits. Anyhow, you wouldn't have a noggin of brandy to ease a soreness in my innards?'

With a display of reluctance the Colonel produced a decanter and splashed a small measure into a crystal glass. McAra slurped down the brandy and inspected the empty vessel with disapproval, holding it up to the light to confirm it had been drained.

'Did you ever hear of a lady called Albertine Burgess?' he asked.

'How does that concern…? Oh, never mind. Yes I've met her. She had permission a long while ago to do some drawings and paintings here. About a year or two back that would be.'

Before the Colonel could probe the basis of the enquiry further a brisk sergeant came clumping in, saluted and delivered into the CO's hands a folded piece of paper. Grant scanned its contents quickly and turned his attention to McAra who was receding into gloom at the rate at which the prospect of further supplies of some very fine cognac was disappearing.

'Allow me to explain what's going to happen,' the policeman began, 'when the Queen and her consort…'

'Yes, yes, McAra, but I've had the dubious pleasure of being treated

HIDDEN

to your ruminations before now. Now I'm told Colonel Roland needs to consult me urgently. Please take yourself and your cluster of fragrances off to some other arena.'

With a shrug McAra shuffled out of Grant's office. Wandering with a disconsolate air towards the Grassmarket he was diverted from that destination by the sight of a pub on the West Bow. Not taking too seriously Haining's injunction to remove himself from the city at short notice he made himself comfortable at a dark corner table and with a vague notion of his own itinerary in mind set about alleviating his thirst. It was evening before that operation had been successfully concluded and, tears streaming down his face, he was embarking noisily on the second verse of "My heart's in the Highlands":

"Farewell to the mountains high–covered with snow,
Farewell to the straths and green valleys below,
Farewell to the forests and wild–hanging woods,
Farewell to the torrents and loud–pouring floods."

The essence of patience and good nature, the landlord suffered this invasion of the civilised ambience of his establishment for longer than reason or fortitude could have been expected to support. But even by the time his guest's incontinence – both vocal and bodily – had become conspicuously obtrusive the rest of the clientele remained an appreciative audience and, sympathetic to their entertainer's condition and carefully avoiding various areas of his person, they carried him shoulder high onto the pavement and left him clinging to a gas street–light to gather himself, shed his unruly emotion and totter off down the slope to the Grassmarket. It was there that misfortune struck. A great fatigue had crept over him and the temptation to pause for rest became irresistible. With a sigh he lay down in a foetal position facing the wall of a five storey tenement and, with the way ahead now seeming to be clear, he once again exercised his predilection for lassitude and fell into a contented sleep.

Sometime later Breccan Donnelly was hurrying up the slope towards the High Street when he noted what appeared to be a discarded bundle of well–worn, by no means intact but probably wearable old clothes. But he was discouraged from availing

HIDDEN

himself of this sartorial windfall by the cry of "*Below*" from the third floor, which was accompanied by the generous spilling of the contents of a slop–pail. As soon as these had settled on what Donnelly now saw to be the recumbent occupant of the heap of tattered apparel he removed himself in haste from the stirring dump of hazardous waste.

'Jesus, Mary and Joseph, it's McAra the walking dung pile. I took you for dead by now with them fellows from London at your arse.' Rendered coherent and cunning by repose McAra, his hair medusa–like, his eyes like pools of putrefying sludge, steadied himself against the wall and said, 'Them were my pals. Saved me from some murderous midget called Newsome. They let on I better sleep somewhere the wee bastard and that razor of his can't find me.'

'Newsome? I know him. Why's he after your stinking hide?'

'Grundy thinks I warned you that the dwarf was out to slit your filthy neck. Trapp and Wallace got the word out of a copper called Laurie that let Newsome back on the street after he was jugged. Grundy's covering all his tracks from the killing of yon fellow Hopkin, and Laurie's his man.'

Donnelly rewarded this duplicitous assertion with a sneer. Ignoring the expiration McAra breathed that combined onion, gin and gastric reflux fumes on top of his scatological and urinary decoration, he assured the officer, 'I'm not feared of Newsome. He's only handy with the horses. And he's only any good with a blade when your back's turned.'

'That's what I just said. Sooner or later your back's going to be turned. One late night more than likely and you'll be in a pit in the Canongate graveyard.'

A cloud of irresolution drifted over Donnelly's charmless face and McAra proceeded with his embroidery of the truth.

'Tell me where Grundy is the now,' McAra persisted, directing a blast of oesophageal effluvia into the other's unprepossessing face, 'and I'll set the pair of us free.'

'No idea. Haven't seen him for days.'

'Well hear this – the whole business is to do with the Queen and Peel coming here and youse are a long way out of your depth.'

'Me and who else?'

HIDDEN

'There was Haggerty. And there's Josiah Dicken and Sebastian Bradley for a start. And don't say to me you never heard of them.' Donnelly cupped a hand over his nose and mouth in an effort to ward off the bombardment of miscellaneous essences radiating from the sickening presence in front of him.

'I never heard of them. And I'd have the throat out of that midget Newsome before…'

'Ah, no. He's a killer. It was him, wasn't it, drove the coach that mushed up Hopkin? Hopkin found out what Grundy and his crew was at. You'd do well to make a run for it from that little butcher. You'd be no match for him.'

This derisive dismissal produced the riposte McAra was aiming for.

'No match! If I could find that undersized ratbag I'd hack the head off him.'

'You're just talk, man. Newsome's in a place in Anchor Close, but I've seen you shite your breeks at the sight of my chum Balthazar so…'

'Anchor Close? I'll show you, you Scotch cur. What door is he at?'

'I can tell you that but he'll not open up without you let on you're somebody else. You'd need the nous to change that fucking voice of yours. And give him two words – Felix Athol. Would you mind them and say them in the dark?'

'I can mind them. I'll slit that goblin from his balls to his gob.' And Donnelly allowed his knife to slip from the sleeve of his burlap cutaway. 'You seen this before, McAra. I know the use of it.'

'Right enough. But you better be a damn sight quicker with it than you were when Balthazar was having a good look at you.'

'It'll be done this night. I'll not be spending my days watching the back of me.'

'Then good luck to you for he's a dangerous wee fucker.'

McAra watched the now sanguinary Irishman stump up the cobbles muttering. While the policeman was taking time out to reflect on his own astuteness Colonel Grant was pondering the demands that the Royal visit were placing on the Castle garrison and on his nerves. His men had had a good deal of recent experience in handling agitation in the country's main cities but none of this had so preoccupied him as the complexities of the present convulsion.

HIDDEN

He was inclined to dismiss McAra's vague admonition about fire-ships in the harbours along the Forth; it sounded primitive and ridiculous. And yet there was something about the repulsive little braggart that made Grant uncomfortable with the notion that he could safely be disregarded. Although he could ill afford to deploy a squadron to both Leith and South Queensferry he reluctantly decided that early in the day of the *Royal George's* arrival in the port he would further deplete the force stationed at the Castle itself to carry out an inspection of the two locales.

Meantime a relieved Hebe had shed the near–comatose, McAra in the yard of the Halley estate. And Casper and Officer Cassels had, with great distaste and greater heroism, once more peeled off his smeared and bespattered apparel and tossed him into a stone trough full of water intended for Hebe and her like but which quickly became so polluted by his flailing presence that any equine enthusiasm for aqueous refreshment was quickly dispelled. When his sister, braced against the sight, came to find him reclining in bed a couple of hours later he managed to prise open one eye and complain, 'Out there I had to pee from a recumbent position. I think I've scraped the top off my pizzle.'

'William Haining sent a man up here earlier to tell me you've been ordered out of the city so listen to me, Mac – you have to go tomorrow or you'll be flung into the Calton. And I can't say I'll be devastated to see the last of you for a long, long while.'

'Take a peek at it, would you? A little massage, maybe.'

'I've completely lost track of what's been going on with the Hopkin business. So let's forget the whole affair and try to get on with our lives. Preferably four hundred miles apart.'

'My dear Emma, all is an open book to me. The Queen is safe. Prince Abelard is safe. Sir Robert Peel is safe. I have swooped on the impious like an avenging angel.'

'Prince Albert. And all you've been swooping on is a lake of liquor.'

'You're familiar with the man Grundy?'

'No – I never met him. Alaric had dealings with him, though. Why?'

'He's always been a step or two ahead of me. I'd like to lay hands on him. Before I go can you get Casper to go to that place in Leith and find some sailing notices? They can tell what boats are moving out of every big port in the country. I'll tell you the ones I want.

HIDDEN

You wouldn't have a bob or two that would slide into my purse?'
'If they'd help you on your way – you and that Balthazar thing. I've packed some clothes for you, so try to keep them in a half–decent condition until you're well out of Edinburgh.'
'Send that lazy bastard Cassels up, would you. It's time he was away somewhere.'
'So you'll go early tomorrow?'
'One other thing. Remind me – when's Latimer away with your Hudson man?'
'Thursday.'
'You have word of Sebastian Bradley and Josiah Dicken?'
'It seems they've gone off today on some sort of expedition. Sir Hudson has been none too pleased to be bereft of your Mr Grundy's acting as a buffer between him and that pair.'
'Good. Very good. Now remember what Casper's to do for me. By the way my haemorrhoidal affliction is cruel tonight.'

HIDDEN

CHAPTER 19 AUGUST 1842

What was puzzling William Haining about the murder of the dwarf Newsome was neither the fact of the killing nor the ease with which the perpetrator was caught. It was that Newsome had been detained some time earlier on the instruction of the odious McAra, but had almost immediately been set at liberty by order of Haining's own deputy Laurie. The killing in Anchor Close had been bloody and brutal. Newsome's throat had been slashed more than once, but it was clear that the dwarf had not died without a fight – his own weapon had been found by the side of the corpse, the blade dripping with gore. And within minutes the crime had been reported to the beat officers by a lurching, loud–mouthed drunk reeking of ordure who had disappeared while the Irish killer was apprehended dashing from the Close still carrying his knife, his clothes saturated in his own and – presumably – his victim's blood.

Andrew Laurie had some explaining to do and Chief Constable Haining decided that he himself would conduct the interview. In the event his deputy was in no condition to respond to his questions, nor did there appear to be the slightest chance of his ever doing so. As to any motive for the attack on Laurie and the subsequent demise of Magnus Wallace nothing had been discovered except that it appeared to be true, according to junior officers at police HQ, that McAra had given Laurie a pepper–pot pistol and a bottle of brandy. Draped in vegetable detritus and the worse for strong drink, the London detective had insisted loudly that the gifts were intended as a gesture of reconciliation after their previous, extended acrimony.

The following day, shortly after dawn, Cassels set off from the city, having dumped the severely hungover McAra at Haymarket railway station and Emma Halley breathed a sigh of relief, a sentiment shared elsewhere by Chief Constable William Haining, Colonel Grant, Earl Bonaly, Hiram D T Stuart, Sir Hudson Smart, Colonel Roland and assorted traders and publicans throughout the city.

Two days later – Thursday 1st September – the Royal party sailed

HIDDEN

into the Duke of Buccleuch's private harbour at Granton. Because of anxiety over the safety of the Prime Minister, the Queen and her consort exact details of their arrival had been kept from all but a small number of officials directly involved. The consequence had been that preparations for the visit had been made for the Wednesday and the disappointment of the crowds expecting to catch sight of the Monarch and her entourage had been mitigated by mixed amusement and disapproval at the premature antics of the demonstrators who had taken to the streets in several areas of the city to express their collective grievances.

Josiah Dicken and Sebastian Bradley, now nowhere to be found, had set their tactics to run under the supervision of a caucus of trusted lieutenants who were quick to realise the mistiming of their events and withdrew their legions for a more effective operation to be mounted the next day. At eight o'clock the *Royal George* emerged from a low-lying fog on the Forth and berthed at the bunting-decorated pier. Joined by the Duke and Prime Minister – who had arrived in Edinburgh earlier – Victoria and Albert descended the gangway from the yacht to cheers from the modest but enthusiastic crowd. Some minor inauspicious alarums invaded the decorum of the jamboree. Neither the city's Provost nor its Council had been made aware of its commencement and so missed the grand entrance. The Earl of Errol was almost run down by the Queen's barouche; and amid the atmosphere of subdued tension the phalanx of her protection officers took the city's Honour Guard for potential assassins and engaged in a brief but violent brawl with them. Discouraged perhaps by the shenanigans of the Chartists, trades unionist and various anti-government agitators together with the intimidating heavy presence of the police and military the population had not turned out in the numbers anticipated.

Nevertheless the procession to the heart of the Old Town went off without further unwanted incident, partly because Colonel Grant had dispatched a small force of his cavalry to both Leith and Queensferry where they had discovered, as McAra had predicted, a number of boats stacked high with flammable materials intended to be launched at the *Royal George* and at the ferries and corvettes further up the river. To the south, east and west of Edinburgh every available man in Haining's police force and Grant's Scots Greys

HIDDEN

confronted and, with sustained effort, controlled the violence ignited *in absentia* by Dicken and Bradley.

With most of the garrison deployed in three cities Colonel Grant had spent the early part of the day hurrying between the guard posts at the Castle and repeatedly reminding the sentries of their duty to ensure that Victoria and Albert would be cocooned behind a screen of absolute security. On his orders and despite the careful monitoring of all visitors the surrounding ramparts and buildings were manned by as many armed troopers as could be corralled. Some weeks earlier the Earl of Bonaly had, at the request of the Colonel Roland, volunteered his services to facilitate the transfer of the Honours from the Crown Room to the exhibition area. By daybreak his coach had been drawn up inside the portcullis gate and a brass chest brought from the vehicle. A pair of Sergeant Rannoch's men stood sentry at the entrance while Colonel Roland loaded the jewels into the huge case and when summoned the troopers carried the cumbersome casket to the temporary lodging where the crown and other accoutrements were prepared for display under the regal eyes. Seeing the unsightly crate dumped casually on the site of the exhibition, the Colonel waxed furious at what seemed to be a minor infraction.

'Their Majesties tripping over that would see you tossed in the Tower, you oaf,' he warned Rannoch. The bulky item was loaded back on the coach which trundled off into anonymity after the guards had poked around inside and confirmed there was nothing to be seen in either the vehicle or the chest. But it was with the fear of assault on the Royal party while in their safe–keeping that most conditioned the disposition of the garrison's senior officers. In the event the occasion of the Royal visit went off without a hitch. Recent attempts on the life of the Queen ensured that her personal bodyguards formed a protective cordon around her even in the Castle's comforting embrace. If more severe threats were to be present beyond these prodigious walls, Colonel Grant asserted with a sigh of relief that that was hardly his concern.

'Lock up the display chamber,' Colonel Roland instructed Rannoch, 'and we'll move the Honours back to the Crown Room tomorrow. I'm away now to Holyroodhouse.'

But the Sergeant was staring at the crown jewels with an intensity

HIDDEN

that was strange to him. A moment later he was hissing to the corporal at his side, 'Get a troop mounted and after that damn coach of Bonaly's and catch the bastards before they get away.'

With a shrug Corporal Denning threw his hands in the air.

'Jesus, man, what's got your dander up? The coach is away hours ago and look – there's nothing missing there.'

'Do what you're told, you stupid shite. Find that bloody coach and everybody in it. Do it now!'

'But I'm telling you we stopped the thing at the gate and had a damn good look…'

'The crown, you fool – there's no blue stars on the monde. It's a fake! Get your arse moving. Get every man available and ride down yon coach. And tell the coppers on the esplanade the jewels are away. It's Bonaly's folk that have took them for sure.'

'I'm telling you – we searched…'

Rannoch's impatience gave way to fury.

'Do what I say or by Christ I'll see you flogged.'

Already mounted on his horse Colonel Roland, purple with rage, descended on this altercation.

'Rannoch, control yourself. You'll issue no such threats here. Now take your time and tell me what's got your goat. The Honours are there in front of you, so what's all this shouting about? And you, Denning, stand fast till I make sense of this.'

'Every bloody second, Colonel – every bloody second we stand here bawling the odds – these fuckers are riding the Crown Jewels right out of our hands.'

'Mind your language, Sergeant, or it's you'll be the one on the wheel.'

Rannoch narrowed his eyes and, inspecting his commanding officer with frank suspicion, took hold of the reins of the Colonel's thoroughbred.

'You know every quarter inch of them, sir. Look at that crown and tell me it's right.'

With a show of irritable reluctance Roland looked down at the glass case beneath which the jewels rested and, leaning forward, spent a long time concentrating on the collection. Unable to contain himself Rannoch turned on Corporal Denning and repeated his order. Denning hesitated, torn between obeying and waiting for the

HIDDEN

Colonel's endorsement. But Rannoch's seething urgency won out and, without further delay, the Corporal was off running towards the Castle's main gate.

'Another five fucking minutes you went and gave them,' Rannoch shouted recklessly at the Colonel. 'I'll have Colonel Grant hear the whole story.'

Roland climbed into his saddle, appeared to debate whether to drive his mount in the direction of the gate, but with a resigned shrug abandoned the idea.

'Oh, God, you're right, Rannoch. There's treason here. On my watch there's treachery.'

'Aye,' Rannoch called over his shoulder as he rushed off in pursuit of Denning, silently complimenting himself for having absorbed McAra's remarks about Albertine Burgess's paintings of the Honours. 'And there's a reckoning going to be had.'

For the next two hours the police and military authorities cavorted with pandemonium and contended with bedlam. Ashen and unsteady on his feet Culver Roland paced the length of the esplanade muttering to himself. Meanwhile his apoplectic colleague Colonel Grant was closeted with Chief Constable Haining in a temporary command post set up in the Queen Anne building. Mounted troops of the Royal Scots Greys were speedily withdrawn from their attempts to disperse the marchers and rioters and dispatched to guard such exits from the city as the roads leading east, west and south; and at the Haymarket Railway Station and the docks of Leith and Granton all traffic was instantly halted. The river Forth was blockaded by the navy and the Popham signal system relayed instructions to Glasgow and Dundee to require all departing vessels to be searched before being permitted to set sail. The estuary of the river Tay was also to be closed to shipping and the docks in Glasgow to be picketed. The police officers who could be spared from similar duties elsewhere were posted to their familiar beats with instructions to find the Bonaly coach at all costs. An urgent search for the Earl himself resulted in his being led undignified and humiliated from the royal reception at the Palace of Holyrood. Almost fainting with uncomprehending horror he surrendered to an aggressive interrogation by Haining himself. The Earl's tearful explanation that his coach – handled by a temporary

HIDDEN

driver now lost to sight – had been made available to the Castle authorities at the specific request of Colonel Roland was confirmed by the Colonel. The elegance of the vehicle, the eminence of the owner and his conspicuous loyalty to the Crown had combined to make the choice appropriate. As this inquisition was taking place Colonel Roland elected to disappear from the scene of the mortifying malefaction.

It was late afternoon before the vehicle was traced off Leith Walk, empty of passengers and luggage. There was no sign of the huge chest, and houses, shops and every other establishment in the area were searched with a brutal enthusiasm; but the coach's early and speedy departure had delayed official reaction long enough to permit the fleeing plunderers to make good their escape well before either cordon or search parties could be readied and operational. At the exits from the city soldiers and police stopped and searched every vehicle. But with the enormous increase in traffic occasioned by the Queen's visit none of this was revealing. The small number of additional mounted troopers available at short notice were posted to ride the main routes out of the capital at high speed. These included the roads to East Lothian, the direct road to Glasgow, the ferry crossing of the Forth River and the southern part of Midlothian. This was the best that could be achieved in a short time and less obvious or less likely pathways and tracks had to be left unattended.

'How in the name of Christ did Culver Roland contrive this affair? There's nobody other could have done it.'

To Haining's livid enquiry the only response was a helpless shrug from Colonel Grant who was too well aware that the ultimate responsibility for safeguarding the Honours rested with him as garrison commander. Sitting with head in hands Haining said, 'It may be what that little shite McAra was trying to tell me. Why in hell couldn't he just have come straight out with it?'

'McAra? How could he have known anything about this? The idiot's an out–and–out drunk.'

'Maybe, but I should have given him a bit more credit. I'll say that to you and nobody else, mind you.'

'Well, neither one of us is a mind reader.' Grant paused and then confessed, 'The wee man set off to give me some story about all

HIDDEN

this but I shut him up before he could get it out. If I'd sent my lads out to the Ferry and Leith yesterday the way I think that repulsive bobble was telling me I'd have had a cohort here for damn quick deployment today. But he's such a horrible bloody shrimp...'

'So there never was an assassination plot. It was all to keep us too busy to see what was going on. But how did the bastards get the Honours away out of the Castle? If they were in the Earl's coach why did the sentries not see them?'

'No idea. And what about Bonaly himself? Surely you can get the truth out of him? And what about whoever organised all those crowds that were set up to keep my lads and yours busy all over the place?'

But if the Earl was involved in the plot it was going to be difficult to prove. He had been at Holyroodhouse with the Royal party when the theft of the Honours had taken place; and he was known as a favourite of Prince Albert's. His credentials as a loyal and trusted subject were impeccable. The fact was, though, that Bonaly's vehicles had been used first to run down Bertram Hopkin and then to spirit the jewels away from the castle. And several days previously Laurie had reported that he and McAra had uncovered the presence of a rare type of rifle concealed at Granton. So far, enquiries of the dealers in the city had suggested that the only purchase of such weapons had been on behalf of the Earl. How that could relate to the theft from the Castle remained a problem if the intention of the plotters had all along been to steal the jewels and not to attempt to murder the Monarch or Sir Robert Peel. Unless, Haining decided, the objective had been to further divert manpower from the Castle itself. And since the discovery of the gun at Granton several officers had been preoccupied with observing the Earl's activities when they could far more usefully have been deployed elsewhere.

'True enough,' Grant said, 'the jewels would be worth a fortune in the right circumstances but there must be few who could afford them and even fewer who would have the gall to buy them. And the stuff could never be shown off to a soul.'

Haining kept to himself the conviction that the treasure was lost beyond recapture. He was of a mind that the trove had been sequestered somewhere within the city and would be moved only

HIDDEN

long after the hue and cry had died down. Short of invading every property in Edinburgh – not a practical enterprise – the best that could be done was to continue the search of all the homes and commercial properties within a tight radius of where the abandoned coach had been found.

'I'm going to have to have serious words with this Colonel Roland of yours,' he told Grant. 'You'll keep him under guard till I'm ready for him.'

'The man is broken. He was a fighting soldier for years so minding the Honours wasn't the greatest thing in his life. All he wanted was proper military duty. The man is boiling with resentment. And now he's weeping like a two year old.'

The Chief Constable was not inclined to sympathy.

'That'll fool nobody. A few minutes more and he'd have been well on his way. The sooner I have him and Bonaly shut up tight at the High Street the sooner I might get an admission. And a clue about where the jewels have been taken.'

'Tread warily,' Grant counselled. 'The Earl has many friends in elevated places.'

Despite the desperate activity by the forces of the law and the military night fell on the city without any trace of the missing Crown Jewels and no hard evidence had been unearthed to implicate anyone in the crime. In light of Grant's words of warning Haining had refrained from arresting Bonaly and instead he had posted officers to keep watch over him. Having spent the rest of the day in the august company of assorted nobles and statesmen at the Palace of Holyrood, the Earl was now cloistered at his estate on the outskirts of the city.

'I want him to know that he's being watched,' the Chief Constable told Grant. 'When the time comes he'll be that much easier to break down when I have him run in.'

Colonel Roland was not allowed the same freedom of action. No–one else had had the opportunity or the latitude to effect the replacement of the real jewels with the counterfeit ones. And Sergeant Rannoch's report confirmed that the Colonel had been on the verge of galloping out of the Castle before the hue and cry was raised. He had remained isolated in his rooms in the barracks until Haining burst in to discover the old soldier crouched in a corner on

HIDDEN

the floor. Unable to extract anything meaningful from the hysterical Colonel the Police Chief gave up and left him under guard. An hour later the sound of a pistol being discharged brought Sergeant Rannoch running. Roland had blown his own brains out, but not before penning a cryptic note acknowledging his guilt in the affair and expressing remorse for the weakness wrought in him by some vague promise of riches. It went on, somewhat incoherently, to curse the authority that had left him a half–pay nonentity and to confess his fear that under robust interrogation he might betray his co–conspirators and their plan of escape. He would not permit himself to such an act of betrayal.

'Betrayal?' Grant was incredulous. 'Jesus, what are we to make of that? Was he honourable or treacherous to the end? Does the Queen know what's happened?'

Haining shook his head with some vigour.

'Good God, no. Let's see what your lads or mine come up with before we go down that dark road.'

'Much as I hate the man I need to get hold of McAra,' Haining said, inconveniently aware that he himself had ordered the little detective out of his sight and purview.

'I doubt,' Grant told him, 'you'll find him. Or find him forthcoming after the way you and I both…'

Long before this inconclusive termination of the debate at the Castle the coach driven by Felix Latimer had thundered at breakneck speed along the back roads of West Lothian and headed through small towns and villages far from the principal route leading from the capital to the west side of the country. As arranged many days before, teams of fresh horses, generously paid for in advance, had been prepared at regular intervals and were standing ready at each stop. The changes were completed with a rapidity and efficiency that impressed even the feverishly excited passengers. Sir Hudson Smart and Hiram D T Stuart had been tossed around inside the vehicle like autumn leaves in a gale but no word of complaint had issued from their constricted throats. Hanging on to the leather straps and with their eyes often closed tight against the sight of the countryside rushing dizzily past them they shared in jubilant silence the triumph of their clandestine undertaking. Smart himself had much earlier floated with the American the notion of

HIDDEN

secreting the Honours in Edinburgh until the clamour had died down and then moving them at leisure when the search had been called off. Hiram had been dismissive. He had a strict timetable to observe and needed for his own reasons to be back in California as soon as possible. Now that the most nerve-wracking part of the flight would soon be behind them, Sir Hudson could hardly contain his delight that the high-risk strategy had borne such satisfying fruit. Despite the frenetic character of the ride he felt himself basking in a condition of euphoria.

The dwarf Newsome's disappearance had alarmed and disheartened the two men but at the third halt they were able to congratulate each other and the absent Sebastian Bradley who had spotted this consummate replacement. Latimer had proved cheerful, unquestioning, a virtuoso at the reins and more than a mere substitute. He had been invaluable not only in his handling of the four-horse teams but also in ensuring that the vast crate was properly and professionally secured in the boot to resist the rigours of the high speed passage. As to its contents he had manifested no concern or curiosity.

In rather less than five hours the vehicle had reached the village of Buchlyvie, slightly more than half way to its destination. Sir Hudson and Hiram climbed down and made a great show of stretching their limbs and yawning as if the frantic speed with which this landmark had been achieved was nothing other than what could have been expected. After a hasty late breakfast during which Latimer uttered not a single word and signalled his presence by little more than a jaunty smile the party was back on the road to Drymen and on to Balloch with another couple of changes of team. Having left Edinburgh shortly after first light the coach had been subjected to the wildest ride it was possible to imagine and yet the driver showed no sign of fatigue or discomfort. For some time he had had to content himself with the sedate transportation of Emma Halley around the city. Now he was able to enjoy the recaptured thrill of his racing days which, combined with the financial reward, made for a perfect day. And despite the velocity of the excursion it was to take the best part of the day to reach first Portincaple and then Coulport on the shore of Loch Long. Nevertheless this destination was arrived at somewhat ahead of the most optimistic

HIDDEN

schedule while the rays of the western sun were still glazing the surface of the loch with a gold and silver refulgence under a gathering of low purple clouds.

By the shore the exhausted passengers were discharged on the deserted village beach. On the hectic journey Sir Hudson had been driven to contemplate the possibility that Latimer might return to Edinburgh by a more direct route with almost the same dispatch as had brought them away from the city, and that their whereabouts and possible onward passage would be divulged before their escape could be ensured. To avoid this hazard he had concocted a lie that he hastily recounted.

'Some colleagues of mine,' he told Latimer, 'will be travelling back east from here in about six or seven days. I hope you can await them here.' And he handed over a sum that was more than double the driver's monthly remuneration. Delighted with the windfall Latimer had no hesitation on agreeing to wait for the fictitious arrival.

'Mr Latimer,' Hiram D T Stuart intoned, adjusting his sporran and ill–fitting kilt, 'I pronounce you noblest knight of the Kingdom of Alta California. Quarters are prepared for thee in yonder tavern but before you depart our regal company let me…'

And Hiram bent over the chest that Sir Hudson had freed of its ropes at the rear of the coach and with much scrabbling and cursing finally succeeded in opening the lid, shooting the bolts which secured the false bottom and laying a hand on the still hidden Sword of State of Scotland.

'Kneel, my loyal vassal, and prepare yourself for advancement in the ranks of the New World aristocracy.'

But before the ceremonial weapon could be exposed and brandished by the plainly unbalanced colossus Sir Hudson edged the large American aside and slammed the case shut. There was no reason, he thought, for Latimer to be made aware of the illicit freight. It appeared to him sensible that nothing should point even belatedly to their plunderous venture. Uncertain of what was going on Latimer presented an uncomfortable bow and, repeating his gratitude for the prosperity bestowed on him, led the coach and horses off in the direction of the inn at which Smart was pointing.

'There will ever be a place for you at the Palace,' he heard Hiram

HIDDEN

cantillate but chose to disregard the decree and raised the tempo of his retreat.

Hiram was triumphant and was only dissuaded with difficulty from a further swoop on the crown and sword in their concealment in the hidden compartment of the chest. Disappointed, he settled for joining Sir Hudson in carrying the considerable burden as far as the deserted bothy overlooking the loch. An energetic push opened the door and the two men struggled into the narrow lobby and deposited their load in the deserted sitting room. Bouncing off sharp–angled furniture in the gloom Sir Hudson set about finding and lighting candles and cursing the non–appearance of DeWitt who was supposed to have got the cottage ready for their brief stay. It had been the Major who had, with Smart, designed the circuitous escape route from Edinburgh and who had made provision for a boat for the penultimate leg of their flight from Scotland to the Americas. His non–appearance was more than troubling. At least, though, there was good reason to expect Culver Roland to keep to the pre–determined plan and join them in Bristol within the next few days.

'Where the devil is DeWitt? Are we to row the bloody thing ourselves?' Sir Hudson continued to fulminate, the rhetorical question unheeded by the wide–eyed Hiram who was busy contemplating his heroic future in the flickering light.

'Yon Latimer fellow,' Stuart said, 'managed to get us here with nearly three hours to spare. I would never have believed it was possible. Your lieges Bradley and Dicken should be on the *Esmeralda*. And now – we Jacobites, we Stuarts have returned. The King will be over the water. I am he!'

Exasperated but aware of his own pecuniary interest in the American's peculiar, real or imagined world Sir Hudson refrained from the acid comment that had oscillated on the tip of his tongue. There was a long trip in front of them and huge reward to be had at its terminus and there was no point in putting so much at risk by trying to dampen the crackbrain's spirits.

HIDDEN

CHAPTER 20 SEPTEMBER 1842

Rain was starting to fall which did little to improve Sir Hudson's disposition. The cottage was cold, there was nothing to eat, only some brackish water to drink and Hiram's increasingly weird behaviour, which Smart attributed to the imminent completion of his long–planned project, was threatening to become a capitalised index of his declining rationality. Setting about foraging for the *Ceasg* in the approaching dark and torrential downpour Sir Hudson was thrown into a state that combined anger with fear when he came on the vessel and found a hole in the hull that he could have put his head through.

'Then you'll have to find us another, my Lord,' Hiram, temporarily engaged with reality, instructed with an air of regal calm.

'If I knew where I could get a boat at this time on a filthy night I'd do it.'

'The *Esmeralda* will be here soon. How are we supposed to get out to her? Can she come near enough the bank?'

'God no. She'd be stuck in the mud forever. I'll try to light a fire to guide her as close in as she can come and maybe they'll have a tender they can send in.'

'A fire in this rain?'

'One must try, Your Majesty. This is our sole chance to get away.'

While Hiram remained perched on the vast trunk Smart set about a task for which he was little prepared by humour or experience. Quarter of an hour later, however, Hiram pronounced himself content when the window was lit by the leaping reflection of flames.

'How long will that fire last?'

'A good hour or two,' Sir Hudson estimated as he pulled a blanket around himself and stood watching for some sign of the *Esmeralda's* arrival while the large American hummed *The Liberty Song* and annoyingly tapped the beat on the lid of his locker. Just as the whole affair was about to drive Smart to a mental condition not much removed from that of his companion he caught sight of the navigation lanterns of a vessel heaving to fifty yards offshore.

HIDDEN

Ignoring the pulsating rain he dashed to the beach and standing in the glare of his beacon waved his arms and shouted into the growing storm. The surface of the loch was turning dangerously rough but with so much at stake Sir Hudson was prepared to take any chance to make good their escape.

To his relief he was able to make out a boat being lowered and figures scrambling into it and he called on Hiram to join him at the water's edge. As the American dragged the huge case down to the bank the dinghy, rolling ominously from side to side, edged into the shallows under no power other than that provided by the rower's broad shoulders. Sir Hudson was taken aback to see Sebastian Bradley and Josiah Dicken leap from the bow and haul the little boat hard onto the sand.

'It was for us to make sure the right folk was being collected,' Bradley announced without any preliminary greeting. 'Where's DeWitt?'

'No idea. The man's gone. The brains of the pair of you must be in bits getting off the ship in this weather.'

'I told you – we was ordered. And this is the thanks we get for making sure you and George Washington there are safe and sound? Now tell me this – is the thing done? Peel – is he...?'

Sir Hudson ignored the urgent but unfinished question and looked in alarm at the rising and falling of the loch, braced himself and tried to take proper control of the situation.

'What in the name of Christ is that?' Bradley demanded, scowling at the trunk and not pursuing the greater issue. 'Who's brought a fucking wardrobe with them?'

'None of your concern. Give Hiram a hand to load the thing on board. Then let's all be on our way.'

'I wager this is what the police and soldiers was after – there wasn't a boat getting away from the Broomielaw that wasn't searched. And I heard the same thing's going on at Leith and even up at Dundee.' The oarsman was waving his hands at the imposition and delay.

'I'll take your box and your big chum there, but that's the lot. We'd never make it back to the ship with all of youse at the one time. I'll be back for the rest of youse, but you'll have to damn well hurry up for this weather's going to get worse.'

Smart hesitated and even Hiram, *non compos mentis* as he was,

HIDDEN

understood the suspicion that coloured Sir Hudson's demeanour.

'Have no fear, gentle knight,' he declaimed. 'I will not countenance the *Esmeralda's* departure without all of you on board. You will be my Palace Guard.'

'Hurry up, for fuck's sake,' the oarsman said. 'I'm not here for the night.'

With a good deal of groaning and cursing the great trunk and Hiram D T Stuart were loaded onto the boat which, with a shove from Dicken was launched into the seething waters of the loch. The three men on the shore then watched with anxiety as it made its precarious way out to the *Esmeralda* swinging on its anchor. The distance was not great but negotiating the brief voyage was a tricky operation achieved only via the skill and determination of the one–man crew. Through the slanting rain Smart could see the box and the American finally pulled safely up over the gunwales of the ship.

'We'll still make it to Bristol for the *Great Western*, will we?' Sir Hudson asked Dicken on whose familiarity with things nautical he had to rely.

'Be still. She doesn't sail for nearly a week yet and nobody's going to be looking in *her* hold for this freight of yours. But aye, the sooner we're all on the *Esmeralda* ourselves the better for our wives are on her, and Grundy as well.'

'Josiah, get down there and douse that fire before the whole of Argyll sees it. It'll be ten minutes before our man gets back for us, so we'll signal him in with a light instead,' Smart said. 'Come on, Sebastian, let's get out of this weather for a bit.'

The duo scuttled back into the building and Bradley had just lit a lantern when a long, unearthly shriek from outside froze them in a tableau of appalled consternation. Exchanging incredulous glances they were compelled down the corridor when the brouhaha was transformed into a pitiful wail followed by a screeched exclamation: 'My heart! My great heart! I am afflicted! I am sore afflicted! Sore afflicted!' and silhouetted against by a flash of lightning a small, desolate figure, drenched and clutching its chest staggered into the lodge.

'Hell and damnation, McAra, what are you doing here?'

'I'm not a well man. The pain is unspeakable. I'll likely pass on before your very eyes.'

HIDDEN

'My God,' Bradley said, moving even further back, 'what the fuck is that all over your clothes, you dirty wee savage?'

'My apologies, gentlemen, I'm no sailor. Came down the Clyde yesterday and the weather was rough. My lunch was evacuated.'

'I repeat,' Sir Hudson shouted, 'what is it that brings you down here like this?'

'I shouldn't be out in these conditions. My constitution won't stand up to them.'

'What are you doing here, McAra?'

Before McAra could offer explanation Bradley pointed over the new arrival's shoulder.

'What in the name of God is that?' And he pointed to an array of lights coming round the headland, rising and falling but moving with some speed directly towards the *Esmeralda*.

'I have matelots and legions at command. That,' McAra said, vainly trying to wipe the long–dried regurgitated matter from his waistcoat, 'would be my cohort from the Trongate police station away up the river.'

Before either Smart or Bradley could persuade themselves of the grotesque reality of this Josiah Dicken had come rushing back from putting out the fire on the beach and instantly saw his hated adversary who was busy coughing up what he was preparing to assert were the contents of every nook and cranny of his interior. With a roar of unbridled loathing the sailor launched himself at McAra's undefended rear only to be halted in his tracks by a blow to his throat from Hughie Cassels who emerged from the shadows with half a dozen other officers none of whom appeared anxious to avoid a brawl. As Dicken, still choking and gasping for air, reeled backwards Cassels caught hold of his arms in a grip of ferocious vigour.

'If I hang on to this bastard,' he told McAra casually, 'you might want to plant a boot on him.'

'I'm not a man given to violence,' McAra answered but chose anyway to aim a kick at the captive's groin. While the objective struck him as laudable the execution lacked finesse and the result of his enthusiasm was his missing the target by a considerable margin and leaving him sprawling on the ground while a handful of coins were scattered from his pocket.

HIDDEN

'That's my money, you thieving shite,' he snarled at Dicken and spent the next couple of minutes scrabbling in the sand for his capital. As this retrieval operation was under way it was possible to see the *Esmeralda* being secured alongside the paddle sloop which had been engaged by the Glasgow police and Sir Hudson Smart collapsed on the stone step with a gurgling cry. Sebastian Bradley was a big man and handy with his fists but he gave no thought to resistance to the louring posse.

'You can marvel at my investigative prowess at your leisure, gentlemen,' McAra said getting to his feet and peering at the money he had picked up to make sure that not a farthing was missing. 'Meantime you'll appreciate that I needed that trunk of yours to be put on your boat there so that not one of the whole gang of you has a claim to innocence. I am the finest, most...'

'Oh, for fuck's sake, somebody shut that wee insect up in a jar,' Cassels said, and for good measure twisted Dicken's arm up his back until it cracked.

'We never had nothing to do with killing Peel or the Queen or whoever...' Bradley bawled as he was being led off.

'Neither did anybody else,' McAra took some satisfaction in telling him. 'And the mysterious Mr Grundy should be in irons by now. He must be a right clever kind of fellow to have got the lot of you pulling together, eh?'

Sir Hudson, by now weeping profusely, was yanked to his feet by one of Cassels' squad and the motley group made its way through the pouring rain to the inn where the police had established themselves the previous day. Under Latimer's uncomprehending eye the cellar was by midnight accommodating around twenty prisoners, an unhappy and increasingly quarrelsome group composed of Sir Hudson's intriguers and the crew of the *Esmeralda*. To the chagrin of their captors there was one significant absentee from this incarcerated company: Walter Grundy had leapt into the churning waters of the loch and there was every likelihood that he had plunged to his death.

In the bar, however, the atmosphere was conducive to festivity, in the middle of which McAra succeeded in disporting himself with dignity for almost ten minutes before the temptation of excess overcame him. Later, lying crumpled in a corner, a puddle of red

HIDDEN

wine spreading artistically from his chin across the soiled expanse of his putrefying finery, he managed, in the seconds before languor overtook him, the first verse of Thomas Hood's Song:
"The stars are with the voyager
Wherever he may sail;
The moon is constant to her time;
The sun will never fail;
But follow, follow round the world,
The green earth and the sea;
So love is with the lover's heart,
Wherever he may be."

HIDDEN
CHAPTER 21 SEPTEMBER 1842

On McAra's return in triumph from Argyll two days later he collected the impatient Balthazar, bade farewell to the ever–vigilant Mrs McGinty and apprised his sour–faced landlord of his imminent departure. Neither of these worthies seemed devastated at the prospect of his less than ambrosial retreat. Gathering together his decomposing belongings – including the interesting paperwork Casper had obtained for him – he was on the point of setting off to slake his customary thirst when the door was thrown open and the hulking Horace Trapp came thundering in. Artfully concealing his sudden terror McAra leapt to his feet without hesitation and threw his arms round the giant's towering form.

'Horace, my friend. I'd given you up for dead. I heard about... you know.'

Trapp shoved him aside and sat down on the soiled bed flexing his massive fists.

'I never seen what happened. Poor Magnus got his head near blowed off and now there's a hue and cry out for me. I've been hid in every shite–pit in this godforsaken Scotch hellhole. I'm lost, Mac, lost.'

'There's coppers will be on the lookout for you. You'd be welcome to lie low here, but it's not that safe. Folk watch out in this damn place.'

Trap twisted his fingers together and scowled savagely at the floor. 'I still can't...' he began but McAra could swiftly out–think the big man.

'Best to get away before the word's too wide. I can sort that for you, but there's something you need to know.'

'Jesus, what fucking else is there now?'

'That Laurie copper that you done over – he never was the *thinker* behind what got done to poor Arthur Bowler. My snitch at the High Street has found out the whole truth of it. He knows the fellow that planned Arthur's killing so Laurie got the easy way of doing of it. It was the same one came to Laurie's rescue and did for our pal Magnus and nearly had you too. And my man's learned how it is

HIDDEN

that fellow's got rewarded.'
Trapp's face turned purple with a combination of rage and hate.
'Tell me the whole of it. Tell me how I can get at the fucker. Then tell me how you can get me out of this rat's nest else it's a rope for me for sure.'
Balthazar made a scratching sound of disapproval at the unfavourable rodent reference while McAra set out his invented and somewhat speculative narrative.
'Are you in funds enough for a long journey?'
'Money's never short.'
McAra produced a piece of paper covered in hand writing and, waving it under Trapp's nose, launched into his elaborate fiction.
'I can't wager you'll get your revenge but there's a good chance of it. What I *can* promise you is this: a way get yourself safe out of the hands of the law and a fine place to make a new living,' he said and, *ad libbing* with his routine perfidious skill, outlined the tale he had concocted on the spur of the moment. Winding up the convoluted fabrication he added, 'There's money by the bucket–load to be had, and more. And for a clever fellow like yourself there'd be no need to be getting your hands dirty lifting it, if you get my meaning.'
Leaving Horace to find his own benighted way on a long and risky journey, McAra mounted the faithful Hebe, who kept her muzzle averted, and rode like a dilapidated Don Quixote out to the Halley residence. Deposited in his usual corner of the lounge Balthazar demonstrated his recently acquired proficiency at smoking the tiny clay pipe that his master wedged between the bars of his cage. The wheezing cough was not to be alleviated by the practice but, 'It'll do him good,' McAra explained knowledgably to Emma. 'He's not been right for a long time with all that fancy stuff you've been feeding him but the smoke will kill off whatever's been poisoning his insides.'
'I assume your veterinarian skills have been widely acknowledged.'
'And the unhappy Colonel Roland?' the visiting Lord Bonaly asked as Emma's loyal retainer Casper brought in a tray of drinks on the ungenerous measures of which McAra cast a cold eye.
'Left for heaven with the barest warning. Sped on his way by my genius. He likely thought the stealing of the Honours would never

HIDDEN

be found out, the fakes were supposed to be that good. But I told yon Sergeant Rannoch what he should be on the lookout for,' McAra said, reaching for the brandy bottle rather than his glass and having his hand struck away by his sister 'Obviously I had the whole of the thing right from the start.'

'And I gather it was you who mounted the expedition to Argyll to nab the whole gang red–handed?'

'Aye, none other. I've been magnificent.'

'Well,' the Earl said, 'I'm grateful to you for getting me free of all that suspicion that was thrust on me. What I don't understand is why I was chosen as the stalking horse.'

'This talking horse? Surely there's something shaken loose in your head.'

McAra was prepared to be in expansive mood so long as the cognac remained almost within reach. While he was debating how best to order his account and to divert Emma's attention from his surreptitious assessing of the distance between himself and the alcohol his crony Balthazar emitted a staccato wheezing hack which caused him briefly to turn aside from his pipe and scrabble on the cage floor with his forepaws as he tried to catch his breath. When the bout had subsided he returned to inhaling the black smoke with renewed eagerness.

'An open book to me from the beginning,' McAra claimed, examining with visible concern something perched on the end of the finger he had withdrawn from his nose. 'Oh, God, no – that looks like a tadpole. You don't think...'

'The Stuart plot,' Emma reminded him. 'Get on with it.'

'I have a brilliance in these matters, as in most things. And you, Mayor Bonallak, poor devil, were set up as a diversion from the antics of your cronies. It wasn't just police manpower that was being spent – it was making sure everybody was too busy peering into the affairs of the best shot in the country. And protecting Victor and Arabella.'

'Victoria and Albert,' Emma corrected with a roll of her eyes.

'But there was never a danger that I'd follow the breadcrumbs to your door. A false trail was laid. It was like yon Shakespeare play that's called Hamlet but nobody called that ever turns up in it.'

'Oh, Mac, just tell the story.' Emma glanced in supplication at

HIDDEN

unresponsive heaven.

'It was that big trunk thing I nearly fractured my fundament in back in March. You'll remember, Em? At Alaric's place in London. It had the motto of the Kingdom of Scotland on it. In Gaelic, of which I'm an adept. It had a false bottom. It was on a bit of a lend to Roland, the very fellow responsible for minding the Crown Jewels. Loaned to him by a loon descended from the Royal House of Stuart. That's what Major DeShitt had told him anyhow.'

'I must applaud you, sir,' Bonaly told him, 'but that would constitute only the most issuable of evidence.'

'My methods are much admired by the forensic cognoscenti. Only *hoi polloi* aren't up to getting a good hold of them. Hiram Stuart is a man with something fractured between his lugs, but rich enough to buy anything in the world that he wants. And he haled my brother–in–law and the rest of them into his scheme – bought them.'

'Bought them? These are all wealthy in their own right.'

'Not on Hiram's scale. And not on the scale they used to be. They fell foul of some flimflam and lost a fortune. Hiram was offering land, gold likely, and a seat at his round table in that California place."

McAra could possess himself no longer and lunged at the brandy bottle swiftly enough to evade his sister's intervention. Bonaly remained dubious.

'I still can't see how you could tie all this together and arrive at the plan to steal the jewels.'

'Is nothing stirring in that skull of yours? The coppers and everybody was going to be too busy looking at you and them Royals to worry about the Honours.'

'But what about that business of wanting to kill the PM because of him changing his mind and supporting the Catholics?'

'More smoke to hide the real thing.'

'It still makes no sense,' Bonaly complained. 'Why would they make up motives? Just drawing attention to themselves, old chap?'

'Aye, but that's not evidence, is it? Just enough to keep the law fussing about the wrong thing. But when they tried to pull the eyes over my wool – that could never work.'

Balthazar had over–exercised his partiality for cheap tobacco and had retired to the back of his cage to retch noisily in the expectation

HIDDEN

of some sympathetic consideration that would not be forthcoming while his master was preoccupied with a combination of strong drink and the exposure of his own sagacity.

'Look,' McAra went on, 'that brooch of Emma's – she told me months ago it had come from Hiram – he had it made by his own jeweller. So making a copy of the Honours from Albertine Burgess's pictures is no problem. Albertine is smitten with me and lets me know of the cat's arse she'd made of the paintings. So Hiram's plan is to grab the originals and go off to rule his new kingdom on the Pacific.'

The Earl's brow was furrowed as he tried to pursue McAra's rambling narrative.

'The gaps are great yet...'

Impatient, McAra waved away the objection.

'Then poor Bertram Hopkin, him that got himself run over in the Grassmarket – squished by a coach with your crest on it – the only one of your fleet that had it. Now, you'd have been a right idiot to be leave a clue that size at your tail–end if you'd been behind the thing. Somebody wanted the blame put on you.'

'And Bertram had a secret to impart.'

'Right enough. And who did he do work for? Sir Hudson Smart among others.'

'It fell to you to investigate.'

'Then everybody knew fine that it was one of your wee wagons that was going to the Castle with the chest for the Honours – again you'd have been a bonehead to be that obvious about the business.'

'The ploy spotted as quick as you like by none other than Achilles McAra, of course,' Emma said.

'Your name is Achilles?' The Earl sounded surprised.

'I discover who arranged Hopkin's killing,' the irritated McAra hurried on, 'and hear about guns bought and a gunman's hide is brought to my attention. Your cutter – that *Bellerophon* thing – seen at the same place collecting a fellow called Donnelly that left a gun that was supposed to be found. That was Andrew Laurie trying to mislead me. Mislead me, the poor bastard!'

'Oh, Mac, can't you for once...'

But McAra was in full flight.

'It was Colonel Roland that left your coach handy at the yard in

HIDDEN

Low Calton to get stole. And it was out of that coach that the gun was got. All that evidence pointed to you, your worship.'
'But you still took me to be innocent?'
'When you told me that the missing Dreyse rifle was in your stolen coach and it was Josiah Dicken had your wee boat out on the Forth at the time I made out you were just a pathetic dupe. I knew all about Josiah Dicken and him being a pal of Hudson Smart from their days in the East. And anyway I never took you bright enough for the job.'
'Thank you. But the others...?'
'And if it was you going to put a plug in Peel, say, it would have been for him doing his wee bit for us Papists. But then you told me without thinking about it that you didn't have the curse of religion about you – so why would you care a hare's dropping for the emancipation business? I had you in the clear. And right away I work out Stuart's and Smart's plan to get away with their haul. It has to be full–pelt and roundabout to dodge the soldiers. They need yon poisonous dwarf Newsome with great driving skill to bring it off. I set it up so that same midget has to be got out of jug so that he can ride the getaway vehicle. Who sorts that but Andrew Laurie?'
'The Deputy Chief Constable? I don't believe it.'
'Aye. It's a pity but the law's finished with him – mind and body gone. Lucky for me, you might think, for at any minute he might have given out my description to Bradley or the rest. Not likely, with him thinking me being just another copper out of London to look after Her Majesty, but possible all the same. But somebody must have thrown a pigeon among the cats, eh? That was a happy coincidence, him getting that hiding, eh?'
'But Sir Hudson and Hiram Stuart and Colonel Roland? Who could...?'
'Stuart filled in some of the gaps himself. Quotes something about wearing a crown; says the mermaid will be waiting...'
'The mermaid? What on earth has that...?'
'Stuart told Em the mermaid would be waiting for him. The wee boat I found at Loch Long was called the *Ceasg*. It's Gaelic for Mermaid.'
'Yes, you said have the Gaelic?'

HIDDEN

'Need I repeat myself? Everything. Every language known to man. I mastered Akkadian and Sumerian at the age of four.'

'Mac, for God's sake…' Emma prodded her sibling in the chest and withdrew her finger in revolted haste.

'Then there was that keeping the police and soldiery scattered all over the place.'

'So a minimal deployment at the Castle, obviously!'

'I picked up a lot from what I heard in a pub called The Red Herring. You can learn much in pubs, Lord Bonhomie.'

'You might,' Emma suggested, 'at least learn how to behave properly in one.'

'It was Emma here told me that the Esmeralda Sir Hudson spoke to Alaric about was the *Esmeralda* – a ship heading to Bristol out of Glasgow. I checked her out at the Broomielaw quay so we knew when she was due to set off.'

'And you're telling me that Alaric Halley – your own brother-in-law, was mixed up in all this skulduggery?'

'Exactly – dulskuggery. The man was loathsome. A money grubber too.'

'*Was*? You don't think he may already be away in America?'

McAra contemplated the Earl's earnest enquiry in wry silence.

'I think you'll find poor Emma's a widow.'

'Well, yes, I suppose he *has* been gone long. But my acquaintance Major DeWitt? He's nowhere to be found either.'

'No? Maybe he fell in yon loch over in Argyll.'

'And there never was a plot to assassinate Sir Robert or the Queen?'

McAra suppressed a yawn.

'Their Majesties, the Prime Minister, you, the Chartist folk, the trade unionists – all a diversion from King Hiram's coronation.'

Lord Bonaly waved his dimpled hands in appreciation while McAra guzzled down the brandy and brandished his perspicacity with the half empty bottle.

'It could all have been a lot less bother,' he announced. 'But every time I started to explain it to the army or the police they shut their lugs.'

'Splendid work, sir. And what will you do now?'

McAra shifted his weight to one side the better to set free a long sigh of vile gastroenteric breeze.

HIDDEN

'I need to get back to London. I'll wager crime has been running wild while I've been away. And I have to drop in at Rydal Mount to give old Mr Wordsworth a few lines for some poems he's revising. I got him started with *"Far across the fields the lowing sheep."* He's never bothered to use it – he no longer has my gift for the pastoral. And another wee stop–off elsewhere.'

'I suppose your colleague Mr Cassels' efforts will be rewarded in some way?'

'I've given him a wee holiday. There's a chum I'd like him to catch up to.'

'You have that authority?'

'My dear Lord Bohemian, the powers invested in me are without limit. Prince Adalbert himself...'

'Mac, look at Balthazar,' Emma told him before he could expatiate further, 'he's being very sick. Poor thing, he shouldn't have had to listen to you.'

But McAra was in triumphalist mode. Filling his glass to the brim from the dregs in the bottle and clutching it out of Emma's reach he announced, 'I'll be away in the morning for wee bit business on the way,' he concluded as he polished off his drink with a melancholy waving of a trembling hand. 'Then back to Whitehall Place to make sure the Commissioners of the Metropolitan force have been carrying on my work with me away.'

The ventosity ejected from the depths of his entrails was so violent and enduring that even Emma, who was accustomed to her brother's colicky idiosyncrasies, drew back with a gasp.

'Better,' McAra announced with satisfaction. 'I feel better now.'

'The Chief Constable,' Emma reminded him, 'is no less keen to see the back of you than I am.'

Three days later, with the morning sun bathing the busy port of Avonmouth Harold Wax, the clerk on duty at the pier office of the Great Western Steamship Company, was giving vent to his irritation. The visitor had been persistent in pursuing information that Wax felt it unprofessional to divulge.

'I would let you see these,' the intruder told him, holding out a small leather case the contents of which were evidently weighty, 'so that you'd know the truth of the thing. You're an honest man for sure but you'll understand that I can't leave it in the care of anybody but

HIDDEN

himself – it's nearly all of my cousin's worldly wealth in there.'
Though the gesture was unnecessary, Harold heaved a sigh and ran his finger down the passenger manifest. Walter Grundy had left no more than two hours previously bequeathing him a complicated tale of inconvenience.
'And you're Mr Grundy's cousin, you say?'
'I am. Parthis Mendacior by name. Walter likely passed it to you. The arrangement we have is of long standing.'
'No, he never said nothing about it. But –' a pause to express reluctance to comply – 'very well. Mr Grundy has been obliged to meet the cost of a possible alteration to his plans. He now possesses a ticket for passage either the day after tomorrow or for next month.'
'Yes, yes. I am aware of his difficulties. And they will compound without him having all this.'
Mendacior once more waved the small heavy valise.
'He fears his urgent affairs,' Wax went on, 'will detain him in the city until late tomorrow night. If that happens he may well miss the following morning's departure. That's why…'
'Why he has been compelled to make provision for the later sailing. Good God, man, I comprehend that. What is at issue is how I can fulfil my obligation to pass this treasure on to him.'
Wax recoiled from the man's testy impatience.
'Contain yourself, sir. If Mr Grundy is to catch the *Western* the day after tomorrow it will not be, he thinks, until the very last moment. He will have to make all haste to the port from Weller's Hotel in town. That's where he has lodged his baggage, though not himself. With luck he expects to be at the Hotel half an hour after midnight to collect it. But one minute too late here and he will miss the departure. Unfortunately timing must be strictly adhered to.'
'Weller's Hotel? Good. But didn't Walter tell you where he could be found all day today or tomorrow?'
'No, sir. Why would he?'
'Then thank you. I'll ensure Walter is aware that you have done everything possible to assist him.'
'There would be a modest token of appreciation?'
'Certainly, as soon as Walter is in possession of his resource.'
At which point Mendacior was gone and for more reasons than one

HIDDEN

it was an encounter that Harold Wax would not want to repeat. His eyes streaming he waved his hands furiously at the rank air.

That evening McAra, having a couple of days earlier bade farewell to his sister, who resisted any temptation to delay him or lament his going, arrived at the Bristol boarding house where Cassels was already installed. Without pay for a lengthy period McAra had as usual fallen back on Emma's good offices. But when he suggested to Cassels that to keep their collective outlay to a minimum they share a room the nauseated Glaswegian drew a very pronounced line.

'Don't you ever wash?' he asked. 'The stink off you would knock over a horse a mile away.'

'Weakens the sinews, shrinks the mind, atrophies the genitals. A touch of bay rum on the oxters and crotch and you're fresh as a dewy morn.'

'No, you're fucking not.'

'Right, if you're dead set on separate rooms you can buy me dinner at the Ostrich Inn. I had a decent afternoon in the place.'

'The Ostrich?'

'It's one of these stripy things that look like cows. You get them in Canada.'

'I mean the inn. Why there?'

'They do meat pies.'

Popular with merchant seamen the Ostrich Inn on Lower Guinea Street was a harbour–side pub from which a clear view was to be had of the comings and goings of traders, crew, victuallers, merchants and wrights. The huge dinner McAra had insisted on was several tankards of Burton beer reinforced by large measures of port. While Cassels made his laborious way through the courses that constituted the more usual definition of the meal McAra slipped into a state of urbane semi–consciousness out of which he was prodded his colleague's heavy boot.

'Tell us, then, you miserable sot, what we're doing here apart from spending your sister's money.'

'Before I was the most celebrated police officer in the land I was many things.'

'That sounds about right. And a thing you still are.'

'After a career in the military…'

HIDDEN

'Emma told me you was a boy soldier and you was in the army for less than two years.'

'After a career in the military,' McAra persisted, loosening his waistcoat so that his could accommodate the lagoon of intoxicants he was applying himself to, 'I was in great demand as master of the poetic art. Folk like that Shelley that drowned himself when he was bysshed. And yon Aberdeen fellow the Duke of Byron with the one leg. They got their best lines off me for next to nothing. But the main thing was not the money – it was the anonymous generosity of my youthful genius.'

'Are you going to tell me what we're after in this godforsaken hole?'

'And then after that I graduated from the Faculty of Arts at the Sore Bone – in Paris.'

'That's not what it's called, you idiot.'

'Aye, it is. It's for they teach a lot of doctors there. Anyhow, after that I became for a wee while a travelling intellectualist, but the compulsion to bring order to the lawless streets of London was strong. I...' McAra's eyes were rolling in his head and confusion derailed his train of thought. 'What the fuck was I talking about? There's a lot *you* can learn from it.'

'Just your usual lying shite. McAra, you got me sent here so you might let me know why.'

'By any estimate I should be beloved by everybody – personable, amiable, a devoted relative, a staunch upholder of the law, a champion of the downtrodden. Yet everybody hates me. Every bastard hates me. And I'm getting old, and there's been no begetting,' McAra mumbled, lapsing into a self–pitying torpor. 'If I don't breed shortly there'll be no apostolic succession.'

'One more chance – say to me what in the name of Christ we're up to in the godforsaken hole.'

'A wee while ago I had Emma's fellow Casper find out about departures for the States from here.'

'You're wallowing. I'll get you a coffee.'

'God, no, I'd fill my breeks. Here, you haven't been shagging my sister, have you?'

'If you don't tell me what's going on I'm going to belt that obnoxious chaft of yours through the back of your skull.'

McAra tried to raise a glass in an ironic toast but discovered that

HIDDEN

he no longer exercised adequate control over his limbs. Sitting back with a whimper and a look of stupefaction he peered slack-jawed at Cassels.

'He did it,' he said. 'It was all his handiwork. Me and you, we never set an eye on him but it was him all right.'

'Now what?'

'Slippery as an eel. The fucker never drowned.'

'You're on about that Grundy lad, then. You're off your head, man... Grundy's in the loch and there's herring tasting the pelt off him.'

'The *Great Western*'s for New York the day after tomorrow. You can see her from here.'

'And even if you were right about Grundy, it's like you say – neither you nor me ever had a look at him. We'd never know him. More than that – why would he come here when the rest of the gang have been jugged?'

McAra was swaying dangerously in his chair but managed to steady himself by closing one eye and gripping the edge of the table with both hands.

'Where else? Every bobby from John O'Groats to... to somewhere else will be on the lookout for him. It's at the other end of the Atlantic that his fortune is. But I'm the one will nab him.'

At which point the master detective's forehead crashed against the table sending tankards and glasses scattering and smashing on the floor.

'He's on duty,' Cassels explained to the irate landlord, left a handful of coins and hoisted the barely conscious inebriate to his tottering legs and carted him unceremoniously from the pub into a night of lashing rain and a cold autumnal wind.

'I should drop you in the fucking harbour, you putrid tosspot,' the gloomy Glaswegian muttered, struggling to keep McAra on his feet long enough to reach their lodgings. 'I'm away home tomorrow and I hope you get your throat cut before then.'

Cassels was making the most of a decent breakfast when the ashen-faced McAra emerged from a sleep that had been signalled all night by such stentorian snoring that few others in the establishment had been able to close their eyes never mind close their ears to the thunderous din.

'A big day in front of us,' McAra said as he slumped into a chair

HIDDEN

opposite his overtly hostile colleague. 'The *Great Western* sails at one tomorrow morning, but we'll have Grundy this very night.'

No longer surprised by anything McAra was moved to pronounce on, Cassels ignored the claim and continued to eat as if he was alone in the world.

'He's a dangerous man,' McAra went on, his trembling hand reaching for a cup of coal black coffee that the sour–faced maid dumped in front of him. 'We'll stay on the safe side and carry these.' And he passed a pepper–pot pistol across the table.

'God in heaven, put that away, you glaikit ignoramus. You're shaking that much you're likely to blow my head off.'

'It's a wee present. I gave it to yon fellow Laurie in Edinburgh but he never had the use of it so I got it back. Put the thing in your jacket and you'll bless me for it.'

'And shut your mouth about bloody Grundy. The man's dead and gone. And I'll be gone myself soon. I'm for Temple Mead to get the railway to London. After that I can get to Newcastle by the train and I'll find a coach out of there to Glasgow. So away and die of a good dose of scurvy.'

McAra was busy sniffing his own armpits and completed the exercise with an enigmatic shrug.

'The head of the Constabulary here is a Superintendent Bishop. You get along to see him and tell him we're here to detain an escaped criminal from Scotland. If he wants to know more give him just a few vague wee bits and pieces. Make them up if you like. I know him from the London force and he'll not be too bothered so long as his lads don't have anything to do with it. I'd go myself except him and me wouldn't be the best of pals.'

Cassels stared blankly at McAra.

'Are you deaf altogether? We're finished, you and me. I'm scunnered. You need locking up for your own good. Now – not another word or you'll have my fist in your gob.'

'And while you're at it find out from the local enforcers of order where Weller's Hotel is.'

Cassels set aside his cutlery and leaned forward with a glare of loathing fixed on his face.

'Go ahead,' he hissed. 'Say something else other than cheerio and I'll rip the tongue out of your head.'

HIDDEN

McAra edged out of range but continued to try talking his way out of the severity of the previous evening's aftermath.
'Mr Grundy's favourite cousin Parthis Mendacior turned up at the purser's office yesterday with a wee bag that was holding all the valuables Walter has in the world.'
Cassels began to take a mild interest.
'How did you find that out?'
'And something as tempting to the light–fingered could hardly be left just sitting there.'
'Will you in the name of Christ how you got the word on all this.'
'So this is what Parthis got out of them at the office – Grundy's told them he might not manage to catch tomorrow's sailing. If he does it'll be by the skin of his arse…'
'I can't make out how they gave out all this to you.'
'Anyhow Grundy's ticket will be good for next month's passage if he misses this one.'
'I can't waste four weeks picking you out of the gutter in this godforsaken town. We'll have to…'
'Grundy's baggage is stored at this Weller place so Parthis can catch him there tonight with his jewels and watches and stuff.'
Cassels was now paying proper attention.
Good,' he said, 'we'll grab him by the balls when he turns up at the gate right before the boat leaves.'
McAra rolled his eyes and made a dismissive gesture.
'And if he doesn't turn up? He could have his bags out of Weller's and be away somewhere out of sight for a month.'
His colleague frowned, thought for a moment and nodded.
'Well, then, we'll get to this Weller place tonight and lay hands on him there. But what about this Parthis fellow and the jewels?'
'That would be me, and the jewels are a brick in my poke.'
For once Cassels was prepared to offer a compliment.
'You're a right sly wee bastard.'
'You don't have the Latin, then?'
'What's that got to do with anything?'
Duly chastened Cassels hurried off to Constabulary headquarters to discharge the mission McAra had delegated to him. When he returned late in the morning he found his colleague without socks or shoes and probing the gaps between his toes with a fork from

HIDDEN

the dining table.

'Look at that. I thought I was well rid of it.' McAra was frowning at the diffusion of pestilent–looking purulence accumulating on the bare floorboards. 'That can't be right. I'll need to get that seen to.'

He replaced the implement by a plate on the table which was set up for the lodgers' lunch and was pulling on rotting socks and holed footwear when he spotted the dust of grey specks on the shoulders of his worm–eaten jacket.

'Bugger – dandruff.'

He began to pat the stuff off but stopped abruptly when he had examined the derris.

'Oh, no. You'll have to help me,' he whined, 'that's not dandruff. It's eggs of some kind.'

Repulsed by this vision of desolation Cassels removed himself to the furthest corner of the room and reported that the Weller place was one of low repute where rooms were let by the hour and little heed was paid to the conduct of so–called guests. It also served as a holding bay for baggage at low cost. It was located close to the river and more than a mile from the port.

'You damn well keep your throat dry until we get this sorted out,' he told McAra who was tentatively trawling through his hair with the none too clean fingers of both hands. 'This Grundy fellow must be real sharp the way he's run things so far. I'm not going to be busy holding you up when he's waving a pistol in my face.'

'But it's hours before we can grab a hold of him. I'm parched as it is.'

'If you have one drink I'll belt you from here to the Clyde.'

'A bit of lunch, then.'

A few of the other residents were trickling into the dining room and Cassels made sure that he was seated as far as possible from the setting with the recently misused fork. The postprandial afternoon seemed interminable to McAra who made a single attempt to gain the hospitality of a neighbouring pub and found himself painfully shackled to the heavy oak bedstead, alternately moaning and begging and finally upsetting himself so much that his bladder overcame his mewling resistance. His discomfort was not eased by the fact that the autumn night again fell wet and chilly and two gig drivers declined to accommodate the police officers, one in

HIDDEN

seething bad temper and the second reeking of urine and an assortment of other bodily odours. The cost of persuading the third cabby to carry them as far as the Weller Hotel included the charge for cleaning the vehicle and acquiring a powerful dose of *sal volatile* for the driver.

'I still can't make out how Grundy…' Cassels shook his head as the pair concealed themselves in shadow across the street from Mrs Weller's.

'Because yon fellow called DeWitt said the man's as much at home in the water as a mackerel. What time is it?'

Before Cassels could extract the watch from under his coat a figure appeared out of the drenching gloom, tugging a heavy cape around him. For a moment the man cast about with an air of suspicion and then knocked on the front door which was opened with a rattle of bolts and chain. Against the flicker of a lantern the new arrival cut a sinister silhouette as, loudly announcing the name Grundy, he plunged into the lobby with a confident gait that struck McAra as faintly familiar.

'Will we grab the bastard the now?' Cassels asked, patting the pocket where the pepper–pot was lodged.

'No. We'll wait till he comes out with his bags. That'll keep his hands busy.'

For several minutes the officers waited in the teeming rain until a cab came trundling into view. The driver, hunched against the rising wind, bellowed the name of the intending passenger, waited and called out a second time which brought the client out into the street toting a pair of large bags.

'Right,' Cassels hissed, 'I'll have him.'

And he dashed from his hiding place before McAra could restrain him. Catching sight of the sturdy policeman making a headlong dash for him the man dropped his luggage and in a second was tearing off into the streaming dark. Not devoted to the notion of exercise promoting wellbeing McAra joined reluctantly in the chase and within twenty feet was convinced that the rasping in his throat and vice–like pain in his chest were indicators of imminent expiration. Giving up the patently useless endeavour he dropped to his knees with a pitiful wail followed by a series of squeals for instant assistance, but neither Mrs Weller, watching the pursuit

HIDDEN

with indifference, nor the cab driver, irate at the loss of his fare, offered any succour. Meanwhile Cassels and the fugitive had disappeared into the filthy night.

'You have to help me,' McAra was bleating. 'I've never been so ill!' Mrs Weller took the trouble to emerge from her shelter in the doorway to stroll to the stricken officer and bludgeon him on the side of the head with a washboard with which she was unaccountably equipped and then, without a word, stalked off back to her lair. Confused by the infirmity imposed by unwonted exercise and the brilliant lights flashing in front of him occasioned by the woman's assault, McAra cried out, 'Seize her, Balthazar! Kill!' just before he pitched face down in the mud. But Balthazar was ensconced a couple of miles away, comfortable in his cage and lacking only the pipe tobacco to which he was now addicted.

Cassels was no sprinter himself but he had the ability to jog on at a moderate pace for a considerable distance, and anyway his quarry lacked any noticeable capacity for prodigious velocity. Conditions were treacherous and both pursuer and pursued found themselves sliding dangerously and repeatedly until the race came to a conclusion when the fugitive cannoned into a sapling rendered invisible by the atrocious weather and the late night pall. The collision hurled him backwards and more or less into Cassels' encircling arms.

'Right, you bastard,' the policeman snarled, 'go on and give me one tiny wee reason to snap your neck.'

And a moment later, having spun his prey around and stared into his bruised and bleeding face, added, 'What the fuck…'

Twisting the other's arm painfully up his back he conducted his prisoner the quarter mile to where McAra was gradually reassembling himself but still looking as if he had been trapped beneath an indisposed rhinoceros. Peering through the soaking brume at the two approaching figures he stepped back in shock at the sight of Cassels' prisoner.

'Jamesie?'

The Argyll fisherman was bent forward by the excruciating grip inflicted by the policeman.

'You better have a damn good story to tell me or by Christ I'll have Cassels here rip the arm off you.'

HIDDEN

'I was only doing what I got paid for,' Jamesie protested. 'Mr Grundy said youse might be after him for telling the law about how you was taking money off pubs and breaking them in bits if they never paid up.'

'And how did you come to be away down here with him?'

'I got the fare off him and him and me got here quick as you like. He said you would be after him to shut his mouth for good because he put the right coppers on youse. He sorted it for me to come to this place tonight and lead you on a wee while and he'd get clean away or you'd slaughter him for telling the magistrates about your thieving.'

A pause.

'And – oh, aye – I got enough off of him to buy a new boat. You seen what happened to the old one.'

'Where's the bastard now? You better speak up or you'll be too old to sail your boat by the time they let you out of Newgate.'

With a trembling hand Jamesie produced his watch and screwed up his eyes to read the dial.

'He'll be on the *Great Western* by now. Look – he gave me this for youse.'

From his pocket he drew an envelope which McAra grabbed.

'Never mind that,' Cassels shouted. 'If yon driver over there goes full tilt he can get us to the dock before the ship sails.'

With less than fifteen minutes to go the trio scuttled to the hansom and squeezed into the narrow vehicle.

'Five times the fare if you get us to the port before one o'clock,' McAra yelled and the fly set off at a terrifying rate through the insistent storm, sending up a great spray of rain water and mud and an evincing alarmed response from the few late–night pedestrians braving the miserable weather. Several times the coach almost heeled over and the driver lost his cap to the chilling wind but the promise of so generous a reward kept him cracking his whip at his careering horse. Holding on for dear life with one hand McAra unfolded the document Jamesie had been instructed to pass to him. Cassels steadied the swaying side lantern and McAra succeeded in reading the single page.

"Whoever you are, if you're reading this – my compliments. Maybe my star–crossed comrades in crime have owned up to their plan to

HIDDEN

sail into the sunset with the Honours. And maybe you've been thinking all along that Grundy's not languishing in the deep after all. Either way you'll see by now that I had to have a plan to get on the ship without being taken at the dock. That idiot butler Samuel Spark booked passage for all of us in our real names. That left me vulnerable. So I gave you a present of myself at Mrs Weller's. I made a great noise at the shipping office about me getting to the pier as near sailing as was possible, or even missing the sailing altogether. Jamesie was to keep you busy long enough for the Western *to get safe away with me on her. And just so you know – I was aboard the ship with hours to spare.*

It was a shame the stealing of the Honours was found out so quick. I'd have liked to know how that happened for I thought it might take months or years. Now I'll leave you with a bit of a boast – that unhinged Hiram Stuart and the others thought they had come up with the scheme to lift the Jewels and it suited me well enough that they did. But it was all mine. I had pushed him into the Isaac Graham affair and then I saw to it that he thought he was the reincarnation of some Jacobite princeling. Nothing could have been simpler with the centenary of that lost cause coming up in a year or two. And with him being so soft in the head.

I'd been helping myself to thousands of Hiram's dollars and he never knew the difference, there's that many of them. Just for the fun of it, I moved the whole gang around to suit myself. I had Bradley and Dicken understand nothing of the real game – I sowed the idea that it was maybe the killing of the Queen or the PM so if they got taken the only truth they could tell the law was the lies I fed them. Smart and the rest saw Stuart was for giving them gold and a country of their own to run. Stealing the Honours for Hiram was the small price they would pay in return for a gilded future at his court. And poor Hiram! I had him thinking he'd be replacing the usurper Victoria on the throne in the years to come.

Regard me, sir, to be your perdurable enemy. Do not believe you may rest easy in the days and years to come.

Walter Grundy."

Despite the cold of the late hour steam was rising from the galloping horse which clattered and whinnied through the now deserted streets. Jamesie was pale with fright at the momentum of

HIDDEN

the rocking vehicle and McAra and Cassels clung grimly to the straps on either side. The driver was shouting encouragement to the tiring animal and bawling assurance to his passengers that they would arrive ahead of the time of the ship's departure.

'We'll all be killed stone dead,' Jamesie muttered through his chattering teeth.

'My bowels are coming out of me,' McAra complained. 'I'm a ruined man.'

'In the name of God will the pair of youse just hold your tongues for one bloody minute,' Cassels complained. 'Or I'll heave the pair of youse out on your mazard.'

'I'm going to be sick,' the ashen McAra announced. 'And I'm telling you the other end is loosening and all.'

'Well, I'll tear your head off and ram it in your arse,' Cassels said. 'That'll solve that wee problem top and bottom.'

Trapped between the warring factions and with only the remotest notion of what was going on, Jamesie tried to recoil from the threatened disgorgement on one flank and the snarling bruiser on the other. But the narrow bench afforded no room for manoeuvre and he was obliged to sit rigid with fear and loathing, praying that the hurtling cab would arrive in Avonmouth before either viscera or blood were spilled. By the time the hansom reached the dock the rain had eased and the wind dropped to the merest breeze. Tossing money at the driver McAra led Cassels racing towards the water front leaving the uncomprehending Jamesie to instruct the driver to conduct him to any lodging house in the city so long as it was in an obscure back street.

'Bugger, shite and fuck,' Cassels growled as the two men came to a frustrated halt at the gate and watched as smoke belched from the ship's funnel, the huge paddle wheels churned white foam from the black waters and the berthing lines were hauled aboard. The ticketing clerk made a half-hearted gesture to detain the officers but there was no point in pursuing them. The vessel was some yards from the pier and gathering speed, her sails furled and flags flying from all four masts. And from the slightly raised stern a passenger clad in a heavy coat was raising both arms in ironic valediction and the breathy wind carried a jeering laugh. Cassels brought the pepper–box pistol out of his pocket and raised the weapon in a

HIDDEN

steady double–handed grip but McAra pushed the gun downward. 'Not at this range,' he said. 'You don't have my prowess. You'd as like hit Rockall.'
'Then you have a go, you lousy wee runt.'
But even he could see that the proposed target was now well out of range despite still being triumphantly visible.
'How many passengers on her tonight?' McAra asked the clerk at the dock gate as he led Cassels away.
'One hundred and three, sir.'
'And the voyage?'
'A fortnight that would be.'
'Come away, my friend,' McAra ordered his companion, 'and we'll get a noggin to celebrate. There's a place called the Llandoger Trow I put my eye on.'
'Celebrate? You bring me all the way down here to put the arm on that Grundy bastard and he goes sailing off to a new life with not a bother on him? And you want to celebrate!'
'Aye – well, that new life is like to be brief enough so get your hand in your pocket and let me have a few of Emma's shillings.'
The rain was starting to fall yet more heavily again and the breeze was quickly becoming a raw wind. Bending their heads the two men hurried in the direction of the pub only to find its doors long closed against them.
'Disaster,' McAra yelled and began banging on a window. A shutter was thrown open on the upper floor and an irate face appeared.
'Police! Let us in or you're for the Bridewell and a flogging that'll tear the lungs out of you.'
'Hold on a minute, then.'
'I like a man that sees the power in me,' McAra informed his colleague as they stood waiting. Waiting, that is, until a bucket of freezing water drenched McAra while Cassels nimbly dodged out of the cataract.
'Come back in the morning,' a voice shouted, 'and I'll dry you out.' And the shutter crashed shut.
Seething with rage McAra hurled himself in vain against the oak door until he was restrained by Cassels' muscular arm and discouraging snigger.
'Come on, you wee shite and we'll get you a hot toddy back at the

HIDDEN

diggings. Tell me, though – what makes you think your man Grundy'll not last long out there on the water?'

Still scowling but warmed a little by a consoling ebullition of self-admiration McAra linked his arm through that of his associate as they threaded through the unpeopled streets.

'There's a beast of a fellow called Horace Trapp on yon same ship that thinks Grundy is the man that did for a good pal of his. You never saw somebody as wild with hate as big Horace when I told him it was Grundy shot a Mr Wallace one fine night. Somewhere on that Atlantic sea our Mr Grundy is going to be screaming his last when he topples off the hind quarters of that fine boat.'

'So you knew Grundy would be on that boat?'

'Couldn't be sure at all. Just a wee idea.'

'But even if it turned out that way how was your Horace man going to know which one was Grundy?'

McAra was effusive in his own praise.

'Look, I told him that *maybe* Grundy would be on board – no guarantee, and no guarantee that he'd be using that name. But how many folk were going to be on the *Western*? A hundred, say, and a half of them likely women. And how many of the men would be Scottish? And anyway for a man of Horace's talents there was a fortune to be made across the ocean and well out of reach of the law here. See? Horace was on a winner easy enough, if Grundy was sailing or not. My ingenuity is prodigious.'

'Hiram Stuart's bound for the asylum, like enough and Grundy for water a lot deeper than Loch Long. But the rest – and the Honours: when did you…?'

'Weeks ago. For instance, I knew long since that Smart and Dicken were in cahoots.'

'How did you know that?'

'Yon Dicken fellow served on the East India Company ship *Nemesis* at Chuenpi. Smart was one of the bosses on her at the time.'

'How did you find that out about Dicken?'

'He fell over outside a pub in Portobello.'

'How would that…? Oh, Christ, never mind.'

'And folk like Halley and Smart would never have been with some gang that was going to murder the Queen or the Prime Minister.'

HIDDEN

'Regicides.'
'Reggie Sykes? The man wasn't involved. Anyway, it was always the other thing. The Crown Jewels. Nothing's hid from McAra.'
'Why didn't you say so – to me or Haining or Grant or…?'
'No fucker gave me the time so I gave up. I have secrets. Secrets.'
'You're a strange little fellow, right enough,' Cassels told him with a satisfied chuckle.
'I'm the wee man with the big brain.'
'No you're not. You're a big bag of wind with a skull full of havers.'
'And I have a deep understanding.'
'What about?'
'Everything. And I'll tell you this – all human life is a tragedy unfolding.'
'God, Mac, you're a happy soul – that's right philosophical, especially coming from a disgusting, stunted troll like yourself.'
'"Αίδώς τον καλλους και αρετησ πόλις."'
'What?'
'Modesty is the citadel of beauty and virtue. Here, did you ever clap eyes on Emma's tits?'
Sighing his irritation into the bitter night Cassels led the way back through the empty streets.
Tagging along in his wake McAra said, 'There's a tooth in my pocket.'

****